Praise for *Exit Strategy*

"Forget roller coaster rides—*Exit Strategy* speeds like a bullet train. Sharp-eyed and sure-footed, it's the fastest-paced action thriller this side of the cineplex."—Bonnie MacDougal, author of *Angle of Impact*

"Filled with hairpin plot turns, charismatic characters, violent action . . . races through the contemporary realities of international terrorism and organized crime, against a backdrop of the federal government's roster of security forces caught up in their own self-absorbed bureaucratic agendas and turf battles."—Richard Gid Powers, author of *Broken: The Troubled Past and Uncertain Future of the FBI* and *Secrecy and Power: The Life of J. Edgar Hoover*

"*Exit Strategy* starts off like a rocket, accelerates from there, and blasts right through to a completely satisfying ending. Vivid characters, a unique and intriguing story, rich plotting, and a breathless pace . . . what more could you ask for?"—Lynne Heitman, author of *Tarmac* and *First Class Killing*

"*Exit Strategy* is a terrific debut. Mike Wiecek spins his story with propulsive plotting, vivid characters, and a talent for action and surprise. A great read from a writer to watch."—William Landay, award-winning author of *Mission Flats*

"*Exit Strategy* reads like the script for an action-adventure movie—quick, stylish, exciting. The leading man is good, the leading lady is better, and all of the puzzles fit together."—Thomas Perry, author of *The Butcher's Boy* and *Metzger's Dog*

EXIT STRATEGY

MICHAEL WIECEK

J
JOVE BOOKS, NEW YORK

THE BERKLEY PUBLISHING GROUP
Published by the Penguin Group
Penguin Group (USA) Inc.
375 Hudson Street, New York, New York 10014, USA
Penguin Group (Canada), 10 Alcorn Avenue, Toronto, Ontario M4V 3B2, Canada
(a division of Pearson Penguin Canada Inc.)
Penguin Books Ltd., 80 Strand, London WC2R 0RL, England
Penguin Group Ireland, 25 St. Stephen's Green, Dublin 2, Ireland
(a division of Penguin Books Ltd.)
Penguin Group (Australia), 250 Camberwell Road, Camberwell, Victoria 3124, Australia
(a division of Pearson Australia Group Pty. Ltd.)
Penguin Books India Pvt. Ltd., 11 Community Centre, Panchsheel Park, New Delhi—110 017, India
Penguin Group (NZ), Cnr. Airborne and Rosedale Roads, Albany, Auckland 1310, New Zealand
(a division of Pearson New Zealand Ltd.)
Penguin Books (South Africa) (Pty.) Ltd., 24 Sturdee Avenue, Rosebank, Johannesburg 2196,
South Africa

Penguin Books Ltd., Registered Offices: 80 Strand, London WC2R 0RL, England

EXIT STRATEGY

A Jove Book / published by arrangement with the author

PRINTING HISTORY
Jove edition / March 2005

Copyright © 2005 by Michael Wiecek.
Cover illustration by Ed Gallucci.
Interior text design by Stacy Irwin.

ISBN: 0-515-13939-4

JOVE®
Jove Books are published by The Berkley Publishing Group,
a division of Penguin Group (USA) Inc.,
375 Hudson Street, New York, New York 10014.
JOVE is a registered trademark of Penguin Group (USA) Inc.
The "J" design is a trademark belonging to Penguin Group (USA) Inc.

PRINTED IN THE UNITED STATES OF AMERICA

10 9 8 7 6 5 4 3 2 1

ONE

NO ONE SMOKED on the loading dock anymore except Raymond and the drivers, even in bad weather. Rain, snow, freezing cold—everyone else walked down to the curb, just outside the property, where the workplace rules didn't apply. Not because he was the supervisor. Hell, he'd told them every morning for a week before the last quarterly inspection, and still one of the clerks forgot, too slow or too dumb to pitch his cigarette before the district postmaster rounded in on him. "Don't get caught"—what was so hard to understand about that? Their problem, not his, Raymond figured, and since no one had the nerve to file on him, the matter was done with.

In the late-afternoon cool he stood with an overland hauler waiting for the lading to finish, bad-mouthing the mail-handlers' union in a companionable way. The trucker was a private contractor, despite the USPS eagles on his cab, obviously bored but happy to relax while his trailer was binned up. Anyway, Raymond didn't mind carrying a conversation all by himself. He generally found his opinions more interesting than anything anyone else had to say.

Which was maybe why the trucker saw her first, since Raymond usually had a quick eye, especially for pretty ones.

"New girl?" The trucker looked over Raymond's shoulder. "I think I'd remember if I'd seen her before."

Raymond cut his monologue. The woman picked her way through the sorting machinery and sagging canvas carts, headed in their direction. She was tall and blonde and by Raymond's practiced estimate on the near side of thirty, trailing considerable interest from the half dozen other men on the floor. If she knew they were staring, or cared at all, Raymond couldn't tell.

She stopped in front of him, loose and rangy in a faded cotton sweater over khaki shorts. "You the shift supervisor?"

He smiled winningly and flipped away his cigarette, behind his back. "You got me."

"I'm taking the Potrero route."

"Oh, sure." Raymond realized that he'd straightened up, practically at attention, and he was still looking up at her a little. "Molly, right?" He held out his hand. "Saw your bid sheet the other day."

He was hoping for a girl's handshake, the kind he could extend for a few seconds, look into her eyes. But her grip was unexpectedly strong and fast, and he was left with his hand hanging, like a half wit, before he recovered.

The driver grinned and touched two fingers to his forehead in an old-fashioned way. "How do, miss."

Molly nodded at him, one second of attention, just long enough to be polite. To Raymond she said, "Molly Gannon, yes."

"You can call me Raymond." He left the smile on full wattage, but she just waited, maybe raised one eyebrow a fraction. "Or Ray. Sometimes my friends, you know, they get to know me better, they call me Raygun, that'd be okay too."

She seemed to think about it, considering the idea. "I see."

After a moment, Raymond nodded. "All right then," he said, and adjusted his charm level for a longer siege. "The Potrero, right. But you're not on the schedule until Wednesday."

"I thought maybe you could set up a ride-along tomorrow, have someone pull down the route for me before I start."

No way was he giving some sleazebag carrier a free seven hours with her. "Hey, that's a good idea, but I don't think we can make the overtime. Budget, you know."

"Really?"

"The Potrero." He was shaking his head. "Have to say, I'm surprised they're giving it to you."

"I had the first bid."

"Yeah, but . . ." She was too calm; he wanted to impress her. "You know what you're getting into?"

"Park-and-loops, more business than residential. On the sheet, it looked like a good hit."

"Let me show you something." He led her along the dock, ignoring the driver, who just shrugged when Molly gave him a departing nod. At the end of the day local trucks filled the parking apron, all the carriers on their way home. A few second-shift employees meandered about, mostly janitorial and recognizable by their lethargy. The bay was quiet, smelling of oil and canvas and cardboard.

"You're getting Phil's quarter-ton," Raymond said. He pointed to the side of the older, slightly trapezoid postal van, near its rear wheelwell. "Maintenance says they don't have to repair it, nothing mechanical was damaged."

She looked closer. "*Bullet* holes?"

"They shot him up last week."

"Oh?"

"He was finishing a loop and the satchel cart was empty, so they wanted to get inside. He wasn't fast enough, and they tried to hurry him along." Raymond rapped the vehicle with his knuckles, showing it off.

"Hmm." She could have been asking about a flat tire. "How many?"

"Of them? Two—crackheads, probably, looking for credit cards."

"I didn't know the dealers took Visa."

Raymond couldn't tell if she was joking. "The sector's full of them. Carriers have been held up three times just in the last year. Phil's getting two weeks of stress-and-disability for this one."

He watched her as she examined the damage, running a finger lightly around the edge of one puncture, stepping back to check the entry angle. "Did he give them what they wanted?" she asked, distractedly.

"Of course." Whenever the inspectors showed up, fuming about mail depredation, it was Raymond who had to listen to the lecture. They all knew the carriers couldn't care less. "No use getting killed over a lousy stack of strap-outs."

She straightened. "Nine-mil, maybe a .357. No pattern. Not a competent shooter—he could have hit the tire, or even the gas tank."

He looked at her oddly. "You think?"

"Your guy wasn't in any danger."

"Well, I don't know about that." He felt himself losing traction. "You know about guns, huh?"

"Yeah."

"Not part of the job, usually . . ."

She sighed. "I was in the service."

"Got it." Raymond opened up the smile again, back on firmer ground. "I did the reserves, myself. Lots of the guys here are ex-military. Girls, too." She glanced at him. "I mean . . . you know what I mean."

"Yeah, Ray, I know what you mean." She seemed amused, which Raymond, always the optimist, took as encouragement.

"Let me guess." He examined her carefully, head to toe, mock serious but taking advantage of it. "Army, right?"

One of Raymond's rules was that women always

enjoyed close attention from a handsome man, even if they covered it up by pretending to be annoyed or embarrassed. But Molly could have been watching a toaster pop, all the reaction she gave him. "Why's that?" she said.

"You're too tall to fly." Raymond aimed to impress, again. "But the navy, they spend their time firing missiles and torpedoes, not small arms, like you know all about. And you're not a jarhead because you're not wearing the ring."

"How about that." Molly shook her head slightly. "Here, let me try. Your MOS was . . . Motor Transport Operator."

"What, a truck driver? Get out," said Raymond, who had in fact been a tank tread mechanic. "But come on, was I right?"

"Sure. Army." She rolled her eyes. "I was in the MPs."

"Oh." Raymond thought about that. There actually were a lot of former servicemen working for the post office, but few ex-military police—that kind of background, they'd go into the cops. On the other hand, she seemed a little touchy about the whole subject. Best to move on. "Well, I guess you can handle yourself out there, that's the important thing."

"I'll be careful."

Was she making fun of him? "It's a crummy district," he said. "Just about the worst part of San Francisco. Old warehouses, metal shops, that sort of thing. There's a few artists in the lofts, some computer companies, but generally it's just broken windows and junkies."

"If they can buy a stamp, they can mail a letter."

"Most of them probably can't write their own name."

The truck driver wandered past and slapped Raymond on the shoulder, though his eyes were mostly on Molly. "Trailer's loaded," he said. "Be going now."

"See you Thursday," said Raymond.

"Miss." The driver gave her a departing wink, and they watched him climb into the cab. The truck rumbled off, leaving behind a cloud of fumes and several discarded mail sacks spilling off the dock. A man in overalls appeared and began collecting gondola carts, slowly pushing them into a row along the parcel racks. He made it look like the task might require an hour or so, if all went well.

Raymond figured he ought to give it one last shot. "You keep in shape, huh? Beach volleyball, maybe? Or kickboxing, something like that."

She finally turned her full attention on him. "Ray," she said. "You're not about to ask me out for a drink, are you?"

"Um . . ."

"Or ask me how old I am? Or whether I've settled in yet, since I probably haven't been in San Francisco very long? Or what kind of music I like?"

"Well . . ."

"Because the thing is, Ray, you're my supervisor. I'd really hate to get off on the wrong foot, you know?"

"Uh, sure."

"Like with a harassment grievance, for example. That would set a very bad tone to our professional relationship."

Raymond grinned. "Molly—Ms. Gannon?—we don't have a thing to worry about, because if there is one thing I will not tolerate, that is the creation of a hostile workplace environment." He'd seen the training video enough times, like everyone else, after some high-profile settlements had terrified the lawyers in Washington. "Providing the support you need to do your job well is why I am here."

Like everything else, this just bounced off, and her look of amusement flitted past again. "I'm glad to hear that, Ray."

He watched her leave, the rear view no less interesting than the front, and when she'd gone he yelled at the guy corralling gondolas to concentrate on his job, not the scenery. Cooler air drifted through the dock as evening fell. Raymond went to find his jacket and car keys, and as he left he looked once more at the silent bullet holes in the truck.

Now Phil, *he* had found a hostile environment.

TWO

SATURDAY MORNING, PULLING onto a gravel turnout in the hills above Berkeley, Molly was surprised to find Eileen already there. They'd met for a run every week since Molly arrived six months earlier. Eileen generally blasted in ten or twenty minutes late, hair still askew from her bed, coffee or a thermos of grapefruit juice in one hand, wake-up music from KITS a few notches too high. But today she stood talking with another runner, some guy in a sleeveless tee and lycra shorts.

"This is Mark," Eileen said, and Molly vaguely remembered her mentioning bringing a friend along this week. "He works in the hangar, and we got to talking the other day."

"Hey." He wore his baseball cap backwards.

Molly nodded. "You do logistics too?"

"Naw. Aircraft maintenance. Eileen fills them up, we keep them in the air."

Eileen was a supervisor at SFO's Airport Mail Center, lading parcel freight into the planes. She and Molly had met in the army a decade before, and after taking her discharge, she had followed the ex-serviceman's well-worn path into the post office. When Molly left, later on, running through several lousy jobs and making a general botch of civilian life, it was Eileen who'd convinced her to come to California and take the mail-handler's exam.

A mile into the run Eileen drifted back a few paces, leaving Mark to Molly, who glanced back. Eileen grinned and shrugged, like, *He's all yours!*

"Eileen says you were a paratrooper too." He pounded over the scrubby terrain, the muscles in his arms working.

"Airborne, yeah," Molly said. "But mostly as an MP. I didn't jump much."

"I always wanted to do that."

"Military police?" She caught him checking her out and he returned his eyes forward. "It's usually not exciting," she said. "Mostly breaking up bar fights, to tell you the truth."

"Naw, you know. Parachuting. I saw in a magazine about those, you know, high-low jumps? Go out an airplane a mile up and not pull the ripcord all the way down, until just a few seconds before you splat on the ground. That would be awesome."

"HALO," Molly said.

"Huh?"

"But that's more for Special Operations."

The view was spectacular from the ridgeline, a long grassy slope descending to trees and roofs and the distant bay. Mark continued to find her outfit far more interesting.

"You know, I do martial arts," he said. "I been in a few bar fights myself, now you mention it."

"I'm not surprised."

"Yeah?"

"I thought you looked like you have some training."

Eileen, eavesdropping from behind, coughed. Molly looked back. "Right?"

"Sure." Eileen's face was open, guileless. "I noticed that myself."

Molly turned back to Mark. "What discipline?"

"Krav Maga. Developed by the Israeli army, you heard of it? Street fighting, all the way. No belts, even, none of that crap."

"Really?"

"I used to do Tae Bo, but that's like all, you know, suburban ladies who got tired of aerobics. Krav Maga's for when your life is on the line."

"That must be useful."

"Totally."

The hill steepened and Molly gently increased their pace. Mark's breathing gradually became more ragged. Eileen seemed unaffected. Soon they entered a eucalyptus grove, the air cooler in the dappled shade.

"I was wondering," said Mark. "How many guns do you have?"

Back at their cars, six miles later, Molly and Eileen watched Mark drive off in his Camaro, its broken muffler rumbling down the road. Molly drained her water bottle.

"Okay," said Eileen. She picked at her shoelaces, trying to untangle a knot. "Not my best effort, I admit."

"Did you hear him ask how many people I've killed?"

Eileen laughed. "It's a turn-on, and you know it."

"Not for anyone you'd actually want to spend time with."

"So he wants to be a soldier."

"All of them," said Molly. "They all do. They don't want one for a girlfriend."

"We're not soldiers anymore."

But Molly wasn't sure that was true, except in some narrow, literal sense. She and Eileen had been assigned to the same Airborne intake. Of seventeen women who started, they were the only two who finished. Eileen had reenlisted once, Molly twice, and even though they both recognized Molly as the real hardcase, neither of them had been able to abandon the habits—the training, the wariness, the attitude.

In the service, the problem was obvious: they were surrounded by armed, aggressive eighteen-year-old boys being molded to pursue simple goals single-mindedly and without reflection. Well, okay, what did they expect, it was the *army,* after all. Some of the women even welcomed the attention—the kind who remained the same flirty, head-tossing party girls they'd always been. But for Molly and Eileen the real disappointment was outside the base, back in the world. With all the thoughtless, close-minded, and insensitive men in uniform, the law of averages, if nothing else, should have guaranteed a reasonable choice of nice guys among the civilians. Surely someone, somewhere, would know how to talk about something other than football or muzzle velocity or trucks with very large tires.

Well . . . no.

"For what it's worth," said Eileen, "I only met him a couple times, and he seemed okay enough."

"'Okay enough'?" Molly raised an eyebrow. "Thanks, I guess."

"They're out there." Eileen paused, made an annoyed noise, and abandoned the knotted shoelace. "Don't you worry, we'll find one for you."

"Oh, why bother." Molly felt her mood droop.

"Hey, now . . ."

"It doesn't matter."

"Let's not start that again."

"I had my chance and I blew it."

Eileen sighed. "Can I tell you something?"

"Hmmf."

"I know Lance was the love of your life and all, but let's face up to reality here. The question is . . ." She started to grin. "I mean, why didn't you just shoot the bastard?"

"You're as bad as Mark, with the ideas."

"Look, Lance was a moron. You know that, right? You wasted two whole years on a rockhead. Stop moping around, already."

"You're trying to make me feel better?"

On some days, Molly understood that Eileen was right. On most days, though, she knew she was just too tall, too strong, too hard-edged. "For someone like me," she said, "it's always going to be jerks and weirdos."

A few cars passed, leaving a haze of ozone drifting in the light breeze. Eileen rummaged around her back-seat, pulled out a combat knife, and sliced open the knotted shoelace.

"I asked around about your Raymond," she said. "He has something of a reputation, it turns out."

"Way out at the AMC?"

"A real lady-killer." Eileen brightened. "Maybe you should send him my way."

Molly looked at her. Eileen was shorter, but she'd always been stronger, with the cut muscles that came partly from genetics and mostly from years of effort. Standing in the sun, sweat soaking her tank top and cut-off sweats, knife blade gleaming, she looked like a *manga* super-villainess.

"Good idea," Molly said. "You can straighten him out."

Before they left, Eileen asked about work. Molly described her route.

"The neighborhood's fine," she said. "People keep telling me how dangerous it is, but I've never had a problem."

"That's not what the union thinks. I heard they were going to push for paired route assignments, after all the muggings."

Molly nodded. "They asked me about that," she said.

"And?"

"I told them I'd quit on the spot. Getting stuck with a partner for an entire shift, every day—I don't know who it'd be worse on, them or me."

"You might have a point there." Eileen toweled her face and arms, then became more serious. "Lance wasn't your fault," she said. "You really ought to re-member that."

Molly made a noncommittal sound.

"No more than what happened in Afghanistan," Eileen continued. "You can't even call that a mistake."

"I know." Molly leaned into a stretch, one leg on the

car roof, her face to her knee. She eased out of it, lifted the other foot above her head without apparent effort. "I know."

The midday sun was now plainly hot, much warmer than in the foggy depths of the city. Molly closed her eyes and put her face toward it.

"A quiet life," she said. "All I want is a quiet, decent life." She considered for a moment. "And if there's a quiet, decent man in it, so much the better."

MOLLY was sure she intimidated almost everyone, maybe not at first glance, but soon enough. Guys like Mark and Raymond, no, but only because you'd need a claymore to get through their self-absorption. The problem was those nine years in the army—nearly her whole adult life. Unlike the male soldiers, she had to earn respect the hard way. It didn't help that she'd been an MP, basically facing down louts and criminals every waking hour. With her colleagues and friends like Eileen she could relax, but she knew everyone else saw only a blunt and efficient competence as impenetrable as tactical armor. Cosmo Girl she was not.

When they kicked her out after Afghanistan, her last contact the stony faces of the three judge-advocates— all men, naturally—she'd thought, okay, the hell with you, now I can be *normal* again. Buy some sundresses; walk into a bar without scanning for weapons; maybe even cry at the movies if she felt like it. But of course it didn't work out that way. Once a tough guy, always a tough guy.

Which was why she wanted, more than anything else, a peaceful way to spend her days, and why, despite Raymond, the Potrero was increasingly agreeable. She'd previously been working an entirely dismounted route in the Castro. Straight out of her initial training it had seemed ideal: sunshine, a wealthy neighborhood, lots of pleasant people. Soon enough she understood that was the problem, however—lots of pleasant people. They all wanted to chat. She'd tip a bundle into a door slot and suddenly some smiling woman would be asking how she was doing, commenting on the weather, and introducing her yappy little dog. She couldn't find a quiet corner to eat her lunch without someone asking if she'd like company. And even though she wasn't being hit on as often—guys around there were generally checking each other out, not her—it happened enough to be tiresome.

The Potrero was not like that. Further north the district was lived-in and funky in a pre-gentrification kind of way, but down south of Islais Creek Channel it was as Raymond had described: a wasteland. Her first week a burned-out automobile hulk appeared on the street, blocking access to one of her relay boxes. Everywhere the sidewalks were cracked and buckled, making it a chore to push along the low, three-wheeled satchel cart.

On the other hand, once she left the head-out in the morning, she could sometimes go all day without speaking to anyone. A few words with the relay truck driver, or a brief greeting to the Korean convenience store owner behind his steel bars—that was it. The other carriers called her district Baghdad, but for Molly it was perfect.

On a pleasant, mid-October Friday afternoon, that changed.

Late and rushing through the end of her shift, Molly ran down a guy walking out of his office. She had shoved her satchel cart toward the side of the lobby and flicked out her box key in one smooth motion, dropping the front of the cluster unit without looking. At the last second, her gaze swinging around, she saw a rumpled pair of canvas pants dodge the cart as it rebounded from the wall.

"Whoops." He was whippet thin, almost her height, and she recognized his scruffy vandyke beard—he worked in the tech start-up across the lobby. Their office was little more than a room behind a floor-to-ceiling glass wall, and she'd gotten to know him by sight. They were usually slouched around their conference table, disheveled, poking at their laptops and scribbling obscure diagrams on the whiteboard. Letters sandblasted into the glass read Blindside Technology.

"Sorry," she said. What was his name—Jeff? Jack? Something like that. "I was trying to make up some time."

"Forget it." He glanced at the open rank of mailboxes, then around the deserted lobby. "Folks here, I don't think it matters much if their mail's late."

The building was an old warehouse, renovated at the peak of the bubble in expectation of dot-coms fleeing rents in nicer parts of the city. The slate floor gleamed; the distinctive interior glass walls were set in repointed brickwork under brushed-nickel ceiling lamps. But most of the offices sat empty, and Molly had never seen anyone manning the lobby's reception booth.

"Just trying to keep on schedule." In fact, Molly was headed for her third stuck in four days, with more mail than she could deliver before her shift ended. Raymond had grumbled when she called him at 4:30, but agreed to clock her out before he left, since the backlogs looked bad on his stats too. "Anyway," she added, "are you okay?"

"Sure."

"I mean . . ." She noticed that his coworkers across the lobby were watching through the glass, two of them laughing.

"It's nothing." He shrugged and walked off, swinging a key attached to a large wooden block marked M.

Molly watched him go for a moment and shook her head. "Smooth," she muttered to herself. "Real smooth." She turned to the box unit and began dumping in strapped bundles of mail.

She had just popped the rack back into place when two men in postal uniforms came in from the street.

"How's it going, guys?" Molly said, and they glanced at her, briefly surprised.

"Special delivery," one said, and they kept walking, reaching inside their shouldered mailbags as they approached Blindside's glassfront.

Later, Molly realized that she'd unconsciously

observed three incongruities at that moment. She'd glimpsed their truck outside the door, another quarter-ton just like hers—a vehicle that was never used for express mail logistics. Second, carriers never worked in pairs, and they certainly didn't have a third man to drive. And except in *Andy Griffith* reruns, no one ever, ever said "special delivery."

But when the guns came out, she simply froze, all her training forgotten, watching like a gape-mouthed civilian as the men began firing into Blindside's glass wall. Somewhere, deep and muffled, her brain was processing: suppressed submachine guns, Heckler & Koch MP5s, their shape and sound too familiar. The men were shooting to kill, a proper ten feet between them, holding the weapons in professional, stock-to-shoulder stances, no wasted motion. Molly just stood there, a single envelope drifting from her hand to the floor.

After an eternity—five seconds, perhaps—her years of drill and combat finally took over. Two steps and she dove over the satchel cart, tucked into a tight roll that brought her behind the reception desk. Sensation reappeared, as if she was surfacing from deep water. She heard pops and glass shattering. Shards rained on the floor with the shell casings, and a bank of lights blew out. Someone screamed, abruptly cut off.

After slamming into the counter Molly let her momentum carry her forward, sliding along the floor to peek around the corner of the desk. She had a glimpse of the killers, one reloading and the other firing paired taps—not indiscriminate auto, but neatly targeted shots that all found their mark. The entire glass wall was in ruins, jagged shards reaching in from the frame.

One of the victims pulled out a handgun—a Glock?—and got a few rounds off before he was shot down. The two men kicked out the remaining glass and stepped into the conference room, then separated, one moving to an open door in the back wall. As he disappeared through it he slung his weapon and reached back into the mailbag. The other killer circled the bloody room to put one more bullet into each head.

Carnage: blood splashed everywhere, on the walls, the table, the ceiling. The killer appeared indifferent. As he changed magazines, pushing in the new one with a soft click, he scanned the area, and when his eyes locked on Molly's his expression didn't change. He raised the HK and she ducked back, squeezing her eyes shut as the spattering bullets threw slate chips from the floor in front of her face.

A sudden series of small detonations erupted from Blindside's back room, and Molly heard one of the killers say something—an unintelligible word, a grunt. Then their footsteps. In that moment she knew they would shoot her as they came past the desk, but she had nothing, no weapons, no armor, no backup. She was already crouched on hands and knees, so she simply leapt straight up, like a cat. She caught the edge of the desk and pulled herself into a sideways spider roll across it as the killers appeared, one on each side of the desk, firing into the space she'd just vacated.

She crashed off the other side and pushed off again immediately, her motion fueled by pure adrenaline. The man there twisted around, bringing the HK to bear, but Molly struck his knees, knocking him backwards as she crumpled. He was fast, faster than her, and he recovered immediately, rolling into a crouch and raising the weapon, which he'd automatically pulled flat into his chest as he fell. In this half-second Molly thought: *Now I die.*

Instead, there was a shouted command from the other man. "No! Cease fire!" And only then did Molly realize just how well trained they were: the first man to decide and give the order, and the second to follow it, all in an instant.

No shots came. The second man bounded around the desk and struck her on the back of her head, probably with his gunstock. Pain exploded inside her skull, and she blacked out for a moment, coming to in a helplessly woozy state facedown on the slate.

"What the fuck?" The man sounded angry.

"Move! We're out of time."

"What about her?"

"She goes in the truck." A few moments later Molly's wrists were taped behind her back, palms out, her ankles and knees similarly secured. One man picked her up at the waist one-handed, holding her like a drooping carpet roll, and they jogged out of the building.

Everyone else was dead.

THREE

FRIDAY EVENING THE office was deserted, silent but for
the buzz from cheap fluorescent lighting. Behind the
chrome and walnut of the public foyer, a cubicle warren
crowded inside the ring of offices that claimed all the
floor's windows. Like the carpet, stained and worn down
to a grimy sheen, the fabric on the cube walls was long
overdue for replacement. Someone had let the coffeepot
evaporate on its hot plate, and a smell of burnt dregs
permeated the stale air. It could have been a workspace
for any of the numerous agencies occupying the Federal
Building—except for the large firearms locker inside a
floor-to-ceiling cage against the back wall.

Sampford was restless, eager to get to the gym, but
he'd resolved that as the youngest agent in the office he
would work harder and stay later than anyone else. He
was completing a report on one of the bullpen's common computers, making sure that every word was
spelled correctly. The Special Agent in Charge—his
boss, and everyone else's too, in the Bureau's flat hier-
archy—was rumored to be as weak on book learning as
he was strong on politicking, but who knew where one's

paperwork might end up? Sampford believed in delivering 100 percent, all the time.

Which was why he hadn't yet been able to figure out Norcross, who was pecking slowly away at another keyboard, frequently grunting in annoyance and banging the backspace key. Sampford did the calculation: twenty-eight years in, Norcross had probably filed something like four thousand reports. But he'd never learned to type? To be fair, his hands were unusually large—blocky and scarred, like the rest of him. Still.

Sampford had detoured behind Norcross's chair earlier, and seen a Form FD-117 on the screen, "Request for Parking Authorization." So maybe he just hated the bureaucracy, like any other agent, and was taking it out on the machine.

The only other person still in the office was Clain, in the death throes of his third marriage, who evidently preferred staring glumly at the wall to driving home. The cleaning crew—responsible only for the thirteenth floor, having been hired specifically by the Bureau in a mid-nineties round of security paranoia—wouldn't show up until 9:30, since the SAC assumed his staff would usually be hard at work until then. As they would be, of course, when he was also.

Clain was the first to notice the flash bulletin on the TV in the corner, tuned permanently to Channel 2, "The Bay Area Is Watching!" ever since someone neglected to renew the cable subscription.

"Hey," he said, without much excitement, and clicked on the sound. The three of them watched as the reporter tried to shove her way through a police cordon, using words like "massacre" and "assault weapon" and "terrorists." In the crush of bystanders the cameraman must have been jostled, because the feed was jerky and badly lit.

"Where's the SAC?" asked Norcross, glancing around the empty floor.

"Washington." Sampford checked his watch. "Actually, probably in the air—his appointment with the Director was 1:30 this afternoon."

"Out of touch," said Norcross. Sampford nodded; recent cost-containment measures had prohibited in-flight phone calls. "What about Barker?"

They both looked at the ASAC's office, smaller and glass-fronted, but it was dark.

Clain shrugged. "He said something about a liaison meeting with ATF, over at the Civic Center. A few hours ago."

They watched the TV for several moments. The camera panned up the street, showing at least two dozen emergency vehicles—police cars, gray tactical vans, fire and rescue, ambulances.

"We ought to have someone there," said Norcross, but Clain only grunted and Sampford was quiet. Abruptly Norcross snapped off the computer and looked around until he found his jacket crumpled on the floor beneath the desk. "Did you get the address?"

Sampford glanced at Clain. "Uh, the Potrero somewhere," he said. "Near the container terminal." But he didn't stand up.

Norcross had been transferred in only two months before, his face famous from news reports and his reputation within the Bureau approaching legend. In the aftermath of Springwater he was radioactive; the Pierce County prosecutor, up for reelection, had even filed murder charges. When he showed up in August, rawboned and weather-beaten like a plains rancher, it was clear he had so thoroughly alienated senior management that his new assignment could be understood only as a demotion. Sidelining him in a backwater was exactly what hadn't worked in North Dakota; at least in San Francisco the SAC could hold him on a short leash. A quiet betting pool, kept by an admin officer who also ran the football book, was currently holding 7–4 that he wouldn't last for his thirty-year medal.

So his new colleagues were at best wary, at worst hostile: some because they were following their bosses' lead, some from genuine disapproval, some from envy. They all understood that to get too close would affect their own careers.

If Norcross cared about any of that, it didn't show—
he appeared indifferent, with a quiet self-sufficiency
that had no doubt seen him through winter after winter
on the frozen prairie. His assignments so far in San
Francisco had been utterly mundane, little more than
chasing paper, and he carried them out with exact
competence, neither complaining nor volunteering for
more. Sampford had talked with the other agents, and
they all said the same thing: Norcross was always
on time, unfailingly polite—and never had anything
to say.

But now he stood with an unexpected decisiveness,
retrieving a Browning Hi-Power from a locked drawer
in his desk, checking the load and slipping it into his
belt holster with long-practiced familiarity.

"Come on, kid," he said, and it was suddenly obvious
he'd dismissed Clain long ago.

Sampford hesitated. "You know this really belongs
to Ahearn," he said. "The Counterterrorism Task Force
has jurisdiction—that's why it was set up."

"Right, sure," said Norcross. "Except he's not here
either." He waited.

"It's not even clear what federal violations might
have occurred."

Norcross shook his head slightly, disappointed.
"You're smarter than that."

"Um, pardon?"

"Editor, weren't you—of the law review? At NYU,
no less."

Sampford paused. He'd always been careful to say
no more than "back east" when the occasional inquiry
arose, having quickly learned that academic achieve-
ment earned more disdain than respect from the other
field agents. The SAC had seen his resume, probably,
but he would have sworn no one else in California knew
his background. Clain was eyeing him with surprise and
suspicion.

"All right," Sampford said abruptly. "Let's go."

"Good," said Norcross. "You can drive."

* * *

WHEN Molly was eight years old, her mother took sick. For a while she insisted it was nothing, kept right on with her chores, until one day she collapsed in the kitchen, overcome after a long, hot morning canning squash and corn. Molly's brother Chris found her, semiconscious and moaning slightly, and being two years younger than Molly he had just enough self-possession to run crying to her in the field. Their father was miles away, somewhere out in the wheat, running a combine with the teenager he'd hired as a hand. Molly knew how to dial the operator—no 911 then—and the volunteer firefighters showed up in the ambulance, cool and professional, to carry her off.

By then the malignancy was too far along for the doctors to make any difference. Even so, it probably wouldn't have mattered even if she'd called them the very first morning she couldn't get out of bed. No one survives pancreatic cancer. She was gone before the first frost that fall.

They lost the farm a year later. It was the middle of the 1980s, bank examiners and sheriff's bailiffs everywhere, faces at the diner at seven a.m. drawn and desperate. Molly's father couldn't have prevented foreclosure, not with grain prices lower by half than the cost of growing it, but the medical bills shoved them straightaway into bankruptcy. He grieved, and lost a few months, and for a while it was pretty much just Molly looking after Chris.

For some folks—say, the army recruiter who signed Molly up at a folding table in the high school gym nine years later—that was enough to draw a picture. Broken family, economic devastation, a father who dropped the parenting ball: plenty of other recruits had similar backgrounds. The volunteer military drew heavily from the country's back roads, where kids had dusty clothes and poor teeth, where authority figures were more likely to be found on the football field than at home.

But this would be unfair to Molly's father. For he pulled himself together, found a job at the towering grain elevator down by the railhead, stayed away from liquor, and did the best he could to raise his children. Sure, their new house was too small, and rented, but he cleaned it every Saturday and kept the lawn trimmed. He'd never been much of a talker, and sometimes he'd drift off into an hour or two of silent melancholy, but he tacked Chris's drawings on the wall and never failed to read Molly's homework. Most nights he cooked dinner. When Molly was on the rifle team, he missed only three of her competitions—all early in the fall, when the elevator was still busy from the harvest, and he couldn't get away.

Which isn't to say Molly was unaffected. After watching her mother and father struck down, by different events but with equally unexpected and overwhelming force, the lesson Molly learned was: stay in control. Prepare, anticipate, react. Discipline. Competition shooting was a perfect sport for her, because the only actions that affected the result were her own: her real opponent was herself. When she accepted her medal at the state championships, observers remarked on her self-possession. She smiled at the crowd and walked casually back to her team, apparently no more excited than had she just checked out a library book.

It was an enormous disappointment to her father when Molly joined the service. He had enough friends at the agricultural co-op that its credit union might have loaned him the money for college tuition, but she couldn't bear the thought of indebting him so deeply. And no one was offering shooting scholarships—except the army, more or less. There were few other ways out of town, and Molly made her choice.

She believed she was entering a meritocracy, where success or failure would depend simply on her own effort. Later the irony of it was more obvious—for Molly, control meant self-control, while the military preferred to impose it thoroughly from above—but an unyielding self-discipline was useful anywhere, and she so excelled in the skills of her specialty that her superiors could overlook tendencies of independent thought, even insubordination. Her brother married young, into a little land, and worked himself ragged and grim trying to make his farm succeed; trying, it was obvious to all but him, to succeed where their father had failed, and so to redeem him. He tried to impose order on the earth, the weather, and the vast and distant commodities markets. Molly imposed order on herself.

Her need to maintain control, to remain implacable and in charge, meant she suffered all the more when control was lost—when, for example, she was nearly killed, battered unconscious by unknown assailants, and tossed into the back of a truck. But the same discipline also allowed her to recover, over time. All she needed was an edge, a fingerhold, a chance.

SAMPFORD had to park three blocks away, unable to push closer through streets jammed with TV vans, police vehicles, rescue equipment, gawkers, and a large number of anonymous, dark-colored American sedans with second antennas and government E plates. Two news helicopters drifted noisily overhead, circling restlessly as their camera lenses tracked the activity. Red, yellow, and blue flashers atop various emergency vehicles strobed the scene like a carnival midway at dusk.

Sampford began to bull straight through the crowd, but Norcross detained him with a hand on one arm.

"We'll go around back," he said. "No need to walk through the reporters—they'd be all over us."

They followed the sidestreet left, along a razor-wire fence enclosing a fleet of battered five-ton delivery trucks marked Mun Yoh Trading Co. above handpainted Chinese characters. Police tape stretched along the fence, and uniformed officers stood post at the corners.

Around the next corner a graveled lot backed up against a series of truck bays, now locked down with heavy, graffiti-ridden steel shutters. A single tractor-trailer stood under a sodium lamp; the rest of the lot was filled with a half-dozen ambulances and one van marked with the City and County of San Francisco Medical Examiner's seal.

"FBI," Norcross said to the patrolmen standing inside the police tape.

They stared back at him. Sampford could understand why; Norcross looked more like someone you'd hire to dig postholes. Finally one officer carefully examined his ID, checked Sampford's as well, and then nodded wordlessly, pushing the tape down so they could step over.

"Who's in charge?" Norcross asked.

The officer was hostile, like the locals usually were. "Captain Birney," he said grudgingly.

"From Wakefield Station?" Norcross waited for the officer to nod. "Hasn't headquarters sent someone yet?"

"I really couldn't say, sir."

They squeezed between the ambulances, Sampford glanced sideways.

"You know Birney?" he asked, not bothering to add, *After just two months?*

"By sight. I went through the pic books last month." He caught Sampford's skeptical expression. "Situation assessment, isn't that what they call it at the Academy now? Look around in daylight, and you might not break your leg in a gopher hole after dark."

Outside the service door a pair of EMTs piled several empty, black, rubberized bags onto a gurney before wheeling it through. A man in body armor and a visored helmet, assault rifle at ready and no ID visible, nodded briefly when they entered.

"Pretty wide perimeter," said Sampford. "And sewn up tight."

"They're not taking any chances," Norcross agreed. "It must be a real bloodbath inside."

MOLLY thought she had a concussion, since she'd faded in and out for a long time, and her head was pounding with a steady spike of blinding pain. At first, clenching her teeth so she wouldn't cry out, she'd struggled against the bindings. Hardware-store duct tape was basically plastic and would stretch, slowly, if repeatedly stressed. But she quickly realized her captors had used something stronger, probably military speed tape—the kind employed by paratroopers to secure their loads before a jump. Now her wrists hurt too, but they weren't loosened at all.

Panic pushed at her, hysteria lurking beyond.

When the killers had thrown her into the quarter-ton, they'd hopped in as well, jamming down its sliding door with a loud rattle and bang. As the driver accelerated away the van crashed over a pothole, and the men clutched at stanchions as mail trays and loose parcels were flung around the cargo area. Molly's head banged on the metal floor. A wave of nausea almost blacked her out again.

"So why'd we grab her?" The driver spoke in a conversational tone, though it was clear from the pounding and engine noise that he was speeding recklessly down the narrow streets.

"Confusion," rasped the leader. "Lemons into lemonade. With her gone they'll believe the postal thing a bit longer."

"So what?" said the other shooter. "We're clear."

"No." The leader grunted as the van turned a corner, much too fast. "One got away."

"Ah, shit." They were silent for the rest of the ride.

The van pulled up after less than ten minutes, a bump and sudden darkening suggesting to Molly that they'd entered a garage. The driver killed the engine and hopped out; a moment later she heard a sliding metal door descend and clang shut. The other two men left, abandoning Molly in the pitch black.

She could hear them moving around and talking, though the sounds were indistinct. Another wave of panic flowed over her, and she huddled on the van's metal floor. The army had taught her to fight, to move and kill and move again, to overcome pain and deprivation, to survive. But even in the worst firefights she'd never been alone. There were always soldiers nearby, command resources on the radio, heavy weapons on call, in some sense the entire 82nd alongside her at all times. Now she had . . . nothing. No one. The feeling of abandonment paralyzed her.

In the end she went all the way back to the first lessons: Breathe. Wait. Listen. And after a few minutes she had regained enough control to start thinking again. The panic was right there, ready to resurface, but she maintained a narrow focus, one step at a time, and found just enough anger to get herself moving again.

Carefully she worked her way to a sitting position, wincing at the stabbing pain in her skull, and began to feel around the cargo area with her feet.

NORCROSS and Sampford followed the EMTs down a utility corridor, bare bulbs overhead and metal security panels every ten yards. Two more officers stood sentry at the end, in front of a wide freight door standing half-open. Bright lights and bustle were visible beyond. The patrolmen let the medics push the gurney past, closed ranks to check Norcross's ID again, then waved them through.

The lobby was a madhouse. At least a dozen forensic examiners in white coats were dusting, measuring, peering, and noting, even as the EMTs carefully moved bodies into the black bags. Two photographers worked quadrants, one with film and one with a digital camera, making notes after each shot. Other detectives in plainclothes wandered around, while patrol officers stood along the walls.

Sampford restrained his impatience as Norcross simply stood and watched for several minutes.

"Eight casualties," he said eventually, and glanced at the shattered glass. "All in that room." The company's doors, ironically, were untouched. "Blindside Technology—ever heard of them?"

Sampford shook his head, wondering how he was sure of the count.

A tall woman with light brown hair and a hard glare walked up. "Who the fuck are you?" she demanded. "We're trying to keep the scene clean."

"You must be Cathryn Birney—glad to meet you. I'm Special Agent Norcross." Birney's face grew pinched. "This is Agent Sampford." No one shook hands.

"You taking over?"

"Not yet."

"When?"

"Maybe never." Norcross made a who-knows gesture with one hand. "How about we sort out the jurisdictional issues later?"

Birney's expression didn't change. "Do you have issues, Special Agent?"

"You've got the manpower, it's your scene." Silence. "Captain, you know as well as me that our bosses are going to make that decision. Right now we're just trying to help."

"Naturally." She looked about thirty-five, young for a district commander, especially a woman.

"Maybe you can just tell us what you have so far."

"A bunch of dead guys."

After a long moment, Norcross just sighed. "Yes . . . ?"

Birney let it stretch out, but gave up eventually. "Five Asian, probably Chinese, three Caucasian, all shot three times. Twice to the chest, once in the head, the last at close range—every one of them. Explosive damage in the back room."

"Damage?"

"They blew up all the computers. Small charges of some sort on each one."

"Hmm." They watched the medics strap down one of the body bags, overseen by an ME in a blue jacket. "Not your typical workplace violence, is it?"

"Maybe *your* workplace." Birney's face suddenly relaxed, and she brushed absently at her hair, pushing it behind one ear. "Ah, hell, you're right. This has professional written all over it."

"Why do you say the Chinese guys were Chinese?"

"Driver's licenses. Ding Yihui? Yu Xiaoxuan? Probably not Japanese." Her pronunciation sounded accurate to Sampford, who'd had several assignments in Chinatown.

"PRC or Taiwanese?" Norcross asked.

She gave him an interested look. "Taiwan or Hong Kong, if I had to guess. It's hard to say. Ten years ago the shoes and haircut were a giveaway, but the mainlanders aren't such rubes anymore."

Norcross nodded. "Get anything from the security cameras?"

Sampford looked up, finally noticing two fisheyes mounted in the ceiling, but Birney was already shaking her head.

"Broken. The server wasn't running or something. Management company says they were planning to fix it next week."

"Naturally. Any live witnesses?"

"No one inside the building. A couple people down the street say they saw two men carrying a third guy run out and jump in their truck." She paused. "A post office truck."

A moment passed.

"A post office truck?" Norcross said. "Were the guys in uniform?"

"Witnesses aren't sure, but probably."

"Postal," said Norcross. "Three mailmen just shot the hell out of a dot-com." His voice held a certain wonder.

"That's about the size of it."

"No wonder your bosses are keeping their distance."

Birney almost laughed. "Yeah. I can't wait for the headlines on this one." She glanced over his shoulder, and her face abruptly closed down again. "Anyway, speaking of jurisdictional issues . . ."

They turned for the rushing arrival of a bulging man with a mustache a little too thick for his face. His jacket was pushed back from a large semiauto handgun in a quickdraw holster, a Springfield 1911-A1. Sampford noted the beavertail grip and extended slide stop that meant a custom combat rework. The man seemed angry, but his voice was low, pitched to a discreet rumble.

"Captain, I just learned that another witness has been airlifted away by your detectives. Somehow the spirit of cooperation we discussed has disappeared."

Birney pretended they were being polite. "Inspector Kubbos of the U.S. Postal Inspection Service, agents Stanford and Norcross from the FBI."

"Sampford," said Sampford, his first contribution to the discussion.

Kubbos made a dismissive gesture. "Yes, yes. Glad you're here. Now, Captain, my witness?"

"He's not my witness, or your witness, or anybody else's," Birney said impassively. "He's a guy whose coworkers were all just murdered in front of him, and we've taken him down to the station to give him a little distance from the scene."

"Captain." Kubbos paused, his mouth a straight, lipless line. "I don't want to go over your head."

Birney glowered, and Sampford had just decided to interrupt when Norcross beat him to it.

"I thought there weren't any witnesses," he said mildly.

Birney nodded. "He was in the bathroom."

Norcross raised an eyebrow. "Convenient."

"Yeah. He left the room just before the mailmen started firing."

"You don't know they were postal employees!" Kubbos glared.

"Inspector, you can't have it both ways," said Birney. "If they weren't, then what are you doing here?"

As the exchange grew more heated Sampford's attention returned to the room. He soon noticed the satchel cart, which was being examined by two evidence techs near the reception desk, and pointed it out.

Birney caught the gesture. "Yup, belongs to a letter carrier."

"He was in on it," said Norcross.

"Probably. Two guys from the van, one driver, one guy arriving on foot."

"She," said Kubbos.

"What?"

"The carrier—a woman, Molly Gannon. I finally got hold of the route supervisor."

"Really? Has she checked in?"

Kubbos clamped his teeth and shook his head.

"What the hell," said Birney, now openly angry. "I should have heard about her already. Get that supervisor in here."

"I sent two of my inspectors over to his house," Kubbos said. "We'll talk to him."

They glared at each other.

"Okay, stand down," said Norcross. "Inspector, I know your men are fully credentialed law enforcement professionals, same as the rest of us. But let's try to work together on this, all right? Have them bring the supervisor down to the station, we'll do the interview together."

"Fine." Through gritted teeth.

Sampford finally entered the discussion, gingerly. "What about the van? Was it hers?"

Birney nodded. "Good question. We don't think so—there's another one parked down the block."

"Inspector?" Sampford looked inquiringly at Kubbos.

"Yes. She was doing park-and-loops—she'd load up the satchel cart, stop at a few buildings to empty it, then circle back to her van and get another batch. Around here each loop probably covered a blockface or two." He caught Sampford's unspoken question and added, "One side of a city block."

"So are you missing any other trucks?"

Kubbos was irritated by the question. "We're checking," he said. "The city fleet's huge, and most everyone's locked down for the weekend. It's going to take time to figure out where they got it."

"Thank you."

"Where's Gannon's car?" asked Norcross.

After a pause Kubbos said, "I'll have to ask the supervisor. She probably left it near the CPO before her shift."

"Be good to get an alert on it."

When Kubbos finally stamped off, Birney rolled her shoulders.

"When did they begin arming mailmen?" she said. "This is the first time I ever met someone from their Inspection Service."

"Well, they mostly deal with mail fraud," said Norcross.

"Talk about going postal."

"You know, I bet he hates hearing that." Birney's mouth twitched.

Sampford went to talk with a medical examiner he recognized, returning ten minutes later, after Birney left to check with her detectives. He stood, writing carefully in a small notebook, while Norcross walked sightlines from the front doors.

"What'd the ME say?" asked Norcross.

"Very neat. Two rounds to the left torso, and an execution shot in the side of the head—almost the same placement on each one. He figures the double-taps were because the shooter was firing through the windows, the first bullet might get deflected."

"Sniper tactics," said Norcross.

"One of the Chinese victims had a Glock out, looks like he fired a few times before they got him." Sampford tilted his head toward the reception desk, where two forensic technicians were arguing over a long measuring tape. "They're searching for his bullets over there."

"No blood, though."

"Not on the floor. But the witness said one of them was carried out—he probably got hit."

"Or she."

Sampford nodded. "Or she. The mailman. Mailwoman? Mailperson?"

Norcross was looking through the doors to Blindside Technology, squinting at a long whiteboard along the wall, which was covered with scrawled equations and a messy box diagram. "Do we have any idea what this company was up to?"

"Something about encryption, according to the

detectives," said Sampford. "Computer security. You know, unbreakable codes."

Norcross considered the wreckage of the company's office. "Unbreakable," he muttered.

At that moment they noticed a stir across the room. An officer entered and interrupted Birney's conversation with the supervising medical examiner. She examined the paper she was handed, then waved over several other detectives. Their conversation was animated.

When the impromptu conference dispersed, Birney crossed the lobby and showed Norcross a single-page fax. It was cheaply printed on thermal paper, probably from a portable unit in a mobile command vehicle outside somewhere.

"Tentative ID on Ding Yihui," she said shortly. "A fingerprint confirmation from CJIS will take a few hours, but the name off his license came right up when we sent it through NCIC."

"The FBI is pleased to be of assistance," said Norcross, since both the Criminal Justice Information Services and the National Crime Information Center network were maintained by the Bureau, but Birney just grimaced, minimally amused.

"I thought his name was familiar," she said.

"Not to me."

"He was a triad. Belonged to the Wo Han Mok."

At the name Sampford looked up, interested. Norcross frowned slightly. "A gangster?"

"Yeah." Birney sighed. "You guys are going to grab the case for sure, now."

"We always work closely with local law enforcement," said Norcross. "Helpfully. In a spirit of cooperation."

Sampford turned to Birney, waiting for what he was sure would be a cutting rejoinder, but after a moment she smiled shortly and shook her head, apparently already more attuned to Norcross's straight-faced sense of humor.

"I'm sure it will be a pleasure, Special Agent," she said, and Sampford couldn't tell if she was being serious, either.

FOUR

THE KILLERS MUST have stolen the mail van, because it was still half-filled with trays and mail sacks. Some of the strapped bundles had broken open, and loose flats and letters were scattered across the bed. Concussed, bound, and blind in the dark, Molly nonetheless felt a small flicker of hope. She began to move in a circle until she could get her hands underneath the tray rack on the truck's right side. Every vehicle in the fleet—every postal van in the country, for all she knew—was equipped identically, and that meant a simple set of tools would be found in a metal box bolted to the floor.

She froze when a voice sounded right outside the vehicle.

"It's not done until they're all accounted for." Molly thought she recognized the leader's voice. The reply was muffled, unclear to her, but the leader must have been standing beside the door.

"Doesn't matter, he'll be leaving the police station eventually." Pause. "Oh, we'll know all right—they'll tell us." He laughed shortly. A moment later there was a thud against the truck's side, and a minute after that another slam. A car door? Molly decided another vehicle was parked close alongside, and the man had opened its door, banging against the van.

When his voice disappeared, Molly continued her slow movement along the metal floor. By lying on her side and shoving backward she got her hands onto the toolbox. Long screwdriver, pliers, a single-arm lug wrench, a box spanner . . . wincing as the tools rattled against each other, she decided the screwdriver would be sharpest, and pulled it out as quietly as she could.

Cutting the tape took an eternity. She couldn't reach anything holding the screwdriver in one hand, the way her wrists were bound, so she had to jam it in place with her hip against the rack stanchion. Sweat ran into her eyes. She kept pecking away—picking up the screwdriver, shoving it back against the metal, scraping the tape against the blade, groaning silently as it was knocked loose and fell again. Exhausted, her head aching, she became more careless, and her hands were soon slick with blood from slips and nicks.

A bang against the van's wall broke her concentration. The men were back outside, the leader speaking. "We'll take care of him." Pause. "Yeah, he'll want a fucking debrief. Just be there. We'll handle it." A longer pause. "You finish up here. She . . . use a gun then, it doesn't matter, just get moving."

A rush of fear and adrenaline drove Molly to a superhuman effort, and the screwdriver ripped through and gouged her wrist. With the tape torn she was finally able to twist her hands. Ignoring burning pain as the adhesive tore skin and hair straight off her arms, she got her fingernails onto the tape-end and a minute later had unwound it.

Her arms were next to useless, and she gasped silently as she tried to bend them. The garage door rattled open, a little light seeping into the quarter-ton, and Molly heard an engine start and a vehicle back slowly out. As fast as she could she unwrapped the tape from her ankles and knees, then squatted, trying not to black out from the pain in her joints as the blood started flowing again. The car outside accelerated away.

When the van's rear door was unlatched thirty seconds later, Molly had crouched two feet back from it, low to the floor, her feet braced against the rack supports and one hand on the metal truckbed. Her other held the lug wrench, with the socket end sticking out from her fist and the long shank extending down her forearm. She squinted, knowing that after so long in darkness the first light would be blinding.

The door was abruptly pulled up, rattling up its tracks—and without waiting Molly launched herself straight out, uncoiling like a sprinter off the blocks, one arm in front of her face and the other already punching forward with the wrench. She let her panic fuel the attack, riding her fear, coming out of the van like an explosion.

The man was holding a handgun, but his other arm was still in the air from the momentum of raising the door. He clearly hadn't expected Molly to be free. She collided with him straight on, the wrench socket striking his hip and her head going into his stomach. They fell in a jumble, two shots going off, and before they hit the floor Molly retracted the wrench slightly and hit him again with an elbow strike, her forearm reinforced by the heavy iron shank. She felt his ribs go as they struck the concrete, and she tumbled away.

He was injured, but it didn't matter if he still had the gun. Molly arrested her roll by slamming flat, then swung her legs sideways in a sharp scissors. She caught one shin, tripped him up, and threw the wrench without aiming. It struck his shoulder and he dropped the gun, falling down again himself. Molly kicked again, taking a half-second to choose a target this time, and snapped his head back.

He collapsed unconscious and it was over.

For a minute she just lay there, panting, waiting for the pain. When she pushed herself to a kneeling posture, then to her feet, she was dizzy and almost threw up. Fear and anger made it hard to think rationally.

The garage was small, barely large enough for three cars. The walls were corrugated sheet metal all the way around. One space was empty; the third vehicle was a four-door Taurus so bland it had to be a rental.

The man on the floor wasn't moving. In one corner a portable TV muttered, and when Molly focused on the screen she could see a live news report. She recognized the Wakefield police station—it was near the terminus of her route, and she drove past it every day on her way back to the mail facility. She realized where the other two killers had gone, and a renewed sense of urgency got her moving.

She couldn't wait for the police—the assassins were on their way to eliminate the last Blindside employee.

No phone in the garage, of course. She stepped into the street, but it was an alley in a deserted industrial block: a shuttered die-caster loomed next door, then another warehouse, and an empty parking lot surrounded by stained Jersey barriers. She paused, uncertain, before recognition clicked in and she knew where she was. The container terminal boundary was a half mile east, and this no-man's-land extended another quarter-mile west until it neared the city produce market.

Moving quickly now despite the aching stiffness, Molly returned to the man on the floor and patted him down, looking for a cellphone. His pockets were empty. She noticed the handgun—a Sig P226—and picked it up, from automatic habit snapping out the magazine and unchambering the remaining round. Without much surprise she noted that it was a jacketed hollowpoint. She looked at the weapon, then tossed the bullets into the street. The serial number on the frame had not been obliterated, and as Molly continued her quick search, moving to the Taurus, she processed the implication: they were well-resourced and confident enough to arm themselves with throwaways. She glanced at the serial again, memorizing it, and backhanded the gun out of sight under the mail van.

The Taurus was as clean as when they'd driven it off the airport lot at 9:57 that morning, according to the rental agreement on the dash. She ignored the driver's name, knowing it would be fake. A small canvas bag on the front seat had no phone, but the keys were lying in the armrest tray.

Molly looked at the mail van. She could probably drive it, since the entire fleet was identically keyed, just like the relay boxes—she patted her pants pocket, confirming that she still had her key ring. On the other hand, the Taurus would be faster, and Wakefield was a mile away. Without further consideration she slammed the driver's door, grabbed the rental key, and started up, backing into the street with a squeal of tires and accelerating away as quickly as they'd driven her from the massacre.

She was nearly fifteen minutes behind, but Molly thought she could get to Wakefield Station faster—assuming the killers had truly arrived from out of town and had not just rented their cars as cover. If they were unfamiliar with the area, they'd look at a map and go straight down Third. The city had started major roadwork, however, and the blocks south of Oakdale were a moonscape of gravel, trenches, flashing red lights on concrete barriers, and cars crawling along narrowed paths. Even this late—the dashboard clock said 8:34— enough Friday night traffic would be around to slow progress further.

Instead, Molly barreled through foggy sideroads until she reached Jerrold, found Quint, banged across the railroad tracks, and went around the back of Bayview Hill. The residential streets were crowded with parked cars, but actual traffic was light, and she made good time, trying to ignore the constant pain in her arms and shoulders.

She'd passed Wakefield Station a few times before: a low, white gray concrete box with loophole windows and spiked fencing around the garage portal. Broad steps rose to the main entrance at one corner, where the wide doors might have been more welcoming had the glass not been tinted to opacity. Police vehicles were double-parked around the block, the curbside zebra striping taken seriously only near the entrance.

Fog diffused the streetlights. When Molly drove up she hesitated only a moment, then cut the car into a U-turn, squealed across the street, and pulled into the no parking zone. She was surprised to find the area deserted, although a TV van was parked farther down the street, its telescoping antenna raised. Reporters and gawkers must have been allowed into the lobby.

She put her hand on the ignition key and paused, not sure what do. Looking at the station now, grim and silent and fortress-like, she couldn't imagine the killers breezing in as they had earlier. If the sole Blindside survivor was inside, he was safe, and if he'd already left, she had no idea where he might have gone.

Down the street headlights appeared, a vehicle moving rapidly toward the station's entrance. Leaving the engine running, Molly stepped out of her car.

FIVE

JEB PICOT HAD told his story eleven times to a succession of interrogators, starting with the first uniformed officers to arrive at the scene and ending with a pair of plainclothes detectives who'd ferried him to Wakefield Station in an unmarked sedan. The EMTs had cleared him for shock but warned of a delayed reaction. In fact, Jeb still wasn't feeling much of anything except numb. Fuzzy. He'd only peeked at the destroyed office, sideways, as four tactical officers bundled him out of the bathroom, not sure the area was secure, assault weapons aimed and visors still pulled down, barking brief and incomprehensible commands to each other. His brain kept circling around the image of the massacre, not getting anywhere.

"You're not a suspect." They kept telling him this. "You can leave whenever you want." But Jeb didn't walk out, partly because he wanted to help, however he could, and partly because his mind was pushing through molasses. It had been a few years since he'd had to deal with fear and trauma and violence. You needed detachment and clarity, both at the same time; now all he had was the detachment, which didn't help.

A detective named Erikson kept at him the longest. Jeb never left the interview room and the other faces came and went, a blur of white shirts, laminated badges, and guns. That's what he noticed, how every single one of them had a holster visible. Sometimes the weapons banged against the folding chairs.

Erikson seemed unable to decide if he was Good Cop or Bad Cop. A few times he stood up in frustration, raised his voice or slapped the edge of the door, hard. But he was the only one who offered bottled water—the others kept bringing in paper cups of vile vending-machine coffee, none of which Jeb touched—and he commiserated more than he questioned.

"Remarkable," he said. "Everyone else, every single one, shot numerous times, and not a scratch on you."

Jeb looked up. "Because they didn't know where I was, probably. The way you tell it, if they'd seen me, I'd be dead too."

"Just your good luck, you took that bathroom break right then."

"I had to go. That's all."

"Speaking of which, you sure you don't need a trip to the men's now?" Erikson looked at his watch.

Jeb shook his head. "When I heard the shooting . . . there's not a drop left in me."

He'd been friends with the others in a casual way, happy to have a beer after work now and then, but in the end more interested in their work performance than their families or hobbies. It occurred to him to wonder, had any of them lived and he died, what they'd be thinking of him now.

"About the letter carrier," said Erikson.

"I tripped over her cart, she apologized, I kept going. A dozen words, tops, from both of us." Jeb shrugged. "I told you. I didn't see that she was carrying a gun. She looked like she was just, you know, delivering mail."

The questions came and went, reappeared, came back again. To Jeb's surprise, they never asked about his record, and it never seemed like he ought to mention it.

"No," he said. "No one ever said anything about

threats, or strangers, or peculiar business." He felt a weary irritation, at once hungry and completely uninterested in eating. "Believe me, I've been trying to remember anything, anything at all. But no."

Hours later, Erikson told Jeb he could go home. "Get some sleep, if you can. It's the best thing."

"Did someone happen to collect my bike?"

"Bicycle?" Erikson shook his head. "Not that I heard. Probably in an evidence van somewhere. Want me to call a taxi?"

He left, Jeb finally used the bathroom, and an older, rumpled officer who introduced himself as the desk sergeant led him out of the building.

"Just ignore that mob," the sergeant said quietly, as they approached the front lobby. A crowd of journalists stood along one wall, loosely penned by a pair of uniformed officers keeping order. When Jeb appeared the quickest newshounds slung their cameras out, and the piercing glare of a TV camera snapped on. Ill-behaved shouting arose.

"The cab ought to be here any moment," the sergeant said. "We'll hold them back, give you a few minutes to get away."

"Thank you."

"Least we can do," said the sergeant.

MOLLY watched two people push through the heavy doors. The first was the Blindside employee she'd recognized; even from thirty feet away his lean frame and vandyke were distinctive. He started hesitantly down the steps, carrying a black satchel in one hand, while the officer accompanying him pushed back at the door, facing inward and clearly trying to detain the crowd inside.

"Back up—give him room, please!" she heard the officer shout, before adding, "On your way, sir. That's probably the taxi now."

Molly glanced over as she rounded the Taurus, already raising her hand and about to call for attention. In that split second she realized the oncoming car had no taxi light. It accelerated, leaping forward with a roar as the gas pedal was floored, aimed directly at her. By reflex, or training, or instinct—certainly not conscious thought—she dove forward, hit the ground, and tucked into a shoulder roll just as the other vehicle crashed into the rear of her Taurus.

She came out of the roll screaming, "Get down, get down!" and rose to a half-crouch. The other sedan's passenger door opened, not five feet away. One of the killers stepped out holding his HK and immediately began firing, aiming toward the station's entrance. The suppressor was still in place, perhaps refreshed, since the only noticeable sounds came from shell casings bouncing off the roof of the car.

The policeman made a soft, strangled noise, hit in the chest. In an extraordinary display of endurance he pulled his service pistol and managed to fire all eleven rounds at the killers before collapsing. Behind him the lobby erupted in chaos, and Molly had a flashing glimpse of people ducking backwards and away.

"Jeff! Over here!" Even as Molly screamed again, she dropped to her hands and kicked sideways with both legs in a roundhouse, striking the sedan's open door straight on and slamming it into the shooter's side. He grunted in pain as the door closed on his shin, stared at Molly for an instant, and swung the submachine gun her way.

Molly had used the rebound momentum from her kick to hop to her feet. Seeing him raise the HK above the top of the door she did the only thing possible: attacked. She kicked again, this time a right spin-back, adding impetus by shoving with her left leg from the ground. It was the most powerful strike she had, not aimed for anything except to deflect the weapon.

Her foot struck the door's window. It shattered, the safety glass disappearing in a spray of shards. Enough energy remained in the kick to knock the shooter clean into the backseat. An undirected shot went into the car's roof as he fell.

The second or two he was out of action saved Molly's

life. She got hung up in the car's windowframe and fell awkwardly, her foot twisted in the door. But those two seconds' grace also allowed the Blindside employee to get down the stairs, and he ducked toward Molly, confused.

"Get in the car," she yelled, and scuttled back toward her door. The opposing driver had not been part of the attack, at least not since he struck Molly's Taurus, but this was protocol, and she was counting on it: tactical responsibilities were always divided up, the driver was supposed to drive, and probably didn't have a weapon out. In any event, he didn't fire, though Molly gave him a clear target in the seconds it took her to get into the Taurus. She reached across to pull the Blindside guy all the way into the passenger seat, shoving him down as the shooter finally got the HK back in play and bullets stitched through the rear window. The windshield disappeared above her, blown out by the bullets cracking just over their heads. With her face below the level of the steering wheel Molly twisted frantically to get her foot on the accelerator, jamming the shift lever and punching the gas.

The car leaped backwards, surprising everyone including Molly, who hadn't been trying for reverse, and slammed into the other sedan. As they bounced off that impact, she finally found a forward gear and roared away, still not raising her head above the sill. Only after sideswiping two other cars down the street did she look out, a quick glimpse that was enough to set the car down the middle of the lane. Her passenger was curled up, his arms protecting his head. Molly took the next corner too fast, the tires squealing, and roared away, wondering how much of a lead they had.

She still didn't hear any sirens.

SIX

VANDEVEER LEFT HIS house at 5:15 a.m., yawning, and tripped on the crumbling concrete stoop. He noticed another scratch down the side of his eight-year-old Cavalier, and was nearly blasted off his seat when he turned the key and WIYY came on at 110 decibels. All right, now he knew who'd driven the car last, but that only meant another fruitless, accusatory conversation with the loutish stranger his teenage son had turned into. In an increasingly foul mood he navigated the deserted suburban maze of Albertsville, its uniformly ugly split-levels all dark, the only sign of life a vehicle even more dilapidated than his own creeping along as the man inside tossed newspapers more or less toward the houses. From paranoid habit Vandeveer scrutinized the other driver as he passed: dark-skinned, middle-aged, doubtless illegal. Now they were even stealing the paper boy's job. . . . Vandeveer snorted and ran a stop sign, thinking about how much he hated the East Coast. He managed to spend about three-quarters of his time in California, but that only made coming back worse.

He plugged in his cell phone and listened to voice

mail, then dialed into another automated system and let
it read him his recent email messages. The synthesized
voice always reminded him of a fellow he knew whose
larynx had been struck by a bullet and replaced with a
mechanical box. Nothing worthwhile had arrived since
he'd last checked, sometime after midnight. He tried
three direct numbers, all in area code 415, before he got
an answer.

"What?" The man's voice was raspy and irritated,
perhaps because it was 2:30 a.m. in San Francisco.

"Anything new?" Vandeveer didn't bother identify-
ing himself.

"She's gone to ground, looks like. Nothing, not a
trace."

"Police making progress?"

"Not so as you'd notice."

"Rice wants to see me, in about half an hour."

A harsh chuckle. "Padding your expense reports
again?"

Vandeveer grimaced. "Can't you give me anything?"

"She's a looker, what I understand. Charley's in
love."

"Oh, that's real useful."

"What can I say? Everything's just all fucked up."

"Yeah." Vandeveer squinted as the rising sun glared
jaggedly across the strip mall to his left. "Sure, I'll tell
Rice that."

"Better you than me." They hung up.

On the parkway Vandeveer let his speed drift up to
ninety, the Chevy groaning and vibrating from the strain.
A speed trap at this time of day was unlikely, not that it
mattered—he'd been stopped often enough, but the registration was flagged with a federal law enforcement
code that left the troopers gritting their teeth and wishing him a safe trip.

He exited west instead of east, and drove back across
the highway on the National Security Agency's private
bridge to the vast parking lots around the main buildings. Somewhere in the distant east lot was his assigned
space, near a hill covered with a thicket of large and

oddly shaped antennas, but it was a half mile from the blued mirror-glass tower of Ops 2B. Instead he parked in a visitor slot just a few yards from the main doors. The guard at the interior booth was ready to give him a hard time until he saw the clearance level on Vandeveer's orange-and-green pass, then just waved him through the chromed turnstile. Vandeveer nodded and kept the pass out; he'd need it twice more before he reached Rice's office.

Off the elevator on the third floor the corridors were dingy and gray, as uninspiring as when they'd last been painted sometime during the first Bush administration. No Classified Talk warned a sign above a plastic couch placed in a smoking alcove, just off the hallway and with its own air exhaust. Other posters down the hall showed former employees—such as ex-air force Sgt. John Carney, convicted of espionage and sentenced to thirty-eight years: "I lost everything," the quote read, in stark red letters, "my dignity, my freedom, my self-respect."

Thus inspired, Vandeveer continued to a reception area past a cluster of tiny cubicles, entering after stooping to get his eyes flashed in an iris scanner outside the door. The secretarial desks were empty, no surprise this early on Saturday, but the door to Rice's office stood open a few inches. For a moment Vandeveer hesitated: barge right in, bright and cheery? No. He knocked lightly and waited for Rice's grunt.

"Good morning." Rice glanced pointedly at the large clock on his wall, the kind you'd find in a midwestern grade school. "Thanks for coming in."

"Glad to get an early start." Damned if he'd apologize for being three minutes late. "Hey, is there coffee somewhere?"

Rice shook his head and looked down at the mug on his desk, which Vandeveer knew would be half-full of something like barley water, or wheatgrass juice. "There's a bubbler in the hallway," he said shortly.

That took care of the niceties.

Rice kept his office in a state of precise, obsessive order. A flat-panel monitor and keyboard were aligned slightly to the left of center on the desk, flanked by a symmetrically angled pair of halogen lamps on anodized aluminum arms. A walnut credenza sat empty of both paper and adornment; built-in bookshelves above it contained only neat stacks of public access journals, arranged by date. The drawers in three locked, fire-resistant file cabinets against the opposite wall were all unmarked. Two executive-grade leather chairs stood in front of the desk, in parallel, their placement echoing the black and gray telephones at each end of the work surface.

When Vandeveer entered and closed the door behind him Rice clicked off his monitor and gestured at the chairs, not bothering to rise. Vandeveer took the one on the left, knowing that sitting in the right chair put a halogen directly in his eyes.

All in all, it was exactly the sort of office you'd expect for the most powerful position in the Operations Directorate's permanent bureaucracy: the Controller of Budget and Allocation.

Vandeveer, on the other hand, had spent most of his career assigned to Special Collection Services, in locations like Moscow, Tehran, and Khartoum. SCS was a joint operation with the CIA, and now and then Vandeveer would have a beer with one of his old field colleagues. China's Ministry of State Security was craftier than the KGB, he liked to say, and the CIA jobbers in SCS were worse than the Chinese, but he hadn't truly plumbed the nadir of human depravity until his first six months in the headquarters bureaucracy.

"So what happened?" Rice went straight to the point, his tone as pallid and humorless as the rest of him. His bald head was stubbled from a recent haircut around the margins.

" 'What' is easy," Vandeveer said. Long ago he'd realized that bluff and charm had absolutely no effect on Rice, which was too bad, since bluff and charm were what Vandeveer did best. That left competence and honesty, not the easiest performance for him, but most readily simulated by barreling along as directly as possible.

"An operational team of unknown provenance assassinated all but one employee of Blindside Technology and destroyed its computers. 'Why' is harder."

"Who got away?"

"His name's Jeb Picot. Young guy, programmer, hired a year ago. Well, not that young, I suppose—close to thirty, makes him almost the oldest one there. From his resume it looks like he's more coding than crypto but it's hard to know for sure."

"Was he in on it?"

Vandeveer hesitated. "The police aren't sure. At first he was just a witness, though they leaned on him pretty hard. But when he left the station last night, a second incident occurred—two cars, shooting, one officer killed, and now Picot's disappeared."

"This makes no sense," said Rice, in a way that made Vandeveer even more unhappy that he had to be the source of the annoyance.

"No, sir," he said.

"The timing—that's the problem. It can't have been coincidence."

"Um, was the money transferred?"

"No, it's still in escrow. Good thing the Chinese are all dead—they have an access token to the account." Rice grimaced. "Nearly three and a half million . . . why the hell didn't you have someone there in person?"

Vandeveer nodded like this was an easily answered question and not his central, glaring error. "It didn't seem necessary. The terms of the deal were established, the papers were signed—it was just a formality, to hand over the first payment. Twenty-five percent. And technically, Blindside was buying out their main investor. As a third party to the transaction, Dunshire Capital wasn't directly involved."

After a long pause, Rice inclined his head slightly. Vandeveer couldn't help a slight sigh of relief, and he smoothed the crease in his dark wool trousers, neatening the drape above a gleaming loafer. He allowed himself a brief feeling of disdain for Rice's permanent-press shirt, doubtless bought off the rack at Men's Warehouse.

"This pussyfooting around—bah." Rice made a sour expression. "Ten years ago we'd have just declared their technology classified and brought them inside directly. National security used to mean something in this country."

"The climate has changed."

"Indeed." Rice frowned at his blank screen. "Well, now we have to deal with the mess."

"Yes, sir." Vandeveer was back on comfortable ground. "In that regard, we seem to have two different avenues to consider."

"Yes?"

"First, the police—well, actually it's a little confusing who's in charge. The FBI is involved, but the Postal Inspection Service is issuing orders too, and apparently the U.S. Marshals are on their way out as well."

"Postal inspectors?" Rice sat back, leaving his hands on the desk in front of his keyboard so his arms straightened out, as if doing isometrics. "Marshals?"

"It seems that at least one member of the ops team was a letter carrier. New to the job, though—she'd been in the army before that."

"The army." Rice's tone remained flat, but Vandeveer could hear the irritation building.

"Her records haven't been pulled yet, but she had about nine years in, according to her application at the USPS." When Rice just shook his head, Vandeveer continued, "As for the Marshal Service, they're claiming a warrant on one of the dead men."

Rice made a slight choking noise. "Blindside was harboring a federal fugitive?"

"No, no. Sorry, sir. He was one of the original investors—the ones selling Blindside to us. We, ah, we failed to sufficiently investigate these guys, it turns out." He hesitated. "They seem to have been involved with a, well, let's say, a Chinese criminal organization. One of them fled a racketeering indictment earlier this year."

Rice closed his eyes. "Thank God the money's in escrow," he said finally.

"Yes." Vandeveer waited, watching the sunrise through

the windows. The glass was not perfectly clear, since a fine electrical mesh was embedded between its layers as an eavesdropping countermeasure, but the sweeping blue and pink sky was more appealing to look at than Rice.

"Is there any chance," said Rice, speaking slowly, "that we almost paid off the Chinese secret service?"

"Ah, well, the triads work pretty closely with them, from what I understand," said Vandeveer.

"Mother of God."

"On the other hand, we'll probably never know for sure." Vandeveer pushed ahead, thinking he might get past the issue of Dunshire's failed due diligence by dropping bombs everywhere. "But—that may be to our advantage."

Rice waited. "Yes?"

"Look at it from the other direction. Who could have sent in the ODA?" He used the abbreviation for "operational detachment alpha"—what Special Forces called their small units, after the old phrase "A-team" was ruined by the TV show. While in SCS he had used specialists on several occasions, for certain aggressive operations, and he'd picked up some of the vocabulary.

"I see where this is going." Rice's sour expression had returned.

"Yes," said Vandeveer again. "The operation was professional. The killers were well-trained. And the authorities don't have a clue who they were."

"But we do."

Vandeveer hesitated. "Um, well, that's the thing. If someone in counterintelligence decided that the Chinese were doing high-level crypto in Silicon Valley . . ." He let the implication hang.

Rice looked like he'd broken a tooth. "You think it was Langley?"

Vandeveer just shrugged, and Rice shook his head.

"Don't they ever fucking learn?" he said. "You'd think after being dragged up Capitol Hill for all their other stunts they'd figure out how to do a job without mowing down everyone in sight." After a moment, though, he smiled, a brief, scary glint. "I have to say, though, I like their choice of cover. A mailman! I guess they missed *Three Days of the Condor*."

Vandeveer essayed a quick smile, but he was slow, and Rice had already returned to his glare.

"You said, two avenues."

"What?" For a moment, Vandeveer was lost. "Oh, yes. Well, as I mentioned they didn't just try to kill everyone in the company—they also firebombed the server room. Every hard drive in there was incinerated."

Rice stared at him. "Destroyed?"

"Completely."

"It may be," Rice said slowly, "that being in the heart of the nation's preeminent computer security organization, I take certain things for granted. Do you mean to tell me . . . do you mean to say that Blindside was not making backups?"

"No, they were," said Vandeveer. "Every night, full backups—not just incrementals—right onto a RAID array. Foolproof." He now let a slight smile show.

Rice shook his head. "Don't tell me."

"Yes."

"They actually kept it in the same room?"

"Three feet away."

"Unbelievable." A moment passed. "And we were buying these bozos for fifteen mil . . . so you're saying that the company's intellectual property is gone?"

"Utterly."

"So in fact, we have nothing to worry about."

"Um." Vandeveer paused. "Well, let's look at the big picture. Blindside is erased, dead. We wanted their invention under wraps, and that's what we have. Nine people killed so far, of course, including one policeman, and several federal law enforcement agencies involved—so a manhunt is underway. But if they actually find the real killers, who will it be? None other than our, um, friends in Virginia . . . just when Congress is about to finalize the budget appropriations." He didn't smile, but his face was open. "Frankly, sir, I think we just saved $3.4 million, and got a big bonus option in the bargain."

"It's locked in escrow for seven days still, but I see what you mean." Rice paused. "What about the one who's still alive? Picot?"

Vandeveer composed a thoughtful expression, then spoke carefully. "He was hardly more than a contractor, just doing grunt programming for Blindside. He won't be able to recreate it."

A full minute passed in silence. The black, unclassified phone on Rice's desk brilled softly, ignored by both of them, and sat blinking.

"No," said Rice finally. "It's risky. We can't take the chance of having Dunshire's involvement revealed. Picot could know something about that. Your comment about our distinguished congressional overseers—it cuts both ways. They'd be just as interested in us."

"All right." Vandeveer templed his hands, wondering whether Rice kept a tape running in meetings like this. "Here's how I see it. The public attention on this is enormous—I watched TV for an hour last night, and you'd think someone had carpet-bombed the White House. So the police—or the FBI or whoever—are going to be under enormous pressure to close it out, fast and neat. And on top of that, a cop was killed, shot down right on the front steps of the police station." He let his hands fall back to his lap. "Every policeman in San Francisco—hell, every lawman in the country—is going to be after these guys, with a vengeance. Shoot first, sort it out later. See?"

Rice waited, and after a moment Vandeveer continued. "Let's be realistic. The ops team—they're going to disappear, that's how they are, they surface from the deep dark water, do their job, and no one ever sees them again. But Picot, he's a different story."

"He's not a suspect," Rice said finally.

"Not formally," agreed Vandeveer. "Not yet. However, if more evidence comes to light . . ."

They looked at each other.

"This law enforcement effort," said Vandeveer. "All these agencies, plus every cop on his own, the press all over them. Rumors and misinformation are going to be flying everywhere."

Rice was completely still, and then, slowly, he nodded once.

Assured that they understood each other, Vandeveer felt a small but welcome relief. He noticed sweat trickling down his back.

"I was scheduled to go out next week anyway," he said. "But I'll leave sooner."

"On the next flight, you mean."

"Ah, right, of course."

On his way out, Vandeveer paused before opening the door. Now that the interview was over, his usual self-assurance was returning.

"You should come out to Dunshire now and then," he said. "See how our investments are doing. I know we're not really in it for the money, but business is good. Great, actually. We're way ahead of In-Q-Tel."

Rice shook his head.

"No thanks," he said, his eyes devoid of humor. "You venture guys scare me."

SEVEN

WHEN THEY'D SCREECHED around the corner from the station, with most of the windows shot out and the rear end groaning from damage sustained in the collision, Molly hadn't been thinking, just reacting. She'd gone tactical, survival the only objective. The car slewed sideways, banging against a parked minivan, and she yanked the wheel, glanced at all three mirrors, and finally twisted her head quickly to check the road behind.

"They're not following," she said, surprised, and took another left without slowing down. At forty-five miles an hour the wind blowing straight through the broken windshield stung her eyes and she had to keep blinking. "Must have banged them up. Good thing their weapons were suppressed. Full-power rounds would have gone right through the car." She couldn't stop talking.

Her passenger had hunched into a crash tuck, arms over his head and braced against the dash, and now he straightened carefully, looking around like he was still trying to figure out what had just happened. He didn't say anything.

"We'll circle around, I guess." Molly was jittery, her mind chasing its own tail. "Whatever happened back there, it'll be over in a few minutes . . . shooting up a *police station*? What the hell were they thinking?"

"Don't know." His voice was calm, unhurried. "But don't go back."

"What?"

"I only saw one car . . ."

"That's all there was. Two men."

"We don't know who else might have been right behind them."

The street was deserted, a good thing because the damaged vehicle was veering unexpectedly this way and that. Something broken dragged from the undercarriage. Molly forced herself to ease up on the accelerator and looked sideways at her passenger. He sat casually, one arm on the windowsill and the other holding a faded canvas courier bag in his lap, his eyes squinting against cold air through the shattered windshield.

"Could be world war three back there," he said. "Safer to stay away."

Molly had been shot at, banged up, knocked unconscious. She was barely holding herself together, and this guy could have been talking about the weather.

"Fine," she said. "Fine. Next pay phone, we'll call for help. Let the police come to us."

His looked thoughtful, considering the suggestion for several moments. "No," he said. "I don't think so."

"You don't *think* so?"

"They're not behind us?"

"No."

"I guess I'll get out, then."

"Here?" They were on the downhill side of Hunter's Point, where those who couldn't afford to leave shuttered themselves behind barred windows, where crumbling public housing blocks had surrendered to free-fire gangs. The streets were still empty; even the SUVs filled with suburban white kids looking for drugs didn't come through after dark.

"Oh. Well, is there a BART station nearby?"

Molly drove in silence for a minute. Was it shock?—but he didn't appear disoriented, just inappropriately relaxed. He shifted in his seat, getting comfortable.

"I have no idea what's going on," she said. A group of young men on a shadowed corner watched the car as they passed, showing no particular interest in its shot-out condition but staring hard at her. "I want the police here. I want some protection. I want to be safe."

He didn't seem to be paying attention to her comments. "My name's not Jeff."

Molly wondered if she'd gone crazy, slipped into some surreal alternate dimension. "Who cares?"

"It's Jeb." He waited.

A minute passed. Molly shook her head. "Okay," she said. "Jeb it is."

He nodded thanks. "That's why I ducked your way when you yelled, though."

"What?"

"When you called me 'Jeff.' I don't remember thinking it through, but I must have figured that anyone trying to kill me would at least get my name right."

"You," said Molly, "are lucky to be alive." But she thought back, saw him leaping forward off the stoop as the policeman fell to one side. When it counted, he was quick—as fast as anyone she'd served with, and under fire too.

She stopped for a light at Jennings, the crossroad deserted, a single pair of headlights waiting on the other side. At the green she accelerated slowly, trying to ignore the other driver's shocked face as they passed.

"They think you're in on it," Jeb said.

"Who?"

"The police. Kept asking about you—Molly, right?" When she didn't immediately respond, he added, "You're still wearing the uniform, says USPS right on the patch there."

Molly glanced sideways. In the lobby he'd been just another Valley engineer—underweight, the vandyke, shapeless cotton sweater, rockhopper sandals. Now, despite the loose jacket he wore, she realized he was wiry, not scrawny, with sharp edges in his face, and his gaze was much too steady for what they'd just gone through. Molly's head and hands hurt, and cold air bit through the broken glass. The sensations brought a flash of memory: winter patrols through hardscrabble Balkan villages, unheated humvees bouncing on dirt tracks. Jeb looked like the farmers who hadn't yet fled—as hard as their rocky, unforgiving soil.

"You're saying the police . . ."

"Detectives wanted to hear about the other guys, too, your teammates they said, but I didn't know anything about them. I told them I was in the bathroom—I don't know what they thought, like I'd go running out to see what was happening? As soon as I heard the fireworks start, I hid in the last stall and waited until SWAT came through the door."

"Can't blame you, I guess."

"Well, *they* did. Not in so many words, though, and they let me go." His voice had darkened. "This time."

"Wait a minute." Molly was processing about two beats behind. "'Teammates'? The bastards almost killed me!"

"Yeah." The car bounced over a series of potholes, scraping loudly, and he shifted the bag in his lap. "But they didn't."

"That's their proof? I'm still walking around, I'm guilty?" Reality was slipping further downhill. "What is this, the Middle Ages—you drown, you're innocent, you don't drown, you're a witch?" She stopped. "Anyway, you're still alive, too."

"They noticed that." He shrugged. "Fact is, cops aren't sure about me either. They're wondering why I escaped. Was it just coincidence I was in the bathroom? Why did I walk out right then?" He paused. "Why didn't they shoot me first?"

Molly wasn't following. "The police?"

"No. Back there." He gestured vaguely behind them.

"Coming out of the station?" Molly had lost track of the conversation again. "Training, I think. Basic coun- terterrorist tactics—you go into a hostile room, your first target is anyone with a weapon. Doesn't always work, but it's the best way to sort out noncombatants. Anyway, it's a hard instinct to overcome, to ignore the one trying to kill you." She frowned. "Listen, let's get back to the point here. You think you had a bad afternoon—mine was worse."

She told him what had happened at the warehouse. He stayed quiet for her entire account, not even providing the small *hmm*s and *uh-huh*s that most listeners would. But he wasn't ignoring her; in fact, Molly began to realize how closely he'd been paying attention all along. He just didn't bother showing it.

"Forensics ought to clear you," Jeb said finally. "Though it might take a while. Your prints on the gun, no witnesses, all that. The one you clobbered, he was breathing, you said?"

"When I left."

"He probably woke up right after that and took off. Most people don't stay knocked out more than a few minutes. Or if they do, they have the kind of concussion they don't wake up from at all."

"True." Molly wondered how he knew that. What you saw on TV was nothing like getting beat up for real.

She pulled over, stopping in the shadows alongside a high cinderblock wall.

"Oops." Jeb's bag tumbled off his lap when the car stopped. The street was empty, and the light overhead flickered, at the end of its life.

"Sorry."

He picked up the bag and checked inside, Molly glimpsing a dull black laptop, then turned his attention back to her. His gaze was clear and direct, his gray eyes intent. "The cops were right about one thing. You're not a typical mailman."

"Letter carrier," she said automatically.

"Letter carrier," he agreed. They watched each other for a moment.

Then his expression flattened out, and Molly remembered that, what, four hours earlier, every one of his colleagues had been massacred.

"Here's what I think," he said, almost gently. "The killers . . . you and me, we each surprised them, once. I wasn't where they expected, and you weren't *what* they expected. But we've used up our luck. The cops aren't on their side—I don't think, so, anyway—but it doesn't matter, because they're ready to lock us both up on general principles. We go back, guaranteed we end up detained."

"I don't think—"

"Wait." He interrupted her. "Like I said, it doesn't matter. Because being in jail, or just being in an interview room somewhere, we wouldn't be safe. Think about it. Whoever these guys are, they blew up my company like they were shopping for groceries. From what you say, they have all the resources they could ever need. And they're willing to attack a police station with a hundred cops inside, just to get me. If we turn ourselves in, we'll be dead before tomorrow."

For a long minute the only sound was the streetlight buzzing above, and an occasional sputter and clunk from the dying car beneath them.

"Also, maybe I should mention, I have some personal issues with jail," Jeb added.

It was Molly's turn to sigh. "Really?"

"You ever been in prison?"

"Only to visit."

He thought about that. "Maybe helping put other folks in?"

She nodded. "Military police."

"Yeah? Which branch?"

"Army. 82nd Airborne."

"I knew it. Letter carrier, right." His smile reappeared, then faded. "I spent some time inside. I'm not going back."

"You can't just run away."

"No, of course not." He looked surprised. "All I'm talking about is staying out of sight for a day or so. Right now, back at that station, it's nothing but confusion and anger and people yelling at each other. You've done this for a living, you know how it is, they'll be

lucky to get sorted out before morning. Once things settle down they'll be ready for a reasonable conversation,
and they might even listen to what I have to say."

"So you're just going to disappear for a while."

"Pull the covers over my head and get a good night's
sleep. Probably what you should do, too."

"Maybe you're right." They sat in silence for a while,
staring out through the car's shattered glass.

Jeb turned her way, examining her in the dim ambi-
ent light of the silent street, frowning as he noticed her
hands and forearms. "Blood?"

"Yes. Probably on the back of my head, too, where I
got slammed."

He didn't say anything, and Molly, who'd been wondering if she could trust him, realized he was as unsure
about her.

"We have to get out of this vehicle," she said. "It's
eye-catching, and I'm not sure how much longer it'll
last anyhow."

Jeb nodded. "Bernal Heights isn't far. The park up
there is kind of windswept and empty, so we can drop the
car someplace it won't be found right away and walk
over to the 24th Street station. You can catch a cab
there—easier than waving one down on the street."

"What about you?"

"I'll take the train." He pulled off his jacket. "Here.
You've got blood all over your shirt. Someone might
notice."

She hesitated, then took the garment. It was retro oil-
cloth, heavy and worn. "Thanks." And then, impul-
sively, "Got a pen? I'll give you a number where you
can reach me. Not my home."

"I don't need to write it down."

She looked at him quizzically, then recited Eileen's
number. He nodded.

They abandoned the car in a badly lit parking area
off Bernal Heights Boulevard, where it basically ex-
pired. Jeb took a moment to check the floor as he got
out, apparently making sure he hadn't lost anything
from his bag. When he straightened up he looked at

Molly, who'd pulled on his jacket and stood, not exactly waiting for him but not leaving immediately either.

"I'm going the other way," he said.

"Okay." She pushed at her hair.

"You look fine." He hesitated. "You know, I forgot to mention—thanks."

"What?"

"For saving my life."

"Forget it." She raised one hand briefly. "I'm going in tomorrow. No matter what."

"Make sure it's safe."

"Safe." She almost laughed. "I'll look for you there."

THEY split up after crossing Caesar Chavez, Jeb slipping away down a sidestreet and Molly continuing toward the better-lit motley of bars, dollar stores, and takeaway restaurants in front of the station. She wasn't sure Jeb was actually going to board the train, but then she wasn't getting a cab, either. Eileen lived in the Mission, less than a mile away. Perhaps it was overcautious not to tell Jeb that, but she was putting Eileen in harm's way simply by contacting her; Jeb was a complication she didn't want to worry about.

Jeb. After a half block Molly turned into an alley and ran lightly to its end, circling around and looking for him from the shadows. He should have appeared walking in her direction along 25th, but she scanned up and down the street fruitlessly. Wherever he was going, he'd given her the slip. Molly spent a minute looking, then another minute wondering what the hell she was doing. Finally she strode off toward Eileen's. Halfway there she found a pay phone alongside a shuttered donut shop and called to make sure she was in. The rest of the walk took only ten minutes.

Eileen's apartment was on the second floor of a rundown stucco building near SF General, on the wrong side of the gentrification line. Ambulance sirens could be heard around the clock, hauling uninsured gunshot victims to the crowded ER wards. Eileen's building had limited parking so she rented a spot in an alley behind a tiny Mexican grocery two blocks away. The first time Molly visited, Eileen warned her that she'd been mugged three times already, walking between the apartment and her car—twice she maced the assailant, and once she simply kicked the knife from his hand and watched him flee. "But hot water's included, and it gets lots of sun," she said.

Inside the TV was on, volume turned down. When Molly pulled off the jacket, in pain, Eileen just pointed toward the bathroom.

"Alcohol and gauze on the sink," she said. "Want some help?"

"No." Molly leaned over to drape the jacket on a chair, and stumbled as pain racketed from her skull and arms. "I mean, yes."

Years in the service had left the two of them with similar habits of triage. Eileen didn't ask a lot of questions, and Molly didn't launch into her story until she was clean and bandaged and back in the living room, wincing as she lowered herself onto the couch. She closed her eyes, finally overtaken by exhaustion.

"Uh, before you fall asleep," Eileen called from the kitchenette. "Think you might have been followed?"

"No." Molly shook her head, regretting it immediately.

"Still, police could cross-check records and come up with my name, right? So you ought to tell me what's going on, in case they knock on the door." She came into the room and handed Molly a glass of water. "You're on the news, you know. Cable channels are all over it."

"Already?" Molly was tired, so tired.

"They're not waiting for the official line. You're a terrorist, part of a cold-blooded assassination cell, armed and dangerous. Shoot on sight."

"They didn't say that!"

"Well, not the shoot to kill part, though the police chief came awfully close. Just like a bad TV show." Eileen paused. "Which I guess it is, come to think of it."

"I'll tell you what happened," Molly said. "But I don't think it's going to help."

She took a quarter hour, thorough and concise, all relevant details included, her delivery the practiced result of years writing activity and arrest reports. Eileen listened, clarified a few points of timing and description, and then simply said, "For Christ's sake, Molls, what are you doing here?"

"I know, I know."

"You should be talking to the FBI, not to me. You *know* that."

"It's too dangerous."

"More than what you already survived?"

"That's the problem. I don't understand why any of it happened, and that means I won't see the next one coming either. Jeb's right—let them sort it out overnight. I'll go in tomorrow."

"Hmm." Eileen watched her in silence for a while.

Molly drank some water and looked away. It was plain as day, out there between them. She felt a small, rueful smile cross her face.

"I sure can pick them, huh," she said.

"I hope he's good-looking."

"He said he's done time."

"Oh." Eileen rolled her eyes. "Better and better."

"Wade's going to look him up, see what his story is." She was surprised. "Is he out here too?"

"No, no. Still back at Bragg. I called him right after I called you."

Eileen nodded. "Wade's a good guy."

Molly was elsewhere. "It's like I pulled a puppy out of the river," she said. "The damn thing is my responsibility now." But again she saw Jeb leaping from the steps, agile as a cat—then sitting in the car, bullet holes and shattered glass everywhere, as relaxed as if he were driving to the mall for a sundae.

"What puppies do is pee all over the house," said Eileen.

They went through it all again, Eileen questioning more actively this time, trying to elicit details Molly might have overlooked. Halfway through she noticed the TV and interrupted to turn up the volume, and they watched a reporter giving a breathless account from the street outside Wakefield Station. His theory seemed to be that Islamic terrorists had decided to target the heart of America's high-tech community, in order to destroy the country's economic base. Eileen grimaced and clicked the mute again.

"Nothing much useful there."

"Wait." Molly stared at the television. "Turn the sound back on."

"What?"

The screen showed a tall, unsmiling man surrounded by a swarm of microphones, handheld recorders, and reporters yammering questions. His hair was gray and brushed straight back. He'd just stepped out a door, and he hesitated, glancing around at the mob, before nodding once and then walking straight through them. He said nothing, ignored everyone, and carried himself with a remote dignity that might have put off anyone less hardened than an on-air journalist.

He was visible for a few seconds, immediately replaced by a pair of news anchors. A blurry, badly colored face was projected behind them, and Molly recognized her high school yearbook photo.

"My father," she said. After a moment, "I was thinking I'd call him later."

Eileen turned off the television. "Might not be a good idea," she said. "Not with that kind of attention."

Molly's gaze hadn't left the screen, though it was now dark. "I can't imagine what he thinks."

"It didn't look like he was giving anything away."

"He wouldn't."

The room was quiet for a while. "You'll talk to him later," Eileen said finally. "You've got other problems now."

"Yeah . . ."

"Like how the whole world thinks you're Molly the Jackal."

"Maybe I can sue them all for libel." Molly shrugged.

"Wade's going to check the official story on me, too. That could help me figure out who to call in the morning."

"A lawyer might be a good start."

Sometime past midnight Eileen retrieved a sleeping bag from the closet.

"I'll take the couch," she said. "No, don't be silly, you need a comfortable place to sleep. I'm still on first shift tomorrow, so I'll be leaving in the morning."

Molly didn't argue. "I wish . . . I'm sorry about all this," she said.

"Of course not." Eileen flicked open her bedroll with the familiarity of innumerable bivouacs. "It's kind of reassuring, you know? Sometimes I think *my* life is a little out of control . . . now I feel downright suburban." She tucked into the bag and reached for the remote control. "I'm going to see what else they have to say about you."

"I don't want to know."

Despite her exhaustion, Molly tossed in the bed, her mind agitated, watching the day's victims die over and over again. She hadn't been in real combat for two years, and she'd forgotten how to control the playback inside her head. That was the thing about civilian life—all the damned emotions and complications.

She wondered where Jeb was, and how he was sleeping.

EIGHT

CATHRYN BIRNEY MET them at the rented garage before dawn, having had them both paged from there as soon as she saw the postal van. On his way over, Norcross counted out the timing, and determined that she made the call long before a directive to cooperate could have reached her from Washington. She must have contacted Sampford and himself out of professional courtesy and a genuine desire to be helpful. He found the thought comforting.

The SAC, for his part, had been exhausted when Norcross reached him at midnight. He sounded like he'd been briefed by someone who'd only caught the latest news bulletin, and he seemed to have caught cold, though that might have been a bad cell phone connection.

"Any chance this was just a disgruntled ex-employee, or an unhappy spouse—something like that?" he asked.

"Not unless someone was married to an Iraqi terrorist," said Norcross. "Too neat, too thorough. And don't forget there's apparently a Chinese gang involved."

"You're sure about that?"

"Captain Birney seemed pretty confident. But she's waiting for confirmation on the ID."

"Ah, Christ." The SAC coughed. "All right, let me figure out an assignment roster and I'll call you back."

"Sir." Norcross had anticipated this, and he knew that it was his one chance to stay involved; he understood as well as anyone why he'd been desk-bound since he arrived in San Francisco, and he was determined to get back into the field. "There are jurisdictional complications—not just with the locals. ATF we can deal with, I suppose, they're usually happy to let us take a public shellacking. But the postal inspector is a mad dog, and he has federal authority same as we do. Now the Marshals want first crack at the Chinese. And we've got the Chippies, too—something about the van must have been on state roads getting to the site—not to mention the SFPD seems to have internal turf issues of its own." He paused. "What I mean is, this is a swamp."

The SAC groaned. "Don't tell me."

"Yes, sir. They're already talking about a task force."

Nothing was more anathema to an ambitious FBI agent than a multi-agency task force. No matter how clearly the lines of authority were drawn, every participant would be jostling for power and credit, or to shove off the blame if the case went south. If successful, the FBI's accomplishment would be diluted, never a good thing for the agent in charge; and if something went wrong—a few more banks knocked over before the robbers were caught, say, or innocent bystanders killed during an arrest—all fingers would point to the feds, whom everyone hated anyway.

Not to mention how time-consuming the coordination meetings could be.

Norcross could hear the gears grind in the SAC's head. "Look, Sampford and I have already spent half the night out there," he said. "He's a good agent—I think you should give it to him."

"No!" As expected, the SAC's response was immediate. Norcross knew Sampford was much too inexperienced to front for the FBI—and, more importantly, for the SAC—in what was sure to be a very public investigation. On the other hand, the risks were huge. What the SAC needed was someone competent enough to do the job, but who could be tossed overboard without regret when the sharks started chewing through the lifeboat. In this light, there was one clear choice, and Norcross nudged it along.

"Well, maybe Clain then, he was in the office tonight. Whoever it is, I think I should brief them as quickly as possible. I'm just not familiar enough with this district, so the sooner I hand it off the better."

The psychology was so blatant a teenager would have seen through it, but the SAC was tired, and it had been clear he disliked Norcross from the moment they met, which clouded his judgment.

"No," the SAC said again. Then he continued, decisively, "You should keep it. You have more experience than half the office put together. Sampford will be your partner for the duration." He paused to cough. "This is your chance, Tommy. You've been wasted, pushing paper around the thirteenth floor. Clear this case and you'll have your pick of assignments."

By which he meant: screw it up and we can finally get you out of the Bureau. You can get a PI ticket and chase down insurance cheats to supplement your crummy pension.

Or so Norcross figured. "Thank you, sir. I appreciate your confidence. Could you notify the police, since I'll be seeing them again shortly?"

"I'll call the commissioner directly." The SAC coughed again. "He'll be pleased to have someone of your caliber involved."

Now, with the sun just coming up, Norcross was standing outside the police tape with Sampford, sipping at a styrofoam go-cup of coffee and wishing he'd worn a windbreaker. The day would probably clear later, but in the shadowed alley the damp breeze was penetrating and cold. His eyes burned with sleeplessness. Sampford nodded at a uniformed policewoman on the perimeter and drifted over to say good morning.

The captain appeared from an SFPD Explorer with blacked-out windows, looking surprisingly well-rested. Norcross suspected she'd slept in the bunks at Wakefield Station. She slid a notebook into her shirt pocket, buttoning the flap down over her breast, then caught him watching and gave an amused smile. He looked away in slight, unexpected embarrassment.

"Forensic teams are stretched," she said without preamble. "Blindside, then the station, now here."

"But no bodies this time," said Norcross. Seeing her mouth tighten, he added, "Sorry, Captain, I mean no disrespect. I know one of your officers was killed last night. My only point is, the examination here, it's not so urgent."

After a moment her expression softened. "Yes. Thank you. It's been a long night." She paused. "No need to be formal, by the way. Cathryn is fine."

"How did you find the truck?"

She gestured down the alley. "The metal-casting shop. Some kind of big job, so they're working the weekend, and the first guy in this morning drove past the door. It was open, he could see right in, and he was smart enough to connect it with the news on TV last night."

She glanced at his coffee cup. "Throw that away, you can take a look inside. So far we haven't found much."

A single evidence technician was at work, on her hands and knees at the side of the postal van, brushing floor debris into a small paper sack. Plastic bags were only used for completely dry material, since condensation could ruin evidence.

"A little blood on the floor of the truck, in the back," Birney said, pointing. "We'll get it typed as soon as possible, but the obvious guess is it came from the wounded assailant. Kind of a mess back there, it looks like they were driving too fast, no surprise. Tire marks and some exhaust drips suggest two other vehicles, and you don't need a gold shield to figure they were the two cars that hit the station last night."

Norcross nodded. "So what have you found that you didn't expect, so far?"

She nodded. "Right question," she said. "Under the truck, a handgun." She led them back outside to the forensic van, and they looked at the tagged P226 sitting on its interior counter. "It was hard to see. I don't know, maybe they missed it on their way out. The funny thing is, we found the magazine in the street—and two bullets in the wall."

"Hell of an expensive gun to throw away." Norcross considered. "That doesn't make sense."

"Not yet, anyway."

While they talked gawkers began to appear, despite the cold and the early hour. A couple of smokies—scanner junkies, who usually followed fire calls—greeted the officers standing guard, but when a TV van showed up at the end of the alley, nosing around a dumpster, Birney ordered the perimeter reset at the end of the block.

"So we're going to run a task force," she said, when the patrol officers had been dispatched. "Commissioner called me himself, last night. Says we're to, let's see, accommodate the team's requirements as fully and as expeditiously as possible."

"Excellent." Norcross smiled.

"We should have our first meeting later this morning, get all the agencies together. The inspector'll be thrilled, for one. You have a room large enough?"

"For a half-dozen people?"

"It's not the chairs that are the problem," she said. "It's the egos."

Sampford had rejoined them when the policewoman he'd been chatting up left to push back the reporters. He glanced at Birney, obviously unsure whether he could laugh. Norcross grinned.

"In fact, I was hoping you could find us a space," he said.

She frowned. "Why?"

Norcross didn't answer right away, serious again, examining her face. Birney held his gaze.

"Cathryn, I believe I'll tell you the truth," said Norcross, finally, and a bit of north plains drawl had crept into his voice. "The fact is, my boss, the SAC, is going to regret giving me this assignment very soon. If he hasn't had second thoughts already. He doesn't like me and he doesn't trust me. And the more he sees of me, the sooner he'll try to take me off. I don't want that to happen."

Her mouth slowly twitched into a half smile. "You're trying to build up my confidence in you?"

Norcross shrugged slightly. "I'm sure you've checked me out. You'll draw your own conclusions."

She turned to Sampford. "What about you?"

"Uh." He ducked his head, uncomfortable. "That is, I . . ."

"He'd like to learn how real crimefighting is done," said Norcross. "If he doesn't spend more time outside his cubicle, he'll end up an SAC himself."

Birney nodded. "Okay."

"Anyway, you're kind of neutral ground. It'll make everyone else feel better."

"I don't know what I can get. Wakefield's jammed."

"It ought to be downtown anyway," said Norcross. "The farther it is from here, the less often we'll have to meet."

"True." She leaned against the wall, more relaxed. "Special Agent, I'm going to enjoy working with you."

Sampford had been flipping through his notebook, and after frowning at one page, he diffidently interrupted. "One question, if I may?"

"Yes?" She was watching the TV crew filming from the end of the alley.

"Any lead on the two cars yet?"

"From the drips and scuff marks the investigator's guessing they were similar four-doors. Witnesses at the station can't agree on anything except that they might have been dark colored. On the other hand, at least one is probably full of bullet holes—Sergeant Mason fired all eleven rounds before he went down, and only two have been found so far."

"They won't have gone far, then."

She sighed. "City and county are notified, but we'll

probably just have to wait until they turn up. That shouldn't be long, though. I'm sure the cars were either stolen or rented."

"And when they are recovered, they'll be clean," Norcross agreed.

"Even if we get the FBI labs involved?" Her eyes were amused.

"Oh, they'll probably find something—a few threads, some dust—but it's not going to break the case. Might help the prosecutors tie up some loose ends, of course."

"Hmm. Good point. Maybe we ought to have the U.S. Attorney's office on the task force."

Norcross grimaced, but she shook her head. "Hey, only kidding, that can wait until we find some suspects. Anyway, talking to the USA is like opening a direct line to the six o'clock news—he leaks even faster than the mayor."

The sun was just rising above the dilapidated wooden buildings down the street, and an unexpected glare reflected from the Explorer's windows. Birney rubbed her eyes.

"So what do you have on the company itself?" she asked.

"Paul?"

Sampford shook his head. "Not much. The founder's a Russian academic named Astrov, and I ran down some abstracts of articles he wrote. Three were in Russian, and two in the *Journal of the American Mathematical Society*, but even in English I couldn't understand the titles. Washington is trying to find someone smart enough to take a look."

Birney looked interested. "A Russian?"

"Novgorod University, on the faculty of Mathematics and Informatics until 1992. He came to this country on a legitimate visa, then dropped out of sight for several years. He was probably driving a cab—City Hall found a hackney license with his name on it from 1994." He glanced at Birney, embarrassed. "Sorry, I should have gone through SFPD, but I happened to know someone in Records, and it was quicker . . ."

She waved it off and he continued. "Astrov started calling venture capitalists last year, looking for start-up funding. Someone who heard his pitch at a breakfast remembered that it had to do with harnessing together a bunch of off-the-shelf computers into a kind of super-processor . . . a Beowulf cluster, that mean anything to you? Me neither. Anyway, I'm still trying to talk to the VC who ended up giving them money—he's supposed to call me back today."

"Astrov's a number theory genius, and he got out when the Soviet Union fell apart," said Norcross. "But that's all we know."

"Right," said Birney. "All kinds of possibilities there. Mafiya?"

"Just speculation at this point."

Another patrol officer walked up from the perimeter, shaking his head in annoyance as he was peppered by questions from the reporters standing at the tape. He nodded at Birney. "Captain."

"I thought you were off already."

"Overtime." He looked at his watch.

"Go home. We're getting another unit in a few minutes."

"Thanks."

When the officer had left, Norcross thought of something else. "The other employee—Picot?—has he shown up yet?"

"Not to the police, no," she said. "His apartment's empty."

"Got someone there?"

"I wish I had the manpower for that. Local precinct's been alerted, and I put out a BOLO. It sure would be nice to talk to him again."

"He's not a suspect, is he? No matter how you reconstruct it, they were definitely shooting at him last night."

"We don't have any idea what happened, really."

"Yeah." He frowned. "Odd, though."

"That's what my detective thought about him. From last night's interview."

"You weren't there?"

"I saw Picot before he left the station, but only for a few minutes. Erikson had him nearly three hours. He said Picot wasn't acting like you'd expect." She paused, apparently trying not to paraphrase. "Too calm. Someone lands in the middle of a firefight, all his friends get killed, you figure he's going to be angry, or shocked, or disbelieving—something. Picot just took it in like we were running through the box scores."

"People react in all kinds of ways, seeing something like last night. Denial's fairly common."

She nodded slightly. "I know. Anyway, we're checking him out. You might expedite the NCIC requests."

Sampford immediately pulled out his cellphone. "Got it." He walked a few steps away, clicking through the speed dial.

"One mailman killer, two other assassins, a rogue computer programmer, Chinese gangs, and unbreakable computer codes." Cathryn was studying Norcross's face, and their eyes met. "This is your kind of case, isn't it?"

"You know," he said, "for the first time, I'm glad they posted me here."

The forensic tech emerged, carrying several more evidence bags to the van. She stopped halfway to yawn, eyes shut and head tipped back. That set Cathryn off, and then Norcross couldn't help himself, his jaw creaking open in the longest yawn of the three.

"I pulled the public reports on Springwater this morning," said Cathryn.

"Water under the bridge, now," he said after a pause.

"You did exactly the right thing," Cathryn said. "Far as I can tell. But I can see how your bosses in Washington might have been upset."

"They were furious."

The FBI's image, already poor from showdowns like Waco, had been completely shredded after 9/11 by the continuing revelations of incompetence. Morale sagged even further, as agents wondered whether they'd rather be seen as trigger-happy thugs or Keystone Kops. Heavy-handed oversight from the Justice Department didn't help.

So when ten armed, secessionist lunatics kidnapped
their girlfriends and children, took some potshots at the
sheriff, and holed up on a backcountry North Dakota
ranch, nobody wanted a confrontation. The FBI took
over, unenthusiastically, and set up for a long siege.
Norcross was resident agent for the territory, and no one
further up the chain of command had any interest in
getting involved, so he was stuck with it.

The nearest town was forty miles of gravel road
away. Norcross slept in his pickup truck, overseeing a
few dozen other agents, sharpshooters, and support personnel, plus one inspector from Washington, assigned
to document whatever screwups he might commit.

"Why didn't you wait?" asked Cathryn.

"I kept thinking about the kids. How it must have
been for them in there after a week. One was eight years
old."

He went in alone: just walked up, broke open the door,
and disappeared inside. Thirty seconds later he emerged
to wave up the ambulances. No hostages were hurt. Three
of the kidnappers died.

Norcross had no authorization for the action; had in
fact expressly disobeyed an order to avoid all provoca-
tion. On the other hand, he was a flag-draped national
hero, and the Bureau was starved for good publicity.
They milked it for a week, then ordered him to make no
more public statements. Two months later he received
the transfer.

Cathryn opened the door of her SUV, but paused to
look back at him before climbing in. "San Francisco is
fortunate you were sent here, I think," she said.

"I'm not sure the SAC sees it that way," said Norcross.

NINE

WHEN JEB WAS younger he'd always been impatient, and cocky, and generally too smart for his own good. Too smart to buckle down and get decent grades; too smart to settle for a regular job; too smart to think that anyone else might be smarter. His time at Ray Brook took care of all that. By the time he got out, his aspirations didn't go further than a few beers and the sunshine to drink them in.

Inside Ray Brook, amid the unremitting din of too many men in too little room, he'd had to construct a quiet internal space for himself, the only place he would be left alone. He did it by writing code inside his head. Nothing arcane: he wasn't doing complex programming or solving mathematical problems. He just liked structuring the routines. Tightening the logic until he had a nice, elegant algorithm laid out in his mind. Less often he worked on hacks, figuring out the cleanest attacks and tinkering for efficiency and stealth. The particular problem wasn't important; it was the concentration, the mental focus, that mattered. In the beginning he'd simply been trying to keep his skills from rusting away, but

the practice eventually became more like meditation. It
passed the time better than reading, or watching TV, or
listening to the endless cell block arguments.

Now, waking on the floor in a tangled mess of blan-
kets, long before dawn but unable to sleep, Jeb calmed
his agitated mind by returning to this interior plane. He
focused on its pure clarity, cascading down a flow dia-
.gram of if–then logic, retreating to the simplicity of
protocol and machine syntax. His breathing slowed; his
pulse was steady.

When sunrise began to burn off the fog outside the
floor-to-ceiling windows, Jeb sighed and brought his
mind back to the realities of the day.

He hadn't trusted Molly, is what it came down to, so
he'd been vague about where he planned to go to
ground. Now he regretted his caution. The house, a
nineteenth-century Victorian bowfront, sat two blocks
downhill from the most expensive homes along Pacific
Heights, and Darren was out of town for at least three
more weeks. He'd given Jeb a key, to water the plants
and stack the mail inside. It was a perfect hidey-hole,
the more so since Jeb had told no one about it. Molly
might have found it useful.

He'd circled the block looking for her, after they
split up near the train station. It seemed unlikely she
was part of some clandestine team, but she sure wasn't a
regular mailman either. Would she take out a radio and
call for help? Go straight to the cops? Hail a cab after
all? Anything would have been a clue, but somehow she
pulled a fast one and disappeared. After a few minutes
scouting around, Jeb gave up. Pacific Heights was only
three miles uptown, an hour's walk. Despite what he'd
said, he didn't get on a train—bright lights, people staring, no thanks. In the cool night air he missed the jacket,
but that didn't matter. It cleared his head.

Not that anything was making sense yet.

Previous owners had torn out all the walls on the
third floor of Darren's house, creating a vast, single
room. At one end an expanse of glass overlooked a
panorama of the bay and the green hills of Marin

County in the distance; the other end, past the stairwell's rail, was lined with books. Darren's desk was
broad and cluttered, with manuals and industry magazines and plain litter spilling down its length. Two flat-
screen monitors sat dark, their keyboards half-buried
under paperwork. Jeb considered them for a moment.

He wanted to go online, get some answers, see what
the more informed corners of the net thought about the
unknown men trying to kill him. With no editing and little moderation, opinion out there was often paranoid
and fantastical—but it was also much faster, and if you
could filter out the ranting, more useful than main-
stream news.

Darren's computer was probably as messy as his
workspace. Jeb found his courier bag and pulled out his
own laptop instead, which the police had grudgingly returned to him last night.

"Well, I suppose you can have it," Erikson had said,
after Jeb's third request.

"It's hardly evidence."

"You're lucky a bullet didn't go through it." He was
in his Bad Cop phase. "Not so lucky as the other guys,
of course."

Jeb bit off a rejoinder, hesitated, and said, "All my
work is on that computer."

Erikson snorted. "Listen, Picot"—deliberately mis-
pronouncing it Pickett—"I hate to remind you of this, but
you don't have a job anymore. You don't have a *company*
anymore."

But in the end they let him have it, and now Jeb
flipped up the display and nudged the power switch.
The faint whine of the drive started up reassuringly.

A minute later he was staring at the screen, bewil-
dered, at first wondering if the police had messed with it
after all. Instead of his customized boot sequence, a
simple login box sat there waiting—with Chinese characters instead of English.

"They gave me the wrong one?" he whispered to
himself. "Morons."

It was an IBM X40 subnotebook, common enough

among business users with a decent budget. One of the other men around the table must have had the same model. Sure enough, Jeb found an unfamiliar string of numbers etched into the case underneath, some sort of asset-inventory code.

He tried a few obvious passwords—"user," "system," "password"—but none worked, so he powered the computer down again and closed it up.

Okay. He had another laptop at his apartment, along with other equipment. He could go over and pick it up. If the police had his place staked out, he'd just pass on by. Meanwhile, he'd fire up Darren's system after all and see what he could find.

It wasn't much: reporters apparently weren't getting anything from the police on the investigation, so instead they'd drummed up all sorts of uninformed speculation from commentators and pundits. Industrial espionage gone bad? Organized crime moving belatedly into high-tech? No one knew anything, and Jeb soon abandoned the effort, allowing the machine to sink back into low-power hibernation.

After breakfast—cheese melted onto wholegrain bread, the best he could do in Darren's kitchen—he considered how he might travel around outside. So far he hadn't appeared on the news, but that could change. Public transportation was probably not a good idea, and though it would not have done him any good, Darren's car was at the airport. There was a mountain bike in the garage, however, along with a kayak, a windsurfer, and three sets of rollerblades, all equally dusty. Jeb pulled out the bicycle and spent a quarter hour adjusting the fit and tuning the power train. His own bike had been taken from Blindside by the police—no telling when he'd see it again, as Erikson had made clear. Darren's wasn't as good quality, but it was in pristine condition, since he never rode it.

Outside the day had cleared, with a light breeze off the water and bright sun in a cloudless sky. Jeb adjusted Darren's mirrored Oakleys and tied a bandanna skate-style; not as good a disguise as a helmet, but he couldn't find one in the garage. He kicked off, feeling better, even optimistic. Just being on a bike again was relief and distraction and freedom, all at once. Jeb loved cycling.

"I hate bicycles," Molly said.

Eileen shrugged. "I'd give you my car, but I need it to get to work. Anyway, didn't you used to ride a lot? I remember you told me you even had one in Kosovo."

"That's when it stopped being fun." Molly had served six months as an MP among the peacekeepers, when KFOR was still figuring out how to keep everyone from killing each other. One short-lived initiative, the brainstorm of a major from southern California, was a bicycle patrol, modeled after community-policing bike officers back home. No one senior to the major felt like interfering, and no one junior could tell him he was an idiot, so he ordered four specialized Treks and ordered the lieutenant to round up some volunteers. When they weren't stopping gangs of Albanians from assaulting isolated Serbs, or vice versa, Molly and her three hapless teammates had spent all their time fixing flats and bent rims. On the bikes, they often had to dodge rocks, or worse. Molly had finally extricated herself by more or less accidentally skidding her bicycle underneath the wheels of an M-939 five-ton. The driver was apologetic, Molly was reassigned to prisoner protection, and she hadn't been on a bike since.

"You could just stay in the apartment," Eileen said. "You know that."

"No. I have to do this."

"At least let me go with you."

"You have a job." Molly sighed. "I'll be careful."

She'd gone out two hours before and found a pay phone near the hospital, on a corner with cracked sidewalks and a bus stop. Walking up without looking around she faced away from the street and dialed rapidly, holding a handful of quarters. Pedestrians passed by; she kept her voice low.

"MPI," Wade said when he picked up.

"It's me," said Molly. Saturday morning Wade was probably alone in the Military Police Investigations back office, but she stayed careful.

"Jesus, Molly." Wade's voice was raspy. "You're in trouble."

"I know, I know." She had worked with Wade for five years, and had more than once trusted him with her life—exactly what she'd done by contacting him now. "That's why I called last night, remember? Did you run the check?"

"Call me back." He read off a number and hung up.

She guessed it was a cell phone, since the exchange prefix was 305—not a Fort Bragg number, and with the zero, not a typical Fayetteville number either. It didn't ring even once before he picked up.

"You're on the TV, too, you know," he said. "Even out here."

"As what?"

"According to NCIC, there's a multiple-count warrant issued. They must have got a judge out of bed, since the timestamp was just after 3:00 a.m. Eastern. There isn't much narrative detail, but they mention 'armed' and 'in connection with nine murders one.' It's on the network—every cop in the U.S. will be reading this today."

"Great," Molly muttered.

"But that's the legal side, and they seem to be playing by the rules. You've been watching the news, right? Someone leaked just enough of your record for them to completely screw it up—ex-Green Beret, whatever. You sound like GI Jane."

"Funny."

"Not really," he said. "How's Eileen?"

"Still asleep when I left. Listen . . . try to keep her out of it if anyone asks. Just tell them you don't know where I called from."

"Sure." No need for questions.

Molly glanced around, saw nothing. "Now, about this Picot guy."

"What's his story?"

"Innocent bystander. A stray."

"You're sure about that."

"Well." She wondered if she had an answer. "Did he show up in the warrant check?"

"No. They took him in for questioning, then he disappeared, it sounds like. There's a be-on-the-lookout, but no warrant."

"All right." Molly paused as a bus came to a noisy, groaning stop behind her, and she hunched a bit, keeping her face turned away from the women in scrubs who disembarked and headed for the hospital. "From my warrant, what happens if I go in?"

"If they don't gun you down like a mad dog?" Wade almost chuckled. "Lock you up, of course."

"I can't do that."

"I know."

"I mean, it's too dangerous. The operation—you should have seen these guys, they make you and me look like paintball shooters. They're not going to tolerate loose ends."

"You wouldn't be safer?"

For a moment the ragged stress broke through, and her voice cracked. "For Christ's sake, Wade, they attacked a police station in broad daylight!"

Wade paused. "I thought it was nighttime."

Molly was back under control. "Ah, you know what I mean. They were ready to kill Picot in front of fifty cops at Wakefield. I don't think it's any safer inside than out. Not until the police get a better picture of what actually happened."

"The FBI's in now—local agent's name was on the warrant." Wade's voice was quiet. "Are you sure you're doing the right thing?"

"No." The phone buzzed, and Molly put in another quarter. "Look, one more favor?"

"You don't have to ask."

"Run an ATF trace." She recited the serial number she'd read from the third killer's handgun. "A Sig-Sauer P-226. Clean, it looked like it came straight from the factory."

"That's tricky," said Wade. "Requires personal authorization. They can backtrack it."

"Use the squadron code, put . . . is Seaver still Provost Marshal? Put his name on it. He never reads his email, and you can get a copy off the log."

Wade did chuckle this time, briefly. "Unit hasn't been the same without you, Molly."

"I have to go. This the number to use next time?"

"Yeah. I'll turn the ringer off. If I don't answer, it means I can't talk—don't leave a message, just try again."

"Thanks."

"Molly?"

"Yes?"

He hesitated. "You say the word, I'll be there. Next flight. I can wrangle leave, one way or another."

"Thanks," she said again, and closed her eyes. "But that's not necessary. It'll be over quick."

"That's what I'm afraid of."

"I'll call," Molly said and hung up, wondering if she'd be able to. No, she thought to herself, *when*.

Back at the apartment, Eileen was in the shower. Molly ate another banana, prowled restlessly around, and finally sat on the couch. The TV was dark, the radio silent; no answers there anyway. What next?

But after staring at the wall for five minutes, she realized that she'd already made her choice: when she pulled him into the car, bullets smashing around them, one man dead on the steps and who knew how many more about to die.

Eileen came out, dressed in twill work clothes and steel-toed boots. Molly showed her a small piece of thermal-printed paper.

"It was in his jacket," she said. "I can't believe I didn't think to check the pockets until now."

Eileen was looking for her keys. "A clue." She didn't sound impressed.

"Receipt for a DVD rental."

"You can tell a lot about a guy by the movies he watches in the privacy of his own home."

"Pelle the Conqueror?"

"Doesn't sound like pornography . . ."

"You're missing the point here. It's got his phone number."

"You want to call him?"

"No." Though she was reaching for the phone. "But with the number, directory assistance can give me his address."

Eileen waited while she spoke to the operator.

"You're about to do something dumb, aren't you," she said when Molly hung up.

"Let's see, 31st, that's over in the Avenues . . . do you have a street directory?"

Eileen tossed her a map from a drawer. "Maybe you should be thinking more about your own situation."

"Me and him, we're in the same boat, for better or worse." Molly studied the map. "South of Quintara, looks like."

"Bring him on over, we can have coffee, talk about that movie."

"It's too far to walk . . ."

It was Eileen's turn to sigh. "You can use my bike. But at least wait until midmorning, when there won't be so many commuters on the road. If you're not going straight to the authorities, you don't want to be noticed more than necessary."

"Thanks." Molly hesitated. "Hey, I mean it. You don't have to be doing this."

"I'm going to work." Eileen shook her head. "You're the one dodging a hunter-killer team."

"I promise I'll go to the police right after."

"Sure." Taking that for what it was worth; but after a moment she became almost amused. "You hardly even know the guy."

"I just want to make sure he's okay," said Molly.

TEN

NORCROSS WAS WAITING for Sampford outside the Hall of Justice, though they'd agreed to meet in the lobby. The maze of police administrative offices, shoehorned in alongside the county jail, was too depressing inside, even on Saturday. Sullen family members loitered in the worn marble hallways, ignored by civil service clerks and county cops. Outside wasn't much better, since the neighborhood was a rundown postindustrial zone of bail bondsmen, pawn shops, and fast-food outlets. Traffic noise drifted from the elevated highway and a set of concrete on-off ramps at the end of the block.

Still, the sun was out, a westerly breeze brought a slight smell of the bay, and someone had planted a pair of window boxes across the avenue. Norcross watched a jail officer joking with the proprietor of a burrito truck, wondering if he should get an early lunch himself. Since leaving the federal building the night before he'd had only coffee and, that morning, a donut swiped from Birney's command vehicle.

He'd come from Bernal Heights, where a patrolman

had found the shot-up Taurus. Looking at it, Norcross was surprised the car had made it all the way from Wakefield—most of the windows were missing, bullet holes punctured the rear and right side panels, and it was dented and listing badly to one side. The left front tire was flat. One forensic technician had been securing evidence in a bored way, awaiting the arrival of more help before beginning the detail work of dusting and collecting. Norcross didn't think they'd find anything useful, but the damage the vehicle had sustained was an impressive testament to the shooting skill of the deceased Sergeant Mason, surprised and outgunned as he had been.

Sampford was late, double-parking in a red zone and joining Norcross without seeming to notice the annoyed gaze of the county cops, who recognized a federal car when they saw one. He was carrying a portfolio rubber-banded shut, and he'd found time to change into a different suit, this one dark blue. Norcross assumed it came out of a locker in their offices.

"Not in here, is it?" Sampford asked, looking with distaste at the ugly, largely windowless jail.

"No." Norcross decided not to eat yet. "Captain Birney said she found us a room in the annex. Fifteen Marker Street, second floor—you know where that is?"

"Never been there, but Marker's a couple of blocks south." Sampford looked at his watch. "We'd better get going."

As they walked, he opened the portfolio and handed Norcross a stapled set of paper. "Molly Gannon's service record," he said. "Or some of it, anyway. The complete file seems not to be available."

"Why not?"

"The brigade officer said it's because she was discharged recently. He figures her papers are in a crate somewhere between here and the permanent depository at the National Personnel Records Center in St. Louis. This is a fax of what he was able to print from the electronic file."

Norcross flipped through the 201, which hadn't changed much in design since he'd last seen his own, thirty years earlier, except that the computer printing was easier to read. After a moment he stopped, moving to the edge of the sidewalk, so he could scan the sheets without stumbling. It didn't take long; only the most essential information had been summarized. The photo—digitized, printed, and then faxed—was blurry.

"Gee," he said after a minute. "No wonder the reporters love her."

"The brigade officer gave me some detail on the phone," said Sampford. "He wasn't in her unit, but everyone knew her. She signed up right out of high school—no honor student, but she was a state rifle champion. Montana, I think."

"And into Airborne right out of basic."

"Is that unusual?"

Norcross shrugged. "Today, I don't know. Wasn't that common in the sixties."

"They wouldn't give her a combat assignment, of course. That might be why she joined the MPs. But she still ended up stateside for most of her enlistment."

"At Fort Bragg," Norcross pointed out. "So for—what, five or six years—her job was breaking up fights and hauling drunk soldiers out of bars." He paused. "Drunk 82nd Airborne paratroopers . . . this photo's lousy, but she doesn't look like a bruiser."

Sampford shook his head. "Tall, though. Anyway, she joined the Special Reaction Team after that."

"What's that? Military police SWAT?"

"Counterterrorism, special operations, is what the officer said. That's where the record gets really thin, though."

"What's this—Task Force Falcon?"

"Kosovo. The 82nd was dispatched in late 1999, just about the first U.S. soldiers on the ground. She went along as an MP."

"Then back to Bragg for another year and a half, and after that Afghanistan."

"Right. Task Force Panther."

Norcross absently shuffled the pages into order and handed them back. "Something went wrong out there."

"Looks that way. She was back home in June and got her discharge in August, one year shy of serving out her enlistment."

"This officer you talked to offer any details?"

"No."

"Wouldn't or couldn't?" Norcross probed, wondering how good an interviewer Sampford was.

"I'm not sure."

"General discharge. She must have screwed up somehow. Just about anyone who mostly remembers to salute his superiors gets an honorable."

"You saw the last page?" Sampford lifted the portfolio but didn't open it. "Lines in the final block were blacked out."

"That's uncommon?"

"I thought you might know," said Sampford. He paused at a corner, looking for building numbers, before they crossed against a red light. The sun cast a cool shadow down the worn facades on the east side of the block. The street was empty of cars, the sidewalks deserted. "I asked, and right there the brigade officer ended our conversation."

Norcross squinted as he thought about that. "Might not mean anything," he said, without conviction.

The police department's administrative annex was an old brick building three stories tall. Its blank side wall faced an empty lot where another building had been torn down, the space now a small parking area with a few cruisers and unmarked cars. Heavy mesh covered the frosted glass entrance doors. Norcross and Sampford were buzzed in after a metallic voice on the intercom asked them to look up at an armored CCTV camera. The only sign read, in ornate and faded letters, Sweetland Confectionery Co., Ltd.

The bored patrolman at the desk directed them to the second floor, where Captain Birney escorted them past a row of doors looking onto an expanse of drab, deserted cubicles. Ancient linoleum still showed scars where earlier interior walls had been torn down. The air was still and stuffy.

"Accounting," she said, gesturing at the cubicles as they walked down the hallway. "I always wondered why expense reports took so long to process."

"No one works weekends?"

"Just the officer on the front desk. And everyone's gone by five-thirty during the week. It's a lonely assignment."

The conference room was cramped, less than fifteen feet long, and cardboard file boxes were stacked haphazardly against one wall. Dim light showed through windows streaked with dirt on the outside, dust on the inside. A stale reek of cigarette smoke had settled into every surface.

"Perfect," said Norcross.

A brief smile crossed her face. "It may not surprise you to learn that Internal Affairs used to have their offices here," she said. "I'm going to try to find a whiteboard. The finance clerks probably have one somewhere." She disappeared.

Sampford sat down and immediately fell over when the broken chairback gave way. He stood up and tested two more chairs before settling gingerly into a fourth, halfway down the table. Norcross counted seats.

"Someone's going to get the broken one," he said. "If everybody shows up." Moved by a small sense of mischief, he shifted the chairs around, placing the damaged one at the head of the table.

Sampford wandered out to find a water fountain, and Norcross leaned his chair back against the wall, closing his eyes. He was half-dozing, several minutes later, when Kubbos barreled in.

"Hey!" Like Norcross, the postal inspector was still wearing yesterday's clothing, his jacket rumpled and the shirt collar undone, the tie loose and askew. "No fucking coffee! Can you believe it? She says the machine's turned off." Referring to Birney, apparently. "Is this the ass-end of the city or what?" He went directly to the front of the room, sat down in the broken chair, and promptly collapsed, avoiding a fall only by twisting desperately sideways and catching his forearm on the table edge. Swearing, he stood up, glared at the chair, and struck it aside with his foot, pulling another into its place.

Birney appeared with a portable whiteboard, two other men behind her, apologizing insincerely for the facilities.

"Inspector, good to see you again," she said to Kubbos.

Norcross stood. "Captain."

She glanced over. "Cathryn," she reminded him, holding his eye for a moment before introducing the others.

Drake was an African American of average height, in his forties, completely anonymous except for a jagged scar that descended across his forehead. "ATF," he said, his voice relaxed. He looked at the chair Kubbos had kicked over, then sat opposite Sampford. "How're you all doing?"

"I'd rather be on the street, hunting them down." The second new arrival was an obvious weightlifter, and he shook hands with too much force, staring into each person's eyes as he crushed their fingers. Only Kubbos took up his challenge, each of their faces reddening while the grip stretched out for several extra seconds. "Andy Teixeira, with the Marshals," he said, when they finally broke apart. He removed a three-quarter-length black leather jacket to reveal a belt as cluttered as a telephone lineman's: holstered automatic, two extra magazines, steel handcuffs, pepper spray, plastic restraints, cell phone, and a pager.

The chair turned out not to be a problem. Teixeira set it upright, spun it around, and straddled the seat, glancing down with little curiosity as the back fell away and then ignoring it, his posture stiff and upright. His crossed forearms were a relief map of veins and banded muscle, and Norcross could see him unconsciously rippling his pecs as he stared around the table. Cathryn's fleeting smile glinted, and she sat down in front of the whiteboard, pulling out her notebook.

"Right," said Norcross. "Anyone heard from the cowboys?" Meaning CHP, the highway patrol. "Their tactical team showed up last night. Though I'm not sure why, since it wasn't a hostage situation at that point."

"They were just being helpful," said Cathryn. "Perimeter was a zoo—nothing like men with ski masks and automatic weapons to keep a mob in line."

"Uh-huh." Norcross smiled. "Crowd control. I'm sure they loved that. Anyway, weren't they going to send someone?"

Cathryn shrugged.

"Can we get on with it?" said Kubbos, who had clearly run out of patience with the roll call.

"Here's what I don't understand," said Teixeira. "Your mailmen shoot my fugitive. Fair enough. But why everyone else?"

"They weren't—"

"Hang on." Norcross cut off the irate response. "Andy, why don't you tell us more about this guy Ding. I'm a little behind."

Teixeira stood, happy to take the floor, in a parade-rest stance that made him look like a posing bodybuilder. "Ding Yihui. Member of the Wo Han Mok triad." He looked patronizingly toward Kubbos. "That's a Chinese criminal organization."

"I know what a triad is!"

"Where are they from?" asked Norcross.

"Based out of Hong Kong, but, they've been increasing their presence in North America." The more he spoke the more obvious his southwest drawl became. "Mostly the West Coast, Vancouver to LA. Drugs, smuggling, extortion, gambling, prostitution, loan-sharking, you name it."

"Smuggling?" said Sampford. "What, other than drugs?"

"People. Illegals, mostly from Fujian and the southeast coast."

"So what was the warrant for?"

"Kidnapping and murder." Teixeira's jaw set. "They snatched a businessman's daughter in Portland. The father ran a string of Chinese restaurants, but he wasn't nearly as rich as the Wo Han Mok thought, and he couldn't get cash fast enough. The kid turned up raped and dead. It was a sloppy crime from start to finish, and the FBI had Ding in less than a week." He nodded at Norcross. "His pals sprang him from the courthouse, maybe you saw the papers. Brazen's the word—they walked up with M-16s, right in the parking lot, as the guards were unloading him from the prisoner transport van. We've been after him ever since."

"But that was two years ago," said Kubbos. "I mean, how hard—"

Teixeira interrupted, glaring. "The Marshals never close a warrant."

"Ah, it was AR-15s, actually," said Sampford, proving he was the only one who'd been reading the reports.

"Whatever. A couple county screws aren't your most reliable witnesses."

"This explains the Glock," said Norcross, trying to keep the discussion focused. "I was wondering why someone would go armed into a business meeting."

"Didn't do him much good," Teixeira said with a dismissive grunt.

Drake had been watching with a half-amused look on his face, and he now spoke up. "Inspector, what do you have on the postal van?"

Kubbos looked up at Teixeira, who remained standing, and apparently decided to ignore him. "Stolen, like I thought. It disappeared from the district maintenance depot in Oakland sometime Thursday night."

"When did they notice it missing?"

"Well." Kubbos hesitated. "They might not have realized until next week, if we hadn't asked for a check. They're responsible for two hundred vehicles there."

"How was it taken?"

Kubbos paused again. "We don't know. Frankly, security isn't that tight." Teixeira snorted, and Kubbos's eyes narrowed. "They could have just driven it away, if they put a board over the one-way spikes at the gate."

Drake nodded. "Was it hot-wired?"

"No, but that's not surprising. Every quarter-ton is keyed identically." He looked defensive. "Keeps things simple. These aren't exactly BMWs, you know."

Teixeira grunted again, one corner of his mouth rising.

"Fine," said Norcross hastily. He'd grown up with four younger brothers, and sometimes it felt like he was still trying to sort out their nonstop, aggrieved squabbling. "Who was at Raymond Tuck's interview last night? Captain?"

Birney nodded, but the others mostly looked puzzled.

"The postal supervisor," Sampford said.

"Yes," said Norcross. "And your investigators, too, Inspector Kubbos. From what I understand, they didn't learn much."

"No." Cathryn spoke when Kubbos didn't answer. "It was only her second month on the route, and he thought she was having trouble settling in, because she'd been working late to get it finished several days in a row. She called in at 4:30 yesterday to say she needed another hour."

"4:34," said Kubbos. Cathryn rolled her eyes, but she was facing away and only Norcross saw it.

"Is there any reason to think the other assailants weren't postal employees also?" he asked.

"They weren't from this district," said Kubbos shortly. "And I can't believe they flew in from somewhere else."

"How do you know?" Teixeira was being argumentative. "How many mailmen are there in the country? You checked up on each one?"

Kubbos ground his teeth. "Despite what tabloid vultures and ambulance chasers might think," he said tightly, staring at Teixeira, "there are statistically far fewer incidents of workplace violence in the nation's postal system than anywhere else. To assume that any letter carrier could carry out this, this atrocity is absurd."

"Yes. That's what is so puzzling," said Norcross. "The attack doesn't make sense. The triads—why are they involved? Why Gannon?"

"We don't know she was involved," Kubbos said.

"Of course." Norcross held onto his patience but decided to change the subject. "So we need to start with the company itself. Agent Sampford has been looking into their business—why don't we hear from him." He nodded down the table.

Sampford cleared his throat as Teixeira finally sat down with a thump. "Yes, thanks." He straightened another set of papers he'd pulled from the portfolio, the yellow lined sheets covered with his careful notes.

"Blindside Technology. Incorporated just last year, privately funded, six employees, moved into the Potrero in April. There's next to no public information on them at all, just a few press releases last spring, and a puff piece in the *San Jose Mercury News* on the founder, Astrov."

"Nothing from the National Infrastructure Protection Center?" Cathryn asked. Norcross glanced at her, impressed that she'd heard of them.

"Um." Sampford hesitated.

"They're useless." Norcross had no compunctions about criticizing another FBI division. "Too new, too bureaucratic, too much money. They seem to be obsessed with preventing Islamic hackers from attacking the Internet."

"That's good to know." Cathryn smiled.

"Anyway," said Sampford, "when the company was just getting started, Astrov talked to a bunch of venture capital firms. I thought I'd found the one that actually funded Blindside, but when the partner finally called me back, he told me they'd decided not to invest."

Drake interrupted. "Even if they're a private company, some information has to be filed. Either the SEC or California's Department of Corporations should have the names."

"They were flying low," Sampford agreed. "Might have violated a few regulations along the way. We're still looking."

"But you got the answers, in the end." Norcross brought him back on track.

"Yes. This particular VC had spent a few afternoons with them, going over the business plan. He has a pretty good idea of their technology. What Blindside was doing was all cryptography-related."

"Making codes, sure," said Teixeira impatiently. "Heard that last night."

"No." Sampford shook his head slightly. "Breaking them." He looked down at his notes again. "I don't know how much detail you want. There's been a genuine revolution in codemaking over the last twenty years, with the creation of what's called public-key encryption. It's how you secure information on the internet, not just for, say, diplomatic communication, and it's extremely strong, if you use large enough keys. Which are just numbers, by the way, very long numbers. The longer the key, the safer the code."

No one interrupted, so he continued. "You probably remember the debate over the Clipper chip, the FBI wiretapping email, all that. In the end, the government lost. Current encryption systems are just too simple and too powerful to control. It looked like an age of unbreakable privacy had arrived." He paused again. Norcross knew he'd spent several hours on the phone and on the internet, cramming, but he sounded like a computer forensics veteran.

"I can see where this is going," said Drake.

"Yes." Sampford looked around the room. "All ciphers have their weaknesses, of course. Somewhere. Generally there's a tradeoff between security and ease of use. Public-key encryption depends on the inability of a would-be codebreaker to readily factor extremely large numbers. At 1024 bits—the highest level of encryption commonly used—you hear estimates like 'every computer in the world running for a thousand years.' But Astrov figured out a shortcut. And Blindside was the result."

Norcross, amused, noted that Kubbos and Teixeira had identical glazed looks, but Cathryn was paying attention. "How?" she asked.

Sampford was becoming more animated as he

delved into the topic. "Generally, factoring is a fairly primitive process," he said. "You, or rather your super-computer, just tries one possibility after another until it hits the right one. Astrov found a way to simplify the process. Two ways, actually. First, he came up with an algorithm to reduce the polynomial sieve. That was the brilliant part—pure mathematics. The VC had no idea how it worked, the math was too abstract, and anyway Astrov was being vague until he filed a patent. But that alone wasn't enough. He still needed the kind of computing power you'd have to pay IBM or Hitachi two million dollars for. And that was the clever part."

"Brilliant is different from clever?" said Cathryn.

"Absolutely." Sampford leaned back and spoke directly to her. "Brilliant just means an article in some arcane journal and lots of attention at the next AMS conference. Clever means you figure out how to turn a big profit."

"And that's what Blindside was about."

"Like I said, you still need way more power than a single computer has, to run the calculations. Astrov took an idea that's apparently been around a while—a 'Beowulf cluster,' which is a way of tying together a number of small processors to pretend they're one big computer. It sounds easy, but I guess it's awfully tough to get working in practice. Astrov not only figured it out, he managed some sort of nonlinear efficiency increase—somehow his algorithm, working in conjunction with the cluster, didn't just add two processors together to get two times the speed, he got a multiple more like 2.3. Only he was using hundreds of processors, not two. All off the shelf, networked over straight ethernet. The software was the key."

"Doesn't sound like much," said Cathryn. "Two point three."

Norcross, who'd gotten a version of Sampford's explanation earlier, was keeping up okay now, but he knew he'd been slower than Cathryn to understand the concepts the first time he heard them. He was pleased as he watched their exchange.

Drake shook his head. "It's exponential."

"Right." Sampford nodded. "The VC said Astrov's elevator pitch was that he'd found a way to use the cluster to emulate a quantum computer."

Even Cathryn dropped out at this point, but Drake made a slow whistle. "Really?" For the first time he seemed impressed.

"Cut to the chase," suggested Norcross. He looked thoughtfully at Drake, who seemed to be familiar with much more than alcohol, tobacco, and firearms.

"Sure." Sampford straightened. "For $300,000 Blindside could break just about any PKI cipher in use in the world today."

The room was silent. Far down the hall they could hear a faint whistling from a janitor emptying trash baskets.

"That's what Astrov told the VC, anyhow," Sampford added.

"Makes the Chinese connection more interesting, doesn't it," said Norcross.

"Yes." Cathryn was gazing at the filthy windows, thinking. "Wo Han Mok is powerful in Hong Kong, but its connections on the mainland are just as strong. They've been around for decades. Observers usually rank them number three, right after 14K and the Sun Yee On."

Teixeira glanced at her with some suspicion. "You know all that?"

"I was in the gangland unit for two years," she said. "And in Hong Kong on exchange for two more."

He frowned, puzzled.

"I moved to Wakefield three years ago," she said, not waiting for the question. "Away from Organized Crime."

"Policy rotation?" said Norcross.

"Yes." Cathryn nodded. "They don't want you getting too close. Too much chance for corruption."

"It's been a problem," Norcross agreed.

"To be honest, though, I didn't want to get any closer, either. The triads are . . ." She hesitated.

"They're dangerous, violent, and increasingly out of control. Everyone says the Vietnamese and the Cambodians are the real crazies, but I'm not sure. I didn't want to get to the point where I needed a kevlar vest and escorts around the clock."

Teixeira was clearly disdainful of this opinion, though he didn't say anything aloud. Kubbos grimaced and, probably without realizing he was doing so, reached down to stroke the butt of his pistol.

Sampford spoke up. "Back to Blindside, if I may. It's clear the attackers yesterday had the technology as their target. Not only did they kill everyone—well, everyone except Picot, and that wasn't for lack of trying—but they utterly destroyed the company's computers. The lab's not saying so formally yet, but they found iron oxide and aluminum residue in the server room. After shooting everyone in sight the assailants apparently set thermite grenades, or homemade thermite, atop every computer."

"And not just the computers," said Cathryn. "They destroyed the backup power supply and two printers as well."

Sampford smiled. "They weren't computer geeks, right? Probably didn't recognize the difference between a UPS and a PC, just took out everything likely."

Drake stirred. "Nothing can be recovered?"

"The lab says the disks were basically vaporized. It's all gone."

Norcross had turned to the whiteboard and written "Chinese," "Blindside" "Postal Svc," and "Cryptography." Now he faced back to the table, still holding the marker, and said, "Lots of avenues opening up. Let's go back to Picot. Captain, your detectives interviewed him. What do you think?"

Cathryn frowned. "Now that he's disappeared, I'm not sure. He was at Wakefield for two hours, and we were mostly just trying to get more detail on the shooting. Not that he was any help, since he said he'd been in the bathroom the whole time. But his record . . ."

"Record?" Teixeira perked up.

"He's a hacker," said Sampford. "Broke into all sorts of mainframes, got caught, served three years."

"Which is probably why Blindside hired him," said Norcross. "Best resume he could have had."

"Maybe." Sampford wasn't giving up. "Three years, though. You can make all sorts of interesting contacts in prison."

"We'd better bring him in," said Norcross.

"Have to find him first." Cathryn looked unhappy. "Marshal?"

Teixeira shrugged. "Get a federal warrant, we'll take care of it."

"Gannon's the key," said Kubbos. "We'll get her first."

Norcross looked at him, wondering if some sort of postal posse was being saddled up. "Just how many people do you have working on this, Inspector?"

Kubbos clamped his lips together, then said, "We're putting a team together. Probably five or six in the field here, but I'm calling in our Special Operations Unit too."

"I'm afraid I'm not familiar with them."

"Tactical resources," said Kubbos, shortly.

Not just a posse, a mob, Norcross thought. "SWAT, you mean?"

"More like your Hostage Rescue Team."

At this comparison Teixeira grunted a laugh. "Yeah, I bet."

Kubbos glared. "There are more than sixty federal law enforcement agencies," he said through clenched teeth. "Three, just three, train at Quantico—the FBI, the DEA, and our SOU. Everyone else goes down to Glynco. Tick inspectors, for example. The Park Service. Library of Congress guards." He paused. "U.S. Marshals."

Teixeira abruptly leaned forward, placing his massive hands flat on the table and levering himself halfway standing to loom over Kubbos, who didn't retreat an inch. "What are you saying, exactly?"

"That's enough," Norcross said sharply, finally fed up. "Five-minute break. Inspector? Marshal? I want to see you for a moment—outside, please."

THE whole meeting, Cathryn had been wondering if Norcross would crack down on the bickering. Until the end he'd been acting like a diplomat—better than most of her department superiors, and far smoother than any fed she'd met on the job. The performance was an unexpected contrast to his rough-hewn appearance, but probably like everyone else at the table, she'd been lulled by his moderate tone.

When he snapped out the order to dismiss, though, his voice edged with steel, Teixeira and Kubbos subsided without another word, and Cathryn reappraised him yet again. Now she remembered the news photos: Norcross walking up to the cabin in Springwater, sledgehammer in one hand and a carbine in the other, all alone.

She watched him step into the hallway, pulling the door shut in a sharp gesture, then sat back and looked around. Drake, unlike Sampford, seemed to be paying no attention to the barely audible conversation outside the room.

"He'll sort them out," Drake said.

"I wouldn't want to be on his bad side."

"Oh, no." He smiled. "We don't have to worry about that, I don't think."

A few minutes later Norcross led the subdued combatants back in, and the rest of the meeting went quickly. Cathryn handed around more photocopies, packets of preliminary material from the police investigation. Drake asked about the weapons found in the garage, and said he'd follow up on the trace. Teixeira promised to pass along all information he had on the remaining warrants from the raid that freed Ding in Portland. Kubbos clammed up, for the most part, which didn't seem to bother anyone.

"One last thing," said Norcross. "We need a single point of contact with the press. There's too much attention on this case already, I don't want reporters playing us off against each other."

"We can take care of it," said Cathryn, not sure how he'd take what might be considered a usurpation of control. "We have the resources in place. The public information office is already fielding interviews."

Sampford looked up.

"That would be great." Norcross smiled. "Better them in your hair than ours." Kubbos and Teixeira both shrugged, not caring; Cathryn thought they'd both probably had problems with the media in the past. Drake, as seemed to be his habit, acknowledged the decision with an agreeable nod.

"By the way, the funeral for Sergeant Mason is Monday," said Cathryn, as the meeting was breaking up. "The department would be honored if you were there."

"Of course," said Norcross.

Drake poked in annoyance at his cell phone. "I can't get a signal."

Cathryn glanced at him. "Some sort of dead spot here. Sorry about that. The officer at the desk downstairs can let you use a landline."

"It's not that important."

On the way out, Norcross stayed behind to use the restroom, and only Cathryn was still there when he returned to the corridor.

"I took the wrong door at first," he said to her. "Room down there looks like a dry cleaner on a really bad day."

"Oh, you found the evidence room." She knew the tiny space was strewn with bloody clothing, draped on every available surface.

"I figured that out. Everything has to be dry before you pack it away."

"The janitors are used to it now, but we had some complaints at first."

They walked down the hallway, Cathryn clicking off lights as they went.

"Kind of a waste of time, this meeting," she said.

"Oh, I don't know," said Norcross. "It was better than having to clean up another murder scene."

ELEVEN

COASTING DOWN CLARENDON, the long, winding avenue crowded with impatient traffic and slow buses, Molly recognized Jeb before he noticed her. At first she glimpsed only another cyclist, zooming past as she turned onto the busy street, but that brief second was enough; she recognized his face and lanky frame, and then he was gone. The sunglasses were no disguise. She shifted, kicked the pedals hard, and started to catch up, watching him sideslip the slow lane, spinning a nice steady cadence fifty yards in front. Practically sprinting, she started to narrow the gap. He seemed to be riding effortlessly, back perfectly flat, keeping a course so straight it could have been laid down with a transit. Closer, Molly noticed the sharp definition of his calf muscles, one mark of a serious cyclist. No wonder she was having trouble keeping up.

He lost her on Taraval, when the hill leveled off, and gravity was no longer helping Molly out. She could see him shift, the smallest stutter as the chain clacked, and then he simply faded, pulling away in a few seconds. Had he seen her? Molly should have called out, but she didn't want to attract attention from anyone else. He hit a yellow light and a moment later he was gone, while she waited for the green and panted and decided she could still probably out-*run* him, should it come to that. She hoped he'd wait around his apartment for a while.

But ten minutes later, while she was riding slowly and looking for building numbers, he surprised her again, calling softly from the lee of a self-service gas station on the corner of Rivera. He was squatting alongside his bike, poking at the derailleur. She hopped the curb and stopped beside him, looking down.

"Problem?" she asked.

"No." He wasn't the least surprised to see her.

"Convenient running into you here. Couldn't they number the houses better?"

"It's up the block there." He glanced toward the street, then back at her, eyes hidden behind the mirrored glasses. The bandanna gave him a raffish look. "You couldn't have followed me. Not from Pacific Heights."

"Is that . . . no, never mind."

He shrugged, just a little. "Friend's house. You too?"

"Yes." Molly considered him. "How'd you know?"

"That's not your bike. Doesn't fit you right. So you must have borrowed it—just a guess, really."

She smiled. "You saw me back there."

"I wasn't sure. The helmet covers up your hair. But, yeah, on Clarendon."

The bright midday sun cast sharp shadows under the pump island. A man in torn overalls bought a carton of cigarettes at the armor-glass window, receiving the packs a few at a time through the flat, sliding drawer, before returning to his pickup truck and driving off.

Jeb leaned back. "Okay, your turn. How did you know where I live?"

"Your jacket. Want it back, by the way?"

"Ah." He nodded. "No, it looks good on you."

A moment passed. His gaze was calm, and Molly thought he might even be smiling, in a barely noticeable kind of way.

Her whole life, well, since high school anyway, men

had been staring at her, usually and obviously occupied by the same general thoughts. In the army, in Afghanistan—she'd long ago learned to deal, to ignore or deflect the attention without feeling anything about it. But under Jeb's eyes she felt a sensation so unfamiliar it took her a moment to place it. Was she actually *blushing*? "Um, thanks."

He turned back to the bike. "I thought you were going to the police this morning."

"Well, no rush." Molly shook her head, trying to stay focused. "What about you?"

"I didn't commit any crimes."

"Me neither." And like that, her mood darkened. "That didn't stop them from issuing a warrant."

"I'm not surprised," he said. "Oops, sorry, didn't mean it that way—just, the way the detectives were talking last night, it sounded like they'd already decided you were guilty."

"Yeah." She watched him fiddle with the chain. "What's wrong with the bike?"

"Nothing. I wanted to watch the area for a while before I went up to the apartment."

"Hmm." Molly looked around: a few cars were moving on the long street, with more parked along the curb. The gas station was empty, the clerk barely visible behind his window. Nothing looked out of place. "I have to tell you, there could be two dozen tacticals waiting in ambush and we'd never know."

"If there are, they haven't noticed us yet."

"Why are you here, anyway?"

"I need to pick up some things."

"Might not be the best idea."

They were both being so cool about it, they sounded like they were talking about switching to a new brand of toothpaste. Molly had the same sense of dislocation as the night before, in the car: here she was, probably on the FBI's top ten list, every law officer in the country thinking she was a deadly terrorist, and Jeb was relaxed enough to fall asleep.

He looks like a slacker bicycle messenger, she thought,

back from smoking a joint after his last delivery. Wade hadn't come up with details on his jail time yet, and Molly wondered again what he'd done to end up behind bars.

"It'll only take a few minutes." Jeb rose smoothly to his feet and removed his sunglasses, flipping their cord around and letting them drape down his back. "Get my laptop, some clothes, check the answering machine."

Molly put out one hand, resting it lightly on his arm. "You're really, really sure you need that stuff?" His skin was warm. She realized it was the first time she'd touched him.

"Be silly to go away without it." They looked at each other a moment. Without the mirrorshades he appeared almost vulnerable.

"All right. But I'm going with you."

"I'd like that." And his expression agreed. "Look, no need to go through the front door, in case someone really is watching. We can sneak in around back."

Molly frowned. "How? From what I saw riding around already, the houses are connected all up the block, and the back alley is closed off with fences."

The neighborhood's wooden, three-story apartments were built flush against each other, wedged into small lots with no driveways or garages. Their housefronts rose straight up from the sidewalk edge. If the builders had left any space between them it was generally only a foot or two, the gaps closed with planks or chain-link to keep thieves out of the dark, narrow space.

"It's not really an alley," said Jeb. "But you're right. Each house has five or ten feet of backyard, and most of them are walled off."

"And?"

"Come on, I'll show you." Jeb stepped up, clipped his shoes into the flat pedals, and rode ten feet, then balanced the bike in a handbrake trackstand, looking back at her.

They took the long way around, up 33rd, across Rivera, finally stopping again halfway down a block similar to Jeb's: the same seventy-year-old rowhouses, tightly packed but well-maintained, many painted in un-expected pastels. Flowers bloomed in wooden planters, and orchids were common in more secure boxes on the balconies. Jeb made a pointing gesture with his chin.

"Through there, over one fence and we're in."

A piece of wooden garden lattice had been nailed across a two-foot gap between the two houses, but it hung loose from one side. Recycling bins, trash bags, and rusty metal of unclear origin cluttered the tiny walkway.

"We can't leave the bikes here," Molly said. The simple fact of motion, action, had cleared her head, and the question of her motivation, why exactly she was running crazy risks for some ex-con she hardly knew, no longer mattered. But they had no locks, and the side-walk was narrow, exposed. "Maybe at the corner—I saw a dumpster we could put them behind."

The dumpster was temporary, being used by contrac-tors gutting a townhouse, and it was filled with rubble and plaster. An unstructured pile of cinderblocks, most broken, spilled from one end, and the bicycles fit into a narrow space behind them, invisible from the street. Molly left her helmet too, and now, on foot, she felt much more exposed.

"Get your key out," she said quietly as they walked back up the street, taking charge without thinking about it. "What floor are you on?"

Jeb glanced at her. "Third."

"Okay. No running, but move as fast as you're com-fortable with. Once you're through the door, step to one side and stop. Don't move until I'm in and I shut the door behind us."

He nodded and turned into the narrow walkway, shov-ing aside the lattice and restraining it briefly, until Molly took hold and pushed through. They picked their way among the rubbish, emerged into a postage-stamp yard filled with plastic children's toys, and Jeb hopped a waist-high brick wall with one hand, like a gymnast. His yard was less spacious, with nothing but a rusty hibachi on a pair of bricks, under the permanent shade of a third-floor deck overhead. Molly followed, and five seconds later they were inside his house.

Old boots and flip-flops crowded the entryway, a door to the first-floor apartment on one side and narrow, dusty stairs leading up. Jeb shifted his key ring, selecting one without letting any of them rattle, and slipped up the stairs, making no noise. Molly set her feet exactly where he did.

They paused at his door on the landing, the only illumination from a plastic skylight above them. No noise came from behind the paneled wooden door. Jeb raised an eyebrow at Molly, who shrugged slightly. In one smooth motion he turned the key, opened the knob, and pushed the door open—only to have it jam halfway into the room, stopped by something on the floor.

Inside they froze, staring. The small kitchen was in disarray: pots, food, utensils, dishtowels, everything not nailed down had been thrown onto the floor. Cereal boxes and bags of frozen vegetables were torn open, their contents scattered; plates and cups were everywhere, some broken. The oven door hung open, its broiler pan discarded to one side. One of the glassfront cabinet doors had been smashed.

"Stay here!" Molly whispered harshly, and seized the first weapon to hand, a marble rolling pin, long and narrow. She crouched slightly, hefting the club to find its balance, and glided into the next room.

THE next minute was a long one for Jeb. He didn't want to make any noise, so he stood in the middle of his destroyed kitchen and waited, wondering what to do if the searchers were still in the house. He strained his ears. A closet door opened; floorboards creaked.

He was glad Molly was here. At first he hadn't been sure it was her, on the bike, but when she rode up alongside the gas station he felt an unexpected wave of relief. Nothing like having your own special-forces bodyguard, he thought, and immediately felt embarrassed at himself. He'd been watching her face while they talked, the way he'd learned inside, subtle and careful not to let her know. She was tough, all right, hard enough to go unarmed against killers with machine guns and walk away after. But her eyes were kind, the planes of her face softened by laugh lines.

He wondered if he'd ever see them in use.

A moment later Molly was back, standing more relaxed in the doorway, shaking her head.

He started to speak but she put a hand quickly over his mouth and leaned forward to whisper in his ear.

"Place could be bugged, waiting for you. Okay? Find what you need and let's get out of here."

He nodded once and focused on his objective. The living room was as wrecked as the kitchen. Cushions from the long couch and armchairs had been cut open, their batting everywhere. All the books had been pulled from the shelves, and the TV was lying face down, its back torn off. Curtains over a glass door to the outside deck had been pulled off the rod, hanging crumpled to the side. As elsewhere, it looked like the invaders had tried to throw everything into the center of the room.

Jeb sat at his desk, a scavenged door on sawhorses, and stared at his dismembered computer equipment. Both towers had been opened and several boards pulled out; the monitor was shattered; and the printer and scanner were jumbled on the floor. After a moment he dug hurriedly through the pile of junk, then slipped into the bedroom.

It took him more than five minutes, but he returned empty-handed. Molly was crouched by the window, her face just above the lower sill, the rolling pin loose in one hand. Jeb knelt to whisper at the side of her face as she scanned the street below.

"Every bit of memory is gone." He could still hardly believe it. "Every zip, every DVD, every tape, every CD including the music. They removed the hard disks from the computers, and my paper files are completely empty. They must have pulled a truck up outside."

Molly nodded. "You hide anything anyplace? Anywhere they missed?"

"No."

"Okay."

But as she stood she glanced outside again and suddenly tensed, grimaced, and spun around, grabbing his arm. "Uh-oh."

In the street below they saw two cars appear and come to an abrupt halt, a half dozen men in dark caps and jackets jumping out. Most headed for Jeb's building but two split off, one going up the street and one down.

"We're trapped!" Jeb backed up a step, seeking escape. The back window? Down through the cellar?

"What's this?" Molly had released his arm but now she pulled him back to the window. Below, another group of men had emerged from a van parked in front of a hydrant one door up, accosting the more recent arrivals. Oddly, there was no shouting; the confrontation was being conducted almost in silence, though it was obvious that several of the men, inches apart, were speaking low and furiously to each other.

A shattering crash exploded behind them, and they spun around.

A man dressed in what looked like a gray janitor's uniform barreled through the deck door in a spray of glass, his eyes protected by wide, clear goggles. He held a pistol two-handed in an odd, seemingly awkward stance, the weapon close to his sternum and its long suppressor pointing out. But he was moving too fast, and as he swung the gun out to aim at them he caught one foot on Jeb's overturned desk chair and Molly threw the rolling pin underhand, hard as she could. It struck him in the face and his stumble became a collapse. Several *thwp-thwp* pops sounded as his finger yanked convulsively on the trigger, but he fell unconscious and Molly knocked the pistol away.

From downstairs they heard footsteps on the outside stairs and, a moment later, another crash as the front door was kicked in. A confusion of different voices followed, some swearing and several guttural shouts in what sounded to Jeb's untrained ear like Chinese or Japanese. He started to panic, had to fight the urge to scream and run. He spun around, looking for a place to bolt.

"Out," Molly said sharply, and pushed Jeb toward the balcony. They hopped over the fallen intruder and ducked through the broken glass onto the deck, Molly first and moving fast, clearly expecting to find backup waiting. But the deck was empty, and from the railing they saw no one below.

"No fire escape." Jeb pointed out the obvious, but Molly was looking up, examining the guttered edge of the flat roof nine feet above them.

"Is there another way up there?" As Jeb shook his head, she was already in motion, hopping onto the narrow wooden rail a yard from the building's wall, balancing herself with one hand on a light fixture hanging alongside the broken door. With her other hand she grasped the gutter, yanked to test its strength, and pulled herself up one-handed. As she hung with her chin just above the gutter her left foot found the light fixture, she got her other forearm over the edge, and in a moment she had disappeared.

Jeb followed, pausing as he stood on the railing, and Molly's face peered over. "Here!" She held out her arm, they locked hands in a climber's grip, and she pulled him up onto the roof.

From the apartment they could hear banging, the shouting now louder. Flat, graveled roofs extended right and left to the ends of the block. Jeb checked the dome of a skylight but couldn't see through its opaque plastic.

"Which way?" Molly's voice was urgent.

Jeb was trying to think. "Uh, left, I think the other side ends in a four-story drop." They ran along the tarred gravel, slowing as each roof ended to judge the gap and jump up or across or down. Atop the last building Molly crouched to look over a low parapet. No one had appeared in pursuit. The sun was bright, and they squinted in the glare.

"Okay." Molly turned to face him. "There's a bay window on the second floor, it sticks out maybe two or three feet and seems to be shingled. No copper or slate, so it shouldn't be slippery. But it's only about four feet wide, so we have to go one at a time. Me first."

"Wait—"

"I'm sorry," she said. "There's no time." And she rolled over the parapet, hung by both hands, and dropped. Jeb watched her catch herself on the bay window's top, and then she went over that edge too, landing on the sidewalk fifteen feet below and tumbling once in a paratrooper's automatic tuck. She looked up as he hesitated, thinking about how badly hurt you could get landing on concrete from thirty feet up, and then he followed her down.

"Good," she said, helping him to his feet. "You did real good. Ankles okay? Let's go."

The mountain bikes were just around the corner. Molly pulled hers out from behind the dumpster and got out of Jeb's way. As he stepped forward to retrieve the other bicycle, Molly clipped on her helmet—and an Asian man appeared from the other direction, running. He was unarmed, but he came to an immediate halt when he saw them, in a half second converting his velocity into an attack stance, one arm just above centerline and one close to his waist, both hands loose and slightly curled.

Even to Jeb, who knew martial arts only from the movies, the man looked lethal.

"Run!" Molly yelled, "Now!" and lifted one foot to deflect a slashing side kick, grunted in pain, and blocked two more handstrikes faster than Jeb could follow. The third slipped through, smashing into her shoulder, and she fell sideways, feinting a roll and jamming herself upright again, just in time to catch another punch in the stomach. She collapsed, partially blocked another whip kick and then fell for real, face down.

The attacker rebalanced, readying another kick, and Jeb slammed a cinderblock into his back, knocking him clear into the side of the building. He collapsed, unmoving. Jeb dropped the block, crouching to pull Molly upright, practically dragging her away.

"I can ride," she said through clenched teeth, groaning as she put weight on her injured foot.

"I sure wish we had a car," said Jeb, but he was already pulling out his bike and in a moment they were away, building up momentum down a long grade to the next boulevard. He stayed on Molly's left, adjusting his speed exactly to hers. No one followed.

As they turned onto the avenue Molly glanced sideways. "You okay?"

Jeb was still in full adrenaline, fear and confusion and elation at their escape all mixed together.

"You know what I noticed?" he said. "All these guys with guns—did you hear what they were saying?"

"Nothing."

"Exactly. None of them shouted 'Police' or 'Freeze' or anything." He marveled. "Way back when I was arrested, after they kicked in the door, that's all I heard."

"I don't think they were cops," said Molly.

TWELVE

DURING HIS TWO decades overseas, Vandeveer had been caught by unfriendly forces exactly once. It was in Islamabad, and a team of hard men from Pakistan's ISI security service had broken into his listening post, methodically destroyed every piece of equipment, and hauled him off to a stifling, windowless cell. A bucket served for a toilet, unemptied for the three days he was left inside. He was lucky, which he realized almost immediately when they didn't work him over. They weren't even upset to have caught him, really; and later Vandeveer learned the whole affair had been a skirmish in the unending, internecine conflict between the ISI and the country's civilian Intelligence Bureau, which in some convoluted, clandestine way had been assisting Vandeveer's wiretapping operation.

So he hadn't been in any real danger. A U.S. embassy flunky brought him food and cigarettes every day, and one of the ISI officers even shook his hand, grinning and shrugging, when they released him. Still, when Vandeveer walked out into the dust and glare, squinting and unshaven, he paused for a moment before getting into the

Range Rover the flunky had waiting for him. He looked around, listened to the clatter of the street, breathed the acrid third-world city air, and thought: *I have never been happier to be alive than right now, this instant.*

And that, pretty much, was how Vandeveer felt every time he got off the airplane from BWI and stepped onto California soil. Blackouts? Smog? Earthquakes? So what? Back at headquarters he was just another mid-level bureaucrat, sitting in traffic to and from his cheap, vinyl-sided, thirty-year-old dump, one more cog in the vast federal machine. The few neighbors he talked to knew him only vaguely, as a paper-shuffler at Treasury, or maybe the patent office. But 3,000 miles away he had a different life: a life of boardrooms and chauffeured Town Cars, of deals negotiated over filet mignon and sealed with a bottle of Moët. Out here he was a player. In Maryland he had to drive that clanking piece of Detroit junk, lest the agency's security busybodies take too great an interest. In California, beyond their gaze, he drove a BMW X5. Back home a typical evening's entertainment was a shouting match with his ingrate son, followed by recriminations from his wife and, often enough, a night on the couch. Out here he could call an escort or find some company in a hotel bar and enjoy himself without any consequences whatsoever.

Vandeveer was fifty years old, and he knew what he needed: money, and lots of it. Walkaway money.

The problem was, well, the same problem everyone else had. Over the last few years he could have come out further ahead by cashing out all his investments and running the dollar bills through a shredder. For a while, say in late 1999, there were enough zeros in his private, offshore portfolio balance to think about buying an island somewhere; now it had fallen to less than his NSA pension, for god's sake. The little business he was running for the agency kept him in the game, and so far Rice hadn't given him too much trouble about his expense vouchers. But Vandeveer wanted off the leash.

He got the X5 out of long-term parking, irritated by having to take the monorail and then walk through the dank, concrete garage, trying to remember where he'd left it a week before. There was a valet service—would Rice notice the charge? Maybe. He had a jet-lag headache, but he knew he had to drive straight to Dunshire, even though a nap in his beachside apartment in Foxton Cove sure was appealing.

Traffic on Route 17 was slow, and the piercing afternoon sun worsened his headache, blinding him to the coastal scenery south of Santa Cruz on Highway 1. He nearly struck an elderly woman inching across an intersection near Foxton Cove's town square, a quarter-mile from Dunshire's office on the waterfront, slamming on his brakes at the last moment. She swore angrily at Vandeveer, both hands clenching her walker, as he made placating motions through the BMW's tinted glass.

Jittery, he finally arrived and sat down at his desk, pushing aside all the paperwork that had been current when he left the week before. He rubbed his eyes, but as inviting as his full-length leather couch might be, he couldn't lie down. His office had the same glass walls as all the other rooms in the small firm, and several of the younger associates were at work. Like most VCs they regularly put in sixty- and seventy-hour weeks. It wouldn't do for them to see their managing partner dozing, even if it was Saturday afternoon.

Instead, he spent an hour reading carefully through a set of raw intercepts and first-level analysis sent electronically through the Agency's internal, excessively secure email. At two o'clock his screen pinged, the summons he'd expected, and he suppressed a flash of unease as he closed all the files. He moved his monitor, obscuring its screen from anyone who might peer in through the glass, and clicked up the videoconferencing system.

The connection was clear and smooth, despite extremely high levels of encryption guarding the transmission. NSA contractors had installed dedicated fiber directly into Dunshire's offices, bypassing all civilian telecom circuits, and the line provided far more bandwidth than Dunshire could ever use.

"Yes?" Rice answered immediately, sitting in the same chair, wearing the same shirt, tie, and inscrutable expression as he had during their face-to-face meeting eleven hours earlier. From either technical indifference or, more likely, annoying guile, he faced the camera with the room's windows at his back, creating a glaring contrast that made his face blurry and hard to read.

"Got your message," said Vandeveer. "Situation report?" He'd arranged his own camera angle with more care, the background showing only a file cabinet and a blank, beige-painted wall behind his head. Rice knew all about Dunshire, naturally, but Vandeveer still thought it unnecessary to display the mahogany conference furniture or a view of the yachts moored in the marina just outside his window.

"Please." Rice's voice was clipped.

"First of all, the FBI labs have confirmed that Blindside's computers were utterly destroyed. "Slag' was the word used in one description. Astrov's algorithm may turn up in his notes at home or someplace, but the core implementation technology might as well never have existed."

"In one light, that's not the worst result for us," said Rice after a pause.

"Um, yes," Vandeveer agreed. "It might save us fifteen million dollars."

"The initial three-point-four is locked away, though," Rice reminded him. "You can't get it out?"

"Not without a legal process that would be sure to raise some eyebrows. It's only until Friday, the cash is safe enough just sitting there."

"All right." Rice nodded slightly. "Now, what the hell is going on? This just doesn't seem to be ending."

"You heard?" Vandeveer tapped absently at his mouse. "Nothing's come through yet, but I have a call in to the SFPD. Some sort of altercation at Picot's apartment. Neighbors reported a bunch of men crashing around, and when the police arrived they found the place ransacked."

Rice considered. "Presumably someone was trying to tie up loose ends."

"Yes. The police haven't said what they've discovered at the residences of the other employees, but I assume that similar efforts were made to destroy any information related to Blindside's operations."

"But they haven't caught up with Picot himself yet."

"No. He's definitely a suspect now, though."

"Don't they see a logical inconsistency there?" Rice looked down at his desk, then returned his attention to Vandeveer. "Why would Picot tear up his apartment if he was involved in the attack itself?"

"As a diversion, perhaps." Vandeveer shrugged. "No one's really sure about anything at this point, but the fact that he disappeared is definitely working against him."

Rice stared for a moment. "Is anything else working against him?"

"Anything else?" Vandeveer allowed himself a short smile. "In fact, the police—the task force, actually—have needed no, um, assistance, whatsoever. They're making all these connections on their own."

"The press too?"

Vandeveer snorted. "Reporters need everything handed to them." Then, more diffidently, "And in fact, a few suggestions have been. It's possible that Picot's criminal record was faxed to the, ah, more competent journalists out there."

Rice frowned. "Faxed? From where?"

"Caller ID will have shown them a number in the SFPD Public Affairs bureau." Vandeveer spoke carefully, the half smile back.

Rice just nodded. "Good," he said. "Do they have any leads at all, really?"

"Just Picot and the woman, the letter carrier."

"Whom they haven't found yet either." Rice's grammar was, as usual, precise.

"No, but she turns out to be a very interesting suspect." Vandeveer opened a second window on his screen, partially overlaying Rice's face, and called up one of the documents he'd received earlier. "She wasn't just some truck mechanic in the army. Airborne MP, next a counterterrorism specialization, and she finished her enlistment after a tour in Afghanistan with the 82nd."

"And after all that she goes to work for the post office?" Rice shook his head.

"No, it doesn't make sense," said Vandeveer. "Plus there's something odd about her discharge. It was early, she'd signed up for another two-year stint but left halfway through. And the records have no details. Something happened overseas, but no one's willing to say what."

"Well, there's one obvious possibility," said Rice. "She could have been recruited. The spooks are always looking to steal talent for the IAD, and if she was any good they surely would have noticed her. Especially someplace with action on the ground."

"Yes." Vandeveer had worked with operatives detached from the CIA's International Activities Division, and he'd found them invariably quiet, polite, and dangerous as hell. "But I've found no confirmation of that yet."

Rice grunted. "And you probably won't, even if it's true."

Vandeveer felt a yawn coming on, decided he couldn't hold it back without looking foolish. "Sorry," he said.

Rice picked up a glass from somewhere offscreen and sipped. The liquid was clear, nothing more than water—springwater, maybe, at the most.

"All right," he said. "There's nothing to do, but keep all the tripwires up. If we're lucky this will wind itself down without Dunshire becoming involved."

"I'm putting together some preliminary release material, should it become necessary . . ." Vandeveer's voice trailed off as Rice straightened, his eyes boring through the screen.

"Nothing goes public," he said sharply. "Nothing."

"No, of course not. I mean, it's only in case the FBI shows up."

"Even then. If it happens, talk to me first."

"Certainly." Vandeveer kept his face calm, wishing he had his own glass, and not of water.

Through his interior window he saw two of the associates, neat young men in their twenties, debating some point outside the kitchenette. Both were holding sodas, and wearing practically identical chinos and polo shirts. They laughed and went back to their desks. Both had been careful not to look his way for any length of time, but Vandeveer suspected they were wondering what he was up to. He hadn't planned to return to California until Wednesday.

"The Deputy Director called me," said Rice.

"Oh? How did—"

"Dunshire's portfolio list was appended to the last quarterly report he got. We're not exactly Very Restricted Knowledge, you know. Blindside was on it—his staff is sharp, and they made the connection."

"Want me to write something up?"

"No." Rice ignored Vandeveer's irony. "He'd already been asking questions, even before this blowup."

"Really? Why?"

"You're making too much money."

That set Vandeveer back, leaving him speechless for a moment. "Excuse me?"

"How did Dunshire do on Whap Computational?"

"Well, they're awfully strong post-IPO, and I think we'll be fully liquid by November. The net will probably be close to twenty-six million."

"Exactly. And Tetral Systems?"

Vandeveer swallowed and forced himself not to look away. "Sitting pretty, especially now that Blindside's out of the picture." Rice just watched him, eyes unblinking, and Vandeveer finally added, "Too bad Dunshire didn't get a larger piece of the tranche—they look like a home run for their investors."

"All you're focused on is the money."

Vandeveer didn't see the point. "How about Railgun? Hardly more than living dead, they're killing us. Or TrianGL.com—shareholder litigation is probably being filed as we speak."

"Overall Dunshire's running an internal rate of return better than 30 percent."

"We're a venture firm," said Vandeveer, his headache back with a vengeance. "We're here to invest, and if I say so myself, we do a good job."

"Wrong." Rice's voice was a gunshot, even over 3,000 miles of cable. "Keeping a low profile is part of staying in the game. Dunshire is about access, not profit. Let In-Q-Tel do the boasting—they're the intelligence community's public venture fund." He paused. "Of course that's Langley, always angling for PR."

"What do you want me to do, start looking for dogs?" Vandeveer glanced at the slush pile of business plans he could somehow never whittle down. "There are plenty of choices, believe me."

"Stay focused on the mission." Rice, who'd never been in the field that Vandeveer knew of, managed to sound like he was dispatching an SCS team. "Keep an eye on new technology. Some we need, some we neutralize, but that's all that matters. Profitability is incidental."

"Well, yes, of course."

"Listen." Rice had mastered the trick of looking into his computer's camera, not the screen, so he seemed to be glaring directly at Vandeveer. "Don't go native on us. Blindside is a disaster, though Dunshire will probably survive. But remember, at the end of the day the steering committee isn't going to be looking at your profit-and-loss." He clicked off.

Vandeveer sank back in his chair, now truly weary. Outside his windows sailboats bobbed at their moorings in a freshening breeze. He closed his eyes, thinking, *I'll just rest a minute.*

THIRTEEN

AS THE PAIN in her foot increased, Molly could barely keep turning her pedals. She'd been too hurried when she blocked the attacker's kick, not that she'd had any choice, and he had caught her instep sharply from the side. Now it was swelling up. Jeb slowed, taking the whole lane as he rode alongside her.

"Where are we going?" he asked. "It doesn't look like you're going to make it much farther."

They were headed north on 35th, a block off Sunset.

"Golden Gate Park," said Molly after a moment's thought. "We'll blend right in."

They entered near the redwood grove. Cars were parked all along the winding roads, the paths busy with families and joggers. They pedaled slowly through, just another pair of recreational cyclists on a beautiful fall Saturday, eventually finding a place to rest on Marx Meadow, above the polo field. Jeb caught her bike and held it upright as Molly more or less fell off, collapsing with a stifled gasp of pain onto the grass.

"None too soon," she muttered, and carefully removed her shoe to examine the injury. But after a minute of probing and flexing she cheered up. "Nothing broken. Bone bruise, maybe, and the connective tissue is strained. Good as new tomorrow."

"If you say so," said Jeb. He seemed doubtful.

"After fifty or sixty parachute jumps, you start to know your way around leg injuries."

Jeb leaned the bikes against each other and sat next to her. "Would ice help?"

"Probably." Then, seeing him squint at a pair of cart vendors far across the field, she added, "No, wait, you'd only draw attention to us."

The sky was cloudless, the grass warm in the sun, and they could hear the distant sound of children running and yelling. Molly pulled her sock back on.

"Anyway, that confirms one thing," she said. "I won't be going back to *my* apartment anytime soon."

Jeb let it go. "You were right. There was no way to tell they were waiting."

"That's what they do." She glanced at him. "We're lucky to be alive."

"Only one of them had a gun," he said. "And you took care of him."

"Nothing but luck." She wondered how to explain. "Did you see how he came into the room, holding his weapon like this?" She put her hands together in front of her chest like she was praying, the fingertips pointing out. "That's the new 'ready-mobile' stance. Easier to carry, keeps the gun close and safe and fast to fire. They used to do it like this—" she let her arms drop, pretending she was holding a pistol two-handed and pointed at the ground in front of her. "Delta was first, then they started teaching all the special-ops soldiers the new way."

Jeb smiled. "What happened to this?" He made a gun with his forefinger, clasped it with his other hand, and held the pretend weapon to one side of his head, pointing up.

"Hollywood." Molly made a dismissive sound. "Dumb. Blocks your vision, it takes too long to get into firing position, and if you pull the trigger accidentally you're deaf in one ear." She paused. "That gunman was trained by Uncle Sam. Recently."

Jeb sat back. "I can't believe that," he said. "No—I don't want to believe that."

"I might be wrong, but . . ."

"What about Bruce Lee?"

Molly stared at her injured foot. "You saw them on the street. Arguing, it looked like to me—the more I think about it, the more it seems they weren't all together. There was one group like the gunman, all white guys, mostly carrying weapons. And there were the Asians, plus the one around the block."

"So?"

"If they were working together, we'd never have escaped. They'd have come in all at once, all the doors and windows would have been covered." Molly closed her eyes and leaned back into the grass. "They were interfering with each other. I think that commotion we heard as we ran out was a scuffle between them."

"Not one, but two sets of enemies." Molly opened one eye to see Jeb shaking his head. "Or more . . . what are we going to do now?" He didn't seem to expect an answer.

Molly noted the pronoun, tucked it away to think about later. "One question is, who did the search?" she said after a pause. "The toss was professional. The way everything was thrown into the center—that's how we were taught, you begin with the ceiling, next the middle of the room, and then you go around all the edges, pulling everything up. But it was almost too thorough, too destructive, like they were sending a message, too."

"Well, I got it loud and clear."

"It might not have been directed at you."

Jeb started to reply and stopped, frowning.

"It's time to talk about your company," said Molly. "What the hell were you up to?"

"Computer-based analytics, basically. Figuring out cheap ways to run factoring programs more efficiently.

Doesn't sound like much, does it?" He sighed. "It's not like Blindside was, I don't know, simulating nuclear reactions for warhead development or something."

"So why . . ."

"Code-breaking. Astrov—the founder—he was a genius."

A young couple slouched by, the boy's pants hanging much too low and the girl's T-shirt riding much too high, sharing an MP3 player. Each had one of the earpieces in, and they were giggling and mock-fighting over the player's controls, oblivious to everything around them.

"All right," said Molly. "I take it Blindside had working technology. Something worth killing for. Who are your enemies?"

"Enemies," Jeb repeated. "That's all I've been thinking about, every minute since . . . since yesterday." But he hesitated.

"Sorry," Molly said. "I know this is hard."

"It's not that." He leaned forward, stretching. "The problem is, *lots* of people might be unhappy at what Blindside was doing. Cypherpunks, say—there's some overlap between privacy lunatics and survivalists, especially the second-amendment nuts for some reason."

"Fringe militia? I don't think so. Not to run an operation like that. Who are your competitors? IBM? Not that they keep hired killers on the payroll, so far as I know . . ."

"Companies that we know about are mostly little start-ups, like us. Tetral Systems, Whap Computational—you probably haven't heard of them. Could be the big guys have skunk works they're keeping quiet about, especially if they're getting government money, but if that were the case, they might not be planning on going public anyway, so they don't count."

"These competitors, though—how exactly do you compete? Poach each other's employees? Criticize them on the internet? Steal customers?"

"All good ideas." Jeb pulled a water bottle from its cage and offered it to Molly, then drank off the rest.

"But no, none of us have a real product yet. Blindside was awfully close, but it's still a horserace. First one to market is going to make a killing." He winced. "Oops."

"It's all right. I know what you mean."

"The buyers are going to be big corporations, federal agencies, like that—the kind of customer that doesn't want to source from multiple players. First out the door has a good chance for lockup."

"And how much would that be worth?"

"Well, Astrov's always saying 'fifty million in three years.' That's the kind of revenue the investors want to see."

Molly massaged her foot absently. "It sounds good, I guess, but there must be lots of companies doing that kind of business. I can't see where assassins would come into it."

"No."

"Look, who could dispatch a team like that, really? Like I said, you start thinking it through, there's one obvious suspect."

"You mean the government."

"There are some pretty scary agencies out there. I, um, encountered them now and then." Molly remembered Afghanistan for a moment. "And nowadays they're running free and wild, with all that counterterrorism funding."

But Jeb was shaking his head. "No way it was the government," he said emphatically.

Molly was skeptical. "You sound sure about that."

"I am." Jeb hesitated. "Because they were buying Blindside out."

"What?" Molly stared.

"That's what the meeting was about, yesterday. With the Chinese guys. They were our backers, they held a majority interest, and they were selling it."

"Selling," she repeated.

"Yeah."

"Okay." She took a long breath. "Okay. So who were the buyers?"

"Probably the National Security Agency."

"The *NSA?*" Moll fell silent for a time. "You're positive?"

"Fairly positive."

"I didn't know they'd gone into business."

"Well, I can't be certain. Astrov was so cagey about the deal I only learned we were being sold last week, when he sprang these nondisclosures on us. I had to spend a few hours on the phone with someone, explaining exactly what programming I'd been doing, and even he didn't give anything away. But it sounded like a front company, and there was some wink-wink-nod-nod between Astrov and the other employees, so it became obvious soon enough." When Molly didn't say anything, he added, "That's why I can't see the killers being spies or whatever. They were getting the company's secrets anyway."

"Maybe they were trying to save some money."

"No one was getting rich. As an exit strategy it was nothing to break the bank—the selling price was under sixteen million. The Chinese were cashing out an investment, they didn't act like they'd won the lottery."

"Plain old businessmen."

"Sure. They were just, you know, the money men. I never met them before yesterday, but the way Astrov talked about them, I figured they were angels, rich guys looking for the next big thing. Maybe from some Taiwanèse software company."

"Normal businessmen don't carry handguns into client meetings."

"Well, that's true."

"Anyway, you're making the whole thing sound like a simple business deal."

"That's all it was. We had some technology the NSA wanted, they must have figured this was the easiest way to get it." His frown returned. "Until the gang of assassins showed up, that is."

"What was the front company's name?"

"The buyers? I don't know."

"But you were sitting in the same room with them, yesterday? You said the deal was closing."

"Oh, they weren't there. In person, I mean. Someone was on speakerphone, but Astrov had all the paperwork."

Molly shook her head. "I don't know business, but the whole thing sounds screwy. Who were the Chinese?"

"Just investors, that's all. They had some money, they were looking for a high-risk, high-return place to put it."

"High risk, sure enough."

Nearby a group of children had started a T-ball game, laughing and shouting. Bright sun shone down, picnickers dozed, a dog barked happily and ran in circles. Molly ignored it all.

"Knowing all this," she said slowly, "I really can't believe you went back to your apartment."

"I wanted to get my laptop."

"But you were carrying it yesterday."

Jeb explained how the police had mistakenly given him the Chinese computer. "And you can see why I don't want to go back to them, ask for mine again."

Molly began working her injured foot back into its shoe, grimacing as pain lanced up and down her leg. "We have to get going."

"But where?" Jeb made no move to rise.

"It's so out of control." She shook her head. "I don't know."

"Problem is," Jeb said quietly, "I'm scared."

"Yeah." Molly tied her laces, loosely, and stopped. They sat for another minute, silent. "I think I have to ask," she said finally. "About your record."

He answered readily enough. "Three years at Ray Brook Penitentiary."

"What'd you do, pirate a video game?"

A smile, but it didn't last. "I did some hacking when I was a teenager. The usual things—local phone systems, bank servers, the CIA. Nothing black-hat."

"The *usual* things? What would count as unusual—ICBM silos?"

The smile flickered again. "It's not that hard. Mostly

you guess one password after another, for hours. Or you call up and trick some clerk into giving you a hint. Or you just ask your pals, since hardly anyone can help boasting about what they've just done." He sighed. "Anyway, I got caught at exactly the wrong time. The Computer Fraud and Abuse Act had just been passed, Congress was in an uproar, the papers were screaming about viruses taking down the entire internet. They made an example of me. I was twenty-one, and I served thirty-eight months."

"No wonder the police are suspicious about you."

"They didn't mention it last night, during my interrogation. Which is what it was, by the way, however polite they were. But they must have known."

"You don't trust them."

"I don't trust anyone." He paused. "The point is, I'm a pretty decent programmer. Mostly encryption and communications, not much in the hot areas like web development, but I'm good at it. That's all I know, though, and after Ray Brook, that's all I needed to know. You see?"

"What about your family?"

"My parents, I haven't heard from them since the trial. Never wrote me in prison . . . nothing." He rubbed at a stain on his knee. "I had a girlfriend when I went in. She visited twice and then moved to Florida."

"I'm sorry." Molly had an urge to reach out and comfort him, and if she hadn't been so damn tough, she might have done it.

"I pretty much lost everything," Jeb said. "Like I was all the way down to zero, had to build it back up one step at a time. For more than two years I couldn't keep a job. Moving out here, landing at Blindside, I was finally putting it back together." He stopped rubbing his knee. "And now—now that's all gone, and I'm not sure what to do."

"I understand," Molly said, wondering if she did.

"I'm not going back to the cops."

"Well," she said. "We only have to wait until they catch the real killers."

Jeb unzipped the single pannier on his bike and rummaged around until he found his cell phone. He dialed a string of numbers but didn't put it to his ear, instead peering at the small LCD screen he'd uncovered by folding down the mouthpiece.

"Who are you calling?"

He didn't look up. "No one. Checking the news. Wireless web . . . not a lot of content, but I can get the wire services and CNN online."

"Handy." Molly closed her eyes again and slowly willed herself to relax, breathing consciously and slowly, forcing the tension to drain with each exhalation. Of course it came right back . . . gulls cawed far overhead. Several minutes passed.

"Oh, Christ," said Jeb.

"What?" She sat up, wincing as her foot dragged slightly on the ground.

He shook his head at the phone and clicked it off, flipping down the panel with too much force. "Police just issued a statement—they're looking for me now, too."

"That was fast." Molly's mouth tightened. "No, wait, they can't have responded to your apartment already, this must have been in the works earlier. What did it say?"

"Material witness warrant. They think I'm involved."

"Just because you disappeared?"

"And because I'm still alive." If he was being ironic, Molly couldn't tell.

"'Material witness' is different from 'suspect,'" she said, but even she knew that wasn't the point. Jeb was a convicted felon, which for most law officers pretty much meant it was up to him to prove his innocence, not the other way around. After years of antiterror hysteria they'd lock him up without a second thought, and the courts would let them get away with it.

She flexed her foot, grimacing. At the moment, she could barely walk, let alone defend Jeb and herself if they were attacked again.

"It's a lousy choice," she said, the thought itself as

painful as her injuries. "But it might be safer to turn yourself in."

"No." His face hardened. "I know what it's like inside."

"You're not exactly safe out here."

"In prison, gangs run the cells, not the wardens."

"Every time we turn around there are stone killers trying to gun you down."

"Exactly." He'd retreated back into emotionless cool. "Getting locked up would only make it easy for them to succeed." He pulled out his phone again, popped open the back panel, and removed the battery. "Passive auto-location—no use taking chances. We'd better get going."

Molly got up slowly, testing her foot. "I can ride, I guess."

"Good." He helped her onto her bike, and she held her balance with one hand on his back.

"You know," she said, "I think it would be nice if we were both alive tomorrow."

THEY stopped at an ATM in the First National Building, its glassed-in kiosk overlooking a broad plaza paved in hexagonal concrete slabs. The financial district was largely deserted on the weekend, a few people walking through and one slow-moving taxi picking someone up. Wind caught by the skyscrapers whistled shrilly through shadowed canyons, cold where the sun couldn't reach. Molly withdrew $720, emptying her account. But when Jeb stepped up and punched in his code, nothing happened. He waited for the card to return.

"Something funny," he said. Molly looked over his shoulder, saw an error message on the screen and a request that he pick up the service phone. "The card's not coming back."

They stood indecisively. Jeb struck the Cancel button several times. The screen blanked, and a "Sorry, out of service at this time" message appeared.

"Hmm," he said, "that's not good." Molly didn't bother to reply.

Across the plaza they found a bank of pay phones and Jeb dialed the 800 number from his ATM card.

"Oh, hi," he said, his voice casual. "Hey, there's some kind of problem with my card . . . no, I don't think I got the PIN wrong . . . sure." He read off the account number, then tipped the earpiece and gestured Molly close so she could listen in.

"It will take a moment to retrieve your records," the service rep was saying. "The computer is running slow today—"

She stopped, rather abruptly, and Molly thought she could hear a faint beeping in the background.

"Sorry," said the rep. "I'm going to put you on hold for a moment, all right?" Muzak started before Jeb could say yes.

"I think that's our answer," said Molly, her eyes anxiously scanning the empty square.

Jeb didn't hang up. "We need that cash," he said. "A few hundred bucks isn't even walking-around money."

The Muzak cut off. "Sorry about the delay." A new voice, much smoother. "My name is Ellen, I'm the supervisor here. Can I get your account number again?"

Jeb started to pull out his card, but Molly reached over and banged down the phone's hook.

"They're just stalling," she said. "Probably already ran the trace."

"I know, I know." Jeb hastily put away his wallet. "I wasn't thinking, I should have blocked the ANI. Let's get out of here."

Six blocks away Jeb stopped, pulling over to the sidewalk. No police cars appeared, no sirens could be heard, no other vehicles were speeding past.

"We're clear," he said.

"For now." Molly felt bone-cold, not just from the wind and lengthening shadows. "I keep thinking, they'll start to figure it out, get a line on the real suspects, and then it'll be safe to go to the police. But every hour it just gets worse."

Jeb shook his head. "You'll be all right. Military police, right? You must have friends who can help."

Molly thought of Wade. "Not really. Way out of jurisdiction here."

"You said it yourself, though. Whoever they are, they're gunning for me, not you." He looked away. "I'm putting you in danger. Can't have that."

"What?"

His gaze returned to her. "I know how to go to ground. I'm going to disappear."

No more "we," thought Molly. "Look, you don't have to do that."

"With those warrants? We stay together, we're both abetting each other."

"Legally, that's not quite how it works." But she couldn't argue with him. "Where are you going?"

"Away, like I said."

And nothing else. A moment passed.

"Oh," said Molly.

DESPITE years of guff about "the intelligent battlefield" and "autonomous warfighters" and "smart soldiering," most of Molly's initial army experience was about following orders, same as it had been for hundreds of years. Stay in formation, shoot on order, kill anything that moves. Even the paratroopers, nominal elites, simply cut wider paths of carnage. Special forces might be different—Delta commandos went their own way, to the point of generally pissing off any regular units who came in contact with them. But for Molly, it wasn't until she joined the MPs that she finally learned to think things through. To break up a late-night brawl you couldn't just open fire; a hostage taking wasn't going to be resolved with artillery. Staying in charge meant staying in control.

By the time she joined the Special Reaction Team, she already had a reputation for cold efficiency. Three years later, before everything went wrong in Afghanistan, her CO was fending off unending requests for her assistance, from other units who knew how effective she was. Her statistics were good enough, but more important was her ability to settle a crisis. Anyone could learn to shout orders and to sound authoritative doing so. Molly's difference was, her decisions were always the *right* ones: the ones that saved lives, that stopped the assaults, that ended the firefights.

At least, on the job. The better she got at defusing armed clashes, the worse she seemed to be at, say, having a disagreement with a boyfriend. Knowing instinctively when it was time to kick some abusive skinhead in the groin was not much use in sorting out a forgotten birthday or a thoughtless remark. Probably that's why she kept ending up with clods like Lance—they tolerated her slash-and-burn outbursts because they were too thickheaded to care, while the nice guys, the sensitive caring guys, got offended and took off.

Back in civilian life, Molly had been trying to unlearn these habits. In Taos she'd even lasted a peaceful six months with a sculptor, a quiet man with hands roughened by clay and a smile like moonlight, a man who'd even mentioned, once or twice, in passing, maybe, like, should they be thinking about, you know, getting . . . but there were a couple of stupid arguments, then one night Molly found him with his hand on the leg of a college student in a bar, and she immediately went and broke about fifty of his ugly damn pots before she got hold of herself. Since then she'd gone back to basics, trying at all costs to *say nothing, do nothing,* whenever she hit a difficult patch.

Which is what she did now, even knowing it was exactly the wrong reaction, knowing she'd end up glaring at a mirror later, muttering, "You idiot! You moron!" But she was too afraid of saying the wrong thing, so she said nothing.

Jeb held her gaze for a few moments. Later, Molly would know, absolutely know, that he was waiting for her to . . . what? Something, anything more than the brief nod she eventually provided.

"Well," he said. "Be careful." He clipped his foot into the pedal, hesitated once more, then pushed off, smoothly hopping the curb and accelerating down the empty street. At the corner he might have looked back, just for a second. Molly wasn't sure.

"You too," she whispered.

More slowly she got her own bike moving, the other way—south, back towards Eileen's. She wasn't sure where else to go. Her foot ached, and bruises from the night before were making themselves known.

As she rode carefully up and down the long city hills, to avoid more painful matters, she wondered why Jeb's account had been frozen, but not hers.

FOURTEEN

AT DUSK THE blocks around the Hall of Justice were populated with the sort of men who, at this time of day, had just woken up. Small groups idled on the cracked sidewalks, smoking and drinking openly, watching with keen and predatory interest as others passed by. Neon beer signs glowed in dark windows, heavy doors occasionally swinging open as some rummy stumbled in or out. From force of habit Norcross paused at one corner, pretending to dig around in his pockets for a cigarette, while he watched a runner pass a small parcel to a pair of young men in a dented Firebird. The car drove off noisily, its muffler loose, and the runner drifted back to his contacts up the street. Norcross shook his head slightly and walked on.

Sampford was just inside the entrance to the police annex, holding two cardboard pizza boxes with both hands and trying to kick the door closed. Norcross pushed it back open and stepped in behind him. The pizzas were hot and the aroma of tomatoes, cheese, and pepperoni was overwhelming.

"Having a party tonight?" asked the desk officer as he made a note in the log.

"Call a meeting at dinnertime, it's the only way to get people to show up," said Norcross.

"Take a piece if you like," Sampford offered.

"Thanks." The officer was grateful. "You with the captain?"

"Uh, yeah. She's here already?"

The policeman had begun eating immediately and he just nodded, pointing upstairs.

Cathryn was in the conference room, leaning back in a chair tipped against the stack of fileboxes, flipping idly through her notebook. Sometime that day she'd changed into a T-shirt and faded jeans that fit much more snugly than her uniform. Her service pistol, a Beretta 96, sat in a crossdraw holster at her waist.

"Hey." She watched as Sampford began opening the pizza boxes, pulling napkins and plastic knives from his jacket pocket. "Thanks for bringing dinner."

"Tired and hungry is worse than just tired," said Norcross.

"I hope we're not settling in."

"Unless you've been more productive than we have, it's going to be a short meeting." Norcross sat down.

"We can go home now, in that case."

They heard footsteps stamping down the hall, and Teixeira loomed in the doorway, his huge frame filling it, the gold, five-pointed star of his marshal's badge glinting on his chest. "Your dimwit desk jockey downstairs didn't want to let us in," he said, annoyed. He entered and Kubbos strode around him. "The inspector threw a fit."

Before Kubbos could respond Cathryn said, "Sorry. The list was probably misplaced at the shift change." She didn't seem particularly concerned.

Kubbos, his glare fiercer than usual, was holding the evening edition of the *Examiner* in one clenched fist.

"Did you see this?" he demanded, throwing the paper down on the table. "I thought your office was going to handle the press."

They all studied the headlines. "Nationwide Manhunt for Postal Killer; Hacker Also Wanted." A large photograph showed several grim-faced policemen emerging from Blindside's building. Below the fold two smaller pictures had Molly Gannon and Jeb Picot staring out.

"Seems like a fair story," said Cathryn.

" 'Postal Killer,' " Kubbos said sharply. "That's a direct quote from your so-called public affairs officer."

"Yes? Well, let's see. She works for the post office, and she killed a bunch of people. Am I missing something here?"

"She was a letter carrier for less than six months." Kubbos jabbed two fingers at her photo. "She was some sort of Special Forces assassin for ten *years*. That's what your flacks should be focused on."

"Military police," said Sampford. "Not special forces."

Norcross was examining the paper more closely. "That's a good picture," he said. It had clearly come from her service file, and showed her in BDUs and a beret, her face expressionless. "Better than any the army's given us. Why are they always more helpful to the reporters?"

Kubbos broke in. "Hey. Excuse me. The *Pentagon* trained her to shoot people, not the Postal Service. That's my point."

Cathryn nodded but answered Norcross. "It's interesting they provided a photograph of her in uniform. You'd think they'd be trying to minimize the connection, not make it obvious. She looks like a recruiting poster."

"What about Picot?" Unnoticed, Drake had slipped into the room and was standing quietly behind Teixeira, who started, then glowered. Drake's scarred face was placid, and his charcoal gray suit was clean and neatly pressed. "That looks like a BOP mugshot."

"Apparently his release jacket," said Norcross, who'd been reading the article. "Seems like the Bureau of Prisons is as eager to cooperate with the media as the Pentagon."

"Mean-looking bastard," said Teixeira. "But five-ten and one-thirty-five, that's scrawny."

"Two years in a federal penitentiary, he'd have to be tough to survive."

"Ray Brook?" Teixeira scoffed. "Minimum security, right? You know what the Club Feds are like—volleyball net next to the lap pool, veal scaloppini for dinner."

"Not all of them," Drake said quietly.

"All right," said Norcross. "Picot was born in New Jersey. Dropped out of Hunter College in New York City after less than two years. His computer science professor showed up at the sentencing to give a character recommendation, but it seems not to have helped."

"Wouldn't that be like Gannon's drill instructor vouching for what a great shot she was?" said Cathryn.

Norcross smiled. "Anyway, he drifted into something called DisOrder C0de. Disc0? They write it with zeroes . . . six or seven misfits who amused themselves breaking into computers all over the world. It's when they started in on banks that the DA got interested. Picot was the last name on the warrant, but they found stolen credit card numbers on his computer and he took the hardest fall."

Drake had leaned forward to scan the newspaper. "This name he used—I don't get it. Oydog? Oidey-og?" He pointed to where the reporter described Picot's online pseudonym as "ØyDog."

Sampford started eating, holding a slice folded over in one hand while his other kept a napkin underneath. The pizza was disappearing rapidly, without a single crumb or drop of grease landing on his suit. He'd clearly been spending time on stakeouts. After a moment he laughed, then stopped abruptly when everyone looked at him. "It's clever," he said diffidently. "Naughty dog. See?"

Drake nodded and Norcross smiled briefly.

"Let's get to business," he said, and the others pulled chairs to the table, Teixeira landing the broken one again. Everyone but Norcross took more pizza. "All right. How about an update from each agency? Agent Drake?"

"We ran the trace on the handgun from the garage." Drake set his slice aside and wiped his hands neatly with a napkin.

"That was fast." In Norcross's experience it usually required two days or more.

"I put a priority on it." Drake shrugged. "But it was short work. The Sig was brand new—came from Switzerland through a legitimate importer two years ago, sat in inventory, only got to the dealer this summer, and he sold it in September."

"I know it's foolish to ask," said Cathryn, "but who was the buyer?"

"One David P. Williamson," Drake said drily. "He might have been a white guy, maybe, the dealer wasn't sure. Louisiana driver's license."

"Did he run a check?"

"Of course. David P. Williamson has no criminal record. In fact, he has no record of any sort. Not even in Louisiana, as it turns out."

"What a surprise," said Cathryn.

They all knew that Louisiana was notorious as a source of counterfeit licenses. And the background check would only turn up a record if it existed; a false name would come out clean.

"Did Williamson buy any other weapons?" asked Sampford, and Norcross nodded approvingly.

"No. It looks like a one-off."

"Or maybe he's legitimate, and the Sig was stolen."

"Sure. Could be." No one around the table believed it.

"There was one thing, though," said Drake. "My trace was the second one today."

Norcross frowned. "What?"

"The clerk told me, when he called to let me know the fax was coming through. He'd started the trace already that morning, based on a request at 9:30."

"From who?"

"Ah." Drake seemed completely relaxed. "No one is really sure. It came through a legitimate channel, with a perfectly good authorization: one Provost Marshal Seaver,

Fort Bragg, North Carolina. But he denies knowing anything about it."

There was a pause while they absorbed this information.

"Isn't the 82nd Airborne headquartered at Fort Bragg?" Sampford spoke first.

"Yup." Drake nodded. "Their ComSec guys are looking into it, but no one sounded very hopeful. It was all done online."

"Your clerk—he'd already sent the results down there?"

"Yup."

"Doesn't make sense." Cathryn frowned, the pizza on the paper plate in front of her forgotten. "It has to be Gannon, but why?"

"Covering her tracks? Checking to see what we know?"

No one had a better idea, so Norcross made a note on the whiteboard and they moved on. Cathryn described what she called the "confusion" at Picot's apartment earlier in the day.

"His place was a complete mess when we got there," she said. "Tossed up, down, and sideways. Detectives from Taraval Station have been canvassing the neighbors, who don't agree on anything except that a large number of men were running around and shouting, just before noon." She glanced at Kubbos. "No mailmen this time, at least. We found a few bullets in the floor, and someone says they saw two people jump off a roof at the end of the block. Forensic teams are trying to scrape up tire prints and so forth."

Teixeira was frowning. "Didn't you have any officers posted? In case Picot came back?"

Cathryn didn't seem offended. "No. We're not working with unlimited resources here. Taraval had a cruiser swinging by every half hour or so, but they just missed the fun."

"Fine." Teixeira looked scornful, but he just turned one hand up and let it fall back to the table. "Whatever. In any event, we should probably be targeting the Chinese.

Whoever Gannon turns out to be working for, we know the Wo Han Mok are involved."

"They've disappeared," said Cathryn. "Liaison office is still open, down on Grant, but the only staffer left is a receptionist, some Valley girl hired right out of secretarial school. She doesn't know anything."

"Liaison office?" Drake seemed puzzled. "For a criminal organization?"

"Well, that's not what they put on their letterhead." Cathryn shrugged. "They call themselves a benevolent association. Everyone knows it's a front, even though not a single person in Chinatown will say so on record."

"They rub our noses in it," growled Teixeira. "I can't tell you how many times I've tried to get a warrant on that place, but they're as slippery as eels. We could never show cause."

"You wouldn't have found anything even if you did get in," said Cathryn. "They're careful."

"So the Marshals have been on the case two years," said Kubbos, "and haven't got squat. Maybe this task force can speed things up."

Teixeira slapped the table with one massive hand, bouncing paper plates and plastic forks onto the floor. "How many felons have you arrested, postman? Tracking down people who use the wrong zip code? Insufficient postage? Mail fraud, now there's a threat to the republic."

"You need to lay off the steroids, big guy."

"Ah, fuck you."

"You wouldn't know how."

Sampford pushed back his chair, keeping his hands free and his eyes on the two men growling at each other. Cathryn, separated from them by the table, was merely watching, and Drake still seemed completely at ease.

"All right, that's fine, thank you." Norcross didn't stand up, but his voice cut sharply through the room. Teixeira paused and said, still glaring at Kubbos, "Norcross, I can't work with this little weasel."

"Good, we'll get more done," said Kubbos immediately.

"Knock it off!" Norcross's voice rose.

"No, fuck it." Teixeira picked up his jacket. "He stays, I go."

"See you," said Kubbos.

"Just hold it a moment," said Norcross, real anger finally entering his voice. Both men stopped. "Do we have anything further to discuss now? Case related?"

"Judge Conrad," said Cathryn. "Follow-up on the warrant on Picot, there are some scheduling issues if we're to get a hearing before Monday . . ." Her voice trailed off. "Well, nothing that I can't handle, I suppose."

"Good." Norcross stood. "We're all going to go home and cool off, and I'll let you know tomorrow morning when the next meeting will be." He stopped and stared for several seconds at Teixeira, then Kubbos. "Let's try to stay focused on the real issues. Our enemies are outside this room, not inside."

Kubbos nodded first, a short jerk of his head, but he didn't say anything.

"Marshal?" Norcross waited.

"Shit." He pulled on his jacket, letting his huge shoulders flex and strain. After a last look around the room, he excused himself and left. Kubbos followed a minute later.

"Good enough, I suppose," Norcross muttered.

The others were still pulling together their papers and equipment. "They won't be going at each other in the parking lot, will they?" said Cathryn as the footsteps receded down the hallway. "I could call in a local unit."

"Nah," said Norcross. "They both seem more like backshooters, anyhow."

"You saw their sidearms," said Sampford. "Cannons—both of them are carrying .45 ACP. The inspector's is a Springfield 1911-A1, same as our SWAT guys have. And Teixeira is using an HK Mark 23."

Norcross looked at him. "Paul, you're not some sort of gun nut, are you?"

Sampford blushed but held his ground. "I try to stay current."

"He's right," said Drake. "You can knock over small buildings with that kind of caliber. Recoil makes it hard to aim, of course."

"Anyway, you're not one to talk," said Cathryn. "I bet that P-35 you carry isn't standard issue."

Norcross glanced at his holstered Browning. "I've used it since Vietnam," he said. "You all pay way too much attention to this sort of thing."

"The Hi-Power's a great weapon." Drake came to his defense. "So what if the design's seventy years old. It could be lighter, but you're probably used to that."

Norcross shook his head. "You run out of ammo, it makes a good club."

Drake started picking up pizza boxes and folding them into the room's single trash can. "I didn't get a chance to mention," he said. "Clerk who ran the serial? He called me back late this afternoon, wanted to let me know one more thing."

"Yes?"

"Someone else was following up on the trace. Not initiating an inquiry, that is—just calling to see where it was in the sequence."

Norcross looked interested. "And who would that be?"

"He didn't say. Mumbled something and demanded a status. Clerk said he knew all the right words, sounded like a supervisor."

"And?"

"Clerk didn't give him anything, and the joker hung up."

"Interesting."

Cathryn was eyeing Drake with curiosity. "This clerk—he sounds on the ball."

Drake nodded. "He knows me. We help each other out, now and again."

"Your office have caller ID?"

"Of course." Drake looked pleased. "He got the number, and it's dead—you dial it, there's no ringing, no sound, nothing. However . . . the area code was 472."

Norcross and Cathryn looked puzzled, but Sampford got it immediately. "Government."

"Right." Drake finished cleaning up the pizza boxes and smoothed the pressed folds in his jacket. "It's a Washington exchange reserved for certain federal agencies."

"Oh, hell," said Norcross.

"Yup," said Drake, almost cheerfully. "Those kind of agencies."

No one answered. Norcross clicked off the lights and they walked down the deserted, echoing hallway.

"I guess that explains why the SAC is letting me run with this one," he said finally.

FIFTEEN

MOLLY HAD TO stop and rest several times, her foot too painful to push the pedal around, so it took more than an hour to get back to the Mission. When she finally rode slowly down 22nd, though, she noticed a parked sedan with three antennas and a spotlight on the dash, and realized her slow pace might have kept her out of trouble. The sedan had a familiar logo on the side panels—nothing subtle or plainclothes here—and Molly grimaced and kept going, careful not to look at Eileen's building. The car was empty as she passed.

Around the corner she stopped at a pay phone on the corner and pretended to make a call, mumbling into the receiver as she wondered what to do next. Late afternoon, long shadows on the street, the air cool; Molly was hungry, too, and exhausted, and now she had nowhere at all to go.

When Jeb appeared beside her, neatly bunnyhopping his bicycle over the curb, she was so glad to see him she forgot to be surprised. He halted and pushed up his sunglasses.

She hung up the phone. "What are you doing here?"

"You didn't have to quit your call." He looked around. "Are you all right? I figured you'd be here thirty minutes ago."

She ignored the question. "And how did you know where to find me?"

"You gave me a phone number."

"Yeah . . ." Molly frowned. "But she's unlisted. They wouldn't have given you a crisscross lookup."

"Unlisted doesn't matter much online." He shrugged. "Anyway, you shouldn't go back to her place. There's some sort of cop car out front."

"Postal Protective Service." Jeb looked blank, so she said, "USPS uniformed division. Usually they guard the facilities, accompany valuable shipments, things like that. An inspector probably borrowed their car, or he's getting chauffeured around. They like that."

"Mail police."

"Pretty much. Eileen works for the post office same as me, and that's probably why they're involved."

Jeb leaned on his bike's frame, his faded courier bag back over one shoulder, watching her and the street at the same time. "I went to pick up my stuff, and I got to thinking," he said. "You saved my life again, and got hurt doing it. Didn't feel right leaving."

Down the block a woman was arguing with the owner of an open-front vegetable stand, waving at the piles of squash and chilies. Passing cars coughed ozone and burnt oil in the encroaching dusk. Somewhere children were shouting.

"Thanks," said Molly, no other response handy.

"I can help you get someplace safe. Wherever you're going, I mean. Before I . . . what I mean is, I'll sleep better knowing you're okay."

"Me too." Which wasn't the brightest quip, but he grinned and Molly suddenly felt better. "How long did you spend watching Eileen's apartment?"

"Ten minutes, maybe. I don't think anyone's home, though. No movement in the windows, and I could see someone hanging around the foyer. Probably your postal cop."

"Eileen wouldn't get back from her shift until about now." Molly didn't bother asking how he knew which windows to check; he'd proven resourceful enough so far. "I doubt they know where she parks. We can wait there."

Eileen had a spot in a cul-de-sac alley, up against a set of loading doors boarded over years earlier. Flattened boxes and neatly tied trash bags leaned against the wall of the Mexican grocery that fronted the street. Eileen was pulling in as they arrived, her Fiesta's brakelights glowing as she bumped over the rough paving. Molly went first, calling her name quietly and then gesturing for Jeb to wheel his bike alongside also.

Eileen looked him over. "Molls," she said.

"Jeb," said Molly, chin-nodding in his direction. "I told you about him."

"Nice to meet you. Um, why are you waiting here? Lose the key already?"

"There's an inspector at your apartment." Molly repeated Jeb's description.

"Mmf." Eileen didn't seem surprised. "Well, the paper trail puts us together. I hate to say it, but you might be on your own now."

"Anyone else talk to you yet?"

"No." She turned back to the car, leaning inside to retrieve her kitbag. Her T-shirt stretched over her muscles, riding up from the gray uniform trousers and displaying a narrow, tanned waist. Molly glanced sharply at Jeb, who seemed to be looking elsewhere, and immediately felt embarrassed at herself again.

"But my neighbors—I don't know who saw what, this morning," Eileen continued. She straightened up and closed the door carefully, making little noise. "If the police ask, I'm going to have to tell them you were there."

"No problem."

"As for tonight, maybe I'll go out to eat, get a burrito down the street. By the time I'm answering questions you should have at least an hour."

"More than enough," Molly said. "More than you need to do, for that matter."

A security lamp at the head of the alley buzzed and flickered, coming to life and lighting up the stained brick. Around the corner the grocery's screen door slammed as someone walked out, but they must have gone the other way.

"You willing to talk to the police yourself, yet?" Eileen leaned on the Fiesta.

"No," Molly said. "We ran into some trouble earlier." She briefly described the encounter at Jeb's apartment. "These guys . . . they were scary. I'll turn myself in, but not before I know who's in charge."

"What about you?" Eileen looked at Jeb.

He nodded at Molly. "I'm following her lead."

Molly thought, *You are? Really?*

"Why?" said Eileen.

A smile flashed across his face and was gone. "She knows what she's doing."

"Yeah. I'd agree with that."

Jeb nodded. "You're another one, aren't you?"

"What?"

"The way she tells it, Molly has kind of an, um, eventful background for a letter carrier." He was now watching Eileen closely. "You too, I bet."

Eileen laughed. "Eventful."

"I told you," said Molly to Jeb. "Lots of ex-military end up handling mail. Nothing unusual about it."

"Sure." He shrugged. "Well?"

"Yes." Eileen held out her hand, and they shook. "I was in the service."

"Why did you leave?"

"My enlistment ran out, and the bonuses weren't good enough to re-up." She seemed still to be taking his measure, as he was hers. "Why do you ask?"

"Just trying to figure you two out."

Molly listened to their conversation with half attention, also watching the alley entrance, the lights sputtering on, a pigeon settling on a silent extension of ductwork. The bricks at her back were rough and cool, catching the threads of her shirt. She'd been counting on using Eileen's bathroom, ever since she started her slow ride back. Now, realizing it wasn't available, she noticed the pressure becoming too great to ignore.

"I have a problem," she said.

"Huh? Only one?"

"I don't suppose the grocery has a restroom."

Eileen frowned. "No, and you don't want to be asking some stranger for a key, anyway."

Molly looked down the alley, which appeared to dead-end thirty feet in. "No other entrance?"

"I've never seen anyone come out the doors." Eileen dug around her kit bag. "I probably have some Kleenex in here somewhere."

"That's all right." She noticed that Jeb, for once, seemed a little self-conscious. "Hey," she said to him. "If there's one thing the army got me used to, it's a field-expedient privy."

WHEN she'd disappeared around a dumpster in the darkness at the alley's end, Jeb looked back at Eileen, who was still leaning against the car.

"I'm surprised the army let her go," he said.

"Molly? Is that what she told you?"

"Something about not getting along with the chain of command."

"Mm-hmm." Eileen considered this. "You know she was military police, right? Women aren't supposed to serve in combat specialties, but being an MP she saw more action than you might expect."

"She said her last posting was Afghanistan."

"Yeah. Her unit was sent in right after the Taliban collapsed. Peacekeeping, more or less, plus some mopping up in the mountains. But it was still confused on the ground—local warlords did all the fighting, you know, with American special forces just calling in airstrikes. Outside Kabul and a half dozen bases, you could go days without seeing another American. You never knew who the enemy was. Even the mujahideen supposedly on our side were more interested in staking out their fiefdoms than in serving some U.S.-backed national government."

A car drove slowly past the mouth of the alley, and Eileen paused, waiting until it disappeared. She shifted her kit bag.

"Molly was sent to pick up a prisoner, somewhere outside Bagram. POW transport, completely routine, something like a five-hour drive out to where a U.S. infantry patrol had caught the guy sneaking around their camp. If he'd only been carrying a rifle he might have passed himself off as a cowherd, but the rocket launcher was a bit much . . . anyway, the patrol turned him over to Molly, and she started to drive back."

"Okay."

"Like I said, all routine. Until halfway back she was ambushed by a bunch of mujahideen on horses—they popped up, surrounded the humvee, and forced her to stop."

Eileen hesitated. "You have to imagine the scene," she said. "Middle of nowhere, nothing but dust and rock for miles around, and she's completely alone. She gets out of the vehicle and there are two dozen madmen on horses crowding her, pointing automatic weapons and shouting. The prisoner was their guy, and they wanted him back."

"Let me guess," said Jeb. "She killed them all."

Eileen laughed. "Good, but no. Because one of the horsemen was American."

"Special Forces." Molly appeared beside them, looking a little more comfortable. "It was hard to tell at first, with the beard and the scarf and the funny hat—you probably saw them on TV, look like upside-down pie crusts? But he was an SF liaison, and after weeks in the field with those bandits, he was having some clarity issues. Kind of forgot who the good guys were."

"What did he do?"

"Ordered me to uncuff the prisoner, said it was all just a misunderstanding. I'll give him this," Molly said, "he didn't draw on me."

"And that's why they kicked you out?" Jeb didn't see the point.

Eileen shook her head. "You don't think she did it, do you?"

Jeb looked at Molly.

She sighed. "I punched his horse in the nose."

"What?"

"It's a sensitive spot." Molly reached out and tapped Jeb's nose, lightly. "The horse reared up and Buffalo Bill fell off. Fortunately he landed wrong and broke his wrist. He was so pissed he'd probably have started shooting if he'd been able to hold his gun."

"And then they just let you go," Jeb said.

"Sure." For the first time Jeb could remember, Molly grinned. "See, it was a compound fracture—the guy's bone was sticking out, and it's not like the mujahideen had a surgeon on call. So I agreed to drive him back to Bagram . . . but only if the prisoner came along too."

Jeb frowned a bit. "Okay, so you had a disagreement with another soldier, but all ended well. I don't get it."

Molly's grin faded. "He wasn't any old GI. He was a Green Beret. The civilians running the Pentagon are just completely in love with these guys. Rumsfeld gave them their own separate command, you know that? So it was bad enough one of their golden boys lost track of which side he was on—but to lose a fistfight with a grunt, well, that was intolerable."

"A girl grunt," said Eileen.

"You want to be charitable, you can say that they needed to avoid embarrassing press reports which might embolden the enemy. That's what they told me, anyhow. So we cut a deal. I promised not to talk, and they'd give me an honorable discharge along with a little more back pay than I'd really accrued."

"Fair enough," said Jeb.

"Sure. It didn't feel like exactly the right thing to do, but what the hell. Except they reneged. Buffalo Bill had a lot of friends, I guess. When the dust cleared I had a general discharge, a bad reputation, and an empty savings account."

As the last glow of daylight faded away, the sodium

lamp cut sharp shadows on their faces. Eileen locked the car.

"I have to go," she said.

"They didn't treat you right." Jeb hadn't looked away from Molly. "But that life is behind you."

"Somehow," she said, "it doesn't seem that way at the moment."

SIXTEEN

THE OFFICES OF Dunshire Capital occupied a renovated warehouse on Foxton Cove's picturesque waterfront. Weathered graystone buildings had been turned
into condos, boutiques, tourist bistros, and an inevitable
proliferation of financial service firms and plastic sur-
geons' offices. Cars parked along the anachronistically
cobbled streets tended to be shiny, foreign, and expensive. The local convenience store stocked the *Financial
Times* alongside the *Weekly World News,* and you
couldn't find a cup of coffee anywhere for less than six
dollars. Vandeveer loved it all.

Alongside Dunshire's building a planked boardwalk
had been extended out over the water to form a large
deck, with an open-air bar and grill and a dozen tables
scattered around. At dusk colored lights strung along the
periphery created a festival setting to watch the sunset
across the marina, while smoke from the grill's gourmet
barbecue drifted inland. Middle-aged couples in expensive clothing clinked their wineglasses; the only children
in sight were a couple of teenagers piling shopping bags
into the backseat of a Porsche down the block.

Vandeveer's companion at the table didn't fit the picture so well. Short and broad, with heavily veined arms and restless eyes, he'd chosen to sit with his back to the dock's rail, facing past Vandeveer more than toward him. His clothing was dark and nondescript, and his hair had been cut with an electric razor.

"I'm not a fucking lost-and-found," he said now, his voice raspy. "Not my problem, you can't find your decoder ring."

"You know it's not that simple." Vandeveer was irritable, consumed by his jet lag after the long day.

"Hire a fucking private eye, then."

Vandeveer just shook his head wearily.

"Look," the man said. "We're a direct action sort of team. Give us a clear objective and we'll grab it or kill it or blow it up. You want someone to dust for fingerprints and interview fucking witnesses, you got to go somewhere else."

"You *had* a clear target. This problem wouldn't exist if you'd cleaned house properly the first time."

The man shrugged, unoffended. "You screw up the intel, that's not our fault. No one expected Xena the Warrior Princess to step in."

"Yeah, yeah."

A powerboat rumbled into a slip nearby, running lights on in the lowering dark, cutting slowly through the black water. Wash from its wake slapped the deck's pilings.

"All right, I'll see what I can find out," Vandeveer said.

"Just call a fucking target, that's all. Tell us who to shoot, we'll take care of it."

"How's Charley?"

"Fine. He was a little blurry on his way out, but he's straight now. Won't happen again."

"I bet."

They watched a Mercedes pull up to the valet stand. The driver—gray hair and a bush jacket—got out with no more than a nod to the attendant, who quickly drove the car away. A waiter seated the man nearby, and as he meandered back to the grill Vandeveer gestured for their tab.

"I have to go back to the office."

"Go ahead. I'll leave in a few minutes."

Vandeveer pushed back his chair. "There's money involved, you know. Real money. Don't forget it."

The man's mouth curled. "It's *always* money," he said. "Always."

"**FOR** a fugitive," said Molly, "you're living high." She limped through the first floor of Darren's house, noting the plasma flat-screen TV amid antique furniture and some burnished-aluminum floor statues. "Not that I'm complaining."

"Darren was employee number three at a start-up that got bought by Microsoft a few years ago," said Jeb. "And then he cashed out most of his stock before the crash."

"So where is he now?"

"A little consulting, but mostly retired—oh, you mean right this minute? Southern Thailand, some little island, for two weeks. I got a postcard, he said it's nothing but white sand, palm trees, and topless Australians. No electricity. No phones, even."

"Nice of him to let you stay here." Molly returned to the foyer, where Jeb was removing his shoes and stretching. "Me too, for that matter."

She'd accepted without hesitation when Jeb offered, Eileen giving Molly a quick nod of approval and then leaving them. The ride back had been slow, but Jeb paced her carefully the whole way. It was night by the time they arrived, no one on the sidewalk to observe them as they slipped into Darren's garage. Molly let herself relax a degree.

"I could use a bucket of hot water for my ankle," she said. "And maybe something to eat, if there's anything around."

Jeb led the way into the kitchen, snapping a row of chromed switches on the wall. Small, extremely bright spotlights illuminated inch-thick granite counters and polished hardwood cabinets. The stove had six burners and a built-in grill under its hood, plus two ovens.

"Nice," Molly said. She opened the Sub-Zero refrigerator and poked around. "But I think you're supposed to keep bananas at room temperature."

"Hmm." Jeb took the bunch she held out, the bananas completely black. "I'll have to have a word with the help."

"Let's see." She inventoried the possibilities. "Beer, leftover pizza, mustard and . . . a tube of salmon paste."

Jeb shrugged. "I think Darren eats out a lot."

"It does have the feel of a guy's kitchen."

"You cook?"

"Well, no. Ten years in the army, I never had to." She examined the pizza, found mold, and tossed the box onto the counter. "But I'm sure we can do better than that."

"I never learned either." Jeb found a box of noodles in the cabinet. "Spaghetti. How hard could that be?"

"Okay."

He checked another shelf. "Tomato paste—that must be sauce."

"I guess." Molly looked at the small cans. "You better open two or three."

They ended up throwing away the noodles, overboiled and inedible in the thick, gummy paste, and started over with scrambled eggs. Dirty dishes accumulated along the counters.

"Sorry about the smoke alarm," said Jeb.

"If I wasn't so hungry . . ." Molly scraped burnt bits out of the pan and went searching for red pepper in the spice rack.

When they'd eaten, finishing off the last of some stale bread, Jeb eyed the mess and shook his head. "Let's just leave it. We can clean up in the morning."

Upstairs Molly paused as she stepped into the wide-open third floor, her attention arrested by the view of the bay at night. Lights twinkled across the harbor, beyond the sweep of the city below them. In the distance they could see the steady flow of headlights across the Golden Gate, under its illuminated cablespan. Jeb clicked on a pair of desk lamps, but they cast only small pools of light and did little to diminish the panorama through the broad windows.

"Sit on the couch," Jeb said. "I'll get the hot water."

When he returned Molly was sunk into the soft cushions, flipping through a magazine without really seeing it. "No, no, stay put," he said when she started to struggle up. The large metal pot he was carrying sloshed as he placed it at her feet, and he handed her a small towel.

"Thanks."

They sat for a while, Molly resting her foot in the steaming water, Jeb in a futuristic Aeron office chair he'd rolled over from Darren's desk.

"We should have ordered takeout," he said eventually.

"No. Too dangerous."

"No more than what we just ate."

Molly was admiring the room. "My whole apartment would take up about one-quarter of this floor," she said. "And view's not as good, either."

"Well," said Jeb. "It's better than jail."

"Yeah." Molly looked over at his face, shadowed in the lamplight. He was distant again, like he'd half gone away somewhere inside his head, his eyes looking at nothing she could see. A few moments passed.

"How was it?" she asked.

"What, jail?" He came back, focused on her.

"Unless you mind talking about it . . ."

"No." He hesitated, but only, it seemed, to figure out what to say. "They told me it was going to be a low-security prison. I didn't get a decent lawyer until it was almost over. Couldn't afford one, not until there was enough publicity and some civil rights groups knocked together a legal defense fund. So my court-appointed bozo handled the pretrial work, and he pretty much screwed it all up."

He stopped, and they listened to the slow creaking of the house.

"Anyway, Ray Brook formerly *was* minimum security—embezzlers, deadbeat dads, you know. But the whole system was overcrowded, so they were taking overflow, all these low-level drug convictions, and by the time I left the entire block was double-bunked. Every few weeks they'd have to put down cots in the cafeteria. You can imagine."

The first lockup Molly ever saw was an MP drunk tank, and the last was a sand-blasted shipping container where a dozen captured Taliban were left to die; there had been more than she could remember in between. She could imagine. "How did you do?"

"Just lucky." He shrugged. "The gangs weren't too bad, and not so many guys were in for violent offenses. They just wanted to serve their sentence and get out. But the main thing was, I landed in a fight early on. Stupid, an argument in the yard one day and he came after me that evening as they mustered us out for dinner. I had no idea what I was doing, but I was terrified, and I grabbed him and tripped and when we fell over, his head hit the corner of the wall. Blood everywhere. I'd never really seen a head wound before. He got a fractured skull and a week in the infirmary, and after that the predators generally went after other guys."

Molly nodded. "Yeah, that's how fistfights usually happen. It's not like the movies."

"Really? But the way you took on that Chinese guy, that martial arts stuff, isn't that what they taught you in the army?"

"Nah." Molly was amused. "Oh, there are a few tricks we used in the MPs, sure. Come-alongs mostly, ways to bend a guy's elbow or put a stick between his legs, so you can walk him out of a bar in front of all his liquored-up buddies. But when you seriously want to put someone down, it's usually just a question of being first and nastier."

Jeb looked skeptical.

"Most guys protect their groin," she said. "Instinct.

So you hit them in the throat—it's going to hurt regardless, and if you crush the larynx, they'll probably die. Or you can gouge out an eye, which is pretty easy to do. If you're wearing boots, kick them in the side of the knee, keep going, and don't hold back just because you feel some bones break."

Jeb winced.

Molly rubbed her face. "What's happening to us—that's what I feel like. Next time we run into them it'll probably be napalm and close air support."

That got a wry smile.

"We need some ammunition, anything, on our side," she said. "Right now we're completely in the dark, nothing to do but wait for someone to try to kill us again."

"I'm not waiting." Jeb straightened up in his chair. "I'm *running*."

"And see where that got you." Molly paused, considering Darren's palatial home. "Actually, it's pretty darn nice here. But you know what I mean."

"You said it yourself. So many victims, so many attacks, the law is all *over* this. Eventually they'll figure it out, catch the bad guys. Whoever they are . . . the point is, that's when it'll be safe to show up. Not until then."

"Uh-huh." The water in the basin was cooling, and Molly slowly rotated her foot, testing out the ankle. "Two problems there. First, you're counting on the police and the FBI actually solving the crime, and soon, which is kind of a dangerous assumption. Second, we've got serious dobermans on our tail. No way we're safe while they're still out there."

"They won't find me." He glanced at her. "Us."

Molly sighed. She knew that stubborn look. Was it just her, the men in her life? Or did they all do it, driven by inevitable male pride—back themselves into a corner and then refuse to see reason?

On the other hand, usually when a guy got all bullheaded, he was about to do something outlandish and stupid. Jeb was only being excessively cautious, which Molly had to admit was behavior she generally hoped to see more of, not less. He just didn't appreciate that sometimes you couldn't be careful enough—and then, you had to do things differently.

The soak had done all it could for her, so Molly pulled her leg out and dried it on the towel. Jeb scooted over, the chair remarkably silent as it rolled across the varnished floor, to help stretch her leg and ease it onto the coffee table—an unnecessary, chivalric gesture.

"That's some bruise," he said, and Molly noticed how warm his hands were, and how gentle.

"Um," she said.

"But the swelling is down," he continued. "And your muscles feel . . . just fine."

"Yes. They are, uh, fine."

He leaned forward to look more closely, on the edge of his chair, and then let his gaze travel up her bare leg, slowly, up her midriff, finally to her face. She looked into his eyes and everything seemed to halt, her mind aware of nothing but the sensation of his hands and the slow smile starting on his face. Her breath stopped.

And then the chair finally overbalanced, its casters skidding out from underneath. Jeb fell forward with a yelp, crashing onto the coffee table and the pot simultaneously. Water splashed out, drenching the floor, and pain shot up Molly's leg as the chair bounced off it. Magazines flew everywhere.

"Jesus, sorry, what a mess." Jeb tried to sop up the puddle, but the towel was too small. "Are you all right?" Without waiting for an answer he stood, righted the chair, and pushed a magazine away from the spreading water. "I need to find a mop or something."

He disappeared down the stairs and Molly looked at the mess. After a moment she laughed.

THE barriers of uncertainty were back as they straightened up, back where they started, careful again about distance and eye contact. While Jeb took the bucket of soaked towels off to the basement laundry, Molly noticed a TV screen in the shadows of the bookshelves and clicked on the news.

When Jeb returned she was standing, riveted, watching intently as a man fielded shouted questions from the mostly offscreen reporters before him.

"Anything useful?" Jeb said, walking over. "I checked the cable stations this morning but—"

"Shhh." Molly's eyes didn't leave the screen.

"Who is it?"

"My father."

He'd apparently decided talking to the press might get rid of them quicker. Molly thought she recognized the grain elevator behind him; perhaps he'd holed up there, or perhaps he'd just gone ahead and put in his usual workday, refusing to bend to the pack frenzy of the journalists. The lighting was poor, shadows scoring deep lines in his face.

"That is absurd," he said, unexcited. He glanced off-camera, dismissing the questioner with a look of contempt. "She'd never do what you're suggesting."

The confidence, the absolute conviction of his tone, left the reporters silent for a second, maybe two, an eternity. Then the shouting began again.

"You're as much in the dark as me," Molly's father said. "The difference is, I know my daughter, and you never will."

The reporters ignored that. "Did she tell you what she was planning?" someone called.

"Do you think she stole the guns from her base?"

"How many people did she kill when she was in the army?"

"Did she lose a lot of money in high-tech stocks?"

Molly's father just looked at them, slowly shaking his head.

"Good for him," said Jeb when the interview ended a minute later, Molly's father once again pushing silently through the crowd. Molly turned off the television and they settled back into their chairs.

"I'm proud of him," said Molly, surprising herself with the truth of the statement as she said it.

"He stood up for you." Jeb observed her face. "Didn't back down an inch."

"He always did," Molly said. "It took me a while to realize it."

THEY watched the nightscape city below them for a while, not saying much, and as it grew later lights across the bay began to blur with the first faint mists of fog. Molly felt drowsy but unwilling to sleep. Their conversation drifted back to safe territory and stayed there.

"So," said Jeb, "why would they tear up my apartment?"

"It had to be the Chinese investors," Molly said. "Along with the same team that attacked Blindside to start with. But they're working against each other—we just happened to be in the wrong place when they both showed up at your apartment."

"They might both have been waiting."

"Maybe. And our arrival brought all of them out." She looked out over the bay, Alcatraz just visible, its distant ramparts spotlit in the dark. "I was starting to think perhaps the original target had been the Chinese themselves, not Blindside. But if they're both still looking for you, that theory doesn't work."

"Don't forget they destroyed our server room, too."

"Yeah." Molly sighed. "You really don't know anything about the Chinese?"

"No." He looked pained. "I've been thinking about it all afternoon, but the business side never, well, seemed all that important. Not that Astrov shared much."

"Then we have to start from the other side. The buyers."

"I probably know even less about them. I had the one phone call, part of their due diligence, but it was all technical, only about my work." He rubbed one temple. "Believe me, I've been trying to remember . . . he seemed to know what he was talking about."

"Any indications at all who they were? A conversation you might have overheard, some letterhead, visitors—anything?"

"The only thing—I saw we were getting a lot of overnight mail recently. But I never noticed the address, just the blue-and-white envelopes sitting out front when I came in."

"Which carrier? FedEx? Airborne?"

"Not them. It had the blue stripe with the eagle."

"Any red in the design?"

"No, I don't think so."

"USPS Express, then. Makes sense, they'd be more likely to use overnight than third-day." Molly was all the way back to businesslike.

"Do you know someone at the post office who can find out who they were coming from?"

She shook her head. "It's a completely separate system from regular delivery—different trucks, different facilities, different computers. Route carriers like me never see them." She paused. "Computers. Why don't you hack in and look it up?"

He glanced at her. "Oh, no, that wouldn't be easy at all."

"I thought you told me it was."

"Well, sure, if you have enough time, but—proprietary systems? Just figuring out where to start would take all night." He dismissed the idea with a gesture.

They fell silent. A huge container ship moved slowly across the harbor, its deck illuminated by a catenary of strung lights. Near the bridge a casino boat passed it, out for a night's booze cruise, and both disappeared into the outer bay.

Molly wondered how good a hacker Jeb really was. Dangerous enough that the feds sent him away for three years, yes; but careless enough to get caught in the first place. How hard could the postal service be?

She shifted her position, starting to feel drowsy on the couch. "You know," she said, "you want to hide, you still need to understand as best you can what you're hiding from."

After a moment, Jeb nodded. "True enough." He pushed absently at the floor, turning himself around in the chair, then spun twice more, rapidly, like a little kid. Coming to a halt, he looked up. "There might be another way to do it. To get the name."

"Yes?"

"Sometimes the easiest methods are the most obvious. All we need are the tracking numbers from some of the envelopes, right? Then we can just look them up online. They must have a public interface, like FedEx." He slapped at the keyboard to Darren's computer, and the screen came to life, booting back out of hibernation.

"I guess." She hardly needed to say anything; he was off and running. "But no one's going to just give us those numbers."

"It depends how you ask." He pushed off, coasting the chair down the length of the desk. "Who's in charge of Express Mail at your post office?"

"The floor supervisor, I suppose. Raymond Tuck."

"He won't be there now." Jeb glanced at the clock. "Not at eight o'clock Saturday night."

"It's closed until Monday."

"But somewhere mail is being sorted even as we speak, right?"

"Sure. The ADF—Area Distribution Facility—out at the airport runs around the clock. It's combined with the Airport Mail Center. That's where Eileen works, doing consolidation logistics." Molly tried to remember other details she'd been provided at her training. "I think the Sectional Center Facility in Oakland is 24/7, too."

"I don't suppose Eileen would be able to look this up." When Molly shook her head, Jeb continued, "But you know her number out there?"

"Sure." Molly frowned. "But she already left work, remember?"

"That's fine. I'll talk to whoever answers."

Molly recited Eileen's extension and Jeb picked up the sleek desk phone. Just before he dialed he smiled and winked, so quickly she wasn't sure she'd seen it.

"Operator, can you help me place this call, please?" Jeb spoke slowly, his voice tentative and weak. Molly blinked. He sounded ninety years old. "Yes, I'm at home, but my wife is away tonight. I'm afraid . . . I'm sorry, I'm blind. When I try to dial I get the wrong numbers by mistake, and then we have these charges on our bill . . . oh, thank you, you're too kind." He carefully recited a long number beginning with ten.

A moment later, he requested Eileen's number from what was apparently the automated machinery of a long-distance service. A longer pause followed.

"Hi, this is Detective Donald Regan, San Francisco Police Department." His voice boomed out—now he sounded like an Irish stevedore. "This the Airport Mail Center? Thanks. Who's the manager on duty tonight?" Pause. "Can you page her to a phone, please?"

After a moment he introduced himself again. "I'm working on the Potrero shooting yesterday, the massacre, you probably saw it on the news . . . that's right. I wonder if you can help me out. We're trying to run down some of the company's recent contacts. We found some Express Mail packages in their office, but they were pretty well destroyed by the fire . . . you didn't? Well, they never seem to get it right on the TV news, do they?" He chuckled. "That's the problem, we're sifting through embers, and everyone was killed, so we don't have much to go on."

At this point Molly decided he wouldn't get the information; the story seemed to be spinning out of believability. But Jeb pressed on.

"So here's the thing. Raymond Tuck—do you know him? He's the floor supervisor at the Potrero post office . . . well, anyway, he spent most of the day talking with us but now we can't reach him, he said something about taking the wife out to dinner." He chuckled again. "You are surely right, I'd like to be doing the same thing. Now, I know you can't give me the details on the phone like this, even if you could look up the records on your computer . . . of course not, and you're absolutely right. That's why, we're getting a subpoena, we'll do it straight by the book, opposing counsel won't be able to knock the blocks out later, you know?"

He was better, more convincing, than any of the innumerable fast-talkers Molly had dealt with in the MPs.
She couldn't help starting to smile as she watched him
perform.

"I'm sitting in the judge's chambers this very
minute," Jeb continued. "He's the on-call tonight, and
he's going to sign the subpoena as soon as we get the
details. There's some urgency here, so we can't wait until Monday . . . but the judge wants it pretty narrowly
constrained. We have to tell him precisely what we're
looking for . . . right, that's the reason I'm calling you.
If you could give me the tracking numbers, we'll know
the exact documents to request in the subpoena, and
then everybody's lawyers will be happy."

He waited, his eyes now completely shut. "The last
two weeks would be great . . . how many are there?
Hold on." He moved the handset away from his mouth,
half covering it with one hand, and said, as if to someone else, "Is there a fax here? No . . . why not?" After a
pause, he returned to the AMC manager. "I'm sorry,
ma'am, they're telling me the fax machine is broken.
Five numbers isn't that many though, can you just read
them to me?"

When he hung up a minute later, Molly was shaking
her head.

"That's how it's done, huh?" she said.

"Social engineering." He seemed pleased. "Most
people think hacking is all about programming and machine code, but you know what? The weakest link usually isn't inside the computer."

"I'm impressed. What was the business at the beginning, with the operator?"

"I didn't want caller ID to pass this number. Blocking keeps the recipient from seeing it, but the central office still keeps a record of the ANI." He saw her
questioning look. "Automatic Number Identification—
like the same thing they use to locate 911 callers. On an
assisted call, though, the link is broken. Just to be sure,
I added one more layer by going through ATT."

He was already at the computer, opening a browser

window. "For the same reason, I'm going to run this session through an anonymizer—a proxy outside the country operated by privacy hawks. You can't be too careful."

As it turned out, all five overnight packages had been mailed from a single location. Five minutes later Molly and Jeb were staring at the scanty details provided by the USPS database.

"Dunshire Capital Partners," said Molly slowly. "94039—that's Monterey, I think. Where's Foxton Cove?"

Jeb was already opening an online map service. After a moment a jagged, line-drawn road map appeared. "Monterey, all right. North of Moss Landing." His hands were still on the keyboard, but motionless. "Now that I think about it, the name is kind of familiar—Dunshire. Someone must have mentioned it."

"Can we find out anything about them?"

"Let's see." Jeb closed the map window. "We'll start with a meta-search." Scrolling down the list of results, he started opening additional windows faster than Molly could keep up, checking links briefly before abandoning them, following some, going back to the list for more, cluttering the monitor with a proliferation of commercial webpages, messages, and raw posts. He was clearly in his element, but to her it quickly became a meaningless blur.

"I'm going to make some tea," she said. "If I can find any."

Jeb grunted absently. When Molly returned twenty minutes later, a mug in one hand, he had barely moved. The screen showed a PDF document, some sort of report, and he was flicking through it at a rapid scan. Hearing Molly come up behind him, he leaned back, rubbing his eyes.

"We're on to something," he said. "This is a report from a venture capital survey, through July of this year. The appendix lists investments for a number of firms, including Dunshire. Not complete, since apparently they have to rely on public records and news releases and that sort of thing, but . . ." He paused. "It's enough, anyway." He pointed at the screen, scrolling up until a particular page was displayed. "Look. Tetral Systems, Whap Computational, Avenoir, Railgun. Part of Dunshire's portfolio."

"You mentioned the first two earlier. So?"

"They're all doing work related to cryptography. Just like Blindside was."

Molly stared at the list on the screen. "I assume none of them have been, well, attacked."

"No." Jeb watched her in the glow of the monitor. He'd switched off the only other lamp, and the room was dark, though some light came from the glittering cityscape visible through the windows. "Whap is relatively well-known, but they're all secretive. Tetral's doing something similar to what we were."

"So Dunshire is particularly interested in cryptography."

"I guess we already knew that." He clicked the mouse, bringing up another document. "Here are the management bios. Pretty thin, but they do have some pictures. This guy, Vandeveer, he seems to be the chief executive."

They looked at the photo. "Did you ever see him?" asked Molly.

"No." He closed the window.

"I have one more smoker," she said. "While I was downstairs I called Wade back, at Bragg. Don't worry, I did just what you did—pretended I was blind, went through the operator."

Jeb nodded. "What's a smoker?"

"That's what the CID detectives used to say. You know—a smoking gun. Almost literally, in this case. He'd gotten the ATF trace. The handgun I was supposed to be killed with? It was purchased in July from a dealer in Glen Furnace." She sipped at the mug and set it on the desk. "That's in Pennsylvania, just over the Maryland border."

"So?"

"A direct line from Fort Meade," she said. "NSA headquarters."

Jeb scowled. "Oh, no," he muttered.

"It might be coincidence."

"I doubt it."

Molly's tea had gone cold. "Don't worry," she said. "If we can figure it out, so will the good guys." She paused. "Whoever they are."

Jeb just shook his head. "There are no good guys," he said.

SEVENTEEN

HALF-AWAKE AT THREE a.m. Jeb heard the phone ring, somewhere else in the house. He ignored it and pulled another blanket over his head. No one knew they were there; it had to be one of Darren's friends, either drunk or in some distant time zone, confused. If the call woke Molly, she wasn't moving around downstairs.

He finally dozed off, not waking again until the rising sun flooded the third floor with light. The rest of the house was silent. He looked at the computer, decided he didn't have the energy even to check a few news sites. Instead he stared out the window, his mind jumping around. Occasionally he rubbed his chin, now clean-shaven, unused to the feeling.

When Molly had suggested he disguise his appearance the night before, he'd objected that shaving was the first thing the police would expect, but she just shrugged.

"It's still the best way to make a quick change."

"What about you?"

Molly grimaced. "A lot more difficult. My hair's too short to cut much further, and people tend to remember how tall I am."

Jeb considered. "The pictures of you in the news we've seen, they're all from the army. You're wearing camouflage, or a uniform. That's what people will remember."

She nodded. "You're right. Does Darren have a girlfriend? Someone who might have left some dresses here?"

They found some women's clothing in the second-floor guest room, folded carelessly on the closet shelves and smelling of laundry softener. Molly sighed when she held it up to herself.

"Nice stuff, but this woman must be a size four."

"It looks like it would fit, except for the sleeves being too short."

"Six inches too short."

In the end she picked out a sundress that fell just above her knees; on the owner it was probably midcalf, but it would do. She matched it to a silk jacket, dangerously transparent.

"Very good," Jeb said, approving. "I like it."

"Yeah. I guess. Lousy to run in, though." She accepted the compliment awkwardly, glancing at him and then looking away. In the room's rather dim light, Jeb thought, *No, she didn't just blush, did she?*

"Let's hope you don't have to," he said as she dumped the outfit on the bed. "Run, I mean."

"Hobble is more like it." She looked down at her injured foot, then back up, pushing her hair back, and caught his eye.

Jeb looked into her face and suddenly one thought filled his mind, appearing in an instant and driving away all others: hey, there's a large, comfortable-looking bed with a fluffy pink comforter *right there*. And because he was as suave as he'd always imagined, he said, "Gurrk," forgot to breathe, and froze up completely.

Maybe he could blame Ray Brook, or maybe, after the fight-or-flight buffeting of the last thirty hours, his limbic system finally went tilt. She was looking at him, not saying a word. Was there an invitation in her gaze? He might as well have been fourteen again: he stuttered and coughed and abruptly turned toward the hallway.

"I have to, um, ouch," he said, his hand banging the doorframe, missing the doorknob by several inches. "Brush my teeth. Find a razor."

"Oh." Molly's face was unreadable, at least to Jeb at that moment, but he barely knew what he was doing anyway.

"I'll see you in the morning. Good night," and he was away, up the stairs, shortly to conclude he'd just made the biggest mistake of his life.

DURING the long dark hours, in between nightmares of terrifying pursuit and faceless killers, Jeb tossed fitfully and wondered what he could say to Molly in the morning. At eight a.m. he finally slipped downstairs, stopping outside the kitchen when he saw the blinking light on the answering machine. After he heard the message, even before it ended, he turned and ran back up to the second floor, rushing into the guest room where Molly was sleeping, one arm across her eyes.

He tapped her lightly on the shoulder, unprepared for the reaction. She came awake immediately, her opposite hand whipping around to knock his arm away and diving forward off the bed in tuck roll, coming to her feet in a fighting stance a second later.

"Yow! Whoa!" Jeb backed quickly away, holding his hands in front of his chest protectively.

She straightened up, now favoring her hurt foot. "Sorry."

"What do you do when the alarm clock goes off— kick it through the wall?"

"I'm a little tense."

"Uh, yeah, I guess so." He let his hands fall. "Darren called last night, I just listened to his message on the machine. I thought his vacation was going to last another week, but maybe the islanders have TV after all. He heard my name in a report, and he cut his trip short. He's back in Bangkok, wondering what's going on." He abruptly realized that Molly was only half-dressed, nothing but a sleeveless T-shirt and panties.

She glanced at him, then just pulled on the khaki trousers she'd found in Darren's closet the night before, tucking in her T-shirt and looking for her boots under the bed.

"What time did it arrive?"

"What?" He was still distracted. "Darren's message? Um, around three, I think."

Molly muttered and said flatly, "We're compromised."

"He wouldn't call the police."

"We can't count on that. Who knows what he heard, what kind of news made it out there. We have to leave now."

"Uh." Jeb was trying to catch up.

"Grab what you need, but keep it light—we'll take the bicycles." She shook her head. "Christ, I wish we had a car."

They left a rushed ten minutes later, Jeb's courier bag now packed with the Chinese laptop and clothing, Molly carrying a faded duffel strapped to her mountain bike's rack.

"I took Darren's cell phone," said Jeb. "It probably won't be tapped. And his Visa card. I figure he owes me."

"Nice thought, but it's probably too risky to actually use it."

Three blocks away, pausing at a red light, they were passed by two police cars going fast in the other direction, one with lights flashing but neither using a siren. Seeing them Jeb clenched the handlebar grips, knuckles tightening under his fingerless riding gloves. Molly tensed up, too, but she put one hand lightly on his arm, restraining him until the light changed.

"Okay," she said. "No need to panic. We're clear, no one's going to notice us." She seemed to be talking as much to herself as to him.

"Fine."

At the green they pushed off. After a minute Jeb brought his breathing under control.

"We missed breakfast," he said.

She glanced at him. "You're hungry? Now?"

"A big plate of bacon and pancakes sure would be nice."

INSTEAD they had some candy bars and soda, purchased from a bank of vending machines outside a gas station on Van Ness. Waiting at the curb, holding Jeb's bike by the stem while he used the station's bathroom, Molly watched a cloud drift over the sun. In the brief chill she felt their isolation; if it began to rain, where could they go?

But the weather held off. They rode over to the bay and found an isolated stretch of concrete at the water's edge near Pier 10. Chain-link and razor wire closed off the wharf's freight-handling facilities, deserted on Sunday morning. Behind them traffic rumbled back and forth along the Embarcadero. Seagulls cawed past occasionally, but most of them circled the public access pier, two hundred yards away, where Sunday fishermen might lose track of some bait. The cool breeze smelled of brine and fuel oil.

Molly sifted through her duffel, jittery now that they weren't moving. "I can't believe I forgot the skirt. And the shoes."

Jeb was checking his wallet. "Eighty dollars. Our credit cards are useless now."

"I have about seven hundred—not much. Not enough."

"It'll do." He pocketed the wallet. "All right. I'm serious this time. I'm going to disappear. No more nonsense about taking the fight to them."

Molly had drawn exactly the opposite conclusion from the morning's near miss, but it was clear that going round the same argument wasn't going to convince him. "Well," she said.

"That hacking I did, all the time I spent breaking systems—what we're talking about here is just identity theft in reverse, right? It's not hard to run away in this country, but when someone gets caught, it's because they don't know how not to leave a computer trail, somewhere."

"You think you can do better."

"Sure." His confidence was absolute.

Molly sighed. "Actually, most people get caught because they can't leave their past behind. They want to see their kid's graduation, or they send a birthday card to someone. Sentiment is their worst enemy." She looked at Jeb, realized the same might be true of her, and fell silent for a few moments. "Anyway, that's not the issue here. You're not talking about giving the slip to some bounty hunter or a PI. The entire national law enforcement infrastructure has been mobilized against us."

"So?"

A dog barked back at the roadway, behind them, and they were quiet until the owner walked it past. Out on the water a freighter moved slowly by, its long wake slapping and splashing against the piers.

"We can't just dig a hole until this blows over," Molly said. "And splitting up makes it worse. If we keep running, just reacting, they're going to catch up, soon."

Jeb shrugged. "Maybe."

"Our only chance is to fight back."

"Right." He grimaced. "Against the, what, the entire national law enforcement infrastructure?"

She looked embarrassed. "That's what sitting in army classrooms does to you. Anyway, it's simpler than that."

"How?"

"Here's what we know. There were three groups in on the buyout: the Chinese, Dunshire, and Blindside itself. Two of those parties were shot up. The other one wasn't even there at the time. What does that tell you?" Jeb just waited, so she continued. "Dunshire's the key. Unless we assume some hypothetical fourth actor, they're the likeliest suspect, even if we can't figure the motivation. Not to mention, if they're an NSA front, they'd have no problem whistling up a professional assault team."

"Hmm." Jeb absently adjusted his bag's shoulder strap, working the metal bracket down over the heavy webbing, thinking about it.

"We go to them," said Molly. "Next time, they're the ones surprised."

"That'd be suicide. We don't even have any weapons."

"Not yet. But we should hit them on our ground anyway." She paused. "To start, you have to hack them."

"Huh?"

"Break inside. Get us some data, some background—something—so we're not just sitting out here in the dark."

Jeb stared out at the water.

"They'd be hard to crack," he said. "If they're really NSA. Fort Meade was always the ultimate challenge. People would boast all the time, how they broke in, but I never heard a story I could believe."

"Assuming Dunshire's a front, they'll have to be separated from the organization. Maybe security will be a little weaker."

"Maybe."

"You don't know until—"

"Yeah, yeah."

"We're in a box," she said. "We can't run, and I'm not going to just stand out here like a deer in the headlights. We need an edge. You're the only one who can provide it, right now."

A weather-beaten harbor tug chuffed slowly past, attracting some seagulls to its wake. Molly pulled on a nylon shell she'd taken from Darren's basement, and waited.

Jeb shifted, coughed, watched the harbor, and then squared up to face her.

"All right."

"Yeah?"

"I'll take a few runs at them." Just like that.

"Oh. Good." She'd expected—what? More resistance? "Great."

Jeb unslung the courier bag and opened it back up,

removing the Chinese laptop from the light pile jacket he'd wrapped it in. "We might be able to use this."

"I thought you said it was passworded."

"I need a computer, and we can't afford a new one." He withdrew a disk from an unmarked sleeve, slipped it into the laptop's drive, and hit the power switch. They heard the whine of drives starting up. "It's probably running a Chinese-language version of Windows, which means the base code's a year or two out of date, so that's good. I know the hardware inside and out since it's the same as mine. Once it boots off the CD I can crack the operating system, and then we'll have access to anything not encrypted." He paused. "Of course, we won't be able to read files created in Chinese fonts."

Molly considered the laptop as cryptic text began popping up on the screen. "You brought that disk with you."

"I made it last night at Darren's."

"You were already thinking of doing this." She smiled, but he didn't see it.

"Well . . . yeah," he said. He stopped tapping at the keyboard but didn't look up. After a long moment he added, "Not outside on some dock, though."

"Things got moving fast this morning." Her tone was neutral.

Jeb finally caught her eye. "I'm still not taking any chances," he said flatly. "No more confrontations. Someone even looks at us funny, that's it—I'm gone."

"Sure."

"I mean it."

They watched each other, both frowning slightly, until Jeb nodded shortly and went back to work.

He clicked away, muttering now and then. A truck clattered along the road but didn't stop. Gradually the sun's warmth overcame the steady, cooling wind. Molly lay with her eyes closed, resting her head against the duffel.

"Whether or not you find anything useful on the computer, you can use it for breaking into Dunshire, right?" she asked.

"Yeah. I was thinking I'd need to partition the disk, put on my own OS, but even in Chinese this is easy enough to use—all the icons are the same, and I won't be doing anything sophisticated. I'll download some hacking apps from the net."

"Good."

"In fact . . ." His voice became thoughtful. "In fact, that might even be to our advantage. If their security is really good, they might backtrack fast enough to grab some configuration data. Especially if I leave it unprotected. They might get the idea they're being probed by someone Chinese."

Molly opened her eyes and saw him watching her.

"Just to muddy the water a little more," he said.

EIGHTEEN

NORCROSS DROVE AROUND the neighborhood ten minutes looking for Tico's Restaurant, then another ten until he found a parking space four blocks away. He could have parked illegally, since traffic enforcement was much reduced on Sunday, and because most patrolmen would immediately recognize the prefix on his pool car's government plate. But there was some chance Cathryn would notice, and he didn't want to look like a crass fed, ignoring local sensibilities.

When he finally walked up to the diner, Norcross noticed Cathryn's Explorer angled into a narrow space in front of a hydrant, its rear half-blocking an alley entrance. He wondered where Sampford had parked.

Inside, the booths and tables were mostly occupied, late risers still straggling in for breakfast. Light slanted through the plate glass windows, across the tiled floor and wooden chairs, then sank into a deeper gloom at the diner's rear, where banging and a Spanish-language radio station could be heard over the kitchen sounds of frying food. Tubs of dirty dishes filled a busboy's cart abandoned near the waitress station, and a careless patron's stumble had erased part of the day's menu from a chalkboard propped against the bar. Norcross looked around, his eyes adjusting from the sunny glare outside, until he found Cathryn and Sampford against the wall, underneath a long planter cantilevered from the paneling and overflowing with ivy.

"We ordered," said Cathryn. "He was hungry."

Sampford blushed. "Sorry, I wasn't sure—"

"No problem." Norcross sat down, opening the menu as a cheerful waitress appeared. "Black tea, please," he said, looking up. "Toast and, let's see, the fruit bowl."

"Anything on it—trail mix? Goat milk yogurt? Quinoa?" He shook his head. "Honey? Turbinado? Cane juice?"

"Just plain, thanks."

The clatter and conversation from other diners formed a constant background noise just loud enough to feel comforting rather than oppressive. Steam from innumerable coffee cups drifted in the sunbeams.

"Thanks for meeting us," said Norcross to Cathryn. "Your day off and all."

"'Day off'—that must be a federal thing." She glanced at him. "It's not like anyone's waiting for me at home."

"Nicer here than at the station, anyway," Norcross said after the shortest pause.

"They make me carry a beeper."

The food arrived a few minutes later. Norcross watched as the waitress set down a wide ceramic plate covered with rice, black beans, a large egg burrito and a mound of salsa and cheese, along with side dishes of green soup and chips. Sampford tucked in gratefully. Cathryn's half sandwich of avocado and sprouts looked like a Weight Watchers appetizer.

"Anything new from the house?" Norcross asked.

"Not much. We might have just missed them this morning—it looks like they were there last night."

"So they won't get far."

"I keep thinking that, and here we are." Cathryn indicated Sampford's salsa with a questioning look, and when he nodded, his mouth full of burrito, she scooped some onto her sandwich. "Something interesting about Picot, though. I started wondering how the reporters had gotten his prison record so quickly."

"Bureau of Prisons leaked it, probably, like we figured yesterday."

"I don't think so. After those lawsuits a few years ago, they're real careful about releasing anything. My detectives complain about it—in fact, I have to sign authorization forms even for basic information requests. You've never had trouble with them?"

"Never needed their data," Norcross said. "We generally use NCIC records."

"Anyway, I talked to a reporter I know at the *Chronicle.* He was surprised, since he said Picot's file was faxed to them from our own SFPD Public Affairs office."

Norcross was thoughtful. "Let me guess—they don't know a thing about it."

"Right." Cathryn drank some coffee. "The reporter sent me a copy of the fax they received. You know how the machine prints the originating number on top? It was our line, all right, but I had the PA officer go through his call records, and it wasn't there."

"Someone faked it." He looked at Sampford. "How hard is that?"

"Anyone can dummy up a cover page." Sampford hesitated. "Spoofing caller ID is another matter—I think you'd need to hack the telco switch."

"This wasn't some teenage kid," said Cathryn. "The BOP jacket was real, not something an amateur would be able to find."

Norcross grimaced. "I don't like the sound of this."

"A mysterious federal agency was following up on the ATF trace. Could be they're screwing around here too."

"Black helicopters, huh." He seemed more annoyed than concerned. "Assholes."

"I put an investigator from the Computer Forensics Unit on it. He might shake the tree a bit." She shrugged. "It doesn't mean that much yet."

Sampford signaled the waitress to ask for more rice and beans. The room was warm, and Norcross removed his jacket, shifting his chair so the Browning at his hip was concealed by the table.

"I tried to have a conversation with Marshal Teixeira this morning," he said. "Maybe I woke him up, it's hard to say. But he wasn't feeling particularly cooperative."

"I bet."

"I was hoping he could give me their investigation's background file on the triad," Norcross continued. "Despite what Kubbos says, after two years they probably know a good bit. But Teixeira just said he'd be more than happy to talk about it at the next task force meeting and hung up."

"Which is when, by the way?"

"The task force? In a day or two, maybe, unless something breaks. He and the inspector need to settle down some."

"What about Drake?" Sampford mumbled around his food.

"Nice guy, but ATF doesn't have much of an investigative role in this one. I get the feeling he's here on other business, too."

The waitress breezed by with a coffeepot, not stopping when they all shook their heads.

"I know something about Wo Han Mok," said Cathryn. "I've been talking to some of the officers I used to work with in Gangland."

"Good."

She finished her sandwich and pushed the plate away. "Like Teixeira said, they've been moving into North America for the last ten years. They started in Vancouver, which has been taking in huge numbers of Chinese immigrants, mostly from Hong Kong. Ever since Britain gave back the territory."

"Were they trying to get out, too?" Sampford asked.

"No. They're well connected in both Macau and on the mainland, mostly in Shenzhen—the takeover didn't mean much to them. Except for a change in business opportunities. They were just following the money overseas."

"Business opportunities," said Norcross.

"The usual." Cathryn sipped her glass of water. "Within the community, gambling, loan-sharking, and smuggling illegals seem to be their primary activities. But they've also taken a greater than normal interest in what we might call financial services. You know what the chit system is?"

Sampford nodded, but Norcross said, "No."

"At ground level it's not much different from wire centers that poorer people use to transfer money back to their home country. Say you have a few hundred dollars you want to send to your family in Fujian. You give it to the Wo Han Mok here in San Francisco, they notify their office in China, and that office delivers the amount in *yuan*. The trick is that no money crosses the ocean—it's all handled out of operational cash flow in both countries. No taxes, no fees, no banks involved."

"Money laundering," said Sampford.

"Sure," said Cathryn. "But if you're making two-fifty an hour washing dishes in some Chinatown restaurant, you probably don't have a checking account, and the fees on a bank transaction are going to be much bigger than what the triad charges. Of course, you have to trust them, but they have no reason to steal the principal—they make much more by skimming a little off the continual cash flow."

"Still sounds small-time," Norcross said. He had finished his meal and sat back in his chair.

"It's only the beginning. On a much larger level, they do the same thing for businesses. The Chinese multinationals tend to be secretive, family-controlled, and dependent on vast webs of *guanxi*—personal connections. They've always had relationships with the triads, to break up labor unions, collect debts, that sort of thing. Sometimes to remove competitors. Now Wo Han Mok is extending their services, to become a sort of shadow bank. Money laundering is certainly a big part of it." She tipped her head at Sampford. "But they also do more common tasks. Trade finance, commercial lending, investment services. Everything you could get from Citigroup or Chase, but without all the bothersome regulation and oversight."

"They want to be the Medici to the Florentine princes, so to speak," said Norcross.

"Yes. You know, the prosecutor said exactly the same thing?"

"So what does this all have to do with Blindside?"

"Ah." Cathryn waited while a young man with extensive piercings and a bandanna tied crosswise over his scalp picked up their dishes. "Teixeira was right about Ding, the fugitive he'd been chasing. Ding was just a thug, a killer with gang tattoos and a long record of violence. Whoever shot him did us all a favor, frankly. But the other guy, Yu Xiaoxuan, he's much more interesting."

Norcross tilted his head to one side, waiting.

"He was one of their financial officers," Cathryn said with satisfaction. "Over at Wells Fargo he'd be called something like Vice President of Business Development. You can never be sure exactly what the power structure is, since the triads don't publish org charts, but Yu apparently reported directly to Zheng He, the Wo Han Mok's leader."

"A money guy."

"Yes." Cathryn stopped. "Unfortunately that's all we know. Their operations are as tricky as Enron—shell companies on top of shell companies, everything incorporated in offshore centers like Nauru and Bahrain, almost no documentation and what there is generally in Cantonese code. Maybe the Marshals have had better luck untangling it all, but I doubt it. You'd need two dozen forensic accountants working nonstop for a year."

"Hmm." Norcross fell silent, as several people sat down at the next table. They were dressed in tattered clothing and high-tops, unshaven and bleary, not saying much as they wearily pulled up their chairs and waited for menus. Musicians, clubhopping all night, thought Norcross.

Computer engineers, thought Sampford.

"What about the leader," said Norcross, "what's his name? Chung?"

"Zheng," said Cathryn, the pronunciation flowing naturally. "He's been in the U.S. for several months, mostly in northern California. He's not much to look at—I'll make sure you get a photo, we have some from a surveillance team—about sixty-five and short, doesn't smile much. He's tough. Worked his way up from street level on pure smarts." She finished her glass of water. "Well, he's a ruthless son of a bitch, too. Goes without saying."

"Why don't you just arrest him?"

"For what?" She shrugged. "Gangland's been trying. They turned a guy, a low-level enforcer, and ran him for half a year, but he never got close. Even more than most triads, they're just too careful."

"Half a year's not a long time," said Sampford.

Cathryn looked his way. "They knew he was a plant from the beginning. The last day, his body was dumped right in front of police headquarters downtown, with a large manila envelope taped to his chest. He'd been chopped. When the team opened the envelope they found a complete copy of their internal case file. Everything—handwritten notes, interview transcripts, computer printouts. God knows how they got it, but the point was clear."

"The internal police file?" said Norcross. "That must worry your people."

"I'll tell you, I'm glad I'm out," said Cathryn.

A moment passed, and Sampford asked, "Chopped?"

"With a cleaver, right?" Norcross looked at Cathryn, who nodded. "The traditional method."

Sampford had finished his meal, cleaning the plates down to the garnish, and after some deliberation ordered a piece of chocolate cream pie. Cathryn and Norcross watched him eat it.

"We should probably pay you more," Norcross said. "With the food bills you must have."

"Isn't the task force picking this one up?" He seemed genuinely surprised.

The diners at the next table had perked up with the

arrival of their coffee and began arguing about baseball. Norcross realized he had no idea who was in the playoffs.

"So Blindside probably had some sort of business connection to the Wo Han Mok," he said, turning back to their topic.

"The technology," said Sampford. "International finance is all online nowadays, and it's utterly dependent on encryption. Banks are using the most secure technology anywhere. Blindside's cracking ability could be hugely valuable—at least, to a sufficiently unethical competitor."

"Don't forget China itself," said Cathryn. "They'd love to get their hands on this, if it really works. And the triads are in deep with the mainland government."

"I guess I understand why those, ah, mysterious federal agencies are interested too." Norcross sighed. "Every rock we turn over, this case gets more complicated."

"So keep it simple," Cathryn said. "Three people did the shooting. We know who one of them is, and we've got suspicions about the kid, too. Catch them and we're almost done."

"The warrants are out nationwide," said Sampford. "It won't be long."

"Good," said Cathryn. "So let me know when you wrap it up."

NINETEEN

JUST AFTER TEN p.m., dusk settling into night and a gradual overcast obscuring the moon, Molly loitered warily at the end of a row of tightly packed houses on the downhill side of Bernal Heights. The neighborhood was quiet. No one in the streets, old cars above oil stains on the cracked driveways and the television's blue glow in most windows. The residents would be going off to jobs as health aides or construction workers or grocery clerks early in the morning. The block had been deserted since she and Jeb had arrived fifteen minutes earlier.

After leaving the bicycles in a shadowed corner, they split up, Jeb to the junction box and Molly to stand watch twenty yards away. The box sat behind a bus stop. Five-foot advertising posters on the shelter's lexan panels effectively walled Jeb off from the street, and the yard behind him was surrounded by an overgrown hedge that provided more shadow and cover. He crouched in the darkness, invisible to anyone more than five or ten feet away, shielding the glow of the laptop's screen with his jacket.

They had spent most of the afternoon looking for an access point Jeb could use.

"The problem is how fast they trace you, once a trip wire goes," he'd explained, outside the hardware store they'd stopped at just after one o'clock. "Six or seven years ago we could have checked into a cheap hotel and jacked in through the table phone, but not anymore. Pay phones are out, too, at least in the city. It's easy to get at the wires—the base on most PacBell phones is only secured with a pair of plain hex bolts—but they have all sorts of AI software in the central offices scanning for suspicious line activity."

"You still have Darren's cellphone, don't you? Can't you just plug the modem into it?"

"In theory. I've never had it work all that well, the connection is always slow and crummy. Not to mention it makes it that much easier to track us down. Someone else's phone is always best. What we need is a terminal block, a bank of thirty or forty lines."

He showed Molly an example, a low green box bolted to the sidewalk alongside an apartment building, corrosion stains running down the side and an old American Telephone and Telegraph logo cast into the metal. "This would be good, except it's completely exposed, and I'm going to need, well, maybe as much as a few hours."

He packed up the tools he'd just purchased: two cheap screwdrivers, a 7/16 hex driver and a 3/8 boxend, a mini-maglite, a pair of high-impedance headphones, several alligator clips, and a Leatherman multi-tool. The last item had cost twice as much as everything else together.

"A lineman's handset would be nice," he said. "And a pocket dialer, and a ceramic recorder, and what the hell, a wireless transceiver, so we could sit in comfort fifty feet away. But this will do."

"So now what? We just ride around until you find the right spot?"

Jeb settled his helmet. "Good thing it's a nice day," he said.

In fact, the bicycles turned out to be perfect cover, in large part because the weather was so pleasant: seventy degrees and a light breeze, bright sun in a cloudless sky. The streets were filled with Sunday afternoon recreational cyclists; Jeb and Molly were only two more, unidentifiable in their shorts and mirrored sunglasses. They rode through the city's neighborhoods, Jeb scanning the sidewalks and evidently tireless in the saddle, Molly slowly becoming sore from the unfamiliar and uncomfortable seat. They stopped occasionally to rest, in parking lots mostly empty on the weekend, eating plain rolls and peanut butter Jeb bought at a mini-mart in the Mission. He seemed confident that he would not be recognized, beardless under the helmet, and Molly just warned him to say as little as possible.

It was past five when they found the can on Bernal Hill, so well concealed that Jeb missed it entirely. Molly only noticed it because she'd stopped to secure the duffel back onto the rack, where it had rattled loose.

"Perfect," said Jeb, stooping to check more closely. "Now we just need to identify some lines."

They circled the two blocks around the junction box, and found three houses that seemed likely. Two had several newspapers tossed on their stoops; at the third, plastic garbage bags under the side door's eave had clearly missed the last pickup day, one having torn open, spilling out a sheaf of rain-thickened magazines.

"How do you get the phone numbers?" Molly asked. "An online directory?"

"That would work," said Jeb, "but why bother?" He stopped at a pay phone several blocks away, outside a shuttered convenience store on Cortland, and simply dialed directory assistance, giving the names and addresses he'd noted from the mailboxes.

"You haven't been writing anything down," Molly observed when he'd finished.

"No. Safer to keep it in my head."

"You remember all those? Just like that?"

He paused, shifting the bag on his back and straddling the bike's frame. "When I was in Ray Brook, I had

lots of time. Endless hours . . . I don't know if you can
imagine what it was like. One reason I was sitting there
was because the cops found all sorts of records, and not
just on my computer—bits of paper, printouts, notes. I
decided it would never happen again, and I taught myself some mnemonic systems. Parlor tricks, really, like
old showmen used." He hesitated. "Read me a string of
numbers, or names, or cities—whatever. Go slow, and I
can hold fifty or sixty."

Molly stared at him. "Really?"

"It's just a skill. Practice is the main thing." He
shrugged. "How many pushups do you do every day?"

"Two hundred," she answered automatically, then,
"How did you know that?"

"Just guessing." He stepped into the pedals. "We can
wait over by 24th Street Station. It won't be dark for a
few hours."

NOW, standing in the shadows near a broken streetlight,
Molly had effortlessly fallen back into sentry habits.
She remained motionless for ten-minute periods, then
moved quietly to keep her blood active, watching and
listening with equal alertness. Twice pedestrians had
passed by, and each time Molly noticed early enough
that she simply started walking herself, ahead of them,
warning Jeb in a soft voice and circling the block back
to her post while he faded into the hedge. She was most
concerned about dogs, although she hadn't mentioned
this to him, but after a brief barking nearby none had
appeared.

The house containing the phone line Jeb was hijacking was visible from her position, and Molly regularly
cycled her gaze that way, in case the owners returned
unexpectedly. So she was not entirely surprised when a
car drove up to it, two blocks away. But just as she realized that it had stopped on the street, not turning into the
short driveway, another pulled in just behind, this one a
large SUV with fog lights under the bumper. Suddenly
alert, she watched as several doors opened and a half

dozen men spilled out. Light glinted dully from objects in their hands.

Molly immediately slipped up the sidewalk, keeping to the shadows as much as possible, struggling not to run.

"Shut it down!" she said urgently, her voice barely loud enough to interrupt his concentration. "Trouble."

"What?" But he quickly closed the laptop, yanking free the wireclips and sliding the can's large cover noiselessly back into place.

"Forget the bolts," Molly whispered, and he nodded, stuffing the laptop and tools into his bag and looping it over his shoulder one-handed as they retreated back toward the bicycles.

At the corner they paused long enough to look back. A muffled crash came from the front of the house, just audible at a hundred yards, and several of the black figures disappeared silently inside. Two others went to the back. No lights came on inside, though quick, firefly-like flashes against the windows suggested they were using maglites similar to Jeb's.

"Not the owners," said Molly unnecessarily as they pulled the bikes out and moved them hastily down the street, just far enough to ensure they wouldn't be observed when they pushed off. "Not the police, either."

"And not the phone company." Jeb was thinking hard. "Down the street to Jarboe and left. The neighborhood's full of one-ways, we can be sure no one follows."

"What did you do, anyway?"

He just shook his head as they mounted, the bikes already in motion. "I thought I was being careful."

But Molly had stopped listening. "Shit."

"What?"

They were fifty feet from the end of the block and she'd noticed another black SUV parked at the left corner, sitting directly in front of a hydrant and poking into their street. Under the streetlight its heavily tinted side windows were opaque, but a dim figure in the driver's seat was visible through the windshield. The engine was idling.

"Don't stop, don't turn." Her whisper was rapid and tense. They were only seconds from the intersection. "Take the next block instead. Keep your head down."

Jeb immediately accelerated. They shot through the stop sign—just as the SUV's headlights came on, blinding them, and Molly caught an instant of crackling radio traffic through the driver's open window.

"You lead," she shouted and dropped back, hearing the SUV screech into the road behind them. Jeb went another two hundred yards before finally hanging left, their pursuers only car lengths behind. Molly hit a pothole and briefly lost control, veering and sideslipping, her breath short from adrenaline. They were rocketing down the dark, empty street, the rows of small houses silent to either side, moving dangerously fast for mountain bikes at night but far too slow to outrun a vehicle. For an instant Molly was in another frantic, jolting firefight, tracer rounds and mines exploding as her mind flashed back.

With no warning Jeb yanked his bike right and disappeared into a narrow alley running behind a series of crowded bungalows. Caught by surprise Molly almost overshot, braking hard and just swinging in as she sideswiped a plastic garbage can. The SUV locked its wheels and a long squeal of tires cut the night silence before it skidded to a stop, reversed and roared into the alley after them. Cats yowled nearby.

"They'll be calling backup," Molly shouted.

On the alley's rough paving, cluttered with trash cans, children's bicycles, boxes and other junk, they managed to stay about thirty yards in front of the SUV. A passenger-side spotlight held them jerkily in its beam. The alley hit a cross street and without stopping Jeb continued straight across the blacktop and into the next back lane. A moment later, Molly now alongside on his left, the SUV's lights illuminated the narrow stretch before them, bouncing around as the vehicle slammed over potholes and debris.

"Jeb!"

In front of them, two seconds from impact, the alley was blocked by a small pickup parked right in the lane, its tailgate missing and one tire flat. It was facing away from them, snug against a cinder block wall. On its left was a space perhaps a yard wide. With barely time to react Molly steered for the gap, which would just accommodate her bike, and her whole consciousness anticipated a crash as Jeb ran smack into the pickup's rear.

But instead he braked once, cutting his speed slightly, and while Molly flashed past the truck's left he aimed straight on. At the last possible instant he jerked the handlebars up as hard as he could, immediately curling forward and pulling his feet in the clips so the rear tire caught air a half second later. Airborne, he sailed into the pickup's bed, bounced once and repeated the sequence, so that he hopped onto the cab's roof and slid down the windshield and off the hood with hardly any loss of forward speed. He crunched onto the road just behind Molly, shoving his feet down to get the rear wheel to ground first, still upright. She was already coming to a panic stop, looking around in astonishment, and Jeb coasted past her, his momentum finally diminishing.

The SUV braked but too late and slammed into the back of the pickup in a shattering crash, knocking it forward several yards. Lights came on in houses up and down the alley.

"Keep going!" Jeb yelled, and Molly pulled herself together enough to shove off again. A few seconds later they were out of the alley, on a one-way street, riding fast against the direction of traffic. No other vehicles appeared. They hooked a rapid series of turns, Jeb choosing their way with increasing confidence, and after ten minutes the chance of further pursuit had disappeared.

"My God," said Molly, as they rode at a reduced cadence, catching their breath. "How did you do that?"

Jeb didn't bother with false modesty. "I used to

race—cyclocross, and off-road mountain bike. I've bunnyhopped boulders worse than that." He'd even managed to hold onto his bag, which was still in place over
his shoulder.

They crossed Dolores on the Miguel Street bridge
and rode west, keeping to quiet backstreets.

"You're full of surprises," said Molly.

TWENTY

HALF AN HOUR later they found a dark, abandoned supermarket off Portola, not far from Glen Canyon Park. The store had been closed for some time, the plywood nailed over its windows covered with graffiti and weeds growing up through cracked paving. Trash and broken glass littered the concrete loading dock in the rear, which clearly served as a hangout for local teenagers. Near midnight Sunday, however, the spot was deserted. They sat in the shadows beside an empty plastic dumpster, listening to an occasional car drive past on the road out front.

"I didn't get far," said Jeb, trying to find a comfortable position on the concrete. "Some of the references I found last night gave me email addresses at Dunshire, and that led me to their server. I had to download some cracking tools—NMAP for port scanning, NetCat, L0phtCrack, the basics. That took most of the first hour, and then I started running FIN scans against the site. They're all automatic, so I began working on the mail server, pinging it for behavioral information. The scans didn't get anywhere, which means they pay attention to security—in fact, the whole site seemed particularly well-hardened."

"No surprise, if they're really NSA," said Molly. She leaned against the dumpster, which shifted slightly, grating across the gravel.

"Yeah." He paused. "I'm guessing it was the scans that tipped them off. The scripts are sophisticated, and awfully easy to use, compared to back when I was doing this stuff. I used to write just about all my own code, but now you just pull it down from the net, type in an address, and let it run." He shook his head. "Easy. But of course the other side has access to the exact same attacks, so if they're smart, they know what to expect, and they put in their alarms."

"Even so, the response was incredibly fast." Molly watched the shadowed men crash the house again, searching her memory for clues. "They must have had the team fully prepared and waiting, just in case."

"But how would they know we'd try to hack Dunshire?"

"I don't think they did. They were waiting for any kind of a hint, just some indication of where we were. Either one of us, probably." She thought about that. "They might not know we're together."

"The police were at Darren's, and they probably figured out we'd both been staying there," said Jeb.

"That wasn't police chasing us just now."

They were silent for a while. A heavy truck accelerated up a grade nearby, racketing echoes trailing from its poorly muffled diesel.

"It wasn't a complete waste of time," Jeb said finally. Molly thought he might have been willing himself to find an optimistic angle. "The one thing I discovered is that their local network is probably running on 802.11g wireless. Second-generation wi-fi."

"What does that mean?"

"It's an opening." Jeb leaned back and lay down, placing his helmet under his head. "There are some well-known vulnerabilities, like Berkeley's, and I'm sure they're closed, but the protocol is fundamentally easier to access since it doesn't run on dedicated cable.

All you need is a wireless modem and you've at least found the keyhole."

"And they can't track you down that way, right?" Molly watched his eyes, which were closed. "No actual wire connection."

"Well, they can triangulate, but it would be harder."

"So get the modem and we'll try again."

Jeb opened his eyes. "I'd have to be within a hundred feet of the server. In Foxton Cove."

"Oh." Molly felt stupid. "Of course."

They shared the last of the bread and peanut butter, scraping the jar clean with a plastic knife.

"One other thing," said Jeb. "Almost the entire laptop is in Chinese, like I figured, but there are a few applications and files in English. Or in code I can understand, anyway. I got interested in one because it was wrapped in some pretty powerful encryption."

"But you were able to look at it?"

"It was open to local access, to anyone with administrator privileges. Careless of the owner to set it up that way. Or lazy. Doesn't matter, I suppose." He ran his thumb up and down the knife blade, getting the last peanut butter. "It's a bank authorization token."

"What does that mean?"

"It provides software-mediated online authentication to a bank account somewhere."

Molly took a moment to translate that. "So what are we doing here? Let's go download some money!"

"Can't." He finally put down the knife. "The bank name isn't included in the token. One last bit of security, perhaps. It's useless unless we know where the account is."

"Oh." She thought. "Is it a Chinese bank?"

"Probably not, since the interface was entirely written in English, but there's no way to be certain."

"So it does us no good."

Jeb shrugged. "Just another data point."

After their meal Molly scouted up some cardboard and broken styrofoam from a pile of debris against the retaining wall. When she returned Jeb was examining the interior of the plastic dumpster, which was tipped over and about eight feet on a side.

"It's fairly clean," he said. "I'm not sure it ever held any trash, and it looks like kids have been using it for a rain shelter." He swept out a pile of cigarette butts.

"I've slept in rougher hides," said Molly.

"It's like camping," said Jeb, still making an effort to be cheerful. "I guess."

They bundled up, putting on the few extra articles of clothing they'd brought. The dumpster smelled of smoke and beer, but even open on one side it was slightly warmer than on the dock, and the styrofoam insulated them from the ground. Molly was acutely aware of Jeb's slow breathing, his arm and leg a few inches away.

"We have to get out of San Francisco," she said.

"No kidding." Jeb lay with arms crossed, his head propped up on a half-squashed shoebox.

"You were right." She sighed. "This area is radioactive. We can't run forever, but we have to find someplace secure to regroup."

"We're not going to get far. No car, no money, hardly any clothes even. At the moment we're just lucky it's not raining."

"We can try Eileen."

"But they're on to her. They staked out her apartment."

"Not at home. At the airport mail center."

Jeb didn't follow. "What can she do, lend us a postal van?"

"They have mail-cargo planes flying out every night. Eileen told me that sometimes employees deadhead. It's against the rules, but it happens. She'll know how we can sneak on."

Jeb thought about it. "The police will be watching the terminals."

"The USPS has its own hangar—a warehouse, really. I don't think they'll be able to cover every single freight facility. We can slip in tomorrow night, when it's dark."

"Well." He paused. "I guess I can't see anywhere else to go."

"I'll call Eileen when she goes in tomorrow. In the afternoon, come to think of it—she said she's starting a second-shift rotation." Molly closed her eyes. "One flight, a few hours, we can be halfway across the country."

They lay without talking, the styrofoam squeaking noisily when they shifted their weight, listening to cars passing with decreasing frequency as the night grew later. The air was uncomfortably cool and dank. Molly curled on her side.

"At least in the army they gave us ponchos to wrap up in," she muttered. They were just about leaning against each other.

A half hour later Jeb got up, joints creaking, and crawled out of the dumpster. Molly heard his footsteps around the corner of the building, and then, faintly, the sound of him relieving himself against the wall.

"Going to be a long night," he muttered when he returned.

They adjusted the styrofoam again, and pulled their clothing tight. Sleep remained elusive.

"So who was Lance?" Jeb asked.

"What?" Molly looked over at his face, but it was invisible in the shadows. "Who told you . . ." She paused. "Eileen, huh."

"While you were getting your bike."

"What'd she say?"

"Um." Jeb hesitated. "Not much, just . . ." His voice trailed away.

"Yeah?"

" 'You better not be as much of jerk as Lance was.' " He sounded embarrassed.

After a moment, Molly laughed.

"So," said Jeb hesitantly, "what happened?"

"Lance." Molly called him up in her mind's eye: six-foot-five, linebacker's build, aw-shucks handsome, and polite as all hell, except after about three beers. "He and I kept house for a while. While I was still in the service."

"Another soldier?"

"No. That never works. He was a civilian, wanted to be a policeman." In fact, Lance had passed the intake exam, barely, but he kept missing out when the list was called every six months. Which he blamed on affirmative action, naturally. In the meantime, waiting around, he worked as a Tae Kwon Do instructor occasionally, and as a bouncer the rest of the time. "We lasted two years, almost."

"Uh-huh." Jeb waited.

"It's not easy, keeping a relationship going when you're spending half your time overseas. Him working the door at a strip club, that didn't help either." But it wasn't the real problem, of course. "The thing is . . ." Molly paused, and then, surprising herself, she began to explain what she'd figured out only after long and painful reflection. "You see, most men, they're not sure how to deal with me. I mean, not just being in the army, but being drop-certified, and choosing a tactical specialty—it's not like they were afraid of me, but somehow . . ."

"Sure," said Jeb. "You're just better at guy stuff than they are. Lots better. And so what does that make them?"

"Yeah." Molly looked at the dark blur that was his face. He'd gone straight to the heart of the matter, like it was the most obvious thing in the world. "Well, Lance didn't think about it that way. For one thing, he *was* bigger and stronger and tougher. But mostly, he was so wrapped up in himself that it didn't occur to him to worry about me."

"Ah." Jeb leaned up on one elbow. "He sounds like a keeper, all right."

"In hindsight," Molly said, "I'm just embarrassed it took me so long to see where I stood."

After a minute, when she didn't say anything else, Jeb cleared his throat and asked, "And, so, like, how did you break up?"

Molly bit her lip. "Okay," she said. "I'm not proud of what happened." No reaction; he just waited. "It was when I came back from Afghanistan. I was on base assignment at Bragg, killing time at a desk while they figured out what to do with me. Lance got all hinky, because he thought I was going to get court-martialed, and he was convinced that living with a convict would knock him off the intake list for good. Plus he said I couldn't use his truck, which was a problem since I didn't have a car."

She remembered how inconvenient it had been, trying to catch the shuttle around Fayetteville, usually ending up walking miles in the humid North Carolina summer heat. "He loved that truck, too . . . anyway, one day I'm at the apartment, alone, and this woman calls up, wondering if I'd found her handbag. I ask who she is, and it turns out Lance told her I'm his *sister,* and golly she sure does need that purse back because it has her work clothes in it. I say, work clothes? And she starts to get snippy, tells me I've no right, just who do I think I am?"

"I can see where this is going." Jeb sounded amused.

"She was a stripper at the club Lance was bouncing at," Molly said. "I was so naive, or blind, or something, I just didn't get it, not until I found her purse where she said she left it, in the cab of his truck. Her 'work clothes' were, well, you can imagine—some strings and sequins and a tiny bit of fabric. Of course, that wasn't what she was all worried about. There was also this little packet of white powder."

She listened to a siren in the distance. "I'm not sure who I was more mad at—her or Lance. But I was sitting in his truck, which he'd ordered me to stay out of, so a minute later I was driving it down the street. After a mile I threw the G-string out the window, and I was wondering how I could totally wreck the truck without getting hurt. But then I saw a police car parked in front of a donut shop."

"You turned him in for the drugs."

"Sort of." She couldn't help it—she started to smile. "The cruiser was parked nose against the wall, so I put the truck right up against it, bumper to bumper. And when I got out, I realized they couldn't see me from inside, so I deflated one of the truck tires. Just to make sure. I left the dope on the seat."

Jeb laughed softly. "What happened to him?"

"I truly don't know." Molly shrugged. "He was still in jail that evening when I moved my stuff out. I got my discharge a few days later, and I left town. Never saw him again."

They fell quiet. The dumpster creaked. Another siren went by, following the first, fading away.

"I thought it was my fault," she said eventually, quietly. "I still do, sometimes."

"Uh-huh." Jeb nodded in the dark. "He might have *acted* like a thoughtless, conniving, abusive weasel— but only because you drove him to it."

"It sounds dumb when you say it."

"Nope." Jeb leaned back onto his shoebox. "Not at all."

Later he said, "When you meet a guy, my advice is, don't tell him you put your last boyfriend into jail."

"Somehow, after these last couple of days, working on relationship issues isn't at the top of my worry list."

They stopped talking. After a few minutes, Jeb reached out and let his hand rest on her shoulder. For comfort? more?—she had no idea, but she held his arm and snuggled in, tucking her head against his chest. They curled up and lay in silence, listening to the wind.

TWENTY-ONE

THE NIGHT'S FOG was dissipating, leaving a high, thin overcast, as Sampford drove carefully down Grant on Monday morning. The heart of Chinatown was already crowded, with small, battered delivery trucks double-parked everywhere and slow-moving traffic choking the roads and air. Under the neon thicket of Chinese signs, two or three stories high, throngs meandered past: men pushing handtrucks stacked with cardboard crates; elderly women returning from Falun Gong in the park; schoolchildren with their mothers; occasional toughs in leather jackets or shirts neatly buttoned down.

"Because of the gang tattoos," said Sampford, who was providing running commentary. "They're careful not to show off."

Norcross grunted, sipping from the overpriced cup of cappuccino he'd gotten when Sampford insisted on stopping at a coffeeshop near the federal building. The black suit he'd worn for the policeman's funeral no longer fit well, loose at his waist and tight across the shoulders. "Different ethic."

"You still know who they are, though. The sunglasses are a clue."

"Over there." Norcross had been scanning the building numbers, and as they passed a nondescript three-story with an unmarked door, he looked carefully away. "Don't stop."

Sampford drove around the corner and pulled into a space in front of a Golden Mountain Bank branch. The asphalt had been painted in orange zebra stripes, and a large sign in Chinese characters was posted above another, in English, reading "No Parking Ever! Tow Truck On Call Two Blocks Away! $135 Towing Fee!"

"You better stay here," said Norcross. "Explain to the tow truck driver."

Sampford gave him a look and flipped over a placard on the dash, the FBI's seal and On Official Business printed in large black letters. He reached behind his hip, obviously checking his handgun, and started to open the door.

"Before you get out of the car." Norcross was still sitting, holding his cappuccino. "Think about what Cathryn was saying yesterday. Once the triads know you're interested, they'll investigate you down to your underwear and your preschool graduation certificate. They're ruthless. They hold a grudge for a very long time. There's no reason for us both to end up in their sights."

Sampford just shrugged, glancing over as his small smile started. "Cathryn?"

"Captain Birney." Norcross appeared unembarrassed. "You can call me Tommy, if you like."

"Yes, sir." Sampford's grin was now open.

"Fine." Norcross sighed. "I can't imagine anyone's going to miss you."

They locked the car and walked back, Norcross tossing his empty coffee cup into a trash basket outside a shop with roasted duck carcasses hanging in the window. At the building's entrance Sampford finally noticed a small plaque mounted on the door frame. The brass was polished to a sheen, and under five Chinese characters neat lettering spelled out Wo Han Cooperative Society.

Inside they ascended a dark wooden staircase and passed through a paneled doorway into an office overlooking the avenue. Heavy furniture of dark, stained wood sat empty in the small reception area, but a woman looked up at them from behind a modern desk. The society's name was repeated in red characters on the wall above her. The room's only other adornment was a gaudy promotional calendar from an industrial supply company, tacked up underneath, with a large photo of a dragon parade. Norcross thought he smelled incense, faintly. He scanned the room quickly but much more thoroughly than his idle glance suggested, and thought to himself: the sprinkler.

"Good morning." The woman was in her early twenties and blonde, her accent pure southern California.

"Special Agent Norcross, FBI."

"I'm Paul Sampford." They displayed their IDs, Sampford adding a dazzling smile. Norcross glanced at him sideways.

The receptionist was unfazed. "Yes, gentlemen?" Visits from law enforcement personnel were no doubt far from uncommon.

"We were hoping we might—" Norcross broke off, as if he'd just thought of something. "Say, where's the camera?"

She frowned, puzzled, but not before her eyes had flickered involuntarily to a fire sprinkler set unobtrusively in the corner of the ceiling. "I'm sorry?"

"Never mind." Norcross looked up at the sprinkler for a long moment before returning his attention to her. "I just wanted to introduce myself. We're investigating the murder of, among others, two Wo Han Mok associates in the Potrero this weekend—Ding Yihui and Yu Xiaoxuan." Cathryn had coached him in the pronunciation, and he said the names naturally.

"Oh, yes?"

"They were members here, of course."

"They don't sound familiar, I'm afraid."

Norcross continued, "We'll probably be wanting to talk to Zheng He soon."

The receptionist made a show of looking through a printed list of phone numbers. "I'm terribly sorry, there's no one by that name in our directory."

"Ah." He waited, and she waited, and finally Norcross just said, "You might pass the message on. Someone will know him."

"Maybe they will." Her smile was sunny.

He asked a few more questions, with no result, and they left politely. On the street outside Sampford said, "So what was that about?"

"Just letting them know who we are. It'll be easier this way. When we come back, they'll have done their research, maybe we can skip some of the preliminaries."

"Why bother? We could just demand to talk to the guy. The clock's running, remember?"

"We don't know where he is." Pointing out the obvious.

"The gangland unit probably has an idea. That's what they're supposed to be doing."

"Maybe. But he's not a suspect. The Wo Han Mok are more like the victims, so far."

"Gee, I forgot." They turned the corner to find a tow truck backing up to their car. "Hey!" Sampford ran up to the driver, pulling out his ID, and Norcross watched as an argument ensued. When it ended, a small crowd had surrounded the car and the truck, spilling out into the road; many of the onlookers seemed disappointed when the tow operator finally drove angrily off without the sedan, punching the accelerator to cough a cloud of unpleasant exhaust in their faces. The onlookers dispersed without haste, several staring intently at the agents as they got into their car and drove slowly away through the crowd.

"Smooth," muttered Sampford. "All of Chinatown knows who we are now."

"Wasn't that the point?" Norcross relaxed in the passenger seat. "So, are you going to ask her out? The receptionist, I mean—when we come back."

TWENTY-TWO

IF JEB HADN'T learned patience the hard way, staring at light green concrete for three years, he might not have lasted the long daylight hours before leaving for the airport. Molly claimed to be indifferent to the discomfort, having endured worse in the military, but Jeb noticed that her temper shortened as the hours dragged on.

They'd gotten up weary, having been unable to sleep after the temperature dropped during the misty eternity before dawn. For breakfast Molly found some ancient hard candy in the bicycle toolkit. A church down the street, locked and empty on Monday morning, had a garden hose around back and Jeb was able to fill their water bottles.

"I wish we could call Eileen." He was truing his bicycle's front wheel, spinning it, watching the rim ripple, deftly loosening and tightening its spokes in quarter-turns. "She's on second shift, right? She could swing by on her way over, pick us up."

"Her line's probably being monitored. They don't even need warrants for that, anymore."

"Really?"

"But the phones at her job should be okay. We'll call before we ride over."

After Jeb finished overhauling both bikes he tried to doze in the shade of the dilapidated loading dock. Molly determined that a small area behind the dumpster was shielded from view on all sides, and after sweeping out the broken glass and debris, she began a series of stretches and exercises. He listened to her practice, silent but for thuds as her feet struck the wall and ground. The day crawled on.

Midafternoon found them sitting wearily on the styrofoam, ravenously hungry. The Swiss Family Robinson aspect of their situation had long since palled. Jeb rubbed his jaw, noticing stubble.

"Just as well," said Molly. "You can grow it back different, change your look."

"That'll take days." His stomach rumbled loudly. "By the way, we need money. We get off the plane in some other city, we still have to find food, a place to stay, more clothes."

"I know."

"You have a mailbox key, right? Why don't we open one up somewhere and swipe some credit card data? We might even find some bank statements, get the account numbers."

"Good idea." Her voice was testy. "Seems like a lot of trouble, though—maybe we should just steal someone's wallet. Or better yet, mug some little kid and grab his lunch money." But her frown faded quickly. "We're not criminals just because everyone *thinks* we are."

"Oh, right."

They watched a seagull poking at rubbish in the deserted parking lot.

"Sorry." Molly sighed. "I probably shouldn't say this, but I'm not sure about anything, at all."

"Well, me neither."

"Going to the airport could be the worst idea possible."

"It's not like we have options."

She shook her head. "There may be undercover cops

posted at every terminal. We might get on the plane, be found out, and land to face a full paramilitary hijacking response. What the hell, they could decide to blow the plane out of the air."

He looked at her. "You're really cheering me up."

A breeze gusted, scattering some scraps of paper and disturbing the gull. Jeb thought about all the ways they could screw up, how just about anything could go wrong.

On the other hand, here they were, still in one piece, warm in the October sunshine. The gull had noticed them and wandered closer, looking for a handout. Molly made a shooing gesture and it lazily flapped away.

"I think we'll be all right," she said. "But I'm about ready to catch and eat that seagull."

THE San Francisco Airport Mail Center was a squat, ugly hangar connected to a warehouse, several hundred yards beyond a parking garage outside the South Passenger Terminal. A broad apron between the access road and the AMC was filled with postal vans, LLVs and tractor trailers, most dark and quiet under the buzzing sodium lamps. Two of the bays were still lit and active. On the hangar side of the facility, a windowless L-1011 with USPS markings was being fueled, while two heavy conveyors steadily moved palletized mail into the cargo hold. Three smaller jets waited further out on the tarmac, just inside the blue taxiway lights. The penetrating smell of jet fuel hung in the stagnant air, and every few minutes a plane roared down the runway, momentarily bringing to a halt all conversations nearby.

Molly stood restlessly at the window of a small, paper-strewn office, one of several in a row at the rear of the warehouse, fifteen feet above the main floor. She could see part of the truck yard and an elevated walkway that connected the facility to the parking garage. Unlike the tube-like corridor running between the garage and the passenger terminal, the AMC's pedestrian bridge was bare concrete and open to the elements, but it was lit by regularly spaced lamps and had been deserted for the ten minutes since Molly started watching.

"I'm feeling trapped and exposed, at the same time." Jeb sat on a rickety wooden chair near the door. The offices overlooked the long interior of the main floor: sorting and assembly lines, huge racks for parcels, large conveyors ramping up and down, with a maze of box slides and drop points at one end and shuttle carts standing around everywhere. The facility was brightly lit down its entire two-hundred-yard length, but no employees were visible. "Where is everyone, anyway?"

"The planes are almost loaded. Eileen says they usually have a lull until the incoming flights begin to arrive around eleven."

Jeb, nervous, wasn't paying attention to the conversation. "I wish we could have hidden the bikes better." They were tucked into the end of the walkway running along the office-fronts, obvious to anyone walking up the stairs from the main floor. Not that a single person had, ever since Eileen told them to wait and disappeared, forty-five minutes earlier.

"It doesn't matter. They could belong to anyone."

"When is she coming back, anyhow?"

Molly glanced at Jeb's worried face and looked back out again. "You heard what she said. She'll let us know when the plane is ready."

Eileen had asked no questions when Molly called from a pay phone, catching her just going on the clock. She met them at a seldom-used side door, dark and hidden at night under the shadow of a huge air conditioning compressor. She was wearing a stained jumpsuit with a USPS eagle on the shoulder and scuffed, steel-toed boots.

"You are in so much trouble," was her only comment about their situation. Molly just shrugged, and Eileen led them to the office where they now sat.

"We have one plane to Chicago and one to Newark," she said. "The rest are just hops to Mather up in Sacramento."

"Whichever is leaving soonest," said Molly. "All we need is distance."

"Newark. It'll take another hour to finish the lading." She was chewing her lower lip. "I think I can sneak you into the cargo area before we close the rear doors. It won't be comfortable—grab some mail sacks on the way out, to sit on."

"The hold's pressurized, isn't it?"

"Oh, sure. Not heated, though. People hitch rides back there now and then, but they usually bring their own pads."

"We'll manage."

Eileen looked like she wanted to say more, but just nodded. "I'll call you on . . . line two, let's say." She pushed aside some folders on the desk to reveal an old four-button phone, the handpiece chipped and worn from long use. "I'll probably just tell you to come down. Meet me at the double doors labeled Three, over there." She clasped Molly's shoulder and disappeared down the stairs.

Molly turned off the light and moved back to the window to watch the truck lot. The airport's newly constructed monorail hummed past every ten minutes, the glassed compartments mostly empty. Sometimes it carried no people whatsoever, since the controls were fully automated and it had no driver. The concrete passenger bridge to the monolithic garage remained deserted as well, and in the parking lot the trucks were dark, locked up for the night. The only movement she saw was an occasional taxi or shuttle bus on the access road, which ran underneath the elevated monorail track. The emptiness began to seem spooky.

DESPITE her vigilance it was Jeb who noticed the encirclement first. He'd slipped out and walked to the corner, by the bikes, where the wooden stairs led down. The entire facility was visible, quiet and still under the industrial fluorescents hanging from the ceiling thirty feet overhead. At the far end some handlers in USPS overalls had been shifting pallets and large mail sacks onto the loading conveyors, but they'd finished and wandered away fifteen minutes earlier. The floor was empty of people.

Just beyond the head of the stairs a narrow catwalk began, three feet wide and running the entire length of the facility, suspended amid ductwork and machinery for the beam cranes. It ended in the far corner, above a locked, chain-link cage. Near the catwalk's terminus, a raised platform served as a second-level loading bay, and past scattered crates Jeb could see exterior lights through the open freight doors.

He was staring at this distant illumination, his attention caught by an unexpected glare—of headlights? a spotlight?—when he heard the sputter of a motorcycle, quickly shut down, and a muffled metal-on-metal clanging. Fear stabbed his gut, and he glanced around, then ran silently to the other end of the row of offices, to a darkened conference room whose outer windows overlooked the far side of the building. In a moment he was back at Molly's door, his voice cracking in an agitated whisper.

"Police!" He swung one arm behind him. "All around the building—I saw two vans and a bunch of cars, and men running everywhere!"

"Shit." Even as she spoke Molly saw the black-armored figures appear in the truck lot below her. She recognized the tactical gear—ski masks and submachine guns, boots and LBE web harnesses. "It's a siege."

The lights abruptly went out, along with HVAC and the building systems. They could hear low engine noise and a brief shouting from outside. The interior was now eerily dark, lit only by the occasional emergency lamps, which cast inadequate circles of weak blue light.

"Eileen," said Molly, her voice cold. "They got to her somehow."

"We have to get out of here," said Jeb urgently.

Molly was motionless for another moment, struggling to deal with the situation. "No," she said slowly.

"There's a protocol. They won't just attack, they'll open negotiations first."

But even before she finished speaking, a crash sounded from the truck bays, followed by a shattering of glass and several sharp pops as CS gas canisters detonated on the floor. Jeb panicked and started to run for the stairs. Molly grabbed his arm and held him still, her hand a vise.

"Wait!" Her voice was fierce, but she wasn't looking at him. "Where are they coming in?" She waited several seconds, listening. "Okay, they're on both sides and"—another crash sounded below them—"fuck, the lower offices. They know just where we are." She let him go and ran for the corner. "The bikes—our only chance."

She pulled Jeb's out and shoved it at him. "The catwalk!" Without thinking he boarded the bike and jumped to the wobbly metal grating, head lowered in a sprint tuck, accelerating into the darkness, Molly behind him a moment later.

Her eyes started to tear from the gas, but as they rocketed down the catwalk above the truck bays they outdistanced the worst of it. Molly risked a glance below, through the grating, and glimpsed a half dozen tacticals running along the floor, inhuman in their gas masks and body armor. Without thinking she jabbed her chin down, seeking the throat mike they always used in SRT maneuvers, then remembered she wasn't on a team anymore.

Jeb followed the catwalk as it turned out over the main floor, now suspended ten feet below the ceiling by thin cables, a single handrail the only protection from the twenty-foot drop. Molly fell back, unable to keep up with his sprint. Barely thirty seconds had passed since the SWAT team made its entry, and a few of the quicker sharpshooters had now realized where they were. Molly saw the red dots of laser sights dancing on the girders. Bullets spanged off metal around them.

Thirty feet ahead of Molly, Jeb reached the end of the catwalk. The lighting was poor, and he disappeared with a strangled cry into the looming shadows and darkness.

Molly braked hard, briefly locking the rear wheel and for one terrifying instant skidding almost off the edge of the swaying catwalk, but she regained control and shuddered to a stop just before its terminus.

"There's a drop!" he yelled.

A three-foot ladder descended from the catwalk to the cargo area's floor, and Jeb had flown over it, saved only by the instincts of long practice—at the last possible moment he jabbed a pedal kick, got the front wheel up and landed a perfect dropoff, both wheels hitting simultaneously. But he had immediately collided with a pallet lying invisibly on the dark floor and lost control, slamming into the ground while the bike skidded forward.

Molly dismounted, shoved her bike over the drop in a loud crash and jumped down to reboard just as Jeb was pulling his upright. Somehow he'd held onto his courier bag.

"The pedestrian bridge," said Molly, as they reached the freight door and looked through. An elevated truck ramp spiraled up from the access road fifty yards away; in the other direction a raised plaza formed an exposed patio in front of the facility's main entrance. The bridge stretched across the access road to the parking garage, a hundred yards distant. Jeb was gasping, less from exertion than adrenaline.

"Go! Go!" Molly slapped him roughly on the shoulder, and they pushed off.

A sudden racket echoed in the concrete canyon of the truck ramp, and Molly glanced back to see a motorcycle appear at the end of the pad, a man in black kevlar sliding neatly through the last turn, in complete control of his bike. He paused when he saw them disappearing up the bridge, long enough for a second motorcycle to roar up beside him, and then the pair accelerated, following.

The bridge was simple concrete and four feet wide. On open ground the motorcycles could easily have caught up, but in the confined corridor they had to throttle back. Jeb and Molly were in a flat-out sprint, Jeb ahead again, and they still had a fifty-yard lead when they shot into the parking garage. Molly's shoulders were hunched involuntarily, even though she knew there was no way their pursuers could raise one hand from the handlebars to fire a gun at them.

The bridge ended alongside the garage stairwell, ten feet from a battered elevator. They were on the third floor, the spaces about half full, in a dank smell of oil and gas fumes. Molly jammed the brakes and slewed to a halt just past the stairwell, by a pair of large plastic trash barrels.

"Go left!" she yelled to Jeb, then turned without looking and, still straddling the bike, kicked at one of the trash barrels and skidded it back the way she'd come. It took a second to reach the entrance to the bridge, falling in front of the narrow walkway just as the first motorcycle arrived in a roar.

The rider lost control when his front wheel hit the barrel. Molly ducked the crashing jumble of chrome and metal and spurting gasoline that slid across the concrete floor. The motorcycle collided with a monstrous Ford SUV parked in a space twenty feet away and fireballed as its fuel spilled across the spark plugs. In the whoosh of sudden flames Molly saw the rider roll clear—only to be hit by the second motorcycle, which shot off the bridge at that moment, its operator clearly disoriented by the explosion.

She turned away and shoved off again, catching up to Jeb on the other side of the garage and pointing at the entrance to the pedestrian tubeway to the airport terminal. It was brightly lit and protected from the weather by clear plexiglass, broad enough for three luggage carts and curving gently away over the ground two stories below. He had paused to stare backwards at the flames and destruction.

"They'll catch us in a minute if we go out here," Molly said. "Our only chance is the terminals."

Jeb shook his head, muttered something incomprehensible, kicked his feet into the pedals and followed her into the tubeway. They shot past a shocked, elderly couple toiling along with their rollaways, and seconds later flew onto the main departures floor of South Terminal.

To their right a long row of airline desks marched down the vast space, protected by a maze of theater ropes but mostly empty this time of night. A few passengers waited in small clumps, their luggage piled nearby. At the far end of the expanse guards at a security checkpoint were idly passing a small number of people through. Every thirty feet an escalator descended to the baggage claim area.

Molly took this in with one glance, still moving fast, seeing startled faces turn and stare. She was twenty feet in front of Jeb, coasting rapidly down a corridor formed by the airline desks on one side and a row of benches and large potted plants on the other.

"Now what?" he called.

"Keep going!" Molly said, and a trio of Transportation Security Agency guards burst from an unmarked doorway, guns drawn and directly in her path.

She had no chance to react and simply rode straight into the closest of the men, lifting her arms at impact to protect her face and neck, and rolling off the bike as it slammed the guard aside and tumbled away. Shots exploded around her.

Molly fell directly into Jeb's path, and he was unable to evade—instead, he instinctively jerked the handlebars as he shifted his weight back, then forward, curling his forearms and pulling up the rear with his feet clipped in the pedals. As Molly hit the floor, crossways in front of him, he bunnyhopped cleanly over her, the rear tire barely grazing her shoulder as she rolled.

He landed, still moving at speed, and a second guard was in front of him, raising his handgun with two hands to aim straight at Jeb's face. Reacting without thought, Jeb slammed the front brake and the bike lifted up onto its front wheel and pivoted, the rear shooting around in a 180-degree arc. The tailwhip struck the guard's forearms, knocking the gun out of his hands and tumbling him to one side, and Jeb fell to the ground, finally having lost control.

Molly only glimpsed the maneuver as she rolled to her feet, still in motion from her own collision. She came off the floor just in front of the third guard, who was still gaping, and grabbed him front on, locking his arm and dislodging the pistol, then punched him with a short, savage strike to the sternum that left him choking and paralyzed on the floor.

The entire encounter lasted less than twenty seconds, but already other guards were appearing, and more were running from the checkpoint down the lobby.

"Down!" Molly pointed at the escalator in front of them and picked up her bike, boarding just as she coasted onto the moving stairs and trusting that Jeb would follow.

A college student in sweats and a baseball cap was the escalator's only rider, halfway down. "Get the fuck out of the way!" Molly screamed, and he looked up, saw her barreling toward him, and barely leapt aside, staring in amazement as Molly banged and bumped past. Jeb was right behind her. They bounced into the crowded baggage claim area, yelling, trying to clear a path.

Hundreds of weary passengers and heaps of baggage were clustered around the carousels. With little open room Molly had to slow down, though Jeb was able to maneuver more quickly, countersteering through jump turns, once sidehopping an astonished toddler who escaped his mother just in front of him. But after fifteen seconds Molly shouted, "Back up! We have to go back up!" and they turned toward a rising escalator.

She tried to pedal but didn't have Jeb's technique, so they took as long as a standing pedestrian to ascend the escalator. The maneuver had apparently caught their pursuers by surprise, for none were close when they appeared back on the departures level. Molly glanced at Jeb. Forty feet away another pair of guards had noticed them; on the roadway outside the baggage claim they heard sirens and heavy engines roaring up.

"Uh-oh." Jeb swung his head around, searching for escape.

"The monorail," Molly said, even before fully thinking it out, and they took off for the train's entranceway.

They arrived at the portal five seconds later, accelerating, with guards and even a couple of SWAT tacticals now converging on them from all directions. Not slowing, they flew through the short hallway, seeing a train stopped in front of them, waiting as a gaggle of Asian tourists finished boarding. Jeb turned his bike left, aiming for an empty car, and Molly followed. They slammed through with the warning buzzer sounding, just as the doors slid shut. With only seven feet to stop Jeb simply crashed into the car's inside wall, Molly doing the same an instant later.

They pulled themselves to their feet as the train slowly left the station, the autopilot unaware that a crowd of uniformed men with weapons was shouting from the platform. The Asian tourists in the next car were looking through the heavy glass windows, open-mouthed. One SWAT team member jogged alongside the accelerating train, pointing his submachine gun, but he didn't fire, and a few seconds later they were away from the terminal, moving smoothly along in the darkness above the access road.

"They'll be waiting for us at the next stop," Jeb said, and Molly saw that he was on the edge of losing control. "We're actually headed back toward the parking garage."

"There are other garages." She was intently studying the airport map posted above the doorframe. After a moment she looked out the window, down to the roadway below. A line of traffic was halted in front of them, waiting for a red light where an exit from 101 debarked traffic into the airport's roads—taxis and limousines, mostly, with one large shuttle bus.

"Okay, here we go," she said, and Jeb barely had a chance to nod once as she smashed open the emergency stop panel and yanked down the large red handle.

The train jerked to an immediate stop, brakes screaming on the rail, cars rocking violently as their couplings crashed into each other. Jeb was already at the door, prying at the rubber-stripped gap, and when Molly took the other side they had it open in a few seconds. She grasped the door frame and leaned out. The single rail was beneath the train, so no platform or structure was beneath her, just a straight drop to the road below.

Except that here, a quarter mile from the passenger terminal, the shuttle bus was idling in the waiting traffic, its roof less than ten feet under the train. Molly glanced back at Jeb, who just said, "Okay," and then she jumped. Jeb followed, landing heavily beside her as the bus started to move. They scrabbled on the sloping metal roof, halting their slide only when Molly got one hand on a gutter rail and Jeb grabbed the roof-mounted AC unit, his other hand clutching Molly's ankle.

In the darkness, no one saw them, or believed what they saw. When the SWAT vans arrived a few minutes later, the light had changed and the bus had disappeared down the road. It was an hour before an Indonesian interpreter had arrived to translate the astonished babbling of the tourists who'd witnessed the jump. By then, of course, it made no difference.

TWENTY-THREE

NORCROSS CALLED A task force meeting on the spot, 1:38 a.m., right on the tarmac in front of a U-Haul panel van guarded by two SOU officers. The men were still in black combat uniforms, their harnesses laden with ammunition pouches, communication gear, grenades, and small weapons, and they listened intently as Kubbos defended himself against criticism from everyone—even the normally placid Drake. Inside the rented van several large suitcases of ballistic aluminum sat jumbled in a heap, shotguns and tactical equipment strewn everywhere. The tarmac around the postal facility was another circus, with news vehicles parked three deep at the perimeter and what seemed like hundreds of police and TSA personnel crawling over the site.

"No one's dead," Kubbos said again, his arms crossed defiantly.

"Sixteen injured," said Norcross, at the same time that Teixeira growled, "No one's in custody, either."

"Seventeen," put in Sampford, who'd been talking quietly on a cell phone. "One of the Indonesian tourists just keeled over—some sort of delayed stress reaction, they think it's his heart."

"Great," said Norcross. He frowned at the SOU officers until they looked away, no embarrassment evident at having been caught eavesdropping. "Look, we might as well talk this over inside."

Kubbos started to object, more as an automatic reaction than from any reasoned thought, but Cathryn overrode him. "We're only getting in the way out here. Inspector, surely there's an office we can use somewhere?"

They ended up in the package handlers' break room, a dank and windowless area furnished with two ancient plastic couches and a folding table. *No Fumar* signs on all four walls were yellow with cigarette smoke, and a vending machine in the corner was empty of everything but a forlorn packet of honey peanuts. Norcross closed the door carefully and sat on a battered metal chair.

"All right," he said, still seething at the disaster but determined not to let the investigation implode completely. "I'm not going to point out the obvious again. Who knows, even if we'd all been called in, they might still have gotten away. But let me ask—how many of you have heard from your bosses already?"

He waited, looking around. Drake said, "Yup, and they're not happy." Cathryn just nodded, and Teixeira, hesitating, finally said, "He got to me before you did, actually."

"Right," said Norcross. "They're getting pressure themselves, now, and not just from the press. I've wasted at least an hour already tonight, first with the SAC and then with the Director himself. Probably the Attorney General will be ringing me up next." He looked at Kubbos. "You see where this is headed, Inspector? No one died, that's good, but tonight was still a class A fuckup, and someone's going to be blamed."

"He'll be delivering mail in Fargo when this is over," said Teixeira, not without satisfaction.

Norcross gave him a sharp look and continued. "All I want—all we need—is to understand what actually happened tonight. We're trying to catch some murderers, remember?"

Kubbos relaxed slightly, unclenching the fist he'd clamped around a pen. "It was a phone call," he said. "We've gotten, what, a hundred tips since Friday? More? You know what they're worth, most of them."

"But you called out the ninjas for this one," said Drake.

"The caller was one of the package handlers here, Mark somebody. He saw Gannon slip into the office, recognized her from the TV. What made it a more interesting possibility is that another employee, one of the line supervisors, apparently knows Gannon from way back—recommended her for the letter carrier job."

Cathryn looked at him sharply. "You should have talked to this guy earlier."

Kubbos flared, then subsided again. "Her. Eileen Franck."

"Whatever."

"I'm afraid we did, actually—I interviewed her myself Saturday. She didn't know anything."

They just stared at him. Not even Teixeira had a comment to make.

"But it looks like Gannon contacted her later." Kubbos stuck to his guns. "And I don't know what to make of this, but she tried to set this Mark up with Gannon a few months ago. He says he met her but wasn't interested."

"Jesus," Norcross muttered. "Is she at least in custody yet?"

"She's not talking." Kubbos held up his hands. "Yeah, yeah, I know. My inspectors should have called your detectives by now. But I don't think we're going to get anything useful out of her."

"Does she understand she's facing felony misprision?" Cathryn said, impressing Norcross by her use of the legal term but probably losing Teixeira.

"She's being stand-up," said Kubbos, without admiration. "Since she's sure Gannon hasn't done anything wrong, she can't possibly be aiding and abetting."

"All right, we'll keep the pressure on," Norcross said shortly. "Let's get back to what happened here. You were trying to wrap it up yourself, of course. Keep it all in the family."

"They're a little sensitive about their employees going on killing sprees," Teixeira said, gleefully, unable to resist needling Kubbos further. "Of course, after tonight—"

"That's enough." Norcross's voice snapped like a whip. "Marshal, if you've nothing to contribute, keep your mouth shut."

Teixeira stared back. "Motorcycles? U-Haul vans? I mean, what kind of half-assed operation was this?"

Norcross started to speak and paused. "Actually, that's a good question," he said.

Kubbos's mouth was a thin line. "Maybe the Hostage Rescue Team has its own Hercules," he said tightly. "Maybe the Marshals fly everywhere first class. But we make do with commercial transport, if we can't tag along on a postal air freighter."

"So?"

"So it was fastest to rent the trucks when the team got here. The motorcycles we brought on the plane."

Teixeira shook his head. "That is so mickey-mouse, I can't believe it. Maybe you didn't want to call the FBI, but I'm sure the captain's people could have provided decent equipment."

The room was silent, Kubbos glaring at Teixeira, the tension between them approaching a breaking point. But after a long moment it was Kubbos, unexpectedly, who gave in. "Oh, hell," he said, abruptly tossing his pen onto the table, where it bounced and fell into Cathryn's lap. "The SOU team was staying at the Best Western, just a mile away, they were here in less than half an hour. It seemed easiest."

"All right," said Norcross. "It makes sense. You'll have a lot of explaining to do, but let's move on." Kubbos nodded.

With a truce, however tenuous, now in place, Norcross led the discussion to the pursuit through the airport. They reviewed the various reports already collected, tracing the fugitives' flight until they disappeared off the monorail.

"Here's what I'd like to know," said Drake when they'd finished. "How long have they been together— Gannon and Picot?"

Cathryn looked over from the vending machine, where she'd just bought the peanuts. "Since Saturday, for sure," she said. "The ATM security camera caught them both in one frame. And we just missed them yesterday morning—forensics matched both their fingerprints at the house."

"How long had they been there?"

"The friend—Darren something, he was calling from Thailand, of all places—he said Picot had been housesitting for the last week. Gannon's prints were in several rooms. She could have been there for days."

"How many beds were being used?"

Drake's question caused Cathryn to raise an eyebrow, but she only said, "Two. Looks like they're just business partners."

"This is all fine," Teixeira said. "We know where they were hiding out, we know what happened a few hours ago, here. More or less. Bicycles . . ." His mouth twitched as he looked at Kubbos, but he let it go. "But where did they go? They jump off the train, they're on foot, they can't have gotten far."

"We're not allowed to lock down SFO," said Norcross. "The Director seemed to think I was joking when I suggested it."

"I wonder," said Cathryn. "The cargo plane they were trying to board—it was going to Newark."

Kubbos shrugged. "The only other long-haul flight tonight was to Chicago, but it was leaving later. Everything else is short-hop, mostly up to Sacramento, where the primary West Coast distribution center is located. That probably wouldn't have been far enough for them."

"Their photos are posted at every gate and every checkpoint in the airport," said Cathryn. "They won't fly out, not now."

"And we have their bicycles." Teixeira's amusement at the SOU's failure showed no sign of diminishing. Kubbos glared and looked away.

The meeting sputtered along. Cathryn ate half the peanuts, caught Sampford eyeing the package, and offered him the rest. He shook his head, embarrassed.

Norcross began to wrap up. "I don't think there's much else we can do tonight. Captain, let me know if the FBI labs can help out with anything."

"Sure." Cathryn crumpled the wrapper and tossed it vaguely toward a trash can in the corner, missing.

"One more thing," she added. "What were you doing at the Wo Han Mok office?"

"Introductions." Norcross looked at her curiously.

"It's under surveillance. Gangland called me, they have you two on tape from this morning."

"Seems like they're focusing on the wrong people," said Drake. "Why don't they pick up Zheng?" He pronounced it Jang, barely recognizable.

Cathryn paused. "They have their own politics over there," she said. "Not for me to say. It's never as easy as outsiders think, of course."

"The triad will come to us, I believe," said Norcross. "It doesn't sound like the SFPD matters much to them. Sorry, no offense—" He nodded when Cathryn dismissed it with a brief wave. "The Wo Han Mok seem like bystanders in this, not necessarily the perpetrators. Why don't you tell Gangland that's what we're thinking? The message might get through quicker."

"Then what?"

"Then we can talk." Norcross stood, pulling his notebook shut. "They might be able to shed some light on . . . motivations."

Cathryn appeared doubtful. "When the Wo Han Mok discover someone's interested in them, they'll respond in one of three ways. Most people they ignore. Some they buy off." She looked up at Norcross's face. "And the rest they eliminate."

Teixeira snorted. "We're taking them down," he said. "Fuck 'em."

Outside a chill midnight breeze had sprung up, and Norcross zipped his leather jacket as they walked back to the perimeter. Sampford asked a patrolman whether food was available. Teixeira and Kubbos stalked off in opposite directions, each barely grunting a goodbye. Drake made to leave, too, saying, "I have to get some sleep, at least a little."

"Thanks for coming to the funeral this morning," said Cathryn, and, to Norcross, "You too."

"Sure."

Drake paused, looking at the crime scene. Technicians and uniformed officers were visible inside the mail warehouse, along the pedestrian bridge, and all over the monorail, many working under piercingly bright portable halogens. TV crews were still filming, some at the train and some at the main terminal. The activity seemed to have increased since they'd begun their meeting forty-five minutes earlier.

"The marshal was right," Drake said thoughtfully. "It's amazing they escaped."

"Yes," Norcross said. "Or maybe we've just been underestimating them."

"Luck." Cathryn was definite. "And they can't be lucky forever."

TWENTY-FOUR

"**YOU'RE CERTAIN THAT** only this postal SWAT team was involved?"

"And airport security," said Vandeveer. "The TSA. But apart from them, yes—the police didn't show up until it was over."

Rice grunted. Despite the flat and reduced video image, he looked more menacing than usual, perhaps because he'd barely moved during the entire conversation so far. He was staring unblinking out of the screen, his voice soft and uninflected.

"And none of our sister agencies were working with the mailmen?" he continued after a moment.

Vandeveer lifted his shoulders slightly. "Everyone is furious with the SOU for trying to lone ranger it. We're catching all sorts of interesting internal calls, especially over at Hooverville, and the USPS is just flailing around. It looks like their man out here, an inspector named Kubbos, went one bridge too fast. Or too far?" He paused, trying to untangle the metaphor. "Anyway, there's no indication of intel involvement." When Rice said nothing, Vandeveer added, "If there had been pros on the team, it would have ended differently, I think."

"I'm meeting with the deputy director in fifty-two minutes." Rice consciously straightened the cuffs of his suit, just below camera level on the desk, and Vandeveer, who'd been wondering why he was dressed more expensively than normal, had an answer. "He'll be particularly interested in this question."

"Gannon and Picot escaped on bicycles," said Vandeveer, with a small, ironic emphasis but not actually smiling. "Even Langley's muscleheads wouldn't have let that happen."

"All right." Rice finally relaxed enough to glance away from the camera and sip from his waterglass. "Next question, then. 'Gannon and Picot,' like you said. Why are they together?"

Of all the riddles grinding away inside Vandeveer's head since his phone had started ringing ten hours before, this one had kept him awake the longest, and he grimaced with annoyance. "I have no idea. Our hypothesis is that Gannon was working for one of our competitors, trying with their usual subtlety to shut down a Chinese cryptography front." It was clear that "competitors" did not refer to foreign organizations. "At first it looked like Picot was just lucky to be out of the way, but now he seems implicated." He hesitated. "My best guess is that he was part of it from the beginning. He'd only been working for Blindside for a few months, right? He may have been sent in to find out what they were up to, scope out the Chinese connections before any kind of, um, executive decision was made."

"No." Rice shook his head slowly. "I don't think so. If he and Gannon were agents, they'd have disappeared for real by now. They'd be outside the country with burned passports behind them, or hidden away on some deep-cover base. The last place they'd turn up is in the middle of a running firefight." He squinted. "Through a major metropolitan airport, no less."

"That's the key," said Vandeveer. "It was an airport." He paused long enough to glance at the double-chocolate croissant he'd picked up on the way in, warm when he bought it but now cold and stuck to the wax paper wrapping, and decided he'd wait until the call was over. "They were trying to fly away. Away from California . . . and back to the East Coast."

"All the more reason to think they're not CIA operatives. They train them to go to ground, not to run home with toilet paper trailing off their shoe."

"Ah." Vandeveer smiled at last, though only briefly. "What if they've been cut loose?"

Rice opened his mouth, closed it, and frowned. "Hmm."

"We thought Picot would make a good red herring, but the police and the press ended up all over him with hardly any, um, guidance necessary." Vandeveer paused. "From us, that is."

Through the picture window beyond his PC Vandeveer could see a crew taking in one of the sailboats in the marina, lifting it out of the water with a mobile crane near the dockside gas pump. As the hull was winched up, water cascaded from its scuppers, sparkling waterfalls in the brilliant morning sunlight.

"It's spinning out of control." Rice was trying the idea on for size. "And their bosses have made the hard decision." He nodded once, very slightly. "I could see that."

"Here's one more wrinkle. Since we're speculating and all." Vandeveer paused. "What if one of them really is an innocent bystander?"

"Who—Picot?"

"Or Gannon. I could make an argument either way." Rice grunted. "Why?"

"It's easier to explain what they're doing." Vandeveer watched as the hull was cantilevered across the dock and positioned above a high trailer. "But if you're asking why they're together, well, they seem to have, um, complementary skills. They're using each other."

"They're headed east." Rice was forging ahead. "To settle scores? Because they don't have anywhere else to go? Who knows? But they're coming here."

"It looks that way. Probably by land, now, of course. It's going to take them a while."

"And the police everywhere are looking out for them."

"Yes."

"So they'll surely be caught soon. Oh, there may be a few more skirmishes, twenty or thirty more bystanders gunned down, but in the end they're going to be arrested."

Rice was sarcastic so rarely that Vandeveer wasn't sure how to respond, or if, indeed, it really was sarcasm. "Ah . . ."

"And then they'll be in jail, talking to lawyers and judges and the press." Rice was now shaking his head, slowly, though his eyes stayed focused on the screen. "Out of control is *exactly* how to describe this."

"I still think we can keep Dunshire's, ah, tangential relationship to these events a nonstory."

"I'm not worried about the media," Rice said sharply. "But an NSC staffer, or some bright boy on one of the oversight committees, or one of those tenacious damned analysts is going to put the puzzle together."

"There's no link," Vandeveer tried to be reassuring. "We kept the paper to a minimum." He decided not to mention the bank's access token.

"The Chinese." Rice pointed out the obvious. "They're criminals, we know for sure. If they're spies, too, we're headed for a public disaster—the mouth-breathers on Capitol Hill will never let it go. We'll be page one for days."

"Well." The sailboat had been tied down to the trailer, and the crew was lashing its mast in place. "None of this matters unless Gannon and Picot are actually arrested."

Rice watched him carefully. "Matters would certainly be simplified if they weren't."

Vandeveer stared back. "Yes. That's true."

The boat was hauled away, the high truck cab moving carefully along the dock and disappearing behind the clubhouse, and the crew dispersed. About half the marina's moorings were empty, their yachts landed for the winter despite the glorious Indian summer they were having. Vandeveer wondered if he'd have a chance to get on the water before next spring.

"One way or another, we need this to end," said Rice, unblinking, his lack of expression more menacing than any glare could have been. "Soon."

"I'll see what I can do," said Vandeveer.

TWENTY-FIVE

THEY HAD RIDDEN the roof of the shuttle bus halfway around the airport, until it passed the most remote of the long-term parking garages, and hopped off at a corner, sprinting for the shadows as it trundled away. No other traffic was moving along this section of the loop. They heard sirens nearby. The ground was open, with a razor wire fence separating the road from the runways inside the airport's perimeter, bright security lamps mounted every fifty yards. In the distance they could see the main terminals, and beyond them the looming highway ramps and monorail. Several jets were moving slowly along the ground, following the green and blue-lit taxiway paths.

"Nowhere to hide," said Jeb, looking around the deserted stretch of road, feeling dangerously exposed.

"In the garage." Molly was already moving off. "We'll break into a vehicle."

"You don't want to borrow a credit card number, but you're ready to steal a car?" Molly gave him a look. "Anyway, they'll have roadblocks up."

She shook her head. "We're not going to drive away, not yet."

They went to the back of the six-story structure, climbing over the first level's concrete rail. Like the garage they'd passed through earlier this one was only half-full, with vehicles concentrated in the lower levels. Video cameras covered the attendant's booth and the ramps, but Molly led Jeb out of range, through the silent automobiles along the periphery, avoiding overhead lights. They crouched behind a dusty Range Rover as a car drove past.

"A panel truck would be good," said Molly. "Or a pickup with a shell. Even a station wagon if it doesn't have a car alarm."

It was Jeb who spotted the RV first, a thirty-seven-foot Safari, parked neatly across three-end-to-end parallel spaces along the back wall. "See how it's facing?" he whispered. The looming vehicle's right side was to the wall, and they were able to stand in front of the passenger door, eighteen inches in the gap, completely shielded from the sight of anyone nearby.

Molly pulled the handle, which was locked.

"It's just aluminum." Jeb dug through his bag, coming up with the Leatherman and opening it to the pliers configuration. He clamped it on the handle, glanced around and after Molly nodded, yanked downward with enough force to raise both his feet from the ground. The frame around the lockset crumpled, cracking the heavy plastic of the door's window panel, but the handle turned one quarter and Jeb was able to force it all the way open.

"On the other hand, what if the owner comes back?" he asked quietly, crouching to sweep up the shards of plastic.

Molly was inside, looking around the driver's seat, and after a moment she found the garage ticket tucked under the sun visor. She examined it in the dim light coming through the windshield, and said, "Today's the fourteenth, right? They came in six hours ago. This is long-term parking—they won't be back for at least a day."

Jeb pulled the door shut, forcing the broken latch closed, and turned to study the RV's interior. Behind the driver's commanding bucket seat a couch faced two chairs bracketing a fold-down table. A microwave and sink formed a tiny kitchenette, and a wall of plastic paneling angled out, apparently housing the toilet. The end of a bed was just visible beyond the bathroom. Slat blinds covered the long windows.

"All the comforts of home." Molly opened a small refrigerator built in just below the microwave, quickly finding the door switch and holding it down to keep the light off. She pulled out a carton, holding it toward the slightly better illumination from the windshield. "Orange juice? And . . . apples, and this feels like a package of cheese."

Crackers from the cupboard and a large can of chicken noodle soup, unheated for fear of running the RV's power, completed their meal. They said little, eating ravenously but pausing simultaneously at every unusual sound from outside, waiting, before returning to their food as quietly as they could.

Jeb was still amazed at their escape. "I'm exhausted," he said. "But I won't be able to sleep."

"Sure you will." Molly drank off the remaining juice. "We can't do anything until tomorrow, and we're safe here. They won't check every vehicle in the whole airport."

"Maybe." Jeb finished the crackers and brushed his hands on his shirt. Their eyes had adapted to the dim light, and he glanced her way with some embarrassment. "Um."

She looked at him quizzically and said, "You take the bed. The couch is too short, but I'll be comfortable on the floor here."

"Actually, I was wondering . . . do you think we can flush the toilet?"

"Oh." A beat. "If there's water in the basin, I don't see why not. It must have a collection tank. Just be careful of the noise."

He spent ten minutes at the concealed bathroom sink, washing as best he could in the lukewarm water, wishing they could take a chance on running the shower. While Molly took her turn, he found his courier bag and, from curiosity, removed the laptop and switched it on. The screen hummed to life and he shielded its glow from the windows, then tapped through a few menus before shutting it down.

"Still running," he said when Molly emerged. "And I think I can charge the battery off the RV."

"I guess it didn't get banged up as much as we did." She was wearing a clean T-shirt and nylon shorts, toweling off her hair. "I felt funny about it," she said, "but I went through the drawers."

Jeb moved aside to make room for her on the couch. She leaned back and closed her eyes, utterly worn out.

"I'm just going to look around once more." Jeb moved forward and crouched by the driver's seat, scanning the silent ranks of vehicles around them until he'd convinced himself it was still safe.

When he stepped back several minutes later Molly had started to drift off. "Looks okay," he said quietly, and leaned down to gently jostle her shoulder, not sure if she was asleep.

Only half-awake, she reacted instantaneously and on pure instinct, deflecting his forearm and punching with a counterstrike at his exposed throat. A fraction of a second before the edge of her hand crushed his trachea she managed to override her training, but the momentum carried her off of the couch and she knocked him backwards. In a confused tangle, yelping surprise at each other, they crashed against the edge of the table and fell in a tumble to the carpeted floor.

Jeb found himself lying astride Molly's midriff, her T-shirt pushed up to her breasts and her left leg trapped between his knees. He started to scramble off, but found himself staring into her face, six inches away, and there was a vertiginous moment when suddenly all he could perceive was her eyes and skin and faint smile . . . they were completely motionless for another second, and Molly closed her arms around him, pulling him down into a ferocious kiss, even as her knee rose gently against his groin.

It lasted longer than Jeb could hold his breath, and he gasped, trying to lean on one arm so he didn't crush her torso, discovering that his other hand had somehow found its way under her shirt.

"Hey," she said, and her smile broadened. Lying together now they began to yank at buttons and elastic, Jeb running one hand up and down Molly's long back and she tugging off his pants and underwear.

"I . . . I, um," he mumbled, his face buried in her damp hair, marveling at the muscles flowing in her legs and arms around him. He pushed at her shorts, sitting up as he tugged them past her knees, and paused for a moment, simply in awe at the sight of her.

For her part Molly abruptly ripped his shirt, tearing it easily between her hands rather than troubling to work it off more conventionally, and reached up to stroke his chest and shoulders as he leaned above her.

"Nice," she murmured, and then they weren't talking, their mouths consumed, each trying to sense every inch of skin, every bone, every muscle in the other.

TWICE before dawn a patrol car drove slowly through the garage, its spotlight flashing over the RV's windows. They were lying in the bed; Molly didn't move, and Jeb remained silent, but she felt the rigid tension in his frame. As the sound of the vehicle slowly faded away the second time, deep in the night, she stirred, holding him closely across his chest. They didn't say anything, and slowly he relaxed.

"I used to wonder about civilian life," Molly said eventually, her voice low. "When I was breaking up bar fights, or slogging through mud with a combat load, sometimes it seemed like anything at all would be better outside the service."

"This isn't what you imagined, though, huh?"

"I just wanted my own life—a quiet, boring sort of life."

"We can disappear. They won't chase us forever. We'll find a tiny little town in the mountains somewhere."

"I'd rather be on the ocean."

"Okay. Where Darren was, islands in the Gulf of Thailand, sounded really nice."

"I was thinking Polynesia. Some French soldiers I met in Kosovo told me about the Society Islands. Tahiti's overbuilt, they said, but Bora Bora looks like the Garden of Eden, and Raiatea is even better."

"Raiatea." He rolled the name off his tongue. "That's where we'll go, then."

"Sure." She rubbed his stomach muscles. "Lie on the beach all day."

"Snorkel out to the reef to catch our dinner and grill it on the beach."

"Sleep under palm thatch, with a solar-powered refrigerator to keep the beer cold."

"Listen to the BBC once every week or two, just to keep up."

"Get our mail from the inter-island freighter, twice a month."

"We won't need it."

"Or clothing, either." She kissed the back of his neck. "You're all I want." Forty-five minutes later, the sheets even more tangled, they finally fell asleep.

IT was only the soft beeping of Molly's watch that woke her at seven. They were parked deep in the second level of the garage, alongside the rear wall, and little daylight filtered back. In the silent darkness they might have slept until noon.

They ate most of the RV's remaining food—some sugary breakfast cereal, a bag of corn chips, another apple—and straightened up half-heartedly. The bed was a mess.

"Shouldn't we be wiping our fingerprints?"

"Nah," Molly said. "If they think it was us, an FBI lab team will go through here with a microscope. Fingerprints won't matter." She glanced at the bed. "We've left too many samples of hair and skin and . . . DNA to ever clean up."

She'd lost her few possessions when they abandoned the bikes in the monorail. After hesitating she decided to take some of the RV owner's clothing, choosing a canvas jacket and black pants along with some T-shirts and an unopened toothbrush from above the sink. On the dashboard she found a stained baseball cap and a pair of sunglasses.

"All right," she said. "Today we finally get out of the damn city."

"How?"

"We need a car."

"Maybe we can just take Darren's. It's got to be here at the airport somewhere."

"There are what, four separate garages? And the police are probably checking it already."

"Okay . . . what, then?"

"Something boring and anonymous, a Japanese four-door, say, and it can't be red." Molly saw him hesitate. "It's a long-term parking lot," she continued. "We take a car here, chances are good we'll have a few days before someone notices. I don't know how to hot-wire it, but I have an idea."

"It's not that." Jeb seemed embarrassed. "The thing is, um, I can't drive."

Molly stared at him. "At all?"

"Not since high school." He made a small, what-the-hell shrug. "I lost my license when I was inside, and I've mostly used the bike since I came to San Francisco."

"Even an automatic?"

"Well . . . I guess I could try."

"Good." Molly paused. "Not until we're in the desert, though."

They worked their way through the lower levels, Molly studying the possibilities while Jeb kept watch nearby. Twice he whistled, a low and directionless sound, and they crouched out of sight while a car came and went. The solitary collector in the booth at the ground floor exit had a CD player, and thumping hip-hop filtered through the tomb-like silence of the facility. From the airport, more distantly, they could also hear jets taking off and landing with clockwork regularity. The only other sounds were their own footsteps, and now and then a shuttle bus grumbling past outside.

It took less than twenty minutes, and Molly circled back to double-check and confirm her choices.

"The Camry past the pillar, there," she said. "And the one we saw near the RV. They're the same color, and close to the same model year—if we can't tell, most other people probably can't either. Since this one's parked further up, it was probably dropped off later, and hopefully the owner will be coming back later too. We'll take it."

Back in the RV she explained what to say, while Jeb checked the charge on Darren's cell phone. After an extended conversation with directory assistance, to get the numbers of several locksmiths near the airport, he started with AAAA Security Service.

Of the first seven businesses he called, four were answered by recordings and three turned the job down, not so much because they were suspicious as because they didn't want to deal with a credit card over the phone. But the eighth agreed immediately, so quickly that Molly, eavesdropping, wondered how original she'd actually been.

"When do you need the key?" the locksmith asked.

"I'm calling from the airplane," said Jeb, sounding like the harried and overworked businessman he'd claimed to be. "First flight out of Chicago, I should be back at SFO by ten, and the boss wants me in the office for an eleven o'clock meeting. I can't believe I lost my key ring! Is there any chance you can get there by then?"

"No problem." The locksmith was apparently scribbling a note. "Third floor, the long-term garage on the rear access road . . . what was the plate number again?"

Jeb recited it. "It's a tan Camry, and I'm pretty sure I left it in the second aisle, halfway down."

"I'll find it. There's no alarm, right?"

"No." They hoped this was true; Molly could see no status lights through the windows, and the car appeared old enough that the owner probably didn't bother.

The locksmith asked for a credit card, and Jeb gave him Darren's Visa number.

"All right," the locksmith said. "What I'll do is open it up and cut a key right there—my van has all the tools I'll need. Tell you what, I'll throw in a magnetic key box and stick it under the bumper. That would be better than leaving the car unlocked."

"Great." Jeb hadn't dickered over the price, and for a hundred and twenty a key box seemed like the least the locksmith could do. "You won't have any problem with the gate attendant?"

"Oh, I've done this before," said the locksmith. "They don't care."

"I might see you there," said Jeb. "Depends when the plane actually lands."

"I won't wait around." They hung up.

Molly had been listening in. "He's done this before?" she said with a raised eyebrow, as Jeb exhaled, releasing the tension he'd accumulated during the call. "It's easier to steal a car than I thought."

"What about the security cameras at the booth?"

"Good question." Molly thought about it. "You ride on the floor in the back—we'll throw a blanket over you or something. I'll stop a little short, try to keep the windshield pillar in front of my face." She put on the baseball cap, tucking up her hair and pulling the brim low. "Best we can do."

"I guess."

They sat in the RV, switching off every fifteen minutes at the side window while they waited.

"I've been thinking," said Molly. "Your Chinese investors. They carry guns into your meeting. They have a squadron of enforcers watching your apartment, one of whom attacks us without hesitation. And the news reports haven't said a thing about them—you have to figure, if they were legit, they'd be making statements."

"So?"

"The NSA was interested in Blindside. What if you'd attracted other spies, too? Chinese spies?"

"Yeah." Jeb's voice was slow. "I admit, it makes sense."

"Espionage is a federal offense," said Molly. "You can get the death penalty. If these guys really are foreign spies, they're probably pretty interested in covering their tracks. Eliminating evidence . . . they must want that laptop back." She glanced at Jeb, who was silent in the dark interior of the RV. "A lot."

"The computer isn't the only evidence," he said finally.

"No," Molly said. "There's us, too."

"Maybe we can return it, cut a deal with them."

"I doubt it." She sighed. "I think the stakes just got higher."

"Great."

Molly came alert. "There's the locksmith."

Jeb joined her at the window, peeking past the blind, and they watched the van drive past and up the next ramp.

TWENTY minutes later it returned, driving down and departing the garage. Molly and Jeb waited another half hour, to be sure, and slipped carefully out, taking the RV's gate ticket with them. Molly closed the broken door as inconspicuously as possible.

"Hopefully the airport police will think it was kids or vandals."

Before they went up, she took Jeb's Leatherman and used its flathead driver to remove the front license plate from the second Camry they'd found. The car had been parked nose-in, and she was able to crouch unseen in front for the fifty seconds it took.

"They probably won't notice it's missing," she said. "How often do you check your front bumper? And even if they do, it's even more unlikely they'll call the police.

We'll put it on the car we're taking. Gives us one more layer of concealment—if a cop somewhere does run the number for whatever reason, he'll match a tan Camry with no indication of trouble."

"That doesn't help if he's pulled us over," Jeb pointed out. "Like if he asks for the registration."

"It's better than driving a vehicle with an APB on it." Molly slipped the plate under her jacket and they walked quickly up the ramp.

"We're stealing this car," said Jeb. "Right?"

"We don't have any choice."

"Oh. Got it."

She made a rueful acknowledgment. "We'll send them a check later."

TWENTY-SIX

AROUND ELEVEN NORCROSS stopped at Wakefield. He was still groggy despite the takeout cup of coffee, having slept only a few hours after returning home at dawn. The bright sun reminded him of a clear day on the plains, hot and clean and dry, so unlike most of San Francisco's foggy mornings.

Before walking up the steps to the main entrance he stopped and considered the street, trying to reconstruct what must have happened when Sergeant Mason was killed. After a minute, instead of entering, he called Cathryn's direct number on his cell phone.

"You're right outside?" She sounded half-surprised, half-annoyed. "Why not just come up to my office?"

"Tell you what, I'll wait here," Norcross said. "When you get a moment, maybe you can join me. It's a beautiful day."

"It must be nice to be able to enjoy it." She hung up without another word, and Norcross wondered if she'd slept at all.

He was on his way back to the airport, not with a specific task in mind, but he couldn't think of anything more useful. A bonus was that he could avoid talking to the SAC, inevitable if he went to the FBI's offices. Wakefield was more or less on the way, and although Cathryn was probably buried in her neglected responsibilities as station commander, Norcross thought she was probably still the best source for what the investigative teams might have turned up from the previous night's scene.

She startled him, coming up the sidewalk from the garage entrance rather than walking out the main doors. Her uniform was neat but her face was drawn, and Norcross decided that if she had gotten any sleep it wasn't more than an hour or two in the bunkroom.

"Cathryn." He nodded.

"If I'd walked through the main floor I'd still be inside listening to complaints," she said, with a glance back the way she'd appeared. "Well, not all complaints, but you know how it is. Easier to come out through the garage, avoid everyone."

"Not a good morning?"

"The usual." She shrugged. "Cops."

They watched a prisoner transport van park in front of some cruisers, leaving its engine running. A pair of beefy county officers lumbered out and stopped on the sidewalk to light cigarettes, talking idly in the pleasant sunshine. Other policemen were up and down the block, smoking, dispossessed by the city's longstanding clean-air ordinances.

"This was in my mailbox this morning." Norcross pulled a ziploc freezer bag from his jacket pocket and handed it across. Inside the plastic was a 4x6 index card, the blank side printed with several lines of text.

Cathryn read: "Five undershirts, three white T-shirts, eight size L boxers, black webbing belt, gray swimsuit size thirty-eight, three quarters, sixteen pennies, Buck penknife, ring with four keys." She looked up. "I don't get it."

"There's no alarm on my apartment, but the door has a good solid Medeco lockset, and the windows are barred."

"Oh."

"Second drawer in my bedroom dresser. I checked—
the underwear count was off by one, so they must have
been inside yesterday."

"Kind of an odd message, isn't it?"

"Clear enough, I'd say. If they came in with weapons
instead of a notepad, I wouldn't have a chance."

"But it'd be hard to convince a judge this constitutes
a threat."

"Yeah. You can almost admire it."

"Who was it?"

Norcross took back the ziploc. "The triads, I figure.
No one else has reason."

"You sending it to the FBI lab?"

"Nah. It looks like it was printed on an inkjet. I'm
sure there won't be anything useful. Anyway, I think
this is just sort of an introduction. They're letting me
know what they can do."

"I'm telling you, I already know what they can do,
and it's not nice."

"I'll try not to annoy them," Norcross said, leaving
her unsatisfied. He stretched. "This is the first time I've
been here, actually. To your station."

"It's nothing special."

"This is where Gannon showed up, right? When Picot came out."

"Yeah." She pointed. "Her car was right about there,
and the second pulled in behind her."

"That's what I thought, from the reports." Norcross
frowned, looking from the street's edge to the steps
leading up into the main entrance. "Picot came out
there. Mason was behind him, I assume?"

"Yes. He was shot on the top step, in front of the
doors."

"Hmm."

A pair of uniformed officers passed, making half
salutes to Cathryn, who nodded back.

"No one saw the actual firing," she said. "The reporters were all inside, and the technician in the TV van
was watching his equipment. If anyone was passing by
at the time they haven't come forward."

"Right." Norcross looked her way. "Here's what I can't figure. Did you see Gannon's car when it was found? Bullet holes, windshield and most of the windows gone, rear end smashed up."

"They were lucky to drive away. Mason emptied his magazine before he died."

"But look at the sightlines. Mason was up there, Gannon's car was down here. He was shooting down, at an angle, into the back and side of the vehicle."

"So?"

"So how did he blow out the windshield?"

Cathryn frowned, started to speak, and stopped, looking back and forth between the steps and the curb.

"Ricochet," she suggested, finally.

"Off of what?" Norcross shook his head. "Cars are soft, especially against a .40-caliber. The bullets would either pass straight through, or wind up in the undercarriage somewhere."

"But there wasn't anyone firing from in front of her."

"No, I don't think so." Norcross gestured at the street. "But from behind . . ."

Cathryn thought about it. "Who?—wait. The second car, you mean."

"Yes. It's one way to explain it. They were shooting at her—or Picot, maybe—and the bullets went right through, shattered the windshield on their way out."

"CSI didn't find any shells in that direction."

"How far did they look?" He studied the street. "Looks to me like the rounds wouldn't necessarily run into anything for fifty or sixty yards, maybe even into that shrubbery way down there."

"I can ask them to check again." Cathryn was thoughtful.

"Makes you wonder," said Norcross. "If the second car was shooting at Gannon, they obviously weren't working together."

"No." Cathryn paused. "Not at that time, anyway."

"Good point." Norcross nodded. "Double-cross? Changed plans?"

"Impossible to say."

Down the street the county officers had finally disappeared into the station, leaving their van still running. Even with police everywhere, it would have been easy to hop in and drive it away; Norcross wondered if it ever happened.

"We need to talk to them," he said finally. "Gannon and Picot. It feels like they're the only ones who can sort this out, now."

"Let's hope Kubbos doesn't get to them first, then."

"If he's still on the job." At Cathryn's questioning look, he continued, "Teixeira was just running his mouth, but he might have been right. The Postmaster General's office has been leaving me voice mails."

"You haven't called back?"

"Not my responsibility. They have a problem, they should go through the SAC. The FBI's bad enough, I don't need to be dragged through some other bureaucracy too."

"Yeah." Cathryn closed her eyes and turned her face to the sun, the tension lines relaxing somewhat in the warmth. "Speaking of bureaucracy . . ."

Norcross smiled. "The task force? Next meeting's tonight, seven p.m."

"That's late."

"Sorry. Drake said he couldn't make it until then, and I'm hoping Kubbos will be sorted out by that time. One way or another."

"It's all right. I was planning on working through dinner anyway."

"This won't go on much longer." Norcross sounded confident, and Cathryn opened her eyes to look at him. "Oh, the paperwork and the legal stuff will last for years," he said. "But either Gannon and Picot will be caught in the next few days, or they'll disappear forever."

"You sound pessimistic."

"Never." He was amused. "Some cases just don't get solved."

"Like Teixeira and the Wo Han Mok."

"Exactly."

She shook her head. "There you're wrong. There's too much attention on this one—on us, on the fugitives, on everything. You can't do a Bonnie and Clyde anymore, not with this much publicity."

"That's cheering." Norcross placed one hand briefly on her elbow. "Never mind. We'll do what we can. When it's over I'll buy you a drink."

She led the way into the station, taking the front door this time. "We can go over what CSI has come up with so far at the airport."

"That would be helpful. Dramatic, was it, last night?"

"Wild, Wild West. We've already been taking calls from Hollywood."

Norcross's smile faded. "Next time we'll be there."

"If there is a next time."

TWENTY-SEVEN

LATE IN THE afternoon, drained, Molly pulled into a rest stop halfway through Nevada's Forty-Mile Desert. The late-afternoon sun was a blinding glare behind them. They'd hoped to get as far as Lovelock, but heavy traffic and construction through Reno had added more than two hours. She parked on the far side of the cinder block set of restrooms, and opened the door to a gust of alkaline wind.

"Bathroom," she said as she walked off, and Jeb, half-dozing in the passenger seat, mumbled. He opened his eyes, stared dully at the bleak flats surrounding them, and finally got out to stretch.

They had the initiative, they were moving fast, and San Francisco was 250 miles behind them, but Jeb felt no more relaxed. Problem was, they couldn't agree on where to go. Every instinct was telling him to flee, to disappear, to burrow into some large midwestern city and go deep, deep underground. Or Canada, maybe; they could cross on fake IDs with no problem, since the border authorities put all their attention on potential terrorists going the other way. Anywhere, really—but he wanted to be *gone,* the doors all slammed shut behind him.

Molly wanted to attack.

"We know who the enemy is," she'd said outside Sacramento, once they'd stopped checking the rearview mirrors all the time. "You call up Dunshire online, and thirty minutes later there's an assault team shooting the hell out of Bernal Heights."

"That doesn't necessarily mean Dunshire itself is the villain." But he didn't believe it.

"We know who they are, though."

"And they know who *we* are."

"Yeah." Molly glanced at him sideways. The sunglasses she'd found in the RV were an odd greenish blue, their lenses scratched and cloudy, and Jeb couldn't see her eyes. "But we know *where* they are, too."

"You don't think they might figure that out? Be waiting for us to do something foolish, like knock on their door?"

"We'd still have surprise on our side."

"They'd be surprised we'd be that dumb, all right."

Lunch was greasy chicken from a drive-through off I-80, Molly keeping the sunglasses on while she paid. The teenage clerk forgot to include napkins, and Jeb ended up wiping his hands on the paper bag.

"Life on the run," he said.

"Worse than prison food?" Molly had finished hers down to the crumbs of deep-fried batter. "Better than an MRE, anyway."

The broad rangeland of the Central Valley gradually rose to the Sierra foothills, cool evergreen forest dappling the road. Over Donner Pass the interstate began its descent to Truckee, the air warmer and drier in the mountain's rainshadow. The trees rapidly thinned out, diminishing to scattered scrub pine by the Nevada border near Verdi. Jeb looked at the empty, arid terrain stretching out before them.

"Not many people in the desert," he said. "Maybe that's the place to disappear."

She grimaced. "Scorpions. Salt pans. Sharp rocks. The sun's bright enough to give you cataracts, and the nights are freezing. There's a reason no one goes there."

"I'd rather worry about sunscreen than when the next firefight's going to erupt."

Without taking her eyes from the road, Molly reached out her right hand and squeezed Jeb's leg. "We'll be fine."

"We're driving a stolen car in broad daylight with every cop in the country looking for us." Jeb sighed. "At least I'm off parole."

They hit rush hour in the Reno–Sparks sprawl. The highway widened to three lanes, but all were clogged and slow-moving. Molly picked the middle lane and stuck to it, keeping a steady distance from the car in front.

"It's not like we have a complicated decision tree here," she said. "Either Dunshire finds us first, or we find them. And then we settle up."

"Settle up. Right." Jeb leaned back and closed his eyes. "I'm in no hurry to be filled with high-velocity holes."

"Exactly." Molly nodded, like he'd agreed with her. "Our chances are worlds better if we set the agenda."

Outside Reno Jeb lolled drowsily in his seat, too uncomfortable to sleep and too tired to stay alert. After a while Molly laid her hand on his, and he held it, quietly, while the sun descended into an orange blaze behind them and the miles slipped steadily past.

TWO RVs and a pickup truck were the only other vehicles in the rest stop, and the drivers of all three might have been dozing, since the bathrooms were deserted. Traffic on the highway was sporadic. A half mile into the desert a freight train trundled slowly along tracks paralleling the road, an endless set of gondolas and boxcars pulled by three stained locomotives. In between the rushing tire noise of passing automobiles Jeb could hear the train's clanking, rattling progress.

He'd pulled out the laptop when Molly returned, setting it on the Camry's hood while he retrieved additional connectors and his tools from the back seat.

"You're going online?" she said, surprised.

"I'll be more careful this time."

"You're not going after Dunshire." Not a question.

"No. I just want to check my own accounts, see how seriously they're after me." He gathered his equipment. "But I might post some inquiries about Dunshire, in the crypto forums."

"Is that safe?"

"I'll keep it anonymous. Any mention of the NSA is good for rumors—if we can get the hackers interested, they'll direct a lot of unwanted attention Dunshire's way. If nothing else it ought to distract them."

She hesitated, then just nodded, and he walked off to examine the pay phone standing against the building's left wall. A weathered aluminum conduit ran from the phone's base to a junction box at the corner. The box was heavy steel and secured with an exterior-grade ABUS padlock. Jeb made a *tch* sound with his tongue.

Five minutes later he'd unscrewed the phone's base pillar instead, tapped directly into the line and run his wire through the ventilation grate into the men's room. Over the phone's handpiece he'd taped a hand-lettered Out of Order sign. He returned briefly to the car.

"Beep if anything suspicious happens," he said to Molly, who was sitting in the driver's seat, the door ajar for ventilation. She nodded.

Inside a stall for privacy, he laid a piece of cardboard across the open toilet, sat down with the laptop balanced precariously on his knees, and got to work.

MOLLY had fallen asleep when Jeb returned, ten minutes later, moving fast. He didn't take any chances waking her this time, just banged on the trunk as he went around the back of the car, and threw his bag into the backseat with one hand while he slammed his door shut with the other.

"Time to go," he said. "Quick-like."

Molly stared at him, turned the ignition and got them back on the highway in less than ten seconds, rubber marks smoking on the ramp. She accelerated to ninety, flashing past slower-moving traffic in the right lane.

"What happened?"

Jeb was staring at the darkening sky ahead of them. In the dusk about half the oncoming traffic had switched on their lights. "Every one of my accounts was shut down," he said.

"Huh?"

"I wasn't anywhere near Dunshire. But my identities—they'r all locked."

Molly gave him a quizzical glance and let up on the gas. Their speed drifted back to less flagrant levels. "So? That's exactly what I'd expect. The FBI's looking for you."

"No. My secret accounts." He waved one hand impatiently. "I maintain space at four commercial servers, two in different parts of the U.S., one in Holland, and one in Japan. They're for file storage, email drops, some site hosting if I need it. One of the American sites and the Dutch one are aboveboard, I use my own name and pay by credit card. But the other two are my backups, and I thought they were completely anonymous—I signed up using thoroughly anonymized sessions and I make payments quarterly through the mail, with money orders."

"Isn't that kind of paranoid?"

"Apparently not."

"So they tracked you down. I still don't see what's the big deal."

"The FBI couldn't have done it. The only way would be brute force, sifting access records and trying to backtrack my activity. It's a huge job, and not easy. They'd need serious supercomputer time."

"Oh." Her jaw tightened. "I get it."

"Yeah. The NSA again. And they must have put up tripwires. It's possible they've already identified that pay phone back there."

Molly dropped back to seventy-five miles an hour, blending in with traffic. The sky was purple behind them, black in front. Once a minute she checked each mirror— left, right, rearview—looking for unusual activity.

"You know what," she said finally. "I'm tired of this shit."

"Yeah."

"They're too close, and they've got resources to burn. One of these times, soon, we're going to run out of luck."

"Maybe." Jeb looked at his hands, pleased to see they weren't shaking. "Maybe not. Nothing we can do about it."

"Oh, yes there is."

An exit came up, 95 south to Fallon, and she took it without signaling, crossed over, and got back on 80 going west.

"Weapons," she said after several minutes of silence. "We need weapons." The last light of the setting sun glowed on the horizon ahead of them.

THEY found a likely gun shop quickly, faster than Jeb expected.

"You've been here before?" he said, as they drove past a neon-lit row of strip clubs, bars, and shabby gambling houses too modest to be called casinos. Young men in sweatshirts and shaved heads wandered along the sidewalk in small groups, a smaller number of servicemen in BDUs among them. Molly saw an MP humvee but drove steadily past. Sidestreets away from the main avenue were dark and empty.

"Once, when a MAC flight took a layover. But these little towns are all alike. They grow like mold anywhere a few thousand soldiers are stationed."

"Cheery," said Jeb.

"Imagine if you're a woman."

A man was throwing up into the gutter at the next corner, his companions waiting a few yards away. The asphalt glittered under the streetlight, and Jeb realized it was covered with shards of broken glass. An oppressive heat still lingered from the scorching day.

"Hell of a place to put an army base."

"That's the idea. The 9th Mountain Division is head-quartered here. They do desert survival, escape and evasion training, that sort of thing." They were fifty miles southeast of Reno, in the alkaline badlands. "An old-timer told me it wasn't much until the mid-seventies, but it built up fast after the oil embargo, and even more after Desert Storm."

Molly circled through the business district once more, then followed a street that led in a direction opposite the base's entrance. Small houses, most with large, shiny vehicles parked amid junk in sandy and unkempt yards, gradually gave way to open scrub. When the streetlights ended, no habitation visible anywhere in front of them, Molly turned around.

Her second try led them through a similar neighborhood, but a mile on they found a windowless, bunker-like building emblazoned with a huge electric sign reading simply Guns. The gravel patch in front was occupied by a single pickup, an ancient four-wheel drive with lockout hubs and a battered protective grill over the front end. The nearest building, a large metal shed, was two hundred yards away.

"This should do." Molly parked at the edge of the lot, facing out.

"How did you know it would be here?"

"There's always one somewhere nearby."

Jeb looked dubiously at the reinforced metal door. "Why are they open this late?"

"It's kind of like a convenience store."

"Oh."

"Wait for me out here. I can pass myself off as a soldier, but I'm not sure you can."

"I don't think I'd want to." Looking back the way they'd come, Jeb saw a metal sign—Walter City, pop. 1,377—at the edge of the parking lot, and realized the gun shop was located just outside the town's jurisdiction. The sign was pocked with rusty holes. "I thought there was a waiting period on firearms purchases."

"Yeah, if you buy through a regular dealer. But Nevada law makes an exemption for gun shows. You don't need a background check either."

Jeb eyed the squat, ugly building. Brown stains ran down the walls from broken gutters. "Don't gun shows take place in the fairgrounds or something? In a tent at the flea market? This place looks like it's been here since the Korean War."

"You can have one wherever you want, is how I understand the loophole works. And you can run it seven days a week for years."

Molly tied her hair back with a bandanna, pulled on the canvas jacket, and counted three hundred dollars into a bankroll that she shoved into her back pocket.

"This shouldn't take long," she said.

"Have fun." Jeb looked in her eyes, seeing alertness, even excitement. The danger—the possibility of combat that, like any rational person, he feared—was bringing her alive.

He watched her for a long moment, until she finally broke off and turned away. He tried to say something but couldn't assemble the words.

"Buy yourself something nice," he said finally.

"I'd like a Steyr assault rifle." Molly opened her door. "But we probably can't afford it."

WHEN she came out, holding a heavy, wrapped parcel, the car was empty. Immediately she pivoted and sprinted for the building's corner, holding the package close as she dove into the shadows and rolled twice. She came to a stop behind a corroded fifty-five-gallon drum lying on its side and knelt, automatically turning her head in a 360-degree scan.

Silence. A light wind blew off the desert, pushing a fast-food wrapper across the gravel. The pickup truck was gone, their car now the only vehicle in the lot.

Molly waited two minutes, backed out of her cover, and circled the gun shop in a defensive crouch. No one was hidden in the back, no other cars were anywhere nearby. The road was deserted as far as she could see in either direction. Puzzled, she stood up and walked back to the Camry, approaching it from the driver's-side rear.

She found the note folded up and sticking out of the ashtray, just enough to attract her attention.

"It's better this way." The hastily scrawled handwriting seemed to start midthought. "You figured it out: everyone's looking for me, not you. The Chinese think I'm going to blow their operation, the NSA is terrified I'll expose their deal, the police have pinned me for that dead cop. And they're all getting closer. You're right about that, too. We don't have any more time."

Molly closed her eyes tightly for a moment.

"I don't want to fight back. No one's interested in talking. It'll be guns and bullets everywhere, and I just don't see how both of us dead makes things better. You are—" There was an unreadable scrawl. "Don't do anything dumb, okay? We can disappear easier separate than together. Just wait it out. I—" Another scratchout. "I'm counting on seeing you again, damn it."

The signature was small and rushed.

Molly slowly leaned forward, unseeing, until her head rested against the steering wheel. She heard a faint keening moan, and realized it was coming from her only when she finally stopped to draw breath in a ragged gasp. Her mind was empty of everything but pain.

It was several minutes before she stirred, fumbling around until she found the car key in her shirt pocket. On autopilot, she looked blankly around at the empty parking lot, the buzzing electric sign, the darkness of the desert beyond, and started up. She almost broke down completely at the end of the lot, unsure which way to turn and wondering if Jeb had gone left or right, imagining him driving off without looking back—but she pulled herself together, stabbed the accelerator, and squealed away.

For ten miles her mind could only focus on the most

unimportant points: *He stole the pickup? Did that mean he knew how to drive after all? Did he remember his small bag of clothing? How much money did he take?*

And: *What now?*

After gassing up at a self-serve back near I-80, she dumped a pile of loose nickels and dimes into a pay phone and punched in a North Carolina number. Highway traffic whooshed past fifty yards away, making it hard to hear.

"Sorry to wake you up, Wade," she said. "I need help."

TWENTY-EIGHT

WHEN TEIXEIRA PULLED into the dark, shadowed parking lot of the police annex, ten minutes to seven, Kubbos was just getting out of his drab Chevy. Only one of the building's exterior lights was working, and Teixeira could just make out a scratched USPS eagle on the door of the inspector's car. A cruiser was the only other vehicle in the lot.

Kubbos waited for him to get out.

"I was hoping you'd be early," he said. "The others aren't here yet. Maybe we can clear the air, you and me."

Teixeira was wearing a field jacket over an XXL polo shirt, the fabric tight across his massive chest and shoulders, and he stood nearly a foot taller. He showed his teeth, the grimace somewhere between a smile and a sneer. "You have a problem, mailman?"

"I've been doing some thinking." Kubbos stood his ground. "You've been on the Wo Han Mok's trail for what, two years?"

"Yeah. Twenty-five months, almost."

"And not a single arrest, all that time."

"Building a decent case takes time." Teixeira's voice was soft.

"Not a single arrest," Kubbos repeated.

"What about it?"

"What if Picot was working for the triad?"

Teixeira scoffed. "That makes no sense. He's with Gannon, and Gannon zapped Ding and Yu, remember?"

"He could have been the inside guy." Kubbos crossed his arms, staring steadily at the marshal's taut face. "You ever been in a firefight? Bullets everywhere, mistakes happen."

Teixeira just shook his head, still half smiling.

"Well, maybe, maybe not. It's just an idea," Kubbos said. "But this got me thinking about other possibilities. Who else might be allied with the Wo Han Mok? They're completely wired with the city police, according to the captain."

"Yeah. So?"

"So maybe they have someone inside this investigation." Kubbos paused. "Inside the task force, even."

Their eyes locked, and neither spoke for half a minute. A car drove down the street, turned the corner, and faded away. His voice low and steady, Kubbos continued, "And who more likely than someone already close to them? Someone who's been following them around for two years . . ."

"You're making a serious accusation," Teixeira said finally, still speaking softly.

"Yes." Kubbos waited.

"You're wrong." Unexpectedly, Teixeira chuckled.

"What?"

"What if you were right? Why wouldn't I just kill you right here and now?"

"I'd like to see you try." But Kubbos was already beginning to relax.

"I'll show you the case files if you want."

"Nah."

"I think we should talk about it inside." Teixeira stepped past him. "With everyone else. Get this out in the open." He walked toward the entrance. After a moment Kubbos made a small shrug, and followed him.

"I still think you ought to watch fewer westerns, Tex," he said.

"Shh!" Teixeira abruptly cut him off, pointing.

"Wha—?"

The door was hanging slightly open, the lockset loose in the frame and a deep gouge showing in the metal jamb. As Kubbos frowned, Teixeira pushed the door inward, entering quickly and calling to the guard at the desk.

The room was deserted, some papers on the floor the only sign of disorder. A light was blinking steadily on the guard's monitoring console.

"Shit." Teixeira had crossed to look behind the desk, and at the same moment Kubbos saw the blood oozing across the floor beneath it.

In a flash they both had their guns out, turning simultaneously to stare at the open elevator and the stairs leading to the second floor. They could hear nothing.

Kubbos reached for his cell phone with his left hand, then remembered it wouldn't work. He lifted the guard's phone, but set it back immediately. "No dial tone," he whispered.

"Second floor," said Teixeira, his head cocked. "Follow me?" Without waiting for an answer he moved to the stairwell, crouched at one side to stare up, and glanced back.

Kubbos hesitated only a moment, then nodded. Their dispute in the parking lot felt like it had happened last year, faded and irrelevant. He slipped to the other side of the stairs and knelt half-protected by the corner, his pistol pointing up. Silently and with unexpected grace, given his bulk, Teixeira glided to the first landing and paused to let Kubbos join him. In twenty seconds they had leapfrogged to the second floor.

Peering around the firedoor, Kubbos scanned the hallway. The only lights were security lamps at either end of the corridor, and a dim illumination from outside the windows in the offices opening off the hall.

"The evidence room," he whispered, air barely moving through his throat. "Saw a shadow."

"There'll be others." Teixeira was equally quiet.

After a long pause, Kubbos glanced at him with a questioning look. Teixeira shrugged slightly. "Well?"

"Don't want to wait."

A sudden, tight smile broke across Teixeira's face. "Fuck 'em," he agreed, and glanced down to check his handgun once more.

"You first." Kubbos moved to the other side of the doorway, yielding his place, and after another nod from Teixeira, he took a deep breath.

"POLICE!" he yelled. "Hands up, out of the room!"

The response was immediate: before he'd finished, a partial figure emerged from the door to the accountants' cubicles, fifteen yards down the hall, and bullets tore into the firedoor and walls around them. The submachine gun was fully suppressed, with little muzzle flash and only the smallest of sounds. Teixeira dropped flat. Kubbos remained upright after ducking back, the steel door rebounding with loud bangs as the slugs slammed into it, but not giving way.

Teixeira fired back from his prone stance, each .45 round a deafening explosion. He drove the other shooter back, and Kubbos sprinted down the hall, keeping to the other side to avoid Teixeira's sightline. At the door he crouched flat against the wall, pistol six inches back from the frame and pointed three feet above the floor. Watching the darkened end of the hallway with his peripheral vision, he waited for the few seconds it took Teixeira to join him.

Just as the marshal reached his side there was movement in the evidence room, another twenty yards down the hall, and a second man appeared, firing on automatic. As bullets sprayed the walls around them Kubbos and Teixeira, of one mind, dove into the darkened accounting offices, bouncing off each other and rolling in opposite directions. Firing from the hall stopped momentarily, but the first opponent popped up from a cubicle just down the corridor and let off several shots. Kubbos grunted and Teixeira spun around, emptying his magazine. There was a cry, quickly choked off, and a dozen rounds blasted directly through the doorway—someone must have run to stand just outside. Teixeira ducked behind a half-high file cabinet, grabbing another magazine from his belt and reloading without looking.

Kubbos groaned from where he was lying on the floor, barely visible in the street glow filtering through the windows on the far side of the room's cubicles. But he clamped his left arm against his side and aimed the handgun with his right, and when a shadow fell across the hallway door he fired rapidly three times, so quickly the shots sounded like one.

The first opponent appeared, stepping out to shoot at Kubbos from one cubicle further down, and Teixeira twisted to return fire immediately. He wondered how the man had moved—right over the partition? Bullets spanged into the filing cabinet and ricocheted off the desktop above it, shattering a computer monitor, coffee mug, and glass picture frame. Shards of metal and plastic tore into Teixeira's face, blinding him on one side. He grunted in sudden pain.

The firing stopped and Teixeira paused only long enough to wipe the blood away from his good eye before he rose and ran the three steps to Kubbos, hunched over, grabbing him one-handed. Firing came from the doorway again and Teixeira turned just enough to bring his gun arm across his chest, not really aiming, and he snapped off his remaining four rounds backward. He pulled Kubbos away in a crouch, throwing him behind another row of two-drawer file cabinets and diving in on top of him.

They heard footsteps in the hallway and more firing began, most of the rounds absorbed by the packed file cabinets but a few cracking overhead or smacking into the wall behind them.

"I'm hit," said Kubbos, whispering not for concealment but from weakness. In the shadows they could barely see each other.

"I know," said Teixeira. He loaded his last magazine, dropping the empty and kicking it away.

"Reload in my pocket." Kubbos was panting. "Can't reach it."

Teixeira felt around the inspector's jacket, shocked at how much blood had soaked through, and gently pulled out the magazine. He wiped it off and snapped it into Kubbos's pistol for him.

The firing had stopped, and in the lull their opponents started talking to each other, the voices flat, not shouting, just loud enough to be clearly audible across the floor. Radios would have been superfluous in the confined space.

"Clear," said one from the hallway.

"Two, I think." A voice from the cubicles, thirty feet away.

"Colonel?"

"No one outside yet." Pause. "Status."

"Blue."

"Blue."

"Yellow."

"Where are they?"

"On the floor, ten feet in, left five feet. Behind the cabinets."

"All right." Another pause. "I'm calling tag four. Charley?"

"Set."

"Set."

Teixeira was hurriedly trying to clear his face of blood again. "They're coming in," he whispered. He looked around, blinking at the murk, seeing a wall behind them and cubicles to either side, no escape possible.

"We're fucked." Kubbos had pulled himself into a crouch, his left side incapacitated but the gun in his other hand steady.

"One chance," murmured Teixeira. "Surprise them."

They looked at each other. In two minutes blood had completely soaked the carpet beneath them.

"Right." Kubbos tried to smile. "Let's do it."

Teixeira nodded. He wiped his face once more and

reached out to lay his hand on Kubbos shoulder. "You did good, mailman," he said softly. Kubbos started to shrug and winced in pain instead.

Without saying anything further, they adjusted their position, paused, and simultaneously stood, Teixeira firing as he continued into a dive over the cabinet, Kubbos yanking himself around the end and aiming at the doorway. For one instant Kubbos thought, *We're going*—!

They were met by a concerted fusillade, shots pouring from three locations, slamming into them, dozens of rounds in just a couple of seconds. Teixeira was struck full on, knocked flying as one bullet passed directly through his skull. He crumpled backward. Kubbos had just enough time to see the dark men calmly firing at him before he too was hit numerous times. The room blazed in light and went black, an eternity before he fell back across the jagged metal edge of the shattered cabinet.

TWENTY-NINE

OVERNIGHT THE WEATHER turned, with showers and then a damp, heavy fog settling in over the city. Morning commuters hurried down wet streets with raincoats and umbrellas, regretting the clear sunny days, now reminded that November was only two weeks away. The streetlights remained on past nine a.m., glowing in the mist, and even the bicycle couriers donned slicks and tights.

Norcross was waiting for Sampford in an overpriced café off Market, several long blocks from the federal building. The morning rush had passed, but the tables were still half full with laid-off dot-commers nursing overpriced coffees. It was the last place an agent or police officer would ever choose to patronize, which was why Norcross had suggested it.

He'd met with the SAC first thing in the morning, the chief calling him into his office and closing the door firmly behind him before moving back around his desk. He was younger than Norcross, mid-forties, balding and fit, dressed in a dark gray suit bare of all ostentation except its perfect and expensive drape. Somehow they ended up seated, looking at each other across the empty expanse of tropical hardwood, without shaking hands.

"Washington wants me to take over." The SAC cultivated a blunt manner with his subordinates, having long ago misunderstood *The One Minute Manager*. "They have every confidence in you, of course. But the public profile is just too high now."

"I had to come in through the service doors," Norcross agreed tiredly. His voice was rough with exhaustion. "There must have been fifteen reporters in the lobby." He'd known since seven a.m. that he was being reassigned, when two long acquaintances, more loyal to friendship than to their superiors, called him from Bureau headquarters.

"I'm afraid your past fame has brought on even more interest. A distraction, really."

"I understand."

"The reports seem in order." The SAC turned to pull a neatly squared file from the credenza behind him, and Norcross recognized his accumulation of case paperwork. "We'll do a more extended debriefing later today."

The night before Norcross had arrived at the annex simultaneously with Cathryn and two patrol cars responding to an anonymous "shots fired" call. Kubbos was still alive, astonishingly, but he never regained consciousness and died on a gurney despite the paramedics' furious ministrations. Teixeira went straight to the ME. The evidence room was torn apart, files and boxes and paper bags strewn everywhere. The perpetrators had vanished, and Norcross had little expectation that the forensic teams would find anything useful toward their identification.

"Yes, sir," he said, and waited.

"I'd like you to take the rest of the week off," said the SAC. "On Monday you're starting at the resident agency in Crescent City. The RA there is going on paternity leave, believe it or not." He paused to frown absently, clearly wondering when the tsunami of political correctness might be halted. "Anyway, I think you'll do well there, and when he comes back we'll find a permanent assignment for you."

Crescent City was 300 miles from San Francisco, in a county that was mostly redwood forest and national park, the most remote sector of the SAC's district.

Norcross had expected to be taken off, and he knew protest was pointless, but he couldn't leave willingly. "I'm closer to this case than anyone," he said quietly, watching the SAC with a calm gaze. "You know how it works. These guys are too good to fall out of the sky from carelessness. When we finally catch the break, it's going to be because someone on our side puts together the right pieces of the puzzle. You take me out, you're going to have to work twice as hard to get there."

"Agent Sampford will still be on the team." The SAC's tone sharpened. "And Captain Birney is invaluable."

Norcross sighed. They were both just going through the motions. He'd lost assignments before, and he always took it personally. He was able to remain polite now, but he knew he couldn't disengage as easily as the SAC was dropping him. "Is the task force being dissolved?"

"Maybe. Not yet." He paused. "Drake's been recalled temporarily."

"Really?" That wasn't in the script. Norcross frowned, but he received no reply, and after a moment he just said, "All right."

"One thing." The SAC leaned forward slightly, placing his hands together on the desk and frowning, to indicate he was about to say something important.

"Yes?"

"You mustn't go near the Wo Han Mok."

The warning was superfluous, so Norcross immediately came alert. "Why would I? You just reassigned me."

"Stay away from their office, that's all. If they call you or send any kind of message, don't respond, but let me know immediately."

"Do you have some reason to think they will?"

"I'm trying to keep the boundaries of this investigation clearly drawn. That's all."

Norcross studied him and decided he wasn't going to get anything else.

The interview had ended a few minutes later, the SAC remembering to shake hands this time as he saw Norcross out the door. The few agents and staff in the office watched with open interest, but Norcross ignored them and sat at his desk, flipping through files, until everyone drifted back to work. After a while he stood up to leave, stopping only to say goodbye to Sampford, surreptitiously slipping him a note with the café's address before going out the back stairwell again.

He was on his second cup of West Sumatran—"no steamed milk, please, no cream, no sugar, no cinnamon, no sprinkles, no anything"—when Sampford finally showed up, shaking off his raincoat.

"Sorry, I was running down a query." He looked around at the faux zinc and marble decor. At the front counter a sunburned woman in a wrinkled khaki skirt was ordering a complicated drink distantly related to cappuccino; nearby a young man with very small, rectangular eyeglasses was typing two-fingered on a titanium laptop. "I've never been here before. Guess that's the point, huh?"

"Walls," said Norcross. "Ears. You know."

"The SAC talked to me after you left. Explained it just like you said he would."

"The decisions were all made on the Director's floor last night." Norcross shrugged. "A few people were kind enough to let me know."

"I guess if you're around for thirty years, you make some friends."

"Twenty-eight."

"But who's counting, right?" Sampford smiled.

"Something I have to say." Norcross sipped his coffee, the tiny cup almost invisible in his callused hands. "I'm seeing this one through. Doesn't matter what the SAC's orders are." He set down the cup. "I'm not giving up."

"Yes."

"That's not my point." Norcross looked up. "You're still on the A list, far as I can tell. But if you keep talking to me, you're going to have problems."

Sampford waved one hand shortly. "Not important. You think I'm going to walk away?"

"Might be easier."

"No thanks." He didn't seem offended, and the topic was closed. "Anyway, you're right about the funny connections. Take a look at this." He pulled out a single piece of paper, a long list printed on the office laserjet and marked over with scrawled annotations in pen. The numerical strings meant nothing to Norcross.

"It's the SAC's phone log," said Sampford. "All his calls in and out since last night."

"My. Does he know you have this?" Norcross looked more closely. "Does he know you *could* have this?"

"If he thinks his calls are private, he hasn't been paying attention. Our PBX security is a joke."

"Hmm." Norcross noticed that Sampford avoided the question.

"Now, most of these are just what you'd expect. All the 202–324 exchange numbers, those are headquarters in Washington." He'd lined them out. "This one's his home. This is Masa's Bistro downtown—dinner reservations, maybe? This is the Crescent City Resident Agency, and we can guess what that conversation was about. And so forth."

"You figured all that out this morning?"

"Most of the numbers are obvious, or I just looked them up on the internet. Took about twenty minutes." He held up a hand. "Yeah, yeah, I know—in the old days, I would have had to spend three days in the library with the crisscross directories. And then walk back five miles through snow drifts. Times have changed."

Norcross smiled but said nothing.

"Well, anyhow, I pretty much eliminated all except one. And the thing is, if I'd been thinking I wouldn't have had to do even that much—it leaps right out when you're paying attention."

"This one?" Norcross pointed at one line that had been both highlighted and circled in pen, the only one not crossed out.

"Of course. But can you see why?"

It took him about fifteen seconds. "Oh, hell," he muttered. "472."

"Right. Same area code as Drake's caller."

Norcross grimaced. "Same number?"

"No. Just the same area code and exchange. But I think I narrowed it down further than Drake did. 472-688-6524 called the SAC at 8:07 this morning, they talked for eleven minutes. This number I found in the phone book, 472-688-6000. Obviously part of the same agency, right? Their main switchboard, as it happens." He stopped.

"Okay. Great." Norcross gave him his moment of triumph. "So who is it?"

"Crypto City." Sampford couldn't help smiling. "The National Security Agency."

Customers had been drifting infrequently in and out, while squalls of rain gusted against the cafe's tall glass windows. The two counter employees were idle, talking in a bored way about computer games involving shooting and axes and chainsaws.

"So who is it? Do you have a name?"

"No." Sampford looked disappointed. "You call up and some woman answers, but all she says is the '6524.' The extension. I tried twice, and both times I guess I said the wrong thing, because she hung up."

"So they're careful. Probably standard telephone protocol for the whole organization." Norcross thought about it. "Here, let's try something. Who's the current NSA director?"

"Uh . . . what is this, a test?" It took him just under a minute—he called the FBI's main Washington number on his cell phone, switched to the library, and asked a reference clerk, who checked the federal register. "His name's Yount," he said, and spelled it.

"Good. Can I use the phone?" Norcross took it, glanced at the sheet of paper, and dialed.

"Good morning," he said, and continued without leaving the respondent any time to answer. Sampford watched with interest. "This is John Haskell, I have to reschedule my three o'clock next Thursday with Director Yount. An NSC briefing just landed on my calendar—what? It's not? Oh, I'm sorry . . . look, could you transfer me over to his office? Oh, great, thanks."

A thirty-second pause followed, and then Norcross was talking again. "Hi, John Haskell here, is this Anthony? Oh, for Christ's sake, I'm stuck in some sort of forwarding hell . . . I'm sorry, could you just send me back to the last extension? Yes, that's right, 6524 . . . yes, Matthew Rice . . . thanks, that's so helpful." He clicked off.

Sampford grinned. "Gee."

"Matthew Rice." Norcross wrote it on the paper. "Okay, we've got an NSA manager taking an interest. Let's suppose he's involved somehow, and not for the better. Probably helped push me off the task force— why else would he be calling the SAC?"

"We need background." Sampford was straight in his chair, eyes bright.

"The clerk in the library might have something," Norcross said. "But it won't be much."

"What about your friends at headquarters?"

"They can probably dig something up." He nodded. "I'll give them a call."

"If Rice really is involved . . ." Sampford was thinking. "If he's running the kind of operation that involves gunning down dozens of innocent civilians, he might be off the organization chart, right? I bet he's using a personal cell phone for the more sensitive calls he has to make."

"Good." Norcross approved. "Your turn—how do you find out the number?"

"Um." He hesitated. "Your friends at headquarters?"

"No. They won't have that kind of detail. The other way around, if we were the NSA and they were FBI, it might be different, of course." He smiled. "How many cellular providers can there be around Baltimore? Five or six, tops? Just call each of them up, pretend you're Matthew Rice and you lost your last phone bill, which you think is overdue. And you're so darn absentminded, you can't remember the number . . ."

THIRTY

VANDEVEER WAS TRAPPED in an infuriating off-peak traffic jam, no one moving, where Route 1 narrowed from four lanes to two north of Moss Landing. Far ahead, just visible through the rain, blue flashers indicated police cars, and two ambulances had screamed down the breakdown lane ten minutes earlier. Cars on the other side of the median drove smugly past at seventy-five miles an hour. So far the radio stations hadn't picked it up, since the traffic helicopters had been grounded by the weather. He jabbed at the radio's presets, swearing, wondering who had changed all the stations. Probably the garage attendant in his condo building; Vandeveer should have tipped better last Christmas.

When the STE buzzed, his irritation flared up even further, and he scrabbled in his softsided leather briefcase to catch the call before it kicked into voice mail. He kept his regular cell phone in his pocket and rarely used the secure phone, which was heavy and awkward, more than doubled in size by dedicated encryption hardware. And because the special phone, while totally secure against most eavesdropping, had actually been provided by the NSA itself, his conversations were surely vulnerable to their monitoring. Like most of his colleagues, who'd spent their careers intercepting other people's communications, Vandeveer had an extremely developed sense of personal privacy.

"4117." He jabbed the Talk button and recited his extension, holding the phone slightly away from his ear until he saw the orange LED light up, indicating that a fully encrypted link had been established.

"Rice here. Where are you?"

"On the road. There's an accident, nothing's moving."

Rice made an annoyed sound. Their voices were slightly delayed, as if the conversation was bouncing off a distant satellite. "I suppose we don't need the video. Can you talk now?"

"Sure."

"When was the last intercept?"

"Yesterday afternoon. Tripwires on four of Picot's accounts caught him logging in."

"You're sure it was him?"

Vandeveer rolled his eyes but his voice stayed even. "Not certain, of course. But he had to use separate passwords on each, and he's careful about security—I doubt he'd let himself be impersonated so easily."

"They should have backtracked the routing."

"He wasn't in long enough on any of them to do it real-time. And he was using new ISP accounts for the access. By the time the techs got through the providers, he was gone."

"But they know where he was?"

"Yes." Vandeveer paused while a wrecker appeared in the breakdown lane, horn blaring, forcing aside a Lexus whose driver had thought to jump the queue. "A rest area on Interstate 80 in Nevada. Through a pay phone."

Rice said nothing for so long that Vandeveer checked the handset to make sure they hadn't dropped the connection. When he finally spoke, he sounded uninterested and relaxed, a sign Vandeveer recognized as indicating the exact opposite.

"They're on their way out here," said Rice. "The airport didn't work, so they're driving."

"Well, possibly."

"What are they doing? How much do they know?"

The questions were rhetorical. Vandeveer waited, glaring impatiently at the immobilized cars all around him.

"All right." Rice sounded more definite. "We've got a different FBI agent taking over the investigation in California, and they're probably not going to get anywhere fast. It's up to you."

"I know."

"This just has to end," said Rice. "And I'm counting on you to see that it does." He cut the connection.

"Great," Vandeveer muttered to himself, listening to rain drum on the roof. Traffic still wasn't moving. After a moment he shoved the STE back into the bag and opened his normal cell phone, tapping from memory a number he would never have put into the speed-dial.

It only rang once. "Yes?" The man's voice was curt.

"What the fuck." Vandeveer was equally sharp. "How could you not find the damn thing?"

"We were interrupted."

"No shit. You all kind of went off the rails, didn't you?"

"They came in shooting. We didn't have any choice." The man coughed once. "There was a laptop there, a ThinkPad whatever, but the serial number was different and it didn't have the Chinese characters burned into the case. It wasn't the same one."

"So you quit looking when the firing started?"

"We finished the search. I'm telling you it wasn't there."

"You could have missed it."

"No."

Vandeveer didn't say anything for a moment, knowing an argument would be pointless. He drew a long breath, let it out. "Fine. It wasn't there. Where else it could be I haven't the faintest idea, but it wasn't there. Okay."

"So now what?"

"They're moving. Did you know that? Rice thinks they're on the road, headed east."

"Yeah?" Without interest.

"I'm not sure I agree. I think they might show up at our doorstep."

"Could be. They do seem persistent."

"You ought to be down here at Dunshire."

The man grunted. "Charley took one in the side. He can get around, but he's not much use."

"Invalid him out, then."

"That means we'll be down to three."

"But no other injuries, right?"

"Yeah."

"So it'll be you three against a computer geek and a girl. What are you trying to tell me?"

This time the man's grunt sounded more like a laugh. "They're doing pretty good, what I see."

Vandeveer sighed loudly. "Well, if you're not too intimidated, I'll meet you at Foxton Cove, okay?"

"Yeah." The man hung up. Vandeveer muttered again and leaned on the steering wheel. A helicopter rattled past overhead, flying low under the raincloud, and slowed as it approached the accident scene: medevac or news team, he couldn't tell. Either way, it didn't look like the road would be clearing soon.

THIRTY-ONE

NORCROSS EXPECTED CATHRYN to be driving the department's Explorer again, so he was surprised when an undistinguished, five-year-old Honda splashed over to the curb and she rolled the window two inches open. "Get in!" she shouted over the rain drumming down. He and Sampford ducked out from beneath the construction scaffolding where they'd been waiting, both soaked through by the time they slammed the doors. Sampford had the backseat to himself, though he had to shove aside stacks of files, empty plastic water bottles, and a cardboard box with some oily tools clanking around.

"You should have just come to the station," Cathryn said. "I could have had a space held for you in the garage."

"Best this way." Norcross rubbed his hair, shaking out most of the water, and promptly forgot he was wet. Cathryn pulled back out into the street.

"We're off the record, huh."

"Way off," said Norcross. "If you don't mind."

"As far as the desk knows I'm at a meeting downtown." She stopped at a light. "Which is true enough. Where to, anyway?"

"Down to 4th, and across Mission Creek Channel."

They'd waited a quarter hour on the sidewalk across the street from Union Square. In the heavy rain the small park was sodden and deserted, the expensive hotels and department stores surrounding it forlorn and empty of shoppers. Norcross and Sampford amused themselves by watching the newly installed two-story video screens facing each other from building fronts across the square, running silent music video and quick-cut advertising. But the steady drips and gusting sheets of rain had left them wet and increasingly unhappy when Cathryn finally showed.

"I was thinking we might discuss the case," said Norcross.

"The case." Cathryn looked thoughtful. "To start, I understand you're not on it. In fact, I got fairly clear orders to stay the hell away from you."

"That wouldn't be a bad idea, really. Your job and all."

"Right." Cathryn shrugged and accelerated across the intersection as the light changed. "Good, that's out of the way. So. What the fuck is going on?"

"Well, I'm not just off the task force, I may be out of the Bureau soon."

Sampford looked up, surprised. "What?"

Norcross glanced at him. "A vice president in the Personnel Division called me last night, from Washington. Did you know we have VPs back at headquarters? I didn't . . . she told me that if I don't report to Crescent City on schedule they'll start a disciplinary action."

"You're not supposed to be there until next Monday, I thought."

"The SAC changed his mind and made it Thursday. Tomorrow."

Sampford frowned. "That's not how it's usually done."

"No, it isn't." He paused and added, "The Inspection Division is apparently involved, too. I had a message from an IA on my voice mail. Something about expense vouchers."

Cathryn was driving carelessly in the downpour, following a lurching city bus ten feet back. As Norcross was talking she leaned forward to switch off the scanner bolted under the dashboard. "You're being railroaded. Someone wants you somewhere else in a hurry."

"So one might think." Norcross made a raspy chuckle. "As it happens, we think we know who."

"Oh?"

"Sampford here figured out that our boss has been taking calls from the National Security Agency." As Cathryn's frown deepened, he described how Rice appeared.

When he finished, she glanced at Sampford in the rearview mirror. "Hacked your chief's phone log, huh," she said. "That inspector's going to be after you, too, soon enough."

Norcross chuckled again. "He'll be okay. Worse comes to worst he can dime me out, cut a deal."

Sampford was drying off his handgun with a handkerchief. He ejected the magazine to check for dampness. Looking up from the dark, gunmetal components in his lap he said seriously, "Don't worry about me."

"Of course not." Norcross nodded. "Tell the captain about your research."

"Sure." Norcross's sources had come up with basic information on Rice, and Sampford had dug further the previous evening, working well into the night. "Normally we wouldn't be able to get much, since the NSA is about as open as a nuclear repository. They can't even be FOIA'd—the Freedom of Information Act specifically exempts them. But there was a fair amount of open-source information on Dunshire, and even some material in the congressional record, from when Rice showed up for a hearing on spy agency budgeting. He's a green-eyeshade type. Anyway, that's where we made the connection to this guy Vandeveer." He finished reassembling his pistol and snapped it back into his belt holster. "Vandeveer used to work with the Special Collection Service, which is a joint NSA–CIA project, and fortunately for us the CIA is a sieve compared to Fort Meade."

"Hold on," said Cathryn. "You're losing me."

"Sorry." He rubbed his eyes. "The SCS is a black-bag group. Most of the NSA's intercepts are rather distant—satellites listening in to microwave traffic, taps on overseas phone cables, like that. But sometimes they need to get much closer. They want to catch some dictator's phone calls, for example, they need a hardwire bug in a switching station, or one right in his palace. Or maybe they want a device inside a North Korean embassy. Or a French embassy, for that matter. For these jobs, they need technical teams who can break-and-enter under difficult, dangerous conditions. That's SCS."

"And this Vandeveer worked for them?"

"For fifteen years, mostly in eastern Europe, and later in Taiwan and China. A real gunslinger—you can imagine."

Cathryn shook her head. "Boys just want to have fun."

"I don't know if he enjoyed it, but that's a long time in the field." Sampford paused to remember a date. "He was pulled out in 1997, I think, and came back to Fort Meade. For three years after that he served as an NSA liaison to Capitol Hill, doing briefings for the intelligence committees. This is where Rice comes into the picture. I said he's an accountant, but that isn't fair. He's senior, just about the top level of the permanent staff. One of the things Rice is in charge of is a group called the Technology Assessment Working Committee."

"Their bureaucracy sounds as bad as ours."

"My sense is that some turf infighting was playing itself out. There was a full-scale reorganization around then, and the TAWC was formed to take on an assignment that each of two feuding directorates refused to give up."

"Which was what?"

"The NSA finally realized that private-sector technology was getting away from them. For decades they'd been confident that their programmers, their analysts, their computers were the best in the world, and they were right. But by the mid-nineties Silicon Valley was catching up, maybe even surpassing them. They'd had their heads stuck in the sand, and they had no idea how to deal with the cypherpunks, the independent cryptologists, the huge strides taking place outside their sealed world. The TAWC realized they needed a much stronger connection to the scientists and developers outside their walls, and as one avenue they set up Dunshire Capital Partners."

"Sounds like an investment company."

"That's exactly what it is. Venture capital, quasi-independent. In a small way, they buy into various companies, and now and then they acquire a patent or a technology outright. But mostly they're just in the game, sitting at the conference tables, listening to very smart kids think up tomorrow's breakthroughs. A window on their world, more than anything."

"Or a tap," said Norcross. "Which is a better analogy, maybe, given who's doing it."

"So Rice is running Dunshire?" Cathryn asked.

"No." Sampford shook his head. "Rice is the inside guy, still at headquarters. He put Vandeveer in as Dunshire's senior partner."

"Seems like an odd choice, an ex-spook like that."

"He spent three years schmoozing politicians," said Norcross. "Which means he can tell convincing lies with a straight face. That might be closer to the job description."

They were driving slowly along 16th Street in heavy traffic. The rain continued to beat down, and Cathryn wasn't paying much attention to road conditions.

"This is all very interesting," she said. "My tax dollars at work, and so forth. But what's the connection?"

"Ah." Sampford smiled. "Dunshire was buying Blindside out." He explained the deal they'd pieced together from the fragmentary documents and files in the destroyed office.

"I guess I should read the reports the detectives keep emailing me," Cathryn said when he'd finished.

"Drake was the first one to figure it out," said Norcross. "I called him yesterday, he told me what he knew. He's not sure if he's still on the task force or not—I think ATF is getting the same kind of pressure as our SAC. Drake wouldn't say."

"I thought he might surprise us," said Cathryn. "The quiet guys are the ones to watch." She signaled and turned off the main road into an emptier, increasingly industrial area. "We're getting close to the marina."

"Take a right on Illinois," said Norcross.

"Okay . . . so what's it all mean?"

"That's the problem, I can't put it together yet." A rare note of frustration entered his voice. "The NSA is clearly involved, but they certainly wouldn't have shot up their partners. Why would they try to prevent us from catching the killers? All I can figure is that the Wo Han Mok is the key, somehow."

"I was wondering when you'd get around to that." Cathryn looked across at him. "Gangland told me you showed up at the benevolent association again yesterday."

"Really?" Norcross squinted. "It might be convenient if that report took its time getting to the FBI. Don't want to give the inspector any more ammunition just yet."

Cathryn nodded. "I thought you might be off the reservation," she said. "So what were you doing there?"

"I asked for a meeting again, and this time they called me back." Norcross pointed out the window as they were driving past an acres-wide expanse of deserted concrete. "Stop along here somewhere."

Cathryn pulled the car over, and they looked through the rain at the vast, empty parking lot. No Trespassing signs were posted every ten yards on a sagging chain-link fence. The entry gate had been smashed aside long before, and hung in a tangle of rusty steel to one side. In its place a single chain stretched across the gap, secured by a heavy padlock. A metal shed sat at the far side of the lot, a few hundred yards from the Potrero Power Plant, whose ten-story walls were completely featureless beneath massive turbine steam towers.

"I'll be seeing them tonight," said Norcross. "Over at that little shed, if I understood the directions right."

"What time?"

"Eight. This is still in Wakefield's district, right?"

"Sure." Cathryn watched sheets of rain sweeping across the desolation of cracked concrete. Not a single car had passed since they stopped. "We don't get many calls up here, and when we do it's usually just cleanup. Abandoned cars set on fire, illegal dumping . . . bodies, occasionally."

"I wasn't going to argue about the location."

"Why not?"

"I'm sure they're just looking for some privacy." A glint of humor might have crossed his face. "What with Gangland all over them."

"Privacy." Cathryn grimaced.

"If they wanted me dead, they would have tried already."

"Maybe. So why did you bring us up here?"

"Now you know where we'll be. I'll give you a ring when I'm done. If you don't hear from me, you might have a unit swing by."

"Right."

A few quiet moments passed. Cathryn seemed to be glowering out the windshield. Norcross examined her profile.

"They'd spot backup a mile away," he said quietly. "I'm not asking for help."

Unexpectedly, Sampford spoke up. "I'll go with you."

"You don't have to." Norcross shifted his gaze.

"They know me from Monday morning. Like you said, they'll have checked me out just like you, so they won't be surprised if I'm there."

He appeared determined. After a moment Norcross nodded. "All right."

Cathryn put the car into gear, pulled away, and swung

through a sharp U-turn on the empty street. "I have to get to work."

After more silence, Norcross spoke in the same quiet voice he'd used earlier. "You have too much to lose," he said. "I've almost got my thirty, and San Francisco's not my home. The kid's just young." Sampford frowned, but he saw the slight creasing of humor glint across Norcross's face again, and he didn't say anything. "Anyway, we need someone still in the loop. It'd be stupid to blow up all the bridges at once."

He stopped, and finally Cathryn jerked her head once, grudgingly. "Okay."

Norcross sighed. "The other thing is, someone's going to have to be around to explain what's really going on, in the end." He paused. "There are too many powerful interests involved. I'm getting a stronger and stronger sense that when a convenient story finally blasts up at ninety miles an hour, truth is going to be back down the road changing a tire."

"Oh, right." Cathryn suddenly laughed. "That must be how you talk back home."

"I'll tell you something," said Norcross, relaxing. "The reporters love it."

MOLLY had spent the morning dozing fitfully in the car, grateful for the blurring anonymity of the steady rain. The night before, desperate for rest but unwilling to risk a motel, she'd driven all the way back to the Bay Area, the windows cracked open, rain blowing into the car as she listened to AM stations fade in and out. In Stockton, still sixty miles from Oakland, she found a large truck stop and parked deep in the back lot. She bought some chips and bottled water from a bank of vending machines, the tiled atrium echoing emptily at three a.m., and finally slept uncomfortably curled up in the backseat.

At 1:30, half an hour after his flight was due to land, Molly called Wade's cell phone again. He was indeed already on the ground, in fact standing at a rental car counter. She told him where the truck stop was and went back out to wait.

He took less than an hour, but when a tap on the window woke Molly from a nap she hadn't meant to take, she was surprised to see Eileen standing outside the car.

"Eileen?" Molly got out, heedless of the drizzle, for a brief, fierce embrace. "I thought they got you at the airport."

"Someone saw you, but they didn't have anything to hold me on."

"I am so glad you're here." She hesitated. "I was expecting Wade."

"Over there." Eileen nodded, and Molly saw him in a nondescript blue Mazda a hundred yards off, the engine running. "He called me last night, and I met him at the airport."

Molly frowned. "Open line?"

"Of course not. We switched to pay phones, using the dumb little plus-one code, but I'm sure it was good enough to slip through. Don't worry about it." She looked around. "Are we clear?"

"I haven't seen anything."

"Good enough." She made a small gesture toward Wade, not looking in his direction, moving her hand once vertically then sweeping it in a short sideways arc.

He brought up the rental, and rolled down its window. "Ready? You carrying anything?"

Although she didn't move, Molly thought she felt the small, folded piece of paper, buttoned carefully into the innermost pocket of her pants. "Package under the seat," she said. "And the clothes that I'm wearing."

Wade stayed in the car, one brawny arm on the window frame, his eyes hidden behind black sunglasses despite the gloomy conditions. "Where's Picot?"

"Gone." She shook her head. "Later."

"All right. Let's go."

"Wait a minute. You rent this under your own name?"

"Eileen used my sister-in-law's credit card. Relax, it's covered."

Molly sat in the front seat, to navigate, and Eileen
handed up a bandanna to tie over her hair.

"We need a motel," Molly said. "Doors facing right
onto the parking lot, close to a highway ramp, steady
traffic but no reason to stop nearby. Near Gilroy is probably best, we'll be close enough to Foxton Cove we
won't have to move again. It'll be ninety minutes from
here at least, the way traffic is."

"You need to rest, I think." Wade kept his hands on
the wheel at ten and two o'clock, maintaining a steady
five-car distance from the shifting vehicles in front of
him, his speed two miles an hour under the limit. He
looked like someone who broke horses for a living, but
he drove like a Minnesota retiree.

"I could sleep for two days."

"That might not be a bad idea. Eileen and me can do
some recon."

Molly sighed. "It might get . . . complicated, you
know?"

"That's okay." He glanced at her. "We brought some
stuff with us." Molly raised an eyebrow. "Useful stuff,"
he elaborated. Eileen grinned, and Molly shrugged.

"We need to make some plans," she said, and fell
asleep thirty seconds later.

THIRTY-TWO

THE RAIN HAD stopped only recently when Norcross and Sampford arrived, and wide pools of black water sheeted the abandoned lot. A waning moon glowed thinly through the clouds. Few of the streetlamps worked, but the power plant was illuminated to virtual daylight, with glaring mercury-vapor lights at ground level and spotlights trained on the towers. From a half a mile away the generating station looked like a city in miniature, rising from the lifeless barrens and sparkling with diamond lights.

"They're already here," said Sampford, peering at the distant shed. Two dark SUVs were parked openly alongside it, and several figures were standing nearby. The headlights were on, casting sharp contrasts of black and white.

"The chain is down. We might as well drive in." Norcross took his foot off the brake and eased over the bump.

He stopped twenty feet from the group and shut off the engine. Five men were watching them closely, silent and still, not yet hostile but fully alert, all dressed in dark and anonymous clothing. Norcross couldn't see their shoes in the poor light. The sixth man was older, probably twice the age of his guards, with jet-black hair slicked back and a hard, deeply lined face. Norcross had been expecting a grandfatherly Confucian sage, but Zheng looked pretty much like what he was: a Chinese thug tough enough to have fought his way to the top and smart enough to have stayed there.

He left the key in the ignition and the car's annunciator binged loudly until both doors were closed.

"Agent Norcross." Zheng's accent was strong but understandable. "And Agent Sampford."

"Sorry we're late," said Norcross, who'd glanced at the dashboard clock and knew they were ten minutes early. Zheng ghosted a smile.

"I congratulate you," he said. "On your promotion."

Fine, thought Norcross, now we know how well connected you are. "It is a meaningless honor," he said. "But thank you."

"Your transfer is a surprise, however."

"For me also." Norcross matched Zheng's oddly formal tone. "But if you are aware I'm no longer involved in the investigation, why are we here?"

"We read reports. We talk to functionaries." His accent garbled the word, and he paused slightly while Sampford caught up.

"Yes?"

"You are the best policeman, I think. Better than anyone on your task force."

"Drake's a good officer."

"He is not here." Norcross waited, and after a pause Zheng continued. "I need to know what you know."

"About?"

"The assassins."

Norcross considered. "But you say you've read the reports."

"Yes."

"Well?"

"They are well written."

The two older men watched each other. Sampford stood half in shadow, half in the bright beam of an SUV's headlight, his posture alert as his eyes tracked steadily back and forth across the silent guards. A steady breeze rippled the long, dark puddles, breaking the reflection of the power plant's dazzling lights rising above them.

Zheng broke off the stare first. "Of course you left much out. Speculation, guesswork, small ideas. Details. Possibilities not developing. Sources you do not tell others about."

"Raw material."

"Yes."

"Why would you be interested?" And after no answer came, "Then why would I share anything?"

Zheng seemed annoyed. "You will talk." He glanced to one side, and one of his guards immediately stepped forward, his hands inside his jacket.

Sampford didn't wait, turning slightly and bringing out his Glock in a flashing sweep that was as fast as Norcross had ever seen. But as he raised it toward Zheng the soldiers were moving too, weapons appearing in their hands almost as quickly. Two knelt, gun arms braced in a kneeling point stance, while the others matched Sampford's textbook Weaver, one arm straight and one bent, legs relaxed. In less than two seconds the discussion was transformed into a hair-trigger standoff, the two FBI agents surrounded by unwavering gun barrels.

Only Norcross and Zheng remained still, their hands at their sides. A gull cawed and flapped away. Norcross slowly let out a breath. No other sound disturbed the scene.

"Right," he said.

Sampford's Glock was motionless, aimed squarely at Zheng's upper chest. He showed no expression, despite the certain death pointing back at him. Zheng grunted in Cantonese, and still no one moved.

"Now what?"

"There's an outstanding warrant on Zheng," said Sampford calmly. "They aren't planning to let us go."

Norcross sighed. "We're both still alive, did you notice that?"

"Zheng is a dead man if they try." Sampford seemed completely at ease. "Reflex alone will put a bullet in him."

"Take a look, will you? They're in a perfect L, holding us in a crossfire without aiming at each other. I see three, what, Walthers? P-99's, maybe?" Zheng nodded, a smile flickering across his face again. "And two HK submachine guns. Professional weapons in professional hands. If they were amateurs most of us would be lying in our own blood now."

"So?"

"So they're not going to shoot. Go ahead and stand down."

Several seconds passed.

"That's not an order," said Norcross.

"Sir?"

"But I think it would be a good idea."

Sampford finally nodded and lowered his handgun to point at the ground, though he held it in a forward ready, and his eyes remained locked on Zheng. After a moment the guards also relaxed slightly.

Norcross looked at Zheng. "Good enough, I guess."

"Okay." Zheng's amusement remained. "I will explain our problem. We own the Blindside company."

"You were selling it to Dunshire Capital."

"Yes. To receive the payout from our investment."

"Only money, was it?" Norcross said with open skepticism. "Of course, you have Blindside's universal cracking technology already. I wonder if the sale is just a bonus."

"China is signatory to the World Trade Organization. Patent protection is fully guaranteed."

"Oh, right, I forgot about that."

"Anyway, you know about our sale. Good. Last Friday the deal was closing."

"Really?" Norcross tipped his head slightly, his first sign of interest. "So that's why Yu was present at the meeting. Was the payment made?"

"We did not receive our money. No."

"Was Dunshire bringing in a suitcase full of cash?"

Zheng frowned. "That is a foolish idea. We use bank transfers, with external authentication. In one account, then into our account."

"Oh."

A drizzle began to mist down, giving the power station's brighter lights a faint, fuzzy halo. Sampford tilted his head forward slightly, to keep the precipitation from his eyes, but he continued to hold his position, the Glock waiting.

"You know Yu," said Zheng. "In your reports, you write about him."

Norcross nodded. "He was important to your organization."

"He was carrying a computer. Laptop."

"Is that what this is about?" Norcross was surprised. "I'm sure it was collected as evidence."

"No. We checked your evidence logs very carefully. It is not there." Zheng frowned again. "I think, the assassins took it."

"All right." Norcross watched Zheng's expression. "There is important information on it?"

"For us, yes."

Sampford entered the conversation for the first time. "Surely Yu kept backups."

"Oh, yes." For a long moment Zheng said nothing further, then, "He was very careful for security."

"So, no problem, then," said Norcross.

"Very careful," Zheng repeated. "So careful, that he encrypted all his information before each backup."

Sampford got it immediately. "You can't read the tapes."

"CD disks. But yes, you are correct. The computer, we could unlock. But the backups are useless."

Norcross was filling in puzzle pieces. "You were at Picot's house, looking for it."

Zheng paused. "Many people were there, that day. It was confusing."

"You want to find Picot before we do, so you can get

the laptop." Norcross thought about it and decided he was offended. "All this trouble of yours, it's over a lousy computer?"

"Not only," Zheng said with sudden sharpness.

"What?"

"The assassins, they attacked us, killed our men, took our money. That is not all right." He paused, and then said carefully, as if he'd practiced the phrase, "No one fucks with me!"

Back across the expanse of concrete, outside the sagging chain link, a car drove slowly past. Norcross watched its headlights in his peripheral vision, waiting until it disappeared up the road. If anyone else noticed they made no sign.

He shook his head. "Private vendettas get no assistance from us."

"It is not revenge." Zheng scowled. "It is business."

"Not our business."

Zheng became quiet, and his face now expressionless. "Agent Sampford is waiting with his gun. But we are six, and stronger."

"You're not stupid."

"But I think, maybe you are."

The steady drizzle had begun to soak through their clothing, and was accumulating in rivulets on the shiny SUVs. Still no one moved.

"I'm off the case," said Norcross finally, his voice like gravel. "Someone else is in charge. Someone else will catch your assassins. I suggest you leave them to it."

When there was no response, he nodded to himself. "We're going now." He looked at Sampford, who said nothing but began to step carefully backward to their car, his handgun still at ready. Norcross simply walked over and opened the driver's door. With the annunciator binging again, he glanced back at Zheng.

"You can stay outside easily enough," he said. "If you let it go, you're almost as much a victim as Blindside. But if you keep gunning for Gannon and Picot, it won't be just them firing back. Only someone really dumb starts a scrub fire on a windy day."

With that he got in and pulled the door shut, starting the ignition as Sampford joined him. They backed slowly in a half circle, turned forward, and drove back across the vast lot. In the mirror Norcross could see the Wo Han Mok watching them, weapons still ready, until they faded into the mist.

"Think that was Cathryn earlier?" said Sampford as they scraped across the curbcut back onto the street.

"Probably. I bet we'll find her waiting around the block."

"What are you going to tell her?"

"What happened." Norcross shrugged, mostly to loosen tension he was just realizing he'd built up. "Good job, by the way."

Sampford nodded, pleased, but only when they'd driven away from the lot did he holster his pistol. "They're not going to give up," he said.

"Of course not. I wouldn't be surprised if they show up at Dunshire's offices."

"Dunshire."

"They seem to be the focal point."

"Think the SAC is going to figure that out?"

"Not my problem." Norcross slowed as he saw a Honda stopped a few blocks ahead, its engine running. "I'm headed for Crescent City, remember?"

THIRTY-THREE

EILEEN AND WADE had already saved Molly's life once.

The three of them landed in Kosovo with Task Force Falcon, late in 1999. Wade was an MP in Molly's unit; Eileen, who'd trained with them in the Special Reaction Team, had been detached as a advisor, sorting out minor disputes between Serbs and Albanians. At that time, still early, the Albanians were generally considered the good guys, innocent victims of Serb aggression. So the MPs didn't think much about traveling around the Albanian countryside, and one bitter winter afternoon Molly and her lieutenant ended up forty kilometers out of town, on routine patrol.

Routine until they entered a little village called Vranjevo, anyway. The place was wretched, a handful of stone and turf huts along a single muddy road, and there were easily fifty people milling around. All men, all of them angry, blocking the road. The lieutenant spoke enough Albanian to get the story: the village was mostly Serbian Kosovars, and not everyone had fled in time. The Albanian mob had cornered a few refugees in a barn—two old women and a man with a broken leg, the ones who couldn't get away.

By that point the Americans were two hundred yards from the humvee, in a field of frozen mud, surrounded by a hostile crowd, and even as the lieutenant tried to calm things down, weapons began to appear. In the late afternoon, a light snow falling, Molly saw sticks and farm tools—scythes, knives, a few battered pistols.

"We're over our heads here," she said.

"Yeah." The lieutenant dropped his voice. A couple of peat fires had been started, throwing off more smoke than light. "All right, the hell with it. Back to the truck."

The first rock caught the lieutenant square in the face, and he dropped to the ground. Shouting from the mob increased, and that's when Molly realized they weren't going to make it to the humvee. She grabbed the lieutenant, who was too dazed to stand, and dragged him into the ancient stone barn where the three Serbs where cowering. He collapsed to the dirt floor, semiconscious.

Molly had two sidearms—hers and the lieutenant's—and four extra magazines, one hydration pack, and two chocolate bars. The elderly Serbs looked at them without speaking, and Molly heard a few pistol shots, the bullets slapping the stone walls. Darkness was settling fast.

They survived only because back at the base, Wade realized they'd gone missing. He couldn't convince a superior officer that there was a problem—at that point the patrol had been out of radio contact only for an hour, not an uncommon circumstance given the mountainous terrain—so he found Eileen, commandeered a battered MUTT jeep from the pool, and followed the route from the patrol's assignment sheet.

When they got to Vranjevo, Eileen, who'd been trying the radio every few minutes, raised Molly on her portable. At that moment Wade saw the abandoned humvee and the crowd beyond, and he drove straight toward them, right off the road, the MUTT bouncing wildly as the mob scattered. He leapt from the vehicle, roaring, and fired most of a clip from his M4 into the sky, while Eileen took a more sensible covering position behind the open door. One man, probably a KLA irregular, pointed a handgun at them, and Eileen shot him in the chest. Everyone else disappeared, and the field was suddenly quiet. Cordite and peat smoke mingled with the MUTT's exhaust.

On the way back, Eileen driving the humvee and Molly and the injured lieutenant with Wade, Molly checked her Colt's magazine. A single bullet remained. She shook her head.

"Don't cut it so close next time, okay?" she said.

"I knew you'd have it under control," said Wade.

NOW, just past nine o'clock, the three of them sat in Wade's motel room, eating Thai food from aluminum flats. The TV, openly chained to the wall, was tuned to cable news but muted. A jumble of tactical equipment— weapons, armor, stun grenades, gas canisters, spare ammunition—was spread across a plastic sheet laid on the bed. Molly and Eileen had the only two chairs, facing each other at a tiny laminated table by the window; Wade stood leaning against the open connecting door to their other room.

"That's a lousy plan," he said.

Molly had yet to shake off the last of her grogginess after sleeping through most of the afternoon. "I need absolute, rock-solid, convincing evidence," she said. "Tying the kill team directly to Dunshire would do the trick. I've seen them. We just have to wait until they show up, and take some pictures."

"They're not that dumb."

"So what's your idea?"

"Go in and take a look around."

"Oh, sure," Eileen said. "Incriminating documents will be sitting out everywhere. What if they work late?"

"Then we have a hostage situation," said Molly. "You

know, I always wondered what it would be like from the other side."

"We can't just wait outside." Wade had driven through Foxton Cove in the late afternoon, while Eileen cleaned their guns and watched over Molly. "They have their own little building right on the water, in between a dockside cafe and a row of pricey-looking condominiums. Quaint as all hell. No on-street parking, some tourist foot traffic but not much, and the whole place is swimming in money. I saw three local cruisers, all double-manned and not by twenty-year-olds either. They'd pick us up inside thirty minutes."

"What about the cafe?"

"It's open air, maybe ten tables on a wide dock built out over the water. The bar's in the middle, in a covered pavilion open on all four sides, with a grill in its center. Barbecue, grilled vegetables, that sort of thing."

"Did you pick up a menu?"

Wade gave her a look. "Point is, you could sit there easily enough, but you'd be completely exposed. Too dangerous."

Eileen finished off her pik pow and opened the sticky rice with mango. "Why don't we just figure out who the alpha dog is and catch him alone? Follow him home or something."

"You've been making up your own rules a little too long," Molly said.

"They're the ones out of control, sounds like."

"I'm really glad you're here. But even with three of us, if there's any kind of firefight, we'll lose. Even if we walk away, we lose, because they'll be that much closer. Surprise is all I have going at the moment."

"Exactly." Wade found a can of fizzy juice in the mess of takeout containers and popped it open, letting a spray of carbonation splash against the wall. "You can't take a chance hanging around their front door, waiting to be seen."

"Hell, I don't know." Molly set her tray aside. "I don't know what to do."

They watched the local news, lowering the volume again when the sports began. Wade packed the police gear back into the duffels, working with practiced efficiency, and set them on the far side of his bed, in the narrow space between it and the wall. He paused when he came to Molly's package. "What's this?"

"What I got at the gun shop. Go ahead."

He tore open the paper and pulled out an ancient Remington 12-gauge, frowning immediately. "Jesus, there's rust on the barrel. And this—a Vzor?" He examined an autoloading pistol with a dull finish and scratched plastic grips. The frame was stamped Made in Czechoslovakia.

"A 75, yeah." Molly shrugged. "I didn't have much money."

"Tell you what." He laid both weapons back into the paper and bundled them up. "We'll drop this off a bridge somewhere. You need anything else?"

"Just the Colt." Eileen had already given her a .45 Lightweight Commander, identical to the sidearm she'd carried her whole time in the MPs. "I'll sleep lots better."

"Even with Wade next door?" Eileen looked at him. "The only guys who could ever sleep in the barracks with you were the artillery crews, especially after you broke your nose the third time."

"Get out," said Wade. "My snoring never woke anyone up."

"That's because no one ever fell asleep."

"No problem," said Molly. "Right now, I could sleep through an air assault."

LATER, lights out, Molly and Eileen listened to the steady rumble next door, not much louder than a Harley, as it waxed and waned with perfect regularity.

"Maybe I'll put a round through the wall," Eileen said. "Probably won't hit him, but it might wake him up for a few minutes."

Molly, in her bed, was thinking about other things. "It doesn't bother me."

"You need your hearing checked."

Headlights swept across the window as a car passed through the lot. A truck's horn sounded from the highway, the long doppler fading into the distance. After a few minutes Eileen said, "I've been thinking on why you called us."

"I trust you more than anyone in the world."

"So why didn't you ask sooner?" She waited. "Seems obvious to me."

Molly didn't say anything, and Eileen sighed.

"Picot, right?"

After a long silence: "Yeah."

"Where is he? What happened?"

"He decided I'd be safer without him." Molly stared at the dim, stained ceiling. "Maybe he's right."

They listened to Wade snore for a while.

"When this is over," Eileen said quietly, "we can go looking for him too, if you want. Might find him faster than just you alone."

"I'm not sure he wants to be found."

"You know what Wade would say."

Molly smiled in the darkness. "I bet he already said it."

"Yeah."

As Molly was finally falling asleep, Eileen said, "Civilian life is hell, isn't it?"

THEY were woken by Wade pounding on the connecting door in the morning, enough light spilling past the shades to suggest it was around seven.

"It's me," he said unnecessarily, coming through. "Trouble."

"Christ," Eileen muttered, and she lowered her pistol, snapping the safety back on.

"I went out for coffee and picked this up." He tossed the morning edition of the *Examiner* onto Molly's bed. In the dim, early-morning light she could make out little but the headline: TWO FBI AGENTS KILLED.

"Last night," Wade said. "In San Francisco."

Eileen was squinting at the article. "It's connected?"

"Yeah, it's connected. They're saying Molly here did it."

THIRTY-FOUR

HIS PAGER HAD buzzed Norcross awake two hours earlier, long before sunrise, but he'd taken his time getting started despite the SAC's demand for speed. He was worn out, and he decided a decent shower and a slow cup of coffee wouldn't hurt. By the time he arrived at the office, the SAC was impatient and annoyed. The cubicles were otherwise deserted except for Sampford, who was fresh and alert and wearing a pressed suit, as usual. He pointed at the SAC's closed door when Norcross arrived.

"Waiting for us," he said.

Norcross shrugged. "I got here as fast as I could."

"Uh-huh." Sampford closed his laptop and stood. "Have a nice breakfast?"

"Yes, as a matter of fact. Hungry, are you?"

Sampford gave him a look and knocked on the door. This time the SAC didn't even bother with a pretense of cordiality, just said "Sit" and glared at them from behind the desk. His eyes were red, and his white shirt was wrinkled and carried a small stain of food on the pocket.

"Two of our agents are dead," he said without preamble. "You heard?"

"No." Norcross was surprised.

"McKenzie and Wolking. Shot in their car last
night."

"I knew Wolking pretty well," said Sampford quietly,
who'd obviously received the news already. "She was
assigned here just after me."

"She was new," said the SAC. "But McKenzie had
sixteen years in. He shouldn't have been caught nap-
ping."

"Wolking was sharp," Sampford said, a slight re-
proof.

"They were executed."

"Why?" Norcross asked.

The SAC's frown deepened. "They were looking into
Dunshire Capital—Blindside's buyers. They must have
gotten too close."

"Had they reported anything yet?"

"No. Tape recorders and notebooks were missing
from the car."

"The initial scene investigator said it looked extremely clean," said Sampford. He glanced at the SAC,
who had given him a sharp look. "I called him an hour
ago. He knew Wolking too."

"Any suspects?" said Norcross.

The SAC jerked his head once, his jaw set. "Gannon
and Picot. It looks like they're still around after all."

"Really?"

"Witness described a tall blonde woman and a young
guy with a beard. That's not coincidence."

"A witness." Sampford's voice had an edge. "If they
were so professional, they wouldn't have showed themselves. Not recognizably."

"That's what he saw."

"Who is the guy?"

The SAC paused. "It was an anonymous call."

The room was silent. Sampford started to speak, then
decided he didn't have to say anything.

"We're not going to second-guess the investigators," said the SAC with finality.

"Is this what you called us in for?" asked Norcross.

"Not really." He laced his fingers together in front of him on the desk and sat up slightly. "You weren't in Crescent City yesterday."

"I took a personal day. Filed an FD-457 and everything."

"This is your last warning. I've heard from Washington. Either you take the new assignment or you'll be suspended on Monday."

Norcross nodded. "Fine."

For a long moment the SAC clearly wondered whether he should push for clarification of an answer that was intentionally ambiguous, but in the end he just said, "Good."

Sampford had opened his notebook. "When is Wolking's funeral?"

The SAC turned his gaze. "Tomorrow, I believe."

"I'd like to attend."

"The Bureau will be well represented without you."

"I knew her." Sampford didn't blink. "There's nothing I'm on that can't wait a day. I'll do it as vacation if I have to."

They locked stares. In the end, the SAC realized he couldn't reasonably refuse, and he grunted assent.

Outside ten minutes later, the heavy oak door closed behind them, Norcross tilted his head toward the elevator and he and Sampford left.

"That was dumb," said Norcross when they were on the street. The government district was still largely empty, this early, though men were beginning to stir in the permanent encampment of homeless on the square. A cold wind pushed a crushed cigarette box up the sidewalk. "How close were you to Wolking?"

"Barely at all."

"But you're screwing up your career to go to her funeral."

"No. Not for that."

"Then what?" A note of exasperation had entered Norcross's voice.

"I'm going with you."

"To Crescent City?"

"Of course not." Sampford smiled thinly. "You're not leaving either. This is where it's going to end, one way or another. Everything's coming together now."

Norcross, his own expression impassive, watched Sampford's determined face for a long moment. "The Bureau needs agents like you," he said. "Too bad they're about to lose one."

Sampford shrugged.

"I used to be young and stubborn," said Norcross. "See where it got me."

"Yeah," said Sampford. "Old and stubborn."

THEY took Sampford's car, but before they started Norcross borrowed his cell phone and dialed Washington. "One of my friends at headquarters," he said to Sampford as it rang. "You probably shouldn't know about this conversation."

"Right."

"What was Rice's personal phone number again?"

"His cellular?" Sampford repeated it from memory.

"Hang on. George, how are you? You heard about Wolking and McKenzie . . . no, we saw each other around the office, but I can't say I knew either of them." For a few minutes they talked about the agents' histories, what they'd done and where they'd been, a quiet memorial.

Eventually Norcross got to the point. "I'm about to go AWOL." He briefly explained the SAC's orders, leaving out all the backstory, and Sampford understood that George already knew the details, must have been a close confidant. "There's a favor I'd like to ask . . . well, thanks. A follow-me on a wireless number." He looked up at Sampford, who recited it again, and Norcross repeated it to George. "As soon as possible, I guess."

The conversation continued for another several minutes, George apparently providing information, since Norcross mostly just said "Uh-huh" and "Got it." When he finally hung up he dropped the phone in the dashboard cupholder, and Sampford pulled out of the parking lot.

"I thought you needed a warrant for phone records," said Sampford.

"Technically that's true only for listening in. There's more leeway if you're not actually running a tap. Of course, the legalities matter only if you're planning to use the results in court."

"I'm surprised the phone companies will cooperate."

"Oh, George is going back-channel, I'm sure. Calling in favors. We're not going to get any kind of fancy triangulation, but he'll be able to tell us roughly where Rice is, so long as the phone is on."

"It's a digital line, so they can narrow it down pretty well. The analog stations are too far apart to be much use."

"If you say so. Phone service in North Dakota didn't get much more complicated than party lines."

"You had phones and electric up there?"

Norcross ignored the comment. "George had some more detail on these NSA guys, mostly from the CIA. I think he knows someone there."

"Anything useful?"

"Rice sounds like a straight shooter, considering where he works. He's outlasted ten Directors, which has to mean something."

"What about the other one?"

"Vandeveer is, what did George say? Colorful. He took on more and more of the tough assignments when he was in SCS, over time, and his CIA counterparts apparently respected him." Sampford snorted. "Yeah, I know. But they're not all fuckups."

"Right." Sampford, like any new recruit, held his interservice rivalries dear.

"Vandeveer also used Special Forces soldiers seconded

in from the army, more than once, which suggests he was good at maintaining relationships across organizations. He had a reputation as a cowboy in the field."

"I bet. With that kind of background, I wonder how he likes going to work in pinstripes every day."

"Yes," said Norcross. "What happened at Blindside seems more like what he'd be familiar with."

"He and Gannon are maybe not on the same side, right? Could be interesting if he gets to her before we do."

"Maybe the Wo Han Mok will show up too."

Sampford smiled. "I can't imagine how the SAC thought you'd stay out of this."

THIRTY-FIVE

AFTER WADE WENT out again to get breakfast burritos, they decided to spend the morning driving around the county, learning the roads they might need if they had to leave in a hurry. Molly overrode their insistence that she stay inside, out of sight.

"So I'm tagged for another murder," she said. "Hardly matters at this point."

"Two," said Wade. "And G-men, at that."

"They're getting desperate, is what it really means. The agents must have been closing in on something significant, otherwise why kill them? Too much trouble, too much risk, just to frame me up further." She set the burrito aside, not hungry. "And if they were close, well, that tells me we're on the right track."

"Right," said Eileen. "Which is exactly why you should keep your head down. Cops and federals are going to be all over this place. The eighth or ninth one who notices you is going to put two and two together."

"You all are cover enough. I'll ride in the back with a hat on."

"Let's at least take two cars," Wade said, giving in.

Last night he'd lined up four cell phones, unplugging the TV to make room for their chargers, and now he handed one each to her and Eileen. "If something goes wrong we'd be an easy target all together in one."

"Hello? We don't have two cars."

"Wade can rent another," Eileen said. "I'll go out and get you some clothes when the stores open."

"Oh. That's not a bad idea."

"Yeah," said Wade, closing up the duffels of weaponry and locking the zippers. "So you look nice and sharp for the perp walk."

"You leaving those for the maids to find?"

"I'll hang out the Do Not Disturb." He glanced her way. "I'm telling you, those Foxton Cove cops are sharp little beavers. When we go in we'll go in hard, but for now I'd hate to be stopped for some dinky traffic infraction and have them discover our gunrunner's bonanza."

It was past noon when they finally started their reconnaissance. The sun was bright, but a sharp breeze and accumulating clouds to the west suggested that weather was again on its way. Once off 101, driving along dappled blacktop roads winding through Monterey's forested canyons, the air cooled. Eileen drove the Mazda, and Wade took their new car, a Cavalier that he complained reeked of cigarettes.

They stayed several hundred yards apart, drifting further and closer depending on terrain visibility, Molly navigating from one county map and several topos that Eileen had found at a local bookstore. They ran the cell phones off the cigarette lighters, redialing every five or ten minutes and speaking elliptically when the mute button was off. Along the back roads, estates were common, no more than glimpses of cedar-shingled roofs behind stone walls and hedges. Here and there small, well-kept signs announced B&Bs or cozy and expensive restaurants.

"Can't blame Dunshire for setting up shop here," said Molly at one point.

"Wait until you see Foxton Cove." The cell phone chopped down the frequency range of Wade's voice, making him difficult to follow at times. "Hard to believe it's a government operation."

It was soon obvious where the roadblocks would go up, if the state police reacted. To the north Route 1 widened to four lanes and saw its first major interchange with 129 near Watsonville. To the south it crossed a wide, boggy slough before approaching Moss Landing. To the east a half-dozen minor lanes meandered through some meadowed hills overlooking the ocean.

"The best route might be County Road G13," said Molly, studying elevation lines on the topo. "Turn up here—it looks like it runs over a saddle and meets 101."

"It's not paved," said Eileen, peering down the dusty lane.

"Map says gravel, but only for a mile."

They followed the track, which soon became a decent country road, and worked out a route that brought them onto Route 156 ten miles south of Moss Landing. The steep hills were forested with jack pine and alder, here and there only a dented bumper rail separating the roadway from a plunging cliff.

"Good enough," said Wade over the phone, when they'd stopped a hundred yards apart near the Castroville interchange. "Let's find a few more back roads."

By midafternoon the sky had darkened, low clouds blowing in from the north and west, and the air was cooling rapidly. They pulled into a gas station on the outskirts of Salinas, the cracked lot empty but for a sandblasted Escort parked behind the cashier's booth.

"We have to take a pass through Foxton Cove directly," said Molly through her window. She remained in the car while Eileen and Wade filled their tanks. "I need to see the layout around Dunshire."

Eileen just shook her head, and Wade said, "Yeah, I know. Don't like it, though. You're the one they'll recognize."

"We'll drive through once, I'll wear my sunglasses. It looks like it might rain anyway. No one will notice."

"I'll stay a few blocks away, parallel. Keep the phone on."

"Good."

They drove back up 101 for the fourth time. Clouds now scudded horizon to horizon overhead, but as they turned off the highway, the day's last sunlight broke through, illuminating trees and houses and cars with a silver glow against the dark purple sky. As they neared Foxton Cove, glimpses of the open bay, choppy and gray, were visible in the distance.

The last few miles into town were marked by a steep gradient of property values; the estates became larger and greener and even more opulent. Near the village center the houses stood closer together, neatly painted Victorians along clean, tree-lined streets. Even the occasional businesses were discreet: gas station pumps concealed from the road by neatly trimmed shrubbery, a wrought-iron cantilever carrying a small wooden sign with a bank's logo.

"We're a quarter mile from the waterfront," said Wade over the phone, as they stopped in front of an exquisitely designed square, cypress and gum trees along the side and a pavilion empty in the middle. "You go straight through, follow that street until it ends right in front of the cafe, then turn left. Dunshire's about fifteen yards along."

"What do you think, five minutes to drive through?"

"If that. Just stay on the waterfront street until you get to the marina entrance and turn left again. I'll catch up to you there."

"Okay." Molly repeated the instructions to Eileen, and they pulled out as the light turned green. Behind them the Cavalier turned away, disappearing around the park.

The street rose slightly and descended a slow hill to the harbor, which was overlooked by a collection of immaculately maintained stone and shingle buildings. The layout was exactly as Wade had described: Molly could see the cafe before them, a dozen people scattered among the tables, two young men in white jackets manning the bar and propane BBQ grills. Beyond a low wooden rail the harbor kicked up small whitecaps, rocking the marina's ranks of sailboats and power cruisers.

At the corner, the nose of their car ten feet from the edge of the cafe's deck, Eileen looked carefully in both directions and turned left, moving at about ten miles an hour. Molly scanned the area, her eyes moving in steady arcs.

The cafe dock ended with a row of wooden planters, holding flowers and trailing vines. Beyond the planters but not well-concealed by them was Dunshire's small parking lot, its sharp white lines delineating only six spaces. Two were occupied, by identical black Ford Expeditions with multiple aerials and opaque tinted windows. No one was visible in the lot, or through the wide glass doors leading to Dunshire's foyer. The building itself, two stories and narrow, was built of weathered gray stone; its foyer was lit but the other windows were dark.

Despite the storm that seemed to be on its way, the street was not empty of pedestrians; tourists strolled along the waterfront, and a pair of men in white shirts and suspenders were talking animatedly at the corner. The setting sun illuminated the area with a soft light all the more striking against the dark sky above the hills to the east.

"Shit," said Molly.

"They're fucking everywhere," muttered Eileen, her hands tense on the wheel, though she kept their speed steady and slow.

"Wade." Molly's voice was flat. "The whole place is covered."

"So get out of there. I'll wait where we said. You take point."

"No," Molly said sharply, and Eileen looked over, surprised. "Go to the square again. We'll meet you there."

"What?" He sounded angry.

"Just do it! Now!" She looked at Eileen and said, "Go."

"What the hell?"

Molly shook her head. "I don't think they made us."

Eileen opened her mouth, shut it, and drove back without further comment, her eyes jumping between the mirrors and the road. They pulled up under a Sargent's cypress just as Wade arrived, sliding into the space alongside and opening his door but not getting out. He held his right hand low, concealed by the door and his body. Eileen had her handgun out in plain view, pointing it toward the floor.

"What's going on?"

"In the cafe," Molly said. "Four Chinese-looking men, all sitting alone and several tables apart. Two tactical trucks in Dunshire's lot. One sentry on the roof, I think."

"Yes." Eileen nodded briefly. "Behind the HVAC unit."

"Seven possibles in the street—men who could have been loitering, all wearing hip-length jackets or loose shirts."

"So why are we still here?"

"One more person you probably missed," Molly said, her voice still strangely flat. "In the cafe, working on a laptop."

"Oh, Christ." Eileen looked at Wade.

"Yeah." Molly glared at nothing. "I thought he left. I thought he was gone."

Wade made to close his door. "We have to pick up our equipment."

"No. There's no time. It would take forty-five minutes to get there and back."

Eileen shook her head. "Nothing's happened yet."

Impatience flashed across Molly's face. "It's going to explode any minute and you know it. As soon as he moves, probably."

"What's he doing there?" Wade paused. "You're assuming he's operating independently."

"He's not on either side," she said bleakly. "Look, I'm going in. Now."

"You've got no cover!" Wade's anger appeared. "Three sidearms between us and no backup. Hell, there's more of them than we have bullets. Walking in there would be suicide."

"I'm going." Molly stepped out of the car, and a moment later Wade and Eileen were standing as well.

"Goddammit, Molly." Wade looked like he wanted to hit something, but Eileen just sighed.

"It's your play," she said. "But you're not leaving me behind."

"You don't have to do this." Molly checked her Colt, not bothering to be discreet, and placed it carefully in her waistband at the small of her back. "I'm sorry." She hesitated. "Wade, you're completely right. It's suicide. Stay out, both of you."

"No." He seemed to come to a decision. "But we're your only edge, right? They don't know we're here. It's not much but let's not toss it away up front."

Eileen nodded. "We'll each take a car. I'll wait up there." She pointed to the slight rise leading to the harbor. "Wade, you go around and come in on the frontage street. We time it right, we'll both be in position when you walk onto the dock."

"I don't think they'll start a firefight." Molly didn't know whether she believed that or not. "There are civilians wandering around down there too. The hard part's going to be getting out."

"I'll give you a minute," said Wade. "Then I'll pull up, and all you have to do is make it to the door. Eileen can cover."

"That'll work."

"Sure." He grimaced. "You know what? This plan sucks worse than the last one."

"Yeah." Molly looked in his face for a moment, turned and touched Eileen lightly on the shoulder.

"Let's go."

WHEN she walked across the waterfront street, appearing from behind a row of parked cars that had shielded her approach, Molly felt like she'd stepped out onto a firing range, but nothing happened. Even Jeb didn't recognize her until she sat down at his table; then the air flashed with tension as everyone else caught up. In her peripheral vision Molly saw the Chinese look their way, and several men in the street stopped pretending they were passersby. Doors opened in both of the parked SUVs.

She ignored everyone but Jeb. After the first instant's shock, his surprise was gone, replaced with—fear? Relief?

"Molly." He lost his voice for a moment. "I didn't see you coming."

She was wearing an Armani knockoff, dark as midnight, the skirt a couple inches too high and the jacket buttoned once over a sleeveless ivory sweater. Her eyes were disguised by clear eyeglasses with small oval frames. She looked like a Wall Street executive.

"We're surrounded," she said. "I think we have about a minute before someone starts shooting."

"I know. The triads and the special ops guys." Only up close was it clear how tense he was. "Someone has a boat out there, too. The Bertram." He gestured with his chin, and Molly looked away from his face long enough to spot a large power yacht at the edge of the moorings, about two hundred yards off. It was holding its position on the open water, unanchored, rocking in the wind-roughened waves. "I think they're Wo Han Mok. Hard to tell from here but they kind of looked Chinese. See how they don't have their fenders out? They're just sitting there, waiting."

"You idiot." But she was smiling, apprehension and relief and adrenaline all coursing through her at once. She pulled off her glasses and set them on the table, their usefulness over.

"I was getting worried." He closed the laptop. "But now you're here."

She reached across the table to cover his hand with hers.

"It turned out I couldn't just leave," Jeb said. "Knowing you were determined to confront them anyway."

"Might have been a dumb choice." Molly glanced

around and decided that almost everyone nearby was armed, hostile and staring at them. "Odds aren't too good."

"A minute ago they were pretty much zero," Jeb said. "I think I'm ahead."

THIRTY-SIX

RICE WAS FURIOUS but his voice remained polite and controlled, so soft as to occasionally become inaudible over the video connection. He wasn't in his office, and Vandeveer thought he recognized a conference room Rice used for particularly private conversations, a barren tank of acoustic tile, its only advantage the likelihood that it wasn't miked. Most managers kept recording devices in their desks, a manifestation of CYA paranoia understandable among professionals whose lives were dedicated to ferreting out other people's communications. But the electronics were like a keyhole to a locksmith—once they were there, they could be used, perhaps compromised. Vandeveer figured Rice had carried his laptop down the hall and set up the connection himself, an indication of how seriously he was taking his security.

The more pressure Rice faced, the colder and more careful he became. Three thousand miles away he was as impenetrable as black ice.

"An analyst on one of the oversight committees

found some puzzle pieces," he said now. "Those dead
FBI agents were apparently on their way to Dunshire."

"I know." Vandeveer had thought about how to deal
with that question all day. "I'd answered some preliminary inquiries on the phone, and they had set up an appointment."

"You told them your deal with Blindside?"

"Of course not." Vandeveer heard the implication and
winced inside. Pointing fingers were being unlimbered.
"They seemed to know a great deal already, though."

"They were chasing Gannon and Picot."

Because this wasn't a question Vandeveer waited,
suffering Rice's unblinking glare.

"Chasing Gannon," Rice repeated finally. "So how
did they end up at Dunshire?"

"They never got there."

"No. Dead in their car in Hunter's Point."

The cell phone in Vandeveer's pocket vibrated, and
he started, then ignored it. "It was a good spot for an ambush—the middle of an abandoned freight yard next to
the old navy base, acres of rusty equipment and empty
buildings. Gannon must have lured them in somehow."

The lines around Rice's mouth tightened. "An eye-
witness called in the shooting."

"Yes."

"So where did he come from, in this deserted wasteland?"

Vandeveer shrugged, moving his hands wide. "I have
no idea. I got the FBI's preliminary report, that's all I
know, and Gannon's their suspect."

One of Vandeveer's ceiling fluorescents was overdue
for replacement and starting to flicker. He'd sent home
his staff after lunch, ignoring questions, and the deserted
office had felt eerie until the operations team began
drifting in.

"Dunshire is critically important," said Rice emphatically. "To the organization, to the Working Committee, to
our basic mission—and to me." He waited for Vandeveer
to nod and continued. "Because of that importance, you
have been granted considerable leeway in fulfilling your

objectives. Unprecedented flexibility, in fact, as many of my colleagues have repeatedly reminded me. You are aware of this."

"It would have been difficult to succeed otherwise."

"Success." Rice considered the word. "Perhaps. All the more reason, then, for me to remind you that there are, nonetheless, definite limits on Dunshire's mandate. Some defined explicitly in our charter, others I'm sure we understand operationally."

"Of course."

Outside Vandeveer's office a man in a gray janitor's uniform materialized, his eyes shaded by an unmarked baseball cap. He tapped the window glass lightly with the barrel of his P226, and Vandeveer looked up, startled. The man jerked his head and pointed to the outside wall, closed his fist, and tapped his hip once. Vandeveer nodded briefly and returned to the screen in front of him.

"I have to go," he said.

"I think we're done." Rice leaned forward, his face now filling the monitor. "This event has approached a point where I'm beginning to consider options," he said, just above a whisper. "You understand?" After a moment his arm moved and the connection was broken.

Vandeveer closed his eyes. When he opened them the operative was beside his desk, having opened the door and traversed the office in two seconds and perfect silence. Vandeveer blinked.

"The girl showed up," the man said in a raspy voice.

"What? Where?"

"She's talking to the kid outside, right now. They're still on the dock."

"No kidding." Vandeveer stood up, starting to smile. "How utterly, marvelously convenient."

THE interception caught Eileen flat-footed. Thirty seconds later, gun muzzles at her neck and side, her face calm and her mind in overdrive, she decided that her attention had been too narrow, but that even full alertness might not have made a difference. The men who'd taken her were fast and confident, their ambush perfectly timed.

Eileen had waited until Molly was halfway across the park, then drove up slowly and stopped the car just past the crest, looking slightly downward at the cafe a hundred and fifty yards ahead. Wade disappeared to the right. A minute later Molly walked past without acknowledgement, paused at the waterfront street, crossed, and stepped onto the dock. Eileen watched, ready to jackrabbit in if Molly drew fire.

Too focused on the scene in front of her, she forgot her flanks. She had no time to react when a man appeared just behind her door, yanking it open with a single jerk. As she looked up he struck a short, savage blow, punching her left arm just under the shoulder with a single folded knuckle and striking the nerve center with exact precision. Eileen gasped in pain, her arm suddenly numb from the elbow downward. Immediately, on instinct, she twisted away, further into the car, protecting her skull. A fraction of a second later the attacker's second strike glanced off her shoulderblade, just as the passenger door opened and another man slipped into the seat next to her.

She jabbed fiercely toward the second assailant's head. He blocked the blow easily, knocking her arm aside, and showed her a handgun in his right hand. He held the pistol as far from her as the car's interior allowed, and despite the awkward angle across his body he kept it steady, aimed at her lower torso. Eileen stopped moving.

"He also is armed." The man's voice was heavily accented, and Eileen realized they were all Chinese. "Four of us, total."

She couldn't reach the pistol, not before he gutshot her. The man outside the door had stepped back, out of the crossfire, but one glance backward confirmed that he also held a handgun, aimed at her head. A third man was standing on the other side of the car. None of them seemed to care that they might be observed.

Eileen let out her breath and realized the speaker was waiting for her to decide that she was boxed. She nodded, once.

"Good," he said. No one moved. "Please give me your weapon, thank you."

She hesitated, then drew the Beretta from her waist. For an instant the calculus was suspended—but the muzzle brushed her neck, the speaker motioned his pistol slightly, and she knew they could still kill her easily. She sighed and handed over the gun.

"Now, you sit in back, please." He still hadn't blinked.

"What?"

"Quick, please." Following their gestures Eileen got out and opened the Mazda's rear door.

They were settled thirty seconds later. The speaker sat behind the driver, with Eileen at the other end of the rear seat and the third man between them. He was holding his pistol with two hands, twisted in his seat to keep the muzzle pressed into Eileen's side just below her ribs, watching her hands and torso intently, never once looking at her eyes. She sank back into the soft seat.

"Your friend?" said the man who was evidently the leader, the only one who'd spoken so far. Eileen said nothing and the man shrugged. "We want our computer," he said. "That is all."

Eileen remained silent.

"Okay, shoot you now?" The man sounded indifferent.

"No."

"She is going to meet Mr. Picot, yes?" Despite the accent, he pronounced the name correctly. "And Mr. Picot has the computer."

"I don't know that."

"We will watch what can happen, from here."

They saw Molly sit down, too far away to observe her face, or Jeb's. No one came running up; no gunfire erupted; no cars squealed to a stop in front.

A minute passed. Molly and Jeb appeared to be talking quietly.

"You've got this all wrong," said Eileen cautiously. "Molly had nothing to do with the attack on Blindside." No reaction. "She was just caught in the middle. She has no connection to any of you. Since this whole thing exploded she's only been trying to stay alive. You're going after the wrong people, don't you see?"

The leader listened without apparent interest, and his companions gave no indication of understanding English. Now he shook his head once.

"I explain?" He paused. "Maybe she and he are the assassins. We would like proof, yes they are or no they are not. That would be good. But now, here, today, it does not matter. All the police, all America thinks they are. And Mr. Picot has the computer. We have watched Dunshire two days, waiting. It had to be Dunshire, yes? Because only three groups are involved—Blindside is dead, we know who we are, Dunshire is left. So. Now we finish the story."

"Finish the story?" Eileen repeated.

"Yes. Then we all . . ." He hesitated, seeking a phrase. "Then we all move on." He smiled.

Eileen shrugged in frustration. Her weight shifted slightly, and when her hand came back down it was on the door's armrest, half-concealed by her loose jacket. She looked away from the leader's eyes, scanning the interior once more.

The leader grunted, and there was a quick exchange in Chinese between the three men. Down below a large truck drove past; a moment later Eileen saw Molly stand up. The driver started their car, barely waiting for it to turn over before moving away from the curb and accelerating down the hill.

BECAUSE he was facing Dunshire's offices, Jeb was the first to notice when Vandeveer stepped through the front doors, accompanied by two younger men in gray coveralls. All three were holding weapons, casually, alongside their legs so they weren't immediately obvious to an observer. But just as Jeb started to say something, Molly spoke first.

"Wade's here."

The Cavalier appeared up the block, a hundred yards away and driving at the posted twenty-five miles an hour.

"Men coming out of Dunshire," said Jeb. "Armed."

"Move." Molly was suddenly holding the Colt and she stood in a single flowing motion. A half-second's glance had been enough to recognize the two men from the assault on Blindside. Around them she saw abrupt movement as men went into action: some pulling handguns from under their clothing, some also standing, some ducking for cover, some starting to run toward them—

—and a blue Mazda barreled down the street from the town center, its engine roaring. In the parking lot Vandeveer paused, staring, and both men with him raised submachine guns. The car crossed the waterfront road without slowing and slammed over the curb, barely slowing as it crashed into the patio tables.

Inside the car, a block away and five seconds earlier, Eileen had made her move: she jerked her head and shouted, "There!" In a split-second of distraction, she shoved her feet hard against the floor, jamming herself backward. At the same time her left hand caught the barrel of her guard's Walther and twisted it forward. He was already pulling the trigger and the muzzle blast burned her hand but all three bullets passed just forward of her stomach. She grabbed at the door handle.

The sedan struck the curb at that instant, giving her an extra second while the man grunted and tried to force the pistol back into her midriff. As the car jolted Eileen punched the door and kicked herself backward, still hanging onto the man's gun hand. She fell out the door as it swung open, flung sideways as the frame caught her trailing legs, and landed bang on the boardwalk, hauling the gunman out with her by sheer desperate strength. They had all of the car's forward momentum, and he took the full brunt of the cafe table they immediately slammed into. His body folded around the collapsing metal and Eileen skidded away, stunned, sliding across the planks.

In front of the barbecue grills, where he'd been tending a half-dozen steaks, the gaping bartender just managed to leap aside, his jump fueled by terror. The car smashed into the bar, cutting off the driver's scream, as the other man, the leader, rolled out the other door.

Barely two seconds had elapsed since the sedan hit the curb, and firing had begun from all quarters, bullets slapping into the bar even as it disintegrated with the impact of the car's collision. The explosion came a moment later, and Molly could never decide whether it was the gunfire or the car itself that detonated the propane tanks. It didn't matter. The fireball was immediate and immense, destroying most of the bar. The flaming wreckage slid off the deck and tumbled into the bay, secondary explosions sending up huge gouts of water as the remaining tanks blew.

Chunks of metal and burning wood rained down. Vandeveer's team, farthest away, recovered fastest and sprinted up, firing at everyone. The only Chinese from the car to survive the collision—the leader—had landed behind a box planter, safe for the moment, and he clawed out his own handgun despite the blood running freely down his face and arm. His four associates converged on his position from their tables, firing blindly for protective cover.

A few innocent bystanders were starting to scream, one elderly man running for the street, another woman crouched over her unconscious partner and trying to stanch the bleeding from his neck. The two bartenders had disappeared. But most of the people nearby had pulled out weapons and flattened themselves behind overturned tables and other debris.

Jeb and Molly had both dived when Eileen's car crashed onto the dock, scattering tables and chairs. A flaming chunk of metal flew over their heads. By luck rather than design they ended up behind an overturned bench, and splinters and broken wood exploded around them as bullets tore into the wood.

Molly saw Eileen look up as a man in a Hawaiian shirt rose and sprinted toward her, his pistol in two hands, apparently ignoring all the other shooters. Eileen was unarmed and still half-stunned. Molly fired twice and the man jerked aside and down, his handgun flying onto the dockboards.

"Molly!" Over the din of firing all around them they heard Wade roar from the street. He'd pulled up the Cavalier and was crouched behind the open door, trying to keep the engine block between himself and the horde of shooters in the wreckage of the cafe. He attracted the attention of Vandeveer's men, who began raking the car from several directions.

Molly risked a look around, raising her head only enough to get her eyes above the bench, and realized that Eileen was still completely exposed, vulnerable from all sides. Even before this thought was complete, she saw two other men taking aim and she fired immediately, dropping one and forcing the other into cover.

A soft crump sounded, and despite the free-fire clatter Molly found herself tucking into a ball and covering her head before her conscious mind caught up. A fraction of a second later one of the black SUVs in Dunshire's lot exploded, disintegrating in a blast that sent metal shards howling in all directions. One of Vandeveer's men went down, his face half torn away by shrapnel.

"Someone's firing missiles!" Molly screamed at Jeb, who was swiveling his head in confusion.

Another crump, and this time the explosion shattered part of Dunshire's building, destroying one of the offices overlooking the water. The outer wall began to collapse.

"From the boat," Jeb called back, and Molly saw a silhouette on the Bertram's flybridge, recognizing the tube of an anti-tank rocket as it flashed again. She squeezed her eyes shut and there was another blast, Dunshire's outer wall now blown largely to pieces. Someone was thrown into the water, screaming, still clutching an assault rifle.

The Chinese had apparently decided that Vandeveer's soldiers were their immediate problem, and disciplined fire from the four men surrounding their injured leader was taking a toll on the less organized operatives in gray. Two of the latter scuttled to a position closer to Molly, forcing her to use up the remainder of her single magazine keeping them down.

"I'm out," she said, mostly to herself, but Jeb had already realized and was abruptly in motion, rolling across the dock away from the bench. "Jeb!" Molly screamed as she saw him in the open, able to do nothing to keep him alive. Bullets cracked all around them.

His roll ended near the fallen attacker who'd run at Eileen earlier, and just as Molly realized what he was doing he scooped up the man's P226 and slid five more feet to slight cover behind a piece of torn metal. The two men who'd come nearer swung to aim at him.

"Take the damn gun!" he yelled and threw it at Molly without hesitation. She snatched it from the air one-handed, aimed and fired in the same motion. One attacker, fifteen feet away, spun backwards, his chest shattered. The other stumbled, his submachine gun stuttering random fire, and as he fell near Eileen she kicked him and grabbed at the weapon. The brief tug-of-war ended when Eileen punched him sharply on the nose with the heel of her left hand, snapping his head back. At that moment a bullet caught her in the leg and she fell back again in a spray of blood.

Molly twisted around to see Vandeveer himself, twenty yards away, crouched behind one of the planters and aiming his pistol calmly, two-handed, one arm resting on his forward knee. For an instant they stared at each other's eyes, and she fired the last rounds from the Sig, hardly aiming, shooting from a weak stance and the recoil driving her hand backward. He ducked out of sight. Eileen groaned, still alive.

Another crump was followed by a blast inside the near

corner of Dunshire's building, and this time the side wall was reduced to bouncing rubble. One of the Chinese was struck by a rock, or maybe a bullet—he crumpled, and his Walther fell through a gaping hole in the half-destroyed boardwalk.

That splash was followed by an utterly unexpected pause. For several seconds the dazed combatants hesitated, all trying to catch up, unsure what threats remained. Rumbling and sizzling from the burning cafe were the only sounds, and for Jeb and Molly even these were nearly inaudible through the ringing in their ears.

The odd, momentary stasis ended when Molly saw another man running up to Vandeveer's position, holding an assault rifle at his waist. Vandeveer turned and began to shout, "Where the fuck were—" when every remaining combatant fired simultaneously. It sounded like a single, long explosion, all the shots overlapping each other, and Vandeveer and his final soldier jerked like rags on a string and then fell, the automatic rifle emptying its magazine into the boardwalk.

This time the pause lasted nearly thirty seconds. Molly and the triads were pointing their weapons at each other, twenty feet apart, but no one fired. Vandeveer's few remaining men had paused when they saw him fall. Through the long tunnel of her damaged hearing Molly caught the first wailing of sirens approaching. Under the darkening sky flames lit the shattered boardwalk with a volcanic glow.

An unmuffled engine roared, and the Bertram tore up to the dock, rounding in on a sharp turn that sent a high wake crashing over the broken boards. The Chinese ran for it, three men carrying a fourth and helping the fifth.

"Fuck it," Molly finally said, loudly. She glanced to both sides, not moving her head, then stepped back, one pace, two paces, another. In a moment she was at Jeb's side. "Come on." They picked up Eileen, who was clenching the wound in her thigh to contain the bleeding, and ran for the car, Jeb scooping up the laptop on the way. Wade stood holding his pistol, prepared to offer covering fire they all knew would be inadequate, but no one shot at them. The Chinese were scrambling into the boat; Vandeveer's team seemed unsure what to do.

Staring at the devastation Molly shook her head once in amazement, then slammed the door.

"How's Eileen?" Wade was already accelerating away. In the backseat Jeb was helping her shift her leg.

"It's not arterial," Eileen whispered. "Passed through."

"She needs help," said Jeb.

Two police cars—a local cruiser in green and black, and a trooper in dark blue—screamed by as they passed through town, a fire engine close behind. Wade pulled to the side of the road, then continued at an unhurried speed.

"Anti-tank missiles," he said. "Christ."

"With thermobaric rounds, no less." Molly was leaning over her seat, trying to help Jeb bind up Eileen's wound. "We're lucky we weren't strafed by F-16s."

"Even so, it takes some organization to have those available," Wade said. He paused. "What a mess . . . it's not over, you know."

"No."

"Think Vandeveer's dead?" Jeb looked up.

"One of my shots went into his forehead."

"You saw that? Everything happened too fast for me."

"We're trained to pay attention. Practice helps."

Wade spoke without looking away from the road. "I'm sorry, Molly. I have to get her to a doctor."

"I know. You've done more than enough."

"How long do you need?"

"Don't worry about it. Tell them everything, right away. It doesn't matter now."

Wade drove in silence for another mile through the forest canyons. The roads were poorly lit at dusk, little traffic on the smooth blacktop two-lanes. In the end he let them out on an empty stretch on a hill above Route 101, noise from traffic moving along the highway below them just audible. They didn't say much.

"I owe you," Molly said.

"No," said Wade, Eileen shook her head, and that was it.

"I'll be in touch when I can."

When they'd driven off Molly and Jeb collapsed behind several trees edging the gravel shoulder. For several minutes they just sat there, not talking.

Molly finally stirred, checking her torn skirt, wondering if it might pass casual observation. "Eileen bought me some clothes this morning," she said.

Jeb examined her stained, scorched clothing. "Looks great on you," he said.

She smiled, but it faded quickly. "So what were you actually doing there?"

"I was trying to hack their wireless network." He gestured vaguely at the laptop.

"Any luck?"

"Not much. Most of the network traffic was email, which was all too heavily encrypted to crack now. I didn't find anything unprotected on the workstations. I was hammering the architecture, but they weren't swapping files in the clear—I just couldn't get much."

"That's okay."

"One thing to follow up on—this Vandeveer guy was getting a lot of messages from an address at nsa-dot-gov, someone named Rice. He or she, I'm not sure, but . . ."

"It sounds like a lead."

"I got a phone number too, might be his office. Or hers."

"I think we can assume he's a man. He's probably our last chance—at least with the NSA."

"Why didn't you shoot the Chinese guys?" said Jeb. "For that matter, why didn't they shoot us?"

"Me, I was out of ammunition." Molly paused. "Them, I don't know. Maybe they were figuring out that we're not the black hats after all."

"Rice probably isn't going to see it that way. Not with his team all dead back there."

"We have to talk to him."

"I still have a phone."

"No. In person. If we just call, he has no way of knowing who we really are." She grimaced. "The problem is he'll show up with a squad of assassins."

"We make it someplace public, lots of people around, that should be safe, right?"

"We still have to get in and out. And if he decides to use serious resources, we could be in the middle of Times Square and it wouldn't matter. There are only two of us."

"You know," Jeb said thoughtfully, "there might be a way we could set this up."

"How?"

"They'll be thinking with their guns. We can rig some backup."

"If it comes to a showdown, we simply won't be able to kill them fast enough."

Jeb's face was streaked with dirt and blood, his clothes tattered. "I'm tired of people shooting at us," he said.

"Yeah?" Molly looked at him. "Me too."

"But maybe we don't have to shoot back."

THIRTY-SEVEN

NORCROSS, EXHAUSTED FROM the scant four hours he'd slept, drank coffee that their waitress had dropped off without asking. He rubbed his eyes, feeling old, and watched as Sampford brought back his second plate from the buffet. The dish was piled with scrambled eggs, fried ham, and silver dollar pancakes, all of it swimming in generous pools of syrup.

"You're not hungry?" Sampford was neatly dressed in a pressed shirt and gray slacks, his hair still wet from forty-five minutes of laps in a pool nearby just after dawn.

"Maybe I'll have some grapefruit."

The dining room was quiet, a scattering of businessmen in casual clothing at widely separated tables, sunlight spilling through the row of windows along one wall. Forks and spoons clattered occasionally, and they could hear the busboy joking with the buffet's grill man. The hostess stood at her podium near the front, reading a magazine placed discreetly beneath her table chart.

"I'm surprised they picked this place," said Sampford through a mouthful of eggs.

"It's a good choice." Norcross checked the windows again, which looked onto the front parking lot. "A hotel like this, right next to the airport, is going to get a lot of businessmen passing through, Japanese and Chinese among them. Deals are probably cut all the time here. We'll look like just another bunch of executives meeting before a golf game."

"I still think we should just collar Zheng and be done with it."

Norcross smiled thinly. "If the SAC went ahead and suspended me, I don't think I have powers of arrest anymore." He sighed. "Anyway, we want him to talk, and we won't get a word out of him if he's in an interrogation room somewhere."

Sampford shrugged. "Your call."

They'd arrived at Dunshire thirty minutes after hearing the radio call the night before. At the scene, they had a cool reception from the FBI agents already there, who clearly perceived a turf infringement. As they were being relegated to the perimeter, Drake showed up in an ATF van and Norcross waved him over. "I'm back on the task force," Drake said. "Don't ask me why, the chief wasn't doing a lot of explaining." The other FBI agents wanted even less to do with an ATF interloper, but Drake knew one of the state detectives and a rather stiff accommodation, not exactly cooperation, was soon established among the various law officers. A sort of consensus opinion began to take shape. No one wanted their reports to be radically out of line with those of the other agencies, since all were potential media fodder.

That progress was mooted just past midnight, when several nondescript men in dark suits arrived. They were quiet and polite, waiting until each agency's senior officer had called their superiors for confirmation, but within ten minutes a national security clampdown had completely cut off communication with the reporters and news teams. Norcross and Sampford left when it became clear the investigation was effectively over.

Zheng himself had called Sampford's cell phone while they were driving away, so conveniently that Norcross assumed the triad had placed surveillance on the scene. Their conversation was brief, and now they were waiting for him, fifteen minutes early so Sampford would have time for breakfast.

Two watchful young men led the way when Zheng arrived, with two more trailing fifteen feet behind. The hostess intercepted them at the entrance but Zheng made a short remark and gestured toward Norcross. He and Sampford stood as the group approached and nodded at Zheng's greeting. No one shook hands. Zheng sat down and his four companions took chairs at the adjoining table.

"The buffet is acceptable," said Norcross.

"We are not hungry, thank you." Zheng waited until the waitress appeared and asked for black tea.

When she had walked away he looked at Norcross. "Two of my people died," he said.

"I'm sorry." Norcross lifted his hands slightly. "I told you to stay away."

"Too much shooting. Huang almost was killed also. He gave me a report."

"Ah. The detectives thought there was another man involved. They found bloodstains, and some shell casings that didn't match the others."

"He will live. We did not get the computer."

"If Picot was carrying it, either he took it away or it was destroyed in the explosion. The investigators didn't find anything that wasn't blown up or shot to pieces."

Tea arrived. Zheng pushed aside the lemon slice and sugar packets with a grimace. The four men at the next table ignored the waitress entirely, but she just smiled and pointed at the buffet.

"So," Zheng said. He stared levelly at Norcross. "What is next?"

"Now?" Norcross paused. "Well. This has been a complicated case. Now—now it starts to get simple."

"Simple is good, at times."

"Very powerful forces have become involved in the investigation. Last night men arrived at Foxton Cove with ID badges they couldn't actually show us, since we didn't have a high enough security classification. Early this morning, the Attorney General apparently began calling the principal members of the task force. Not me, since my status is somewhat . . . informal, but people are talking, we know what's going on." Zheng's face was impassive, and Norcross couldn't tell if he was being too elliptical. "All right, look. There are two stories here: what really happened, and what everyone is going to say happened."

"I would like to know what really happened." Zheng's voice was harsh.

"For you, basically just bad luck." Norcross sipped his coffee, then pushed the cup away from his place setting. "Dunshire is a front for the National Security Agency, a way for them to participate in private-sector cryptographic research on the sly. Blindside's universal cracking technology shocked them."

"Yes, we realized this fact. We knew we were selling Blindside to the government. In fact, we thought we would get a very high price, because of that."

"Did you ever stop to consider why the NSA was worried about Blindside? Remember, they've had the best minds in the world working on this stuff for fifty years. Whatever Astrov figured out, they probably already have it."

Zheng frowned but said nothing.

"I suppose it's possible that a couple entrepreneurs in their garage could achieve a breakthrough that eluded the NSA's scientists for decades," Norcross said. "But it just doesn't seem likely."

"Then, why are they wanting to buy Blindside?"

"What if everyone could crack codes? Not just the NSA, but any halfway competent network engineer with some decent hardware? Suddenly most of the encryption used today would be useless."

"But that is not a problem for the NSA, I believe." Zheng didn't get it.

"Oh, but it would be, immediately. Because everyone would switch to much more powerful encryption methods. I don't understand it myself"—Norcross nodded to Sampford—"but apparently public-key systems can be made exponentially stronger by increasing the key length. The coding becomes a little more cumbersome, so transmission is slower, but it's easy enough, and at some point even Blindside's system couldn't keep up."

"Ah." Zheng nodded sharply.

"Yes. Encryption everywhere would ratchet up—and the NSA would be out in the cold again, unable to listen in on anyone."

"I understand." Zheng hadn't touched his tea. "Buying Blindside is now very important to them."

"Very. So important, in fact, that someone apparently decided simply purchasing the company wasn't good enough."

The table was silent for several moments.

"Who was killed?" said Norcross. "Your people, and Blindside's." He waited.

"Not Dunshire's," said Zheng finally.

"Right. They were out to erase Astrov's invention completely." Norcross shrugged slightly. "Like I said, just your bad luck."

"My bad luck," Zheng repeated.

"It gets worse. For you, that is."

A pause. "Ah. The story everyone will say, you mean."

"That's right." Norcross spoke without evident emotion. "The government is not prepared to reveal that a rogue intelligence agency went on a nationwide killing spree just to shut down some private-sector competition."

Comprehension was beginning to show on Zheng's face. "I am not happy."

"No, I don't think you will be. The task force is about to announce its conclusion that the Wo Han Mok was itself responsible for all the shootings. Blindside, yesterday, the FBI agents—everything."

"But that is no, not . . . !" In his anger Zheng's English slipped.

"You were covering your trail. First you stole the cracking system for the Chinese government, then you tried to conceal both the theft and the technology itself by destroying Blindside, and then matters just spun out of control."

Zheng spat a few angry words in Chinese.

"I'm afraid that it doesn't have to be completely logical. Remember Wen Ho Lee? Accused of being a spy for Red China by Janet Reno herself—even though he was from Taiwan."

Zheng was furious. His four guards, watching, appeared to be on the edge of violence, one of them already half out of his chair.

"You're the nation's brand new most wanted." Norcross was relentless. "Every newspaper, every TV news program in the country is going to be cheering on this manhunt. The FBI is coming after you with its reputation on the line. They're probably rolling up your low-level operatives while we're sitting here."

Through a clear exercise of will Zheng remained motionless, though the muscles in his face and neck were stretched taut. In a low voice, glaring fiercely, he said, "You die now."

"No." Sampford spoke for the first time. Zheng glanced at him, then looked again, more slowly. Sampford was aiming his Beretta directly at Zheng's chest, the handgun partially obscured by a cloth napkin. "Nine-mil jacketed hollowpoint," he said. "Completely against agency regulations."

"And illegal in California," said Norcross. "But one round will cut you in half."

They all stared at each other, unmoving.

"Why are you doing this?" said Zheng.

"Your best chance is to flee the United States and never return," said Norcross. "And so much the better. Murder, kidnapping, extortion, all manner of organized crime, and financial fraud—good riddance." His voice was still measured, reasonable. "As for Blindside, well, that's one small instance where we might stretch real hard and consider you a victim. So for that, I figure letting you walk away alive is fair enough."

For nearly a full minute Zheng was silent. Norcross knew they'd come to the decision point.

"You're wasting time," he said.

Abruptly Zheng barked a command in Chinese, and the four guards rose. Sampford's handgun didn't waver.

"They go first," said Norcross. "No accidents that way."

Before he left, Zheng paused to look back at them, and for the first time he smiled slightly, utterly without humor. "I will see you later," he said, and walked out.

THEY sat and finished their breakfast, Sampford now too jumpy to eat but Norcross suddenly hungry. He collected a plate of sausage and pancakes and ate cheerfully, more relaxed than he'd been for the entire week.

"We just let them go," said Sampford.

"You wanted a gunfight right here? How many civilian casualties do you think those four thugs would have caused?"

"It doesn't seem right."

"No." Norcross lost his good cheer. "No, but not how you're thinking."

Sampford frowned.

"I doubt they'll make it out of the country," said Norcross. "In fact, I doubt they'll make it out of town." He sighed and set down his knife and fork. "I talked to Drake this morning, while you were in the pool. The task force should be closing in on Zheng right now."

"Oh." Sampford's frown eased. "That's good."

"Perhaps."

"Why not?"

"Drake won't be the one making the arrest."

"I'm not following."

"You heard me describe the, how shall we say, public version of events. Do you really think that if they catch him Zheng will go along? What is he going to say to the court? To the TV cameras?"

"Oh, no." Sampford exhaled slowly.

"If Zheng doesn't get clear, there's only one way the story works," said Norcross. "And that's if he's dead."

Sampford looked away. "They wouldn't shoot him in cold blood."

Norcross found a napkin and wiped his hands. "I'd like to think that was true," he said quietly.

A cell phone rang, startling them both. "Christ!" Sampford had pulled the Beretta halfway out of its holster in an instant, and he hastily replaced it while Norcross excavated the phone from his jacket. Still on edge he watched as Norcross grunted through the conversation. Both of them had forgotten their food entirely.

"Thanks, George." Norcross clicked off the phone and looked at Sampford. "He tapped his line after all."

"What?"

"I asked him to tag Rice's phone line, remember? But he didn't just set up the follow-me, he actually got a recorder in place. And guess who just called Rice." He waited but Sampford shook his head. "Molly Gannon."

"Gannon? She's working for him?"

"It doesn't sound like it. George said Rice didn't know who she was at first."

"So why'd she call?"

"To set up a meeting. Today."

Sampford was thinking furiously. "She's not working for the NSA, she's not working for the triad, so what the hell?"

"I don't think she was involved at all." Norcross pushed his chair back and pulled some cash from his wallet, dropping it on the table. "An innocent bystander all along."

Only when they were outside, standing in the morning sun while they tried to remember where they'd parked, did Sampford think to ask, "Where's the meeting, anyway?"

"Union Square."

He stopped short. "Rice is here in San Francisco?"

"George said he arrived yesterday."

THIRTY-EIGHT

THE INITIAL HACK, the night before, had taken much less effort than Jeb expected. Once he had checked in, unpacked his equipment, and tested the in-house high-speed line, he started by examining the Business Improvement District's website, just poking around before he unleashed a scan. On the directory page he noticed that the BID office's phone numbers were all between 405-2800 and 405-2899. That meant they'd probably reserved the block from the phone company, adding and deleting lines as necessary on their own PBX. On the theory that before kicking in a door you should always try the knob, he opened a wardialer on a separate modem line and had it run through the block, looking for machine tones.

In a few minutes he found three modems and several fax machines. Two of the modems were PCs, connected to the network but running decent security, with no immediate weaknesses. The third modem, however, was a diagnostic port directly into the network's router. When he saw the familiar Cisco prompt Jeb laughed. The router, which handled all traffic in between the BID's network and the outside world, was inside their firewall—and Jeb required only two more minutes to crack its low-grade password. From there it was mere housekeeping to footprint the network's basic architecture and identify the key servers, all of which were sitting wide open to internal infiltration.

By midnight, sitting at the laptop in his underwear, he'd figured out how they were pipelining the various camera feeds. The BID was a private entity, sponsored by most businesses within a few blocks of Union Square, which had taken responsibility for various services inadequately provided by the city: trash collection, for example. They also had their own security officers, unarmed but numerous, whose job was to keep the streets safe and pleasant for the tourists. To this end the BID had also installed two dozen monitoring cameras around the square, discreetly mounted on lightpoles and building facades twenty feet above ground level. A few were on motorized mounts, so they could be moved and zoomed remotely; the others remained focused on busy corners. All were in constant service, streaming realtime to a bank of screens somewhere in the BID's security center.

Once Jeb had tapped the cameras he opened a backdoor in one of the lesser-used servers and departed, confident he could get back in any time he wanted. He shut down his online connection, from paranoid habit pulling the jack, and stretched.

The Beverly Hotel was an ornate, twelve-story sliver between a pricey clothing boutique and a mirrored-glass tower housing media company offices. Rooms started at $350. After taking a cab into the city, paying for one night nearly cleaned out their cash, but Molly figured Darren's Visa card might no longer be safe.

A knock at the door brought Jeb alert, and he was hastily scanning the room to make sure he hadn't left the guns out when Molly slipped in, locking the dead bolt behind her.

"Security isn't bad." She was dressed in her conservative business clothing again, the various rips repaired with the room's sewing kit, the stains brushed out at the sink. "They checked my room key at the elevator."

"Only in the middle of the night, probably." It was after two a.m.

"Yeah." She began removing her outfit, hanging each item carefully in the wardrobe. "The truck shouldn't be any problem. The depot in South Beach is fenced, but there are more vans than fit. They seem to have overflow parking in the alley."

"Good thing you held onto your keys."

"It's amazing they work—I guess I could drive away any postal van in the nation. You'd think they'd be more careful."

"Laziness," said Jeb. "The hacker's most important ally. Speaking of which, look at this." He plugged in the laptop again and opened a pair of video windows. In a few seconds they were watching late-night tourists wandering back to a Marriott on the other side of the square.

"The picture is really sharp." Molly was impressed.

"They're using good cameras. It looks like they're planning to implement face recognition software—I found a system install, but it hasn't been connected yet. When it's up and running the computer will scan the crowd automatically, looking for matches against a database of mug shots."

"That's scary."

Jeb nodded. "When we're done, I might post the details somewhere. Let the world know."

Molly straightened up, pulling off the last of her clothing. "I'm going to sleep for twelve hours."

"We should call Rice early, give him only enough time to get here."

"Fine. But we can't leave the room after that, it's just too risky."

They were looking at each other, Molly naked in the soft lamplight and Jeb nearly so. He reached out to stroke her hair, once, and suddenly they were grappling, holding each other, and stumbling toward the bed.

"I wasn't actually done," Jeb said distractedly, his voice muffled by Molly's neck.

"Later."

"But I haven't cracked the screens yet."

"We'll have all day." And that was the last coherent sentence from either for more than an hour.

THIRTY-NINE

FRIDAY LATE AFTERNOON was the end of a gorgeous Indian summer day, people carrying their jackets, the street vendors selling out of ice cream and big, soft pretzels. A crowd of tourists had accumulated at the cable-car stop on Powell, waiting for their ride up Nob Hill, cheerful in the pleasant breeze. Along the low concrete parapets surrounding Union Square, teenagers with odd haircuts jumped their skateboards in patient, endless circles. Couples sat on the grass, holding hands, in easy coexistence with small groups of homeless men and women. Traffic moved steadily down Geary, the side-lanes kept clear by SFPD cars and a few blue BID cruisers.

Broad walkways entered the park from each corner, converging in front of a monument to Admiral Dewey. Closer to the square's edge several palm trees towered above the neatly kept lawn. Under one of these, not close to any benches, Rice stood impassively, alone, waiting.

He'd arrived five minutes early, walking south on Stockton, carrying the bright orange shopping bag they'd agreed on as identification, since his face was unknown to Molly. When he was standing beneath the tree he looked around, glanced at his watch, and stood still, the bag at his feet, his hands clasped behind him.

"Okay, I've got him focused," said Jeb. He was alone in the hotel room, in front of the laptop, speaking into a headset he'd clipped into the table phone. "No one's with him."

"They're around." Molly's voice was tinny in the earpiece.

"You can go in anytime."

"I'm pulling out now."

Several minutes passed. Rice checked his watch again, casually. A cluster of Latin American tourists stood nearby, craning their necks to stare at the electronic billboards on the buildings above them. Soundless videos played on two-story screens thirty feet off the ground; a five-foot electronic ticker rolled NASDAQ stock quotes. Rice ignored it all.

A half-ton LLV, the workhorse of the postal fleet, coasted to a stop at the curb on Geary in front of the Turnbull building, immediately opposite Rice. Half a minute later the traffic diminished, halted upstream by the stoplight at Market, and Molly stepped out of the LLV. Her slamming door caught Rice's attention, and he watched as she crossed the briefly empty lanes.

"The letter carrier," he said, when she stood in front of him, a yard away. He saw a tiny earpiece and filament mike, the thin wire leading under her collar. "Of course."

"Ground rules," said Molly. "Guys in the truck have you covered. Don't try anything dumb—they're too close to miss." When Rice glanced at the otherwise empty curb she added, "Don't worry, the police aren't going to roust a postal vehicle. We're fine."

"All right."

They waited. The Spanish-speaking tourists had wandered away, to be replaced by a group of suburban kids, smoking and talking loudly at each other.

"According to the news," said Molly, "it was the Wo Han Mok. The triad. They did it all."

"I heard that too."

"But it's not true."

"No?"

"A lot of people tried to kill us this week. Hardly any of them were Chinese."

"Okay."

Molly shook her head briefly. "I was there, at Blindside, remember? When your soldiers came running out of Dunshire last night, it was the same guys. You were behind it the whole time."

Rice sighed. The late, golden sunlight diminished his pallor, but his face was weary. "They weren't mine."

"Vandeveer reported to you."

"He slipped the leash. Yes, I know, it's still my responsibility. But I didn't know what he was doing."

"Sorry, that doesn't add up." In her peripheral vision Molly noticed an eddy in the flow of pedestrians near the LLV. Something was happening on the sidewalk behind it, where she couldn't see. She kept her eyes on Rice. "You blew up Blindside to keep their technology from going to the Chinese. That's a national security objective, not a personal one. And Dunshire's a venture capital firm—Vandeveer wouldn't have a hunter-killer team working for him."

"Not quite right." Rice let his eyes drift around the area and returned his gaze to Molly. "I created Dunshire five years ago as a cover. It was only intended to be another line into Silicon Valley, a way to keep our finger on the pulse of nongovernment cryptographic research. I put Vandeveer in charge because, frankly, he didn't look like a spy. He could get along with people, make deals."

"Yeah, yeah." Molly didn't sound interested. "What's the point?"

"So he turned out to be good at the business. Really good. Unexpectedly, we were earning money, and lots of it."

Molly grimaced. "Good for him."

"Yes. That's what he must have decided. Because he started to cut his own deals, just like a real VC."

"Was Blindside one of them?"

"Oh, no. I told him to buy them out. We had to get their technology under classification, and that was the easiest way."

Despite herself Molly was both puzzled and interested. "I don't get it."

"Vandeveer was doing more and more on the side. He'd been investing his own money, but in other crypto start ups, before he knew about Blindside. One in particular called Tetral Systems. See? Blindside was a competitor—if they got to market first, they'd win, and everyone else would lose, and one of those losers would be Vandeveer. I've had accountants going over his books since last night. It looks like he had about six million dollars on the line."

"Just from Blindside?" Molly's puzzlement turned to disbelief. "This was all about money?"

"I'm afraid so."

"But . . . I thought you were shutting them down anyway, with the acquisition."

"For peanuts. Tetral Systems was lining up to go public, and we were just starting to think about buying them out ahead of time, like Blindside. But Vandeveer had dealt himself in already, with a nice piece of the friends-and-family distribution. He wanted Tetral's IPO—he didn't want Dunshire to knock it off for a tenth the price beforehand." He paused. "Which we could have, with national security to back us up."

"So by blowing up Blindside, he was trying to screw Dunshire too."

"Right. Dunshire can't do anything now, let alone go after Tetral. So Tetral's still on track, and Vandeveer's stock is going to be worth millions." Grim satisfaction flickered across Rice's face. "Not that he'll see any of it now."

"Where did he get the hard men?"

"He was in the agency for twenty years before I tagged him for Dunshire, mostly doing covert operations overseas. He made some unsavory friends along the way, and we think that's how he built his team later."

Molly looked away from Rice to scan the sidewalks across the two avenues from them. Throngs of people were pushing along: tourists, idlers, men pushing handtrucks, couples out for dinner and a show, teenagers, servicemen, a few hustlers, children. Rice could have had two dozen agents nearby and she'd never know.

"I'm still not buying," she said. "I was in the military, I know how tightly controlled operations are. And intelligence is even more bureaucratic, not less. I don't believe he could have gotten away with all that right under your nose."

Rice looked pained. "We tried to cut Dunshire loose from the usual oversight. I thought it was the only way it could succeed. And Vandeveer took advantage. He was careful for a while. Later he must have become overconfident, figured he'd never get caught." He sighed again. "I've seen it before."

"Overconfident? That's what you call this shoot-em-up? How many people dead so far?"

"What I mean is, he didn't take any kind of precautions at all . . . in the end he was even funneling his last deals through the same bank as Dunshire uses, Global Pacific. Just for convenience, though it left a paper trail a mile wide. Stupid."

But Molly had stopped listening to him, hearing Jeb suddenly in her ear: "They're taking down the truck—three, no four men. They're all on the sidewalk side . . . the door is open—" She looked over just as the LLV rocked on its springs, jolted by the men jumping into it.

Jeb's voice was cut off by a loud crash, followed by a confused series of loud noises. Molly shouted, "Status! Status!" into the filament mike, trying to keep track of Rice while also staring at the Beverly's windows, two blocks away. Rice was pulling out his own cell phone, watching the LLV, just as a muscular man in nondescript coveralls and a hardhat came around its side, one hand covered by a large rag. Others were converging on the median from four different points. Molly thought, I can't believe we *planned* on this, and seized Rice's arm in an immobilizing elbow lock.

* * *

INSIDE the hotel room, one minute earlier, Jeb had been focused on the video images tapped from monitoring cameras on the street. He'd run a coaxial cable from an external adapter on the laptop into the room's thirty-inch color TV, and the large screen allowed him to track four tiled camera feeds at once. Rice and Molly were in clear view from two angles; another camera oversaw the postal truck; and the fourth covered the opposite avenue.

He saw the team materialize beside the empty LLV—their decoy—and break through its side window without showing any hesitation. He'd just called to Molly through his headset when the hotel room's door crashed inward. It slammed against the wall and a man in identical coveralls charged in, a square, matte-black pistol in two hands.

"Down! Down!" The man's voice was not loud but it carried a tone of absolute command. Jeb hesitated, the man raised his handgun—

—and another figure dove into the room, crossing the threshold in a combat tuck and rolling immediately to one side as another man crouched just outside, point-ing another pistol around the door frame. The man on the floor, dressed incongruously in a white shirt with a dark blue tie tucked into the second button, was holding a gun of his own on the first intruder. "FBI!" he shouted. "Drop it!"

The first man had reacted with extraordinary speed, spinning around before the white-shirted agent had hit the floor. He fired an unaimed scattering of three shots and ducked, heading for cover behind the unmade bed.

He didn't make it. Two shots each from the second arrivals caught him in the chest, groin, and throat, and he crumpled in a spray of blood.

"Don't move!" said the man in the doorway, coming fully into the room. He was as broad as a truck but moved with an easy grace. His weapon was pointed at the floor, and he took only an instant to scan Jeb's tangle of cables and hardware, the dead man, and Jeb himself.

"Norcross, FBI," he said shortly. "And Special Agent Sampford. Jeb Picot?"

Jeb just nodded, stunned. The explosion of action couldn't have lasted more than fifteen seconds.

"Are you on the line to her?" Norcross jerked his head at the TV. "Tell her you're okay. Quick!"

Jeb looked between Norcross and the monitor, which showed Molly and Rice now joined by five other men, all in dark coveralls, bracketing them in an L from about six feet.

"Molly?" he said. "We have one dead guy here, and two FBI agents who seem to know what's going on. They're not holding guns on me anymore."

"Can you get the pictures up?" Her voice, even through the poor acoustics of the cell phone, was obviously strained.

Jeb looked at Norcross, who nodded and said, "Do whatever you planned. Keep her alive. Is there sound?"

"Sure." Jeb turned to the laptop, started hitting commands. "Twenty seconds," he said into the mike.

ON the street, Molly glared at the soldiers, who were watching her with feral intensity. Rice wasn't struggling, kept still by the barrel of her Colt in his side. No one had a gun out in plain sight, but it was obvious that she would die the instant her attention flagged.

"We thought it might go this way," she said, her voice almost casual. "The truck didn't fool you long enough, though."

"By now, Picot is no use to you," said Rice.

"No." Molly kept her eyes on the other men. "Your guy wasn't good enough. Jeb, are you there?"

"I just patched in."

Molly lifted her eyes and smiled.

"All right," she said to Rice. "I want you to take a look up. Right up there. See?"

The soldiers ignored her, not shifting their attention at all, but Rice raised his head. It took him several seconds, and he said, "Shit."

Above them the twenty-five-foot screen, until moments ago playing a movie trailer, now showed the same video feed Jeb was watching, of Rice and Molly on the square. A slight transmission delay made the effect of seeing themselves even more unsettling.

"Over there, too." Molly inclined her head. The screen across the square showed the same view. A moment later an amber-on-black display similar to a ballpark scoreboard, heavily pixilated, switched from a financial services advertisement to a view of the postal truck, which was listing to one side.

"I take your point," said Rice. "Turn them off, please."

"Leave them up, Jeb," said Molly. To Rice: "It's all being recorded, and Jeb is streaming it real-time to some sort of remote storage cache, too. There's no sound from the camera, of course—but everything you've said was picked up on the cell phone."

"I said I take your point." A few bystanders in the pedestrian crowd had noticed the odd displays, and were pointing upward. No one seemed to have recognized the scene yet.

"So here we are," said Molly. "No need for guns anymore, right? You know what will happen if I die. The networks will love this."

"Yes."

"How we're going to play it: we'll be exonerated, of course. You've already set that up, with all the blame on the Chinese."

"I understand."

"In fact, you may as well spin it that Jeb and I were actually helping the authorities out all along—by volunteering to serve as suspects, we distracted the triad enough that you were able to track them down."

This time Rice didn't say anything, just looked at her.

"Well, whatever you figure out. But it had better be an ironclad assertion of our innocence. Otherwise . . . well, you know."

Jeb's voice came in her ear. "The FBI man says, tell him they missed Zheng."

"What?"

There was a pause, while Jeb conferred in the background. "Zheng is the Wo Han Mok leader."

Molly smiled again. "I get it." She focused on Rice. "Zheng slipped the net. He's still loose."

"So?"

"So if it's ever necessary to distribute our little memorial, and he's still around, he'll get the first copy. Do you think he'd like to know who set him up? Personally?"

It only took another minute for Rice to capitulate, and he called a short series of commands to his soldiers. They tucked their weapons away, displaying only the smallest hesitation, and stepped back. After they'd faded into the crowd Jeb exited out of the screens, returning them to their original broadcasts. Molly put her pistol away and Rice slumped slightly, tension loosening. He looked wearier, even haggard.

"Sergeant Gannon," he said, as she stepped away. "I seem to have underestimated you."

"I'm not a soldier any more."

"I won't make that mistake twice."

Molly glanced back, just once, before she disappeared around the corner. "You'll never see us again," she said.

FORTY

AT THE BEVERLY, police cars already filled the street. Lightbars flashed in the lowering dusk; an ambulance was parked at the curb and onlookers began to congregate. Molly hung back, called Jeb again, and they met around the block, Norcross escorting him out through the underground garage.

"We got here a few hours ago," Norcross was saying. "Then we split up, and just asked for the room logs at one hotel after another. We knew you couldn't have reserved in advance, and there are never that many walk-in registrations on a Thursday night. Rice probably tracked you down the same way. It was a guess that you'd have taken a room, but where else would you go?"

"Lucky guess," said Jeb. "Lucky for us." He placed a hand on Molly's arm, casually, but his grip was iron. She covered his hand with hers.

"Don't think I'm not grateful," she said to Norcross, "but why . . ."

"You figured out the best way to settle things. I'm not going to screw it up." He shrugged one shoulder. "Not to mention, if Sampford and I tried to explain all this on our own, I'm not sure I could make any of it stick. We'd all be dragged behind the horse."

She studied him, then nodded. "Thanks."

He waved one hand. "Get going, both of you."

"Jeb, where's your computer stuff?"

"I left it all up there." He patted one pocket. "Everything except the hard drive. They won't learn a thing."

"Paul's watching the scene, just to make sure," Norcross added.

"The other agent," Jeb said to Molly.

"He's a good kid," Norcross said. "Reminds me of how I used to be, sometimes."

"How's the FBI going to handle this?"

"We don't have to worry about a cover story," said Norcross. "As soon as they run the dead guy's prints, national security is going to land on the investigation like a falling mountain. I'm sure Rice will see to that."

"What about you?"

Norcross was already turning to go back in. "Oh, I'll probably get a suspension and another reassignment. Doesn't matter. I just hope I can shake myself free by nine tonight." A smile broke through his craggy face. "I've got a date."

DOWN the street, as they disappeared into the ceaseless crowds, Molly kept looking around, eyeing faces and hands.

"It's going to be a few weeks before I stop thinking everyone we see is about to pull out a gun," she said.

Jeb nodded. "When they let me out of Ray Brook, that's how I felt—free, and not free at the same time."

"Let's stop to eat. I haven't had anything since breakfast." She rummaged in her jacket pocket and came up with a handful of bills. "A hundred and . . . thirteen dollars. One good meal, and then we have to figure something out."

They found a grill restaurant open to the sidewalk, where early diners sat at wrought-iron tables in the twilight. The waiter brought sparkling water and a menu drawn in brushstroke calligraphy on genuine parchment. Woodsmoke from the kitchen drifted out. Tourists and businessmen ambled past, cheerful in the warm evening air.

After they ordered, Jeb shifted his chair close to Molly's.

"Rice was a piece of work," he said. "While I was upstairs, at the Beverly—"

"It's over." Molly stopped him, gently stroking his cheek once. "I don't want to think about it, right this minute. Let's just enjoy ourselves for a while."

"No, one thing I have to tell you."

"Oh, all right."

"Those FBI agents at the Beverly weren't watching closely while I cleaned up the computer equipment. Too involved with the body on the floor. I had a few minutes to myself online."

She looked at him quizzically. "Yeah? Check your email?"

"Rice gave you the name of Dunshire's bank, right before it got interesting."

Molly tried to remember. "If you say so."

He waited, starting to smile. After a moment she figured it out. "That's how Dunshire was going to pay for Blindside—the account on the laptop!"

"That's right."

"The token worked? The money was still there?"

"Some sort of escrow," he said. "But it had just cleared."

"And?"

"So I transferred it out." He laughed.

"Jeb." She stared into his eyes. "How much?"

The last sunlight illuminated the building tops far above them, reflecting a golden glow downward. Molly's tension and fear were fading away, receding as the future finally lengthened beyond the next twenty-four hours.

An older couple two tables away glanced over, smiling to see two youngsters so obviously happy about something.

"We can leave for Raiatea tonight," said Jeb.